into the
Blue

Drifters, Book Ten

SUSAN RODGERS

*Somewhere there's a silent voice
learning how to sing*
—Amanda Marshall (*I Believe In You*)

*This book is for the silent voices...
I believe in you.*

Contents

Prologue

*T*here's an enigmatic vitality to water that brings peace and healing to those living on or around it. It starts with the gentle lap, lap, lapping of wavelets, a sweet sound that bears no threat and cries out hope, and lasts until the wind builds and a storm comes, bringing with it waves that crash like cymbals and shatter like glass.

On the gentle lapping days, Jacob likes to lie in his bunk and let Sarah May lightly rock him; she lulls him into oblivion with grace and care; she helps him feel safe in her weathered wooden heart.

On the days when the Gods rise up and threaten her lines with ferocious yanks and lightning snaps so that Sarah May's hull rocks mercilessly, Jacob rises up with them. He plants naked toes on the bow, raises one arm to the Gods of wind and rain, and hollers into the fury. Bare-chested, his long dark curls tied back with a red bandana, he rages at the mystical sea creatures lurking in the deepest darkness of the wild sea; he screams at the invisible soul curled up, hiding, in the wrath of his empty heart.

He knows they're the only living things that will listen to his torment.

"Be damned, you!" he curses as he shakes a fist, as he pounds his chest. "You think you know me? You don't know me at all! I am Jacob! I am music, and I am song! And I—am—free!"

Jacob needs to vanquish the terrors that keep him awake; he must send their despairing selves crying to the heartless bottom of the eternal sea. They must be exorcised, these harbingers of fear, these reckless unmerciful tormentors.

There is another outlet Jacob uses to banish the anguish that haunts him— music. Songwriting. Sitting cross-legged on Sarah May's sun-soaked cabin on

1

gentle days, he writes a lot of songs. They come to him like waves to the hull; relentless nudges on his heart that cry *Hear us! Listen!* But when the winds come and the waters begin to stir—like a witch's cauldron, slow to boil but then seemingly unstoppable—Jacob's blood boils too, and he pushes the music aside. There are bigger dragons to slay when the wind furiously sweeps through his curls and stirs up the old demons.

The memories come then, swift and sure, thieves in the night, complete with self-hatred Jacob cannot even begin to process. *Those few perfect moments with Jessie and Dylan at La Casa on Boxing Day; the haunting way Jessie softly gazed at me in the nursery as if she could see inside my soul; the way the light in Talia's green eyes faded when she called off our wedding; the crushing, catastrophic crash as she said goodbye; and then…and then…the sexual violence I unleashed on Jessie in Florida.*

The…rape. Not because, Jacob understands now, he truly blames Jessie for Talia's decision not to marry him. How can he blame her when she tried so hard to let him go? How can he blame Jessie for how he, Jacob, feels about her?

He is learning to take ownership of that. He *needs* to take ownership of that.

No. Jacob's grief now, a few short weeks later, is haunted by the physical, by the image of Jessie beneath him, struggling against him and pleading with him to stop. By his fist rising as if lifted by some unseen power, and then coming down to strike the face of the woman he loves, dazing her, taking the fight out of her, so Jacob can take what he's desired since the Scotland days, when Jessie was Annie and Annie was his.

I could have broken her jaw, is what he tortures himself with, when at three a.m. he lies awake and reruns the violent assault through his mind. *I could have really hurt her.*

It is over now, Jacob knows. Jessie. Jessie and him. They are done. Even if Jessie hadn't come to him at the post-funeral reception with some attempt at civility in true Jessie forgiveness mode, Jacob has to let her let him go. And he has to let go too. The assault was a big ole exclamation mark, a tumultuous love's final farewell.

Life, for him, has been a cycle of loss. And here, in some random Caribbean port on a hapless old sailboat, learning to become one with the unpredictable moods of the water, Jacob plans to live life without entanglements. He will pour his soul into his music and travel to meet Charles and Deirdre at festivals, on tours, at awards shows. Music…he will record more albums and bury himself in music's mystical, eternal grasp. Then Jacob will come back to Sarah May—she is a gnarled survivor of many storms, a windswept woman he already knows he can depend on. He will grow old the way embittered men grow old, in fits and starts and on his own terms. With one hand on the boat and the other cursed fist raised high, Jacob will forever scream out his sorrow to the relentless wind; he will cry out his pain to the sea.

So far, these solitary eruptions in the storms end with him spent and drained, sobbing. Always, Jacob falls to his knees on the deck, his head bowed forward in a Yoga child's pose. Always, the salt spray washes over him, cleanses him of his sins, carries his last words away. And always those last words are, "I'm sorry! I'm so damned sorry!"

And always later—exhausted, emptied—in the cabin below, Sarah May and the little wavelets whispering against her hull rock him back to sleep.

This morning there was no storm in Jacob's heart, nor were a whirlwind of black clouds whipping up a fury outside Sarah May's battered cabin. Today there was only a gentle lapping against the wooden hull, and a rhythmic slapping of the mainsail's line on the mast above. It was a steadfast noise Jacob had already grown to depend on, to love, as the line moved about like a living thing. The muted thwacks drew him awake in the mornings; the calm jingling eased his mind, as multi-colored tropical birds Jacob had yet to learn about dashed and dove alongside, adding their musical stories in counterpoint.

Today there was a new sound. It was a rhythmic snore that came from a body lying next to him. From a woman lying naked on her stomach, her caramel arms wrapped around a pillow, long dark hair splayed out over top like strands of silk, the graceful curve of her back glistening in the early morning heat.

Easing himself up on one elbow, Jacob watched her sleep. She was young, maybe twenty, and he remembered from the port bar the night before that she was beautiful, all dark deep-set eyes and short shorts, and an innocence that, he soon discovered, was a ploy.

He didn't care. He could afford her. The sex had been quick and to the point—it wasn't one of those all nighters he used to enjoy with Jessie. Not with Talia, no, there were no all nighters with her. She liked sex okay but only when it was convenient or romantic. Jessie was always willing; she was often the one to initiate 'playtime.' It was like she knew her body had pleasurable gifts to offer, so why shouldn't she use it and enjoy it?

Jessie, in Jacob's opinion, had no sexual inhibitions. She had started unwillingly at a young age, and learned early on to please others with her body in order to keep the peace or to get what she wanted. Unhindered first love in the most natural way with a boy she still mourned taught her that the physical pleasures of sex were multiplied a hundredfold if she loved the person she pleasured with her body. In Vancouver, she let herself love (and be loved by) a woman while she worked for a short time pleasing others via provocative photographs and erotic films. By the time she met Jacob, Jessie knew her body well, and she knew how to use it.

Charlie? She'd told Jacob sex was nice, with him, but there was always something missing. The soul part, she called it. That intimate connection that, once she found Josh, had lifted Jessie to another level entirely. *With me,* Jacob thought? What was it between us? Serious lust. Desire. That's what. *We occupied each other's souls and bodies with a desperation borne of impending loss right from the start. Like soldiers going to war, never knowing if they would make it home. That was us.*

Sex with Jessie never came free, in Jacob's time. The price had to do with the ring 'Annie' wore around her neck like a noose, and with the sadness imbued within that ring. It had to do with a man who had Jessie's heart long before Jacob entered the fray. There was never a blind belief in a future where he and the woman he loved would grow old together. There was always only desperation, a desperate grabbing and clutching and moving and moaning, intense beyond all intensity, a jet engine on steroids, lust and desire on a level that made sex a drug that Jacob—and Jessie, apparently—just had to have.

The woman beside Jacob stirred now, and blinked herself awake. *I don't know you,* Jacob thought as he reached forward and lifted a strand of the unfamiliar hair, as he moved it up onto her back. *I don't want to know you.* He let his guitar-callused fingers trail down the curve of her sun-darkened back and slip between her legs. Tensing, she closed her eyes and moaned a little.

Jacob could barely understand the girl's English, but now she was speaking a universal language.

Lying back down on the crook of his other arm, he nudged his body closer so he could slip his fingers inside her. In answer, her eyes half-opened with desire as she parted her lips, as she reached for his finger and placed it in her mouth. Sucking, moaning, raising her hips, she rocked herself in a quest to soak up as much of the pleasure Jacob was willing to give as possible. The dark eyes were captivating as they blinked their lust at Jacob now; the girl's body was ready and willing. The anonymous woman was his again for the low port price of a few U.S. dollars.

Jacob removed his fingers from the girl's body, nudged her on the hip to get her to roll over, and straddled her. Grabbing one small set of fingers, he placed them where she could help herself along, because he wanted the job done quickly and efficiently so he could kick her out. A few quick thrusts and Jacob was done, thinking he was generous in that he waited for her to catch up. He had her up the short ship's ladder and off the sailboat before she came down off her orgasm, but neither cared. His whore got her money, and Jacob got his fuck.

The only thing missing, Jacob thought as he lay back down to let Sarah May rock him back to sleep, was everything.

The sounds were different, the body was different, the smells were different. There were no sweet lavender tresses for him to smile into; there was no Talia's innocent, dimpled cheeks to love. The women loved by Jacob Ryan were erased from his life like last night's perfect sunset; they were hues of pink and purple that sank below the distant horizon and disappeared.

It's just you and me now, Jacob told the tough old boat as he stared at the low ceiling. *You and me and a succession of two-dollar whores.*

He rolled onto his side, closed his eyes, and wept.

Chapter One

$\mathcal{A}$ wispy, pale moonlight wafted in through the window of Dylan's room. In a nearby rocking chair, Jessie soaked up its otherworldly glow and watched her baby sleep; she watched his little chest rise and fall in blissful slumber. In her arms was the Gibson Jacob bought her in New York to replace her father's treasured guitar—the one lost in the Langley fire on the fateful day Jessie was found after her abduction a few years earlier.

Plucking at it, Jessie hummed a few notes. The easy sound wouldn't wake Dylan. The guitar had just soothed him to sleep. As with the other two Sawyer children, music was his life. It was in his soul.

Josh crept up behind Jessie and leaned over Dylan's toddler bed. Bypassing her, he reached for the child's duvet and pulled it up just a little further, tucking it just over Dylan's long dark curls.

"It's cold tonight," he warned Jessie as he affectionately touched Dylan's cheek. "This one's always kicking off his blankets. He's gonna freeze." Looking back over at his wife, Josh swallowed. In her expression today was sadness, a longing. Those looks always, of late, came with these evenings spent in Dylan's room picking out tunes, singing to the little guy, watching him sleep and, Josh was well aware, wondering where his biological father was and whether he was okay.

What Josh had no way of knowing was that his comment about Dylan kicking off his blankets had jarred a hard new memory for Jessie. Jacob, sprawled on their bed slumbering in the nude, blankets tangled around his waist, one arm resting on Jessie's waist, a thigh on hers, the leg resting comfortably in between her two legs.

6

Josh saw the look, though. He knew there was some memory lurking beneath the surface. It was evident in the way she blinked, swallowed, and averted his gaze. In the way her eyes landed back on the boy sleeping nearby, and in the way the little bit of blue in her eyes faded and lost their light.

He knelt before her. Some nights it was better if Josh could get her out of Dylan's room, if he could convince her to come watch *Grey's Anatomy* reruns or something, anything, just to get her mind off worrying about Jacob and Jacob's son.

"Jessie," he tried, grasping her fingers, which were suspended over the guitar. "Come on. He's dreaming about teddy bears and bunnies right about now. Let's go watch some mindless TV."

It took her some time to refocus. The sea-pearl blues took Josh by surprise. They were extra sorrowful tonight. "I'm working out a song," she explained carefully. "A new one for the Grammys next month. I'll be late coming to bed tonight, okay Josh?"

"A song about Jacob," he surmised darkly.

She shrugged. "Do you want me to lie?"

"Why, Jess?"

"You know why, babe." She smiled her sad smile at him and strummed a G chord. "I need to say goodbye."

"So it's not a song *about* Jacob, then. It's a song *for* Jacob."

"It hurts, Josh. Knowing he's hurting. Knowing he's alone again. I need to do this."

"And you're going to sing this love song for Jacob live on stage at the Grammys. You're going to tell the whole world you still love him."

"I'm going to tell him I'm sorry. For everything. For hurting him. For having to let him go. It's the only way he'll listen."

"Okay. I know you. I hear you." Cornering right, Josh's voice was edged in frustration. "You're leaving in a week for Brussels, Jessie. I'd like to spend some time with you before you go, and I'd rather Jacob isn't always on your mind when we're together."

"He's going to be on my mind, Josh, for a long time." Accompanied by a deep sigh, Jessie's blue eyes drifted over to her sleeping child. Looking back at her husband a few moments later she added, as she rocked herself with a foot she placed on Dylan's bed, "It's not like you're ever here anyway."

"Kayla's a mess. I'm just trying to get her moved to her new place, that's all. She's exorcising the old memories."

"Thanks for reminding me."

"She needs some time."

"And I'm a cheater too. I get it. She hates my guts." With a scowl, Jessie settled deeper into the rocking chair. Glancing up at her husband, she was sorry to see a flicker of regret pass across his somber eyes. "Do you want to take it back now, Josh?"

"Take what back?" Shifting his creaking knees, Josh held onto his wife's hand, and slowly brushed his fingers across hers.

"You know. Telling me you will never leave me. For what I did."

"I don't want anybody else, Jessie." The simple statement was spoken almost in a childlike pout.

"That's not what I asked. Kayla doesn't want anyone else, either. But she asked Paul to leave."

Josh raised his chin. A tiny sliver of anger loosened itself in his voice. It darkened the liquid brown eyes Jessie adored. "I hate what you did. It makes me sick, thinking of you with him again."

Her defense was weak. "It makes me a little sick too."

"Does it. Just a little, huh?" Rising, Josh pushed on his knees and groaned with the effort. Jessie winced.

"Cut me some slack, Josh, please. None of this is easy."

"It's not going to get any easier if you keep locking yourself in Dylan's room to write sad songs for his father. You might want to consider what this is doing to me."

A few steps and Josh was at the door. Standing, Jessie pulled the guitar over her head and laid it in a soft-necked stand she kept in Dylan's room. She called out to her husband.

"Josh, I do think about what this is doing to you. Every day. It's this constant turmoil in my stomach that just goes around and around and around. And it doesn't help that you're always running off to Kayla to listen to her bitter stream of torment, then bringing your dark moods home to drive the guilt in a little further!"

Stopping at the door, he turned to face her. "You knew what you were getting into when you went to see Jacob in the first place, Jessie. You knew you were making a choice that would affect you and me. We've got a crazy year ahead of us. We don't have the luxury of time to sort out who is hurting the most here. All I can tell you is that I do. I hurt. A lot. What you did really sucked. It sucks. I understand why it happened, but it still sucks. I'm angry, you're sad, and in the meantime my sister is devastated and can't stand the sight of my wife right now."

Jessie was swiping at tears with the back of her hand now, standing in that childish, sulky, proud way of hers that signaled a full-on oncoming melt-down, but Josh didn't stop. Jessie had been moping around the house since the La Casa Boxing Day fiasco, and she would soon be leaving Vancouver for six weeks. Things needed to be said, and now, with the three Sawyer children off in dreamland, seemed to be the time to say them.

"Write all the sad songs for Jacob you want. Sing them in public; tell the world how you still feel about him. Just...why don't you cut off my balls and hang them out for everyone to see, too?"

The light from the hallway backlit Josh, silhouetting him as he stood, trembling, in front of Jessie. The effect was a man who appeared strong, but whom Jessie knew in her heart was very, very vulnerable. She extended a hand to him. To her relief, he took it and stepped back into the room.

"The thing you need to understand about my feelings for Jacob, Josh, is that they are separate from you in every way. I'm sorry for hurting you, but the two of you are apples and oranges. You're not the same thing; you're not the same person. I don't love you the same way."

He cringed.

Jessie squeezed her eyes tightly shut and winced. "Oh, fuck. I take that back." Sighing, she opened her eyes and continued. "I need to do this. I speak through songs. Through music, I let things that hurt go. And I need to let Jacob go. That's the only way you and me are going to be able to move forward."

"I would agree with you, Jessie, but there's one problem. We can physically remove Jacob from our lives, from Dylan's life, if Jacob's in agreement with that, and it seems to me that he is. But you can't just take a knife and cut the guy out of your heart. You said it yourself, he's always going to be there."

Jessie leaned forward and laid her forehead against her husband's. "I know," she whispered, "and right now my feelings for him have destroyed a whole lot of people. But Josh, I chose you. There was never a moment when I was with Jacob that I wasn't missing you with an ache that almost killed me. I will never go back to him. And if all of this is too much for you and you can't bring yourself to love the part of me that will always love him, then I'm here to tell you that I will fight for you. Always and forever, you and me. This is just one of the hard times, that's all. Which means we just have to fight all the harder to survive."

Josh's voice was softer when he spoke again. "I can't imagine my life without you. I need you in it, Jessie. Put the guitar away for tonight. I need some time to reconnect with my wife."

To emphasize his point, Josh wrapped his arms tighter around Jessie and pressed her body against him. She held on for a few extended seconds, but when Josh relaxed his grip and bent in to run his tongue over her lips, she kissed him back but then gently pushed him away.

The blue eyes were pale, accented by the moonlight filtering through Dylan's window, which wrapped Jessie in a ghostly aura. The pallid white light diminished her. It made her look fragile and delicate. "I need to finish the song," she murmured, one hand floating aimlessly in the air between them as if she wanted to take hold of her husband but couldn't.

"Of course you do," Josh responded, the words soaked with a weary irritation. He studied her for a moment, standing there before him all feeble and nervous in pink plaid pajama pants and a lacy white tank top.

Josh's footsteps were loud and hard as he wheeled around and stormed away. He closed Dylan's door behind him, and didn't look back.

Jessie collapsed back into the rocking chair, reached for the Gibson, and quietly retuned.

"Baby boy," she murmured to Dylan as he slept and as she started to strum, "this one's for your daddy. I sure hope he likes it because it's costing me a lot to write."

Outside, a wispy cloud passed in front of the moon and Dylan's room darkened. Jessie bowed her head and got to work.

When she finished the song and climbed into bed behind her husband, it was 1:30 a.m. Josh was sleeping with his back to her. Jessie snuggled up against him and wrapped an arm around his, clasped his fingers, and held on tight. As the new song bounced over and over through her mind she realized, in some ways, that she was also writing it for Josh.

My heart hurts
to know you suffer
My heart hurts
to know you care...

Chapter Two

$\mathcal{A}$ large orange bag of Fuzzy Peaches landed on the pile of neatly folded white T-shirts Matt had laid out on his and Julie's bed.

"What's this?" he smiled, picking up the crinkly bag and ripping it open. Sticking his thumb and forefinger inside, he withdrew two of the sugary treats and tossed one across the room to Julie, who caught it and immediately nipped off a piece. Matt stuffed the entirety of the other in between his lips, and whistled happily while he chewed on it.

"You were supposed to save those for the jet," Julie admonished as she leaned against the doorway and watched her husband pack.

"I'll save the rest," he told her, idly scanning his things to see what he might be missing.

"Did you have a chance to talk to Katy about that tattoo she wants? I'd prefer she consider both of our thoughts on it before she goes ahead."

"What? Oh. Yes. The tattoo."

Slipping into the ensuite bathroom, Matt emerged a moment later with his shaving kit, which he zipped up as he moved. He tucked it neatly into one corner of the suitcase and started to hum as he lifted the T-shirts and placed them in as well, on the opposite side.

"Matt!"

"What?" Rotating around at the waist to look over at his wife, Matt's eyes widened a little in surprise. Julie was frowning at him, sending him that seething look she only used when she was pissed, which, he realized with a start, he'd seen a lot over the last few weeks, when in fact he actually saw her.

Over this last while Matt had been swamped, working first on Jessie's

12

Florida trip and then on Talia's funeral in Nashville. Now Jessie's Belgian shoot was a priority. There were school field trips planned for both Emily-Grace and David, a nightmare as far as Matt was concerned, plus there were the usual family movements to be considered, both for the two older Sawyer children and for their father while Jessie would be away.

Also, Matt, Ulysses and Charles had Jacob back on their work radar since Talia's death. Not that Matt wanted shit-all to do with the lowlife singer and actor these days, at least until Jacob took some responsibility for hurting Jessie the way he had, but at this juncture the singer was still on the Keating roster and had seemingly cut Talia's security loose altogether.

"The tattoo," Julie was saying, her voice growing in annoyance. "Can we talk about this before you go?"

Matt spun back around and resumed his packing. "She's old enough to do what she wants now, Julie. Nothing either of us says is going to matter much to her anymore."

"That's a copout. We didn't stop being her parents the moment she turned eighteen."

"Fine. I told her to consider the long term, to get something small and meaningful to start, and to go from there."

"She wants a frog. A big one, on the side of her leg, so it shows above her boots. Did she tell you that?"

"Why in hell would she want to ink a frog on the side of her leg?"

"She's a musician, she's all about freedom of expression!" Julie's voice was rising further in volume. Clearly, she was exasperated with her husband and her daughter, although Matt wasn't certain which of the two she was the most pissed at.

He needed to keep packing. It was already noon and Matt was supposed to meet Jessie and Charles down on Robson by one. "But why a frog?" he asked without thinking as he rolled up a braided brown leather belt and tucked it into his suitcase behind a stack of neatly folded jeans.

"Matt!"

"What!" Now he, too, was getting frustrated. Facing off against his wife, Matt rubbed a palm against his newly shaved jaw and stared at her. "I need to finish packing, Julie."

"It's a frog! Our daughter loves frogs, and has since she was a small child. Have you seen her bed? It's covered in green frogs, some of which you've brought home from trips with Jessie."

"Okay, then. So a frog makes sense for Katy, for some ungodly reason I have yet to understand. If that's what she wants to tattoo permanently on her leg, then let her."

Julie was near tears. "I don't want her to permanently affix a green frog to her leg! She's just being rebellious."

"Why?" Matt threw his arms out to the sides. "I thought she was past that stage."

"Oh, Jesus. Seriously? This from the man who works with Jessie Wheeler, grown woman, yet still childish Queen of rebellion?"

"Julie, can we not bring Jessie into every discussion we have? It exhausts me." Weary, Matt stooped over and picked up the desert boots he planned to wear today. Setting them on the bed, he tucked the Fuzzy Peaches into his suitcase, then zipped it up and lifted it to the floor. Grabbing the desert boots, he grasped the handle of the suitcase and half-jogged out of the master bedroom and down the stairs.

Julie followed close behind. "This is not a discussion, Matt. We haven't had one of those in a while. This is actually a fight. And Jessie is in every conversation because she is your life. You know her children better than you know your own daughter. You know what they like to eat and where, you probably know what stuffed animals Emily-Grace has on her bed, and I'll bet you know what sexual positions Jessie likes best!"

Dropping the suitcase and the shoes in the downstairs foyer at the same time, Matt whirled around. "Julie, I don't know what brought this on, but two things. One, you have always been okay with me taking these trips with Jessie so I don't know what's upsetting you now, and two, you're crossing a line. I work for Charles, Jessie is my responsibility, and that's that. So stop with the petty jealousy, okay? Preferably now, before I walk out that door for six weeks."

"Three. You said it was three."

"I don't know. I might stay. I don't like the idea of leaving her over there alone."

"You said Arnie was going! He's supposed to switch off with you!"

"He was supposed to but we're sending him down to the Caribbean to find Jacob and see what's up with his schedule for the next few months. I don't know how long he'll be gone. Don't change the subject. What's got you all riled up?"

Julie took a deep breath and started in. "You're going alone this trip. With Deirdre out sick with the flu and Charles staying here to work on his new series, plus Josh staying in Vancouver with the kids, you're going to be spending a lot of time alone with a lonely woman who is very upset over the events of the holidays. And there's something you're keeping from me, too, I can always tell."

"Well, you know a helluva lot, I will assume from Deirdre and Carlotta, so you're not missing much, Julie. Not that any of what's upsetting Jessie has a damn thing to do with you!"

"Oh, but it sure as hell has a lot to do with you, Matt, doesn't it? At least, you make it your business, you make her your business more than you care shit about what's going on in the lives of your wife and daughter!"

Matt took stock of those words and settled. Biting his lip, he studied his wife. Julie was shaking now, running a hand over and over through her new fashionable layered bob. More was at play here than the usual good-natured teasing over the amount of time Matt spent with Jessie and Charles. Sucking thoughtfully on his lip so that he emitted a low *ssstt* sound, he stepped across the bright foyer of their large home and grasped her at the waist.

Unable to meet his eyes, she pushed him away.

"What?" he asked quietly. "What's different this time?"

"She slept with Jacob when she was in Florida. That's what's different."

"So…Deirdre and Carlotta told you this."

"No. Jessie did. Last week at La Casa. Although I have no idea why she would want to tell me that, since my very good looking husband is often alone in her company."

"So what's more upsetting to you, that Jessie was with an old boyfriend she dearly loves, or that she was unfaithful to Josh? And by the way, Julie, your earlier intuition is right. There's more to this story than you know, because I'm guessing Jessie didn't give you the entire unfettered truth about what happened down in Florida."

15

Blinking, Julie took that in, but she discounted it for the time being. "I'm just saying she's going to be lonely in Belgium and you're going to be her usual rock. The two of you live out of each other's pockets, Matt. You've become so close you can practically read each other's thoughts. And from what I hear, she and Josh are barely speaking, and she's cut Jacob out of her life entirely."

"Not entirely, because she and Jacob will often be at the same awards shows and concerts. And as far as Josh goes, they're dealing with it. He has a lot to process, and so does Jessie."

"You're always taking her side, Matt! Why? She cheated on her husband! Doesn't that make you angry?"

"You like Jessie, Julie. Stop trying to crucify her."

"You're too close to her. Call it a gut feeling. Since New York, the relationship the two of you have is far beyond security. It's beyond friendship! I don't want you to go on this trip, Matt. Switch off with Arnie."

"Tell me you're joking, Julie."

"Matt, I understand that you have some kind of driven need to protect her. It's great, it really is after the hell the two of you have been through, and I won't soon forget how much it hurt you to have to walk away from her back when Josh was sick. But sometimes I wonder if you realize just how close the two of you are. It crosses my mind, especially with her history—"

"Don't you dare go there, Julie. Now you're really crossing a line. She's your friend!"

"Come on, Matt. Nice clothes and a fancy house don't erase one's basic nature, shall we say."

"Tell me you didn't just call my client—and our friend—a whore, Julie."

"I didn't call her anything she hasn't already quite publicly called herself."

"Well," Matt said, moisture pricking at his eyes, "she doesn't always see herself the way the rest of us see her."

"The way you see her, you mean. Like a princess always in need of rescue. The rest of us quite clearly see who Jessie really is."

Shaking his head slowly, Matt paused and waited. Julie's words were unexpected and shocking. He felt like she was suddenly trespassing inside his soul.

An angry heat washing over her pixie face, Julie continued crisply pounding nails into Matt's heart. "The way you look at her, the way you touch her, that's what gets me. The two of you are always locked in each other's eyes. Everything's a private joke. Half the time you never even notice when someone else comes into the room! If it's not sex yet, it sure seems like it'll get there someday, Matt." Swiping a finger across her eyes, Julie had one final shot to fire. "She's your best friend, and you are hers. You jumped in front of a bullet for her! And I have a feeling she would do the same for you. If that's not love, then I don't know what is. And I'm just saying that she's in a vulnerable place right now, and you're only too happy to be the one to hold her and help her through it."

Matt's voice was a whisper. "I'm responsible for her safety, Julie."

"Yes. And you can't tell me that you're not still consumed with guilt over mistakes you made that put her and Josh in jeopardy. Matt," she licked her lips as she fought for the strength to say the words. "I challenge you to look me in the eye and tell me you don't love her."

Thrown, Matt made a strangled sound in his throat and replied with, "Of course I do. A lot of people love her."

"You know why I'm really scared, Matt? For you? For us?"

"Why?" A sense of dread started in Matt's gut and worked its way upwards. He closed his eyes for a moment and waited.

"Because it's so easy to fall into bed with someone when you're lonely, that's why. When you spend way too much time alone."

There was a suspended moment while Matt held his breath and regarded his wife. His words, when they finally came, were delivered so quietly she barely heard him. "What are you telling me, Julie?"

It took her a moment to find the words, but Julie had a secret that was eating her alive, that she could not contain for the next six weeks while Matt was in Belgium with Jessie. "I'm telling you that I have been lonely, Matt. I've been very lonely."

"So you…" A slow nausea started to swell over the sense of dread.

"I've been having an affair, Matt. And it's serious."

"Jesus Christ, Julie." Matt grabbed the doorframe for support. "And you're telling me this now? I'm on my way out of the fucking door!"

"That's why I'm telling you, Matt! I'm telling you because you are always on your way out of the door! You're always running off to Jessie! And I've been as supportive as I could be but I got lonely! I'm sorry. It happened, it just happened. I don't see…I don't see how…" She sighed heavily, and dropped down onto the bottom step at the same time that Matt's phone bleeped. Charles was looking for him.

"I'm on my way out of the door," he moaned again, without pulling his phone out of his pocket to see who was trying to reach him. He knew the message would be from Charles. "I'm already going to be late. What am I supposed to do with this information, Julie?"

"I said, switch off with Arnie!" she demanded. "Switch off with Arnie, and stay home so we can sort this out, Matt. So we can try to fix what's broken here."

But as she said it, Julie knew that was not an option. She could tell by the way her husband's eyes dripped sorrow that he was already mourning something that was, in all likelihood, permanently broken. It was clear where his allegiance lay.

"You're going to Jessie," Julie declared, staunchly raising up her shoulders and trying to look stronger than she felt. "And you wonder why I worry about the two of you. You're in love with her. You've probably always been in love with her."

"I'm not—"

She cut him off. "You're choosing her…over me. Over our daughter and myself. After I just told you our marriage is at risk. If that's not love, then I don't know what is."

"Why'd you tell me now, Julie? Why now, just as I have to go?"

A low laugh escaped Julie's lips as she grabbed the banister and hauled herself up. "I guess you could call it a test," she said. "And I guess you could say you failed. Goodbye, Matt."

"So what were the Fuzzy Peaches? You knew I would go." His voice was raspy, strained.

"Call them a hell of a parting gift."

Matt trembled in front of her before bending and pulling on his desert boots. Later, he wouldn't remember tying them, nor would he remember leaving the house and driving to Robson. But what he would never forget was the way Julie looked at him as he backed away, and what she whispered to him as he closed the door behind him.

"You never even asked who it is," she said. "Or for how long I've been seeing him. And you never threatened to go after him the way Deirdre said you went after Jacob in Nashville." She added the repeated refrain that haunted Matt for a long time afterwards. "If that's not what love is, then I don't know what is."

Chapter Three

The Keating Building's thirty-first floor was buzzing. Jessie herself was in a great mood, considering she was leaving imminently to shoot a film in Belgium for six weeks. Unlike a week ago, she wanted the change now. No—she craved the change. The only downside was that it felt a bit like running away again, running away from the sadness, anger, and worry for Jacob, and from the standoffish way Josh had been treating her since Nashville, as if he was standing back and watching her for cues, for signs that she was going off the rails again or sinking into a new black depression.

The other downside of leaving, of course, was the choice to leave her babies behind this time. In consultation with the school and with Charles and Deirdre, she and Josh made the decision to leave Emily-Grace and David in school for as long as possible. Emily-Grace, in particular, seemed to be finally making a friend or two, although over the last few weeks she had gone back to being withdrawn and quiet.

No surprise, Trudy had told them when they brought her in for a visit. *Talia's death and Jacob's verbal assaults outside the church when Dan tried to take Emily-Grace to the vehicle with her booster seat in it were a lot to handle. Emily-Grace needs some continuity and lots of patient love.*

It made sense to leave her home. Jessie, strolling quickly down the hall now to knock on Charles' door and drop off her latest updated itinerary to him, consoled herself with the knowledge that she was doing the right thing in leaving the children home. *Josh will be fine,* she told herself. *He's not drinking; Arnie will be around most of the time so they can go to meetings. Maybe it will be good for Josh and the kids to just be together.* The main worry was Josh's temper. For the most part he was patient, but sometimes the noise and frustration inherent in wrangling three small children got to him. Jessie had asked Charlie to check in with him regularly, and to report back to her.

Now, she dropped the itinerary on Charles' desk and stood in his expansive office waiting for him to disconnect from his phone call, since he had waggled a finger in the air and asked her to come in.

"You're vibrating," he told her with a smile when he set the phone down. "Nervous anxiety?"

Jessie slipped into a wide leather armchair and stuck one leg over the right arm so it dangled over the floor. "I just need to get back to work, Charles. This is a great part—a Belgian bluegrass singer who loses a child and ends up at odds with her husband whose nonexistent spiritual beliefs are opposite hers...I can't wait to sink my teeth into it."

Charles sat back and watched her. True, Jessie was bubbling over with enthusiasm. But there would be fallout from this job she was taking so far away, based on the way she was leaving things at home. She was running away. This was a Jessie special, although Charles accepted some of the responsibility for agreeing with Deirdre that it was a great role for their girl.

"It's going to be a tough part, Jessie. Your character loses her child to cancer."

"I know." Glancing down at her hands, Jessie sighed and studied her new French manicure. One of the white tips seemed a little crooked, to her. "I can handle it. I just hope Josh is okay with my own children at home while I'm away. Anyways, it'll fly by."

Pulling her phone out of the chest pocket of her blue plaid shirt—her ode to Jacob, she told herself when she put it on this morning—she frowned. "It's late, Charles. I wonder what's keeping Matt?"

"That was Matt on the phone. He's on his way." Charles' eyebrows knit together as he stared absently at the itinerary Jessie had dropped in front of him. "He sounded a little odd on the phone."

"Oh. I wonder what's up. I hope he hasn't caught Dee's flu. He's my last hope for Brussels."

"I guess we'll find out," Charles said. "He was just parking the car. He'll be here in a sec. Is Josh meeting you at the airport?"

"Yeah, he is. Then he'll run down to get the kids at school. He has Dylan." She looked up, and her expressive blue eyes became solemn. "You'll stay in touch with him, Charles? Every day?"

"Myself, Ulysses and Arnie, when he's here," Charles confirmed. "Plus Dan and Susanne, of course. And your own posse of Sawyer family protectors. Josh won't have a second to go rogue on you."

"I'm not sure how I should take that, Charles." Jessie shrank a little in her chair and delicately steered the conversation in a safer direction. "How's the series coming along?"

"All set to go to camera in March. The production office team is moving out to Calgary the first of February."

"So Jonathon's involvement gave you and Charlie the last bit of funding you needed."

"Yes, ma'am. Although to be honest, Jessie, it wasn't easy convincing Jonathon to come on board."

"Because of Josh and what happened with *The Wyatt Boys*."

"Because of Josh."

"It wasn't his fault. Not really." A wistful tone imbued the words with regret and sorrow. It always seemed that Josh got such a hard rap. Jessie's belly clenched at the idea of leaving him the way she was today—angry, sad, worried about his sister Kayla, and in charge of their three small children while she ran off to exotic Europe to shoot a film.

"I know," Charles declared staunchly, rising. "But Jessie, Josh is in a funk right now and I agree with Jonathon that he better snap out of it before we go to camera. We don't need a rerun of what happened on *The Wyatt Boys*."

"Jesus Christ, Charles, really? Do you honestly have a single memory of what happened back then? Jonathon is Josh's biological father, for God's sake." Tears stung her eyelids, and Jessie tossed her curls in a half-assed effort to force the moisture to dissipate. This was already an emotional day and, despite the excitement of this new adventure and getting back to work on a plum film role, Jessie dreaded the actual leaving part, the 'flying-through-the-clouds-and-leaving-her-family-behind' part. Josh. It always hurt to let him go, to duck her head and walk away. The kids? Jessie'd already had that cry over sunny David and sweet, quiet Emily-Grace, although Dylan would be at the airport with Josh when they said goodbye.

Skirting his large modern desk, Charles grasped Jessie by the shoulders as she stood. He looked down at her from behind his bifocals. "Do you think any of us have forgotten anything about those troubled days, Jessie? I'm sorry. There's just a lot on the line for this series, that's all. A lot of time and money has been invested in it."

"And a lot of cold hard cash came from Josh's status as an Oscar winning film star, let's not forget."

"Of course. I'm well aware that he's taking a step backwards in some ways to do TV again. And Charlie is on the series as well so Josh will have someone riding his butt the whole time to keep himself together and stay straight. But you have to admit, this last bit with you and Jacob has thrown him."

Jessie swallowed uncomfortably. This was an awkward conversation to be having with her pseudo-father. "Josh is a big boy. He loves me. We love each other. We'll get through this." She couldn't help herself. Partly to alleviate her own worries, Jessie tossed in, "He promised he would never leave me. He said it didn't matter how many lovers I had…"

Charles' eyebrows arched high at that one. "And are you planning to…"

"Jesus, Charles! No, damn it!"

There was a twinkle in the producer's eye. He laughed outright just as Matt stepped quietly into the office and stood just beside and behind Jessie. Impeccably dressed as always, in jeans today, the desert boots, and a crisp white cotton shirt open at the neck underneath an ink-blue Gucci cashmere coat that ended mid-thigh, and his hair spiked just so, he was the picture of formal work mode perfection. But when Jessie rotated around to call out a greeting, it was readily apparent that something was amiss. Matt's usual gentle, wise, light hazel-grey eyes were ringed with a light shade of crimson.

Matt caught Jessie's glance only briefly before shoving his hands in his pockets and focusing on the floor, aware from Jessie's suddenly concerned stare that he looked as badly as he felt.

"Ready to go?" he asked without looking at her.

"Once Charles stops picking on me about all of my future lovers I will be, yes," she answered him lightly, pivoting more fully around on one brown boot so she could wander over to him, her lone accompaniment on this trip.

"Matt?" Touching his elbow so that he would look up and meet her eye, Jessie asked tenderly, "What is it?"

There was a moment when Matt wanted to blurt it all out, to joke about what Julie had suggested about his relationship with the troubled actor and singer in his care; to let down the dam that had been building since Julie's appalling announcement just as he was leaving the house. It was a poignant moment rife with unspoken thoughts that swelled uncomfortably. If Matt took the moment to share what was on his mind, it'd be like sticking a needle-sharp pin into a fully inflated balloon and destroying it forever. The clandestine thoughts, if set free, had enough power to irrevocably, awkwardly, change things between he and Jessie.

Matt knew where the truth would land, at least in the short term. Charles—and Jessie, too, he gave her credit—would insist that he stay at home and deal with the threat to his marriage.

He licked his lips nervously and mumbled, "Little fight with Julie, that's all," intending to leave it at that.

Jessie's eyes softened. "I'm sorry, Matt."

To him, the simple words were Jessie's unwitting bearing of the burden of what Julie had called her. Of everything Julie accused her of—past, present and future.

"I am too," was all Matt could say to those beautiful, sweet, sad expressive eyes. But in that moment, Matt knew beyond the shadow of a doubt that he was making the right choice. He and Julie had felt like strangers for much of their marriage. This woman, Jessie, was someone Matt knew intimately—he was well versed on all of her quirks and issues and pains and past histories and loves, even the one gone badly wrong. In fact, he was the only person besides Jessie who knew the extent of Jacob's treachery just before New Year's.

Trying to force a smile to ease Jessie's concern, Matt wrapped one elbow around her shoulders and gave her a light squeeze, meeting Charles' frown as he did so. Beneath his arm, under the lavender-scented hair, he could feel

Jessie's shoulders relax. Matt couldn't help himself—he closed his eyes as the beloved arms snaked around his waist under the cashmere coat. As Jessie's loving, warm body melted into his.

Friends. We're friends, he told himself. *The best kind, the kind that can tell each other off and still laugh over stupid stuff a few minutes later. The kind that look out for each other when the going gets tough.*

Yet, as Matt released Jessie, touching her cheek lightly with a fingertip and inhaling deeply as her arms lingered around his waist, he knew something underneath his feet had shifted that day. It was spoken by Julie, not by him; nor did he ever voice it, yet upon hearing the words, Matt knew them to be true. Did he love Jessie the way Josh did? The way Jacob did? No, it wasn't like that, it wasn't a sexual craving. It wasn't a need to have her as his partner, to raise children with her, even though a lot of days it seemed Matt shared those things with Jessie anyway.

No, this was a deep abiding love that had grown over time, over shared experiences and tragedies and sadness and hope. It was nurtured in the wings of some of the world's biggest stages, it blossomed during long flights on the jet, sometimes with Jessie's head on his shoulder as she slept, and it grew when she came to him in pain and pleaded for him to understand, like the night when Matt found the blood in Emily-Grace's fine blonde ringlets and realized its origin was Jessie's cut lip.

Yeah. Matt would choose Jessie over Julie. Standing in Charles' office he did just that, in fact, affirming his choice while Jessie's arms were still lightly around his waist. The decision was not one he would have made in the early days, but now there was no question.

He was aware it meant there was a deficit in his character—a lack of honor—that hurt Matt to have to face. Because rarely did Matt let himself dwell on the parts of him he felt were broken.

Jessie was worth it. Her music was worth it.

She was still standing before him now, one ankle turned over, fingers twisting together, curiously watching the thoughts move like shadows across his face. Her usual sad smile was upside down. Matt's faded too, and suddenly a new revelation made itself known.

We can read each other. The thought scared the shit out of him, and he wiped his lip and took a step backwards just as Charles broke him out of his reverie.

"Jessie, why don't you run down the hall and gather your things? Get Magda to call Scott to give you a hand. Matt, a word, please."

"All right," Jessie said, also thrown a little by what she saw in Matt's expression. There was trouble there in her good friend's eyes, no doubt about that, but she had no idea what it meant. *However,* she consoled herself as she skipped down the hall, *we've got lots of time to sort it out.*

In his large office, Charles placed both hands on his hips and stared at the man he trusted with Jessie's life. "What is it, Matt?" The question, although asked kindly, was layered with Charles' usual businesslike gruffness. "I can't have you responsible for Jessie if your mind is going to be elsewhere. Not after what happened before. This will be a very public shoot. She'll need you to be on your toes."

"It's all good," Matt told him, trying to bring his wild emotions under control but not doing a very good job of it. "Julie and I had some words as I was leaving, that's all. I'm not one to bring my home life into the office, you know that."

"Well maybe you should, Matt. You've always played your cards pretty close to your chest, but you're among friends here."

"I know. Thank you." Matt nodded uncomfortably and changed his stance. "Look, we're already running late. Josh will be at the airport waiting with Dylan and I don't know how much patience that child has. Jessie and I had better hit the road."

Charles clapped him on the shoulder as they strode up the long hall together. "Keep an eye on our girl for us, Matt. Keep her safe. And don't get any ideas about jumping in front of bullets. Unless you have to."

"That goes without saying." With a small but cheeky grin, Matt felt his load lighten just a little. *This is where I belong,* he thought as he watched Jessie, down the hall, having an impromptu game of Nerf football with one of Charles' sound engineers. "I'd take a bullet again for her any day." A twinge in his stomach knotted itself around his intestines as a hard thought accosted him. As Matt told himself he would do the same for his wife.

Jessie babbled about silly things all the way to the airport, so Matt didn't have to do a lot of the talking, but he did throw in a few words when she finally stopped chatting and offered him an apology.

"Sorry, Matt. I'm just nervous, I guess." She sat back against the leather seat and exhaled slowly.

"I know," Matt smiled.

Jessie grinned and rolled her eyes. "I know that you know." Chuckling lightly, she grabbed his hand so she could give it a squeeze. Her eyes darted to him when he pulled it away from her. *Okay,* she breathed, but left it alone despite the odd feeling the quick movement engendered in her belly.

Navigating the Audi through the private departures security gate, Matt drove right up to the Keating jet and parked alongside so he could easier facilitate transferring his and Jessie's things from the car to the airplane. He watched as Jessie got out and stretched before sauntering across the tarmac to meet Josh, who had parked the King Ranch closer to the gate, facing the jet.

"Hey," Jessie said to her husband, who opened the driver's side door, slid out, glanced into the back seat, and gently pushed the door closed before walking around to meet her. "I guess I caught Dylan at nap time." Crestfallen, Jessie peeked in the passenger side window. "How long has he been asleep?"

"He fell asleep on the way out here. You guys are late so I'd say about an hour."

"Which gives him about another half hour. Damn. I woulda liked those little arms around my neck one last time before I take off."

"Would you."

Throwing Josh a 'look,' Jessie turned and leaned her back against the truck. Deciding not to take the bait, which Jessie rightly figured Josh intended as a snipe against her indiscretion with Dylan's biological dad, she tossed her curls and watched Matt cart her big suitcase towards the jet.

"We were late because Matt was late."

"Matt's never late."

"Today he was," Jessie responded, as Josh wandered over and took up a post next to her. "Seems Julie picked a fight with him before he left home. He's not really his happy bossy self."

At the jet, Matt passed off the big suitcase to a crew guy in a blue jacket and orange vest, and then he turned to head back towards the Audi. Glancing up, he saw that he was being watched, and looked away despite a wave Josh half threw towards him.

"Hmm," Josh remarked. "Odd."

"I'm sure he'll be fine. You know what it's like when we fight. Sometimes it takes a bit before one of us cools down." Elbowing Josh affectionately in the ribs, Jessie felt a rising gloom take hold. Pivoting towards him on one heel, she grabbed a few handholds of his denim jacket at the waist, took a deep breath, and let the air out slowly while she buried her lips in his neck.

"You're tickling me," she heard him murmur as his hands moved up to her elbows and then around her back.

There was so much that needed saying, but neither knew how to find the words to adequately express the loathsome feelings they had laid bare over small fights and absences from home over the past few weeks. A small grunt was Josh's way of saying how hard this was, to let Jessie go this way. For her, little weepy mewls were all she had to offer.

Matt couldn't help himself. At the jet, behind the Audi, he watched Josh and Jessie say goodbye without the support of words to carry them through. After a few minutes, he saw Jessie lift her head and clutch her husband's jacket at the neck. Josh grabbed a handful of her hair and leaned in for a long kiss, bringing his second hand up to Jessie's left cheek and holding her there, still, while he pressed his lips to hers hard enough to apparently make her knees go weak. She seemed fragile enough for Josh to have to let go with one arm and wrap it around her waist in order to hold her up. They were speaking, but Matt was too far away to hear, although he saw Jessie nod and wipe away tears.

"Great," he muttered to himself. "This is going to be one helluva happy flight."

Bitter, still reeling from his wife's proclamations and announcement, he swung open the door of the Audi, slid behind the wheel, and drove it into a parking spot next to the King Ranch.

"Jessie," he called as he locked it, tucked a key on a tire under the passenger side's back wheel well, and started to move towards the jet, "let's go."

"Hi to you too, Matt," Josh said without looking away from his wife.

Matt didn't answer.

Josh looked up. "Hey! Matt!"

Slowly, Matt stopped and turned.

"All right," Josh started as he dropped his arms from Jessie and moved towards him. "I'm sorry Julie pissed in your cereal today but I'd like to have a word with you before you take off with my wife for the next three weeks."

"Six," Matt corrected him, his lips pressed into a thin line.

"Six?" whispered Jessie as a slow smile spread across her cheeks. "Yay? Yay."

In his peripheral vision, Matt caught her happy reaction. He looked over at her. She gave him a thumbs-up but he grimaced and refocused on Josh while she frowned and shoved her fingers in her back pockets. "What is it, Josh? We need to get the hell out of Vancouver. The sooner the better."

"Just…call me if anything…you know. Just call me, okay?"

"I'm sure you'll hear from your wife every day, Josh. If there's anything you or the kids need, Charles and Ulysses are close by, and you'll have Dan and Susanne on rotation."

"And Arnie?"

Matt scowled. "Arnie's heading south at some point in the next few weeks to rout out Jacob and find out what the hell his plans are. I'm not sure when he'll be back. I guess it will depend on how deeply Jacob's gone into hiding and how long it takes to find him."

At that, Jessie squirmed. She dared a peek at Josh and found his lips working but no sound coming out.

Avoiding Jessie's stare while he spoke, Matt filled in the silence. "I hope he beats the shit out of him when he finds him."

"Thought you got a good start on that at the funeral, if I don't say so myself," Josh finally said, confused at Matt's dark mood and the blatant remark about violence against Jacob. "And may I add remind me to stay on your good side."

"If you want to stay on my good side, find it in yourself to forgive your wife for what happened in Florida. The way I heard it, Jacob's responsible, not Jessie."

"Matt!" Jessie's eyes flashed as she shot him a warning, but Matt just glared back at her. "For fuck's sake! What the hell's gotten into you today?"

Unsure how to interpret Matt's remark, Josh's ears pricked up. He watched the interchange between Matt and Jessie now with a growing trepidation.

They were silent now, but were sending each other telepathic notes, it seemed, which freaked Josh out. Jessie's eyes were tearing up by the time Matt sent Josh a final glare, swung around, and marched towards the jet, calling over his shoulder to Jessie to hurry the hell up.

Stunned, "What the hell was that?" Josh asked Jessie. "I've never seen Matt this angry for no reason."

"I used to be scared of him," Jessie replied as she watched her security and companion for the next six weeks storm away. "Now I remember why." In her head she ran a gamut of questions. *Did I do something? Did I piss him off?*

Josh cut into her thoughts by grabbing her elbow and turning her towards him. The pearlescent blue eyes were dim, covered by a wet sheen now, and Josh realized that it wasn't all just because she was leaving for an extended time. Part of it was her concern for Matt.

"Look," he said gruffly, "we don't want to piss him off further by holding him up. Say goodbye and call me when you get there."

"It'll be like, duh, dawn or something crazy like that when I get there."

"I don't care. I'm leaving my phone on. Got your Gibson?"

"Hell, yeah."

"Good. I wouldn't want to see you all alone in Brussels without your best friend."

"I'm leaving my best friend here, dork. Duh."

"Jess, look—"

Interjecting, Jessie covered his lips with two of her fingers and shook her head. "We've said all there is to say. I love you like crazy, I already miss you, and you suck for staying so mad at me for so long."

A heavy weight almost collapsed Josh. Shoulders sinking, he nodded. "I know. I'm sorry, it's just Kayla and all her shit too. It's a lot, you know?"

She shrugged, and added a slow nod filled with light and hope. "I know," she admitted. "I get it, Josh. But I don't know how many times I can say I'm sorry. There's got to be a point when you accept my apology and we move on."

"I don't know when that's going to be. All I know is, the more I watch my sister cry, the more what you and Jacob did seems to hurt."

"I'm sorry for what Kayla is going through, Josh. But Mandy means nothing to Paul."

"And that's supposed to help me how?" Bewildered, Josh's voice raised in pitch.

"You know how I feel about Jacob. How much he means to me, how much I needed to hold him!"

"Not fuck him, Jessie. You weren't supposed to fuck him, okay? Jesus! You wanted to be all touchy-feely, fine, I get that. Talia was an amazing woman and we're all sorry she's gone. Reminding me how much you love him— love, I said, not loved—doesn't do a damn thing to help my floundering self-esteem right now."

"You said you understood. You said you got the whole 'love isn't a light switch' thing."

"And you said you and Jacob are done. So let's wait to see how that goes, okay? Like, I'm not going to hear about him landing in Brussels, am I?"

"Seriously, Josh? Is this how we're going to say our goodbyes?" Planting her feet apart with a stomp and a raise of her chin, Jessie added angrily, "Am I, like, going to come home and find out you've given one of our kids away, like back to his real daddy maybe?"

"Jesus fucking Christ, Jessie. Get the hell on the jet, will you, before I do something I'll regret!"

The rage building in her husband's eyes was familiar to Jessie, but she was seeing cobalt blue now instead of chocolate brown. Shades of Jacob's anger in Florida were cresting over Josh's indignant frustration at her nasty remark.

At the top of the steps up to the jet, Matt appeared, ready to call his charge again but refraining from hollering since, even from thirty feet away, he could see Jessie swiping at tears as Josh paced and cursed at her.

"What are you going to do, Josh?" Jessie was arrogantly asking her husband as he trembled before her. "You gonna hit me? Cuz if that's your plan, I've got news for you. It's been done. Maybe if you do it with a little more force than Jacob did, you'll actually break my jaw, though. Musicians, you know. Those guys and southern businessmen don't have quite the same strength as Oscar winning actors who wrangle wild horses for a hobby. I'll see you, okay? Take care of our kids. All of them."

At that, Jessie strode off towards the jet. Josh turned and stormed back off to the King Ranch, swung open the door, and slammed his fist into the

hood before he pulled himself up and into the big truck. He got there first—
Jessie was jogging the last few feet towards the jet's stairs when he looked up
at her hunched back. It was easy to tell, by the way she ran holding her hand
up to her face, that she was crying.

"Oh, for fuck's sake," he cursed. "Damn it."

He watched as Matt stepped aside to let Jessie into the jet. She brushed
by him without looking at him. Josh didn't move. Dylan was still asleep, so
Josh flipped on the radio and let music play low while he watched the door
to the jet swing shut. Soon it was taxiing down the runway. Shortly after,
clouds swallowed it up.

Josh started the truck, circled around, passed through the security gate,
and cursed all the way down to West Point Grey Academy to pick up his
two older children.

On the jet, Jessie had dropped into her usual wide seat on the right side
of the plane facing the cockpit, yanked out her iPhone and earbuds, and put
her music on the shuffle setting. Squeezing her eyes tight, she tried not to
let her frustration get the best of her, but the first song to come on was that
old standby she wrote for Josh when they first met.

When Matt had passed her as he made his way to the back of the jet,
Jessie's tears were flowing freely. Any day but today he would have grasped
her shoulder as he passed, or even sat down beside her. But today he felt
the same way she did, and more than a little pissed at the whole cheating
vibe, and he wanted to be alone. Choosing a seat at the far end of the small
couch at the back, he belted himself in for takeoff and turned his head
towards the wall.

It was pitch black hours later when Matt felt something brush by his legs.
It was Jessie, on her way to the washroom. Straightening, rubbing his eyes,
Matt undid his seatbelt and stretched. Momentarily he heard the toilet flush
and the tap come on. The small door opened, blinding Matt with its bright
light, and then Jessie moved towards him. He blinked up at her, and she
dropped down onto an ottoman by the couch and faced him.

"Ain't this gonna be a fun six weeks," she started. "The mood Josh is in
right now, I sure as hell wish Arnie was going to be around more instead of
chasing old wooden sailboats in the Caribbean."

"I'll call Ulysses and ask him to take Josh to a few meetings after Arnie leaves, Jessie. I'm sure he'll be fine."

She grunted. "Fine like 'won't drink at all fine,' or 'fine like I'll just have a few and forget I have three kids fine.' Which fine."

Sighing, Matt looked away and brushed a finger and forefinger against his chin. "Josh will not go down that road again, Jessie," he said, a hint of exasperation in his voice. "He knows what he has. He's not going to be stupid enough to throw it away."

"Again," Jessie moaned. "Don't forget the 'again' part."

Eyeing her carefully, Matt assessed Jessie's state. "What'd you say to him to piss him off so badly?"

Groaning, Jessie stuffed her face into her palms and stared through parted fingers at the floor. "I might've said something about giving one of our kids back to his real daddy or something," she mumbled.

A choked laugh came from Matt's direction. "Jesus, you women sure do have a way with words. Sometimes I think us guys should just move out to ranches in the middle of nowhere and commune with nature instead of trying to communicate with the likes of you."

"Or maybe buy an old sailboat and cruise around the Caribbean, huh Matt? Get the clap instead?"

"You figure that's what Jacob's doing, is it? Sleeping his way around the Caribbean?"

"Hell, yeah. He slept with all kinds of women before he and I got together in Scotland. He was a real man-whore back then. Used to leave his bedroom door open and I'd tiptoe by on my way to the bathroom, you know, the rest of us would be watching movies or just hanging out, and Jacob would be with one woman one night and another the next. He likes sex, that boy. And he's good at it," she muttered without embarrassment or apology. "Most of the time. Well," she sighed, "even that time. Minus the punch and me screaming 'no,' I mean."

Matt was shaking his head when Jessie looked back up at him. He started to take off his warm cashmere coat that, in his hurry to get belted in and hide alone earlier, he'd left on. One of the arms was sticking a bit at the shoulder. Jessie reached up and started to help him, but Matt pushed her hand away.

Hurt, Jessie backed off and studied his face. The usually kind eyes were bloodshot and tired. Matt's face was pale and drawn. Over the hum of the jet, his silence was deafening.

"Matt," Jessie said softly, "I wish you'd tell me what's bothering you. Did I…did I do something? Did I piss you off somehow?"

Matt's right hand was on the left arm of the coat, working at the shoulder. It froze, and hung there, suspended, until Matt got his wits together and exhaled slowly. Finally loosening the sleeve and removing the coat, he folded it, laid it over the ottoman next to Jessie, and looked up at her. She was watching him so seriously now, her face concerned and her lips parted, just a little, as she bent towards him and leaned both elbows on her knees.

"I told you," he said carefully. "Julie and I had a fight. A bad one."

"About…? Can I ask what you were fighting about? I mean…I know it's none of my business, but we're friends, right Matt? You and me?"

Shuffling in his seat so he sat up straighter, Matt sighed and contemplated what to say. In the end he just stared at the floor and mumbled something about Julie not being thrilled with the trip.

"Oh," Jessie said, her voice slightly higher pitched than usual and her shoulders straightening. "I see. You were fighting about me. Seems to be the 'in' thing to do lately."

Matt let his gaze drift up to her face. Almost as if he couldn't help himself, he let his right fingers float up and touch Jessie's cheek. He brushed a thumb under her chin. Her old mask was back, the one that, Matt knew from experience, she put securely in place to cover up the things that hurt. It was her eyes that gave her away. They were floating, and she pressed a forefinger into the corner of one to make sure a tear didn't sneak out.

Matt let his hand drift around so that he could touch her face with the backs of his fingers. Jessie thought nothing of the gesture, except that it was sweet. She took his hand as he lowered it, held it between her fingers—studied it, in fact—and traced one of the lines in his palm.

If that's my marriage line, it's broken, Matt thought quietly as he watched her.

"So?" Jessie's heart lurched when she saw something between fear and sorrow flicker across Matt's eyes. "She's pissed because you're travelling with me. She was never pissed before. Why now?"

"She's got this weird idea that you…that you and I…that we care about each other more than we should." He swallowed. "Since you and Jacob…" Matt let the words fade away.

Jessie's laugh was weird, surprised. "So I'm going to seduce her husband now, is that it? Jessie the whore strikes again. It won't matter how many Oscars I win or songs I write that shoot up the charts to number one. I'll always be the homeless porn star from the Downtown Eastside."

"Julie's been having an affair, Jessie. She told me while I was on my way out of the door."

"Oh. Matt, geez. I'm so, so sorry." Lifting his hand, Jessie brushed her lips against his knuckles. This time when Matt pulled his hand away, Jessie grabbed it back. "Friends hold hands, Spike. It's okay, really. This is not X-rated stuff we're doing here." The blue eyes were shining, glistening in the dim light. They lit up the tiniest bit when Jessie added tenderly, "Julie's right about one thing. I do care about you. A lot. I'd be first in line for you if she let you go, Matt. I told Deirdre that once, and I meant it."

A faint pink blush spread across Matt's cheeks and he let one corner of his lip turn up while, at the same time, a groan escaped from somewhere deep in his throat. "You might want to take that back, Jessie. I don't know where this is going to land, but I have a feeling it's not going to be pretty. Besides," he smiled sadly, "I think you've got your hands full."

"The way this day went, Matt, you and I could both be single by the time we land in Brussels."

"That's not funny, Jessie. It was just a weird day. The stars weren't aligned or something. Everything will be fine."

"I hope you're right, Matt. I really hope you're right."

A diabolical grin lit up Jessie's face. Rising, she dropped down by Matt on the small couch. He made room for her by amicably lifting his arm, and she snuggled underneath. "Although if you're wrong, maybe we should practice, huh? Do a little funky monkey? Some bedtime boogie, maybe?"

Wrapping one arm around his stomach and the other around Matt's lower back, Jessie felt her heart lighten up a little. Easing her body lower, she let one leg fall against his, and closed her eyes. "I'm here if you need me, Matt," she said, realizing as she said it that he'd grown silent again and had not responded to her joke. "You've always been here for me. Maybe now it's my turn to comfort you. Okay?"

Tilting her face up to her friend, Jessie was saddened to see him struggling for composure. Matt tried to look away, but Jessie straightened and reached out to him, tucking her left hand underneath his chin and forcing him to look at her.

"Matt, honey, I mean it. I'm really, really sorry about Julie. I hope she'll come around because I do not know a better man than you. I love you like crazy, and I can't stand to see you hurting like this. C'mere."

His shoulders were shaking when Matt finally let Jessie hold him. She grasped him tightly, one arm around his back and the other behind his head, pulled him to her chest, and rocked him just a little while he cried, all the while letting the emotion from the past few weeks and today's desperately angry parting with Josh leak down her cheeks as well.

"We're a good pair," she whispered into Matt's spiked hair, overwhelmed by this powerful moment in which the man responsible for her safety let his guard down enough to let Jessie spy the pain in his soul. "But we have each other, Matt. We'll be okay, I swear. Everything will be okay."

By the time Matt settled, Jessie had eased him down on the couch next to her. She nudged him onto her shoulder so he could sleep, and she held him and slept next to him until Victoria woke her with a gentle tap and a sweet, "We're landing soon, Jessie."

"Okay," she blinked then, and nudged herself more fully awake. "Thank you, Victoria."

Matt was still asleep, his white cotton button down shirt escaping his jeans and overlapping his belt. Jessie watched him breathe, this man who was her constant companion, security and friend, and she swallowed carefully. A heady wave of feeling swept over her. It wasn't love in the sexual sense, but it was love all the same, accompanied by tenderness and a single-minded determination to ease his hurts as much as she could, if things escalated with Julie and took him down a dark road.

Bending down on one elbow, Jessie let a finger trail lightly along his left cheek.

"Matt," she whispered softly as he stirred, "we're almost there. It's just you and me now, buddy. I hope you don't get sick of me."

A stray lock of Jessie's hair was falling over her cheek. Slowly waking, still half in dream world, Matt reached up and tucked the long, tired curl back into place behind her ear. She smiled, and he smiled back.

"Go," he told her, his voice weary. "Buckle up. I'll see you on the flip side."

"You too," she said, bending to brush her lips across his forehead. "I hope we're not in for a bumpy landing."

She moved up the aisle to her original seat and settled carefully into it. Victoria swept by in her halo of jasmine, and offered Jessie a drink before it was time for her to buckle up as well.

From his seat on the couch, Matt watched the women chat. This time when he fastened his seat belt, a small smile lit up his face and, as the Keating jet touched down in Brussels, Matt felt his heart lift as relief earned by distance and good company passed through his body. Like soothing aloe vera balm, it was cool and moist, and it was very, very welcome.

Chapter Four

While Jessie, with Matt as her shadow, met the cast and crew of the Brussels film, did a table read, and modeled wardrobe for camera testing, Josh held the fort at home. On his third day alone with the kids, he ended up calling Kayla and asking her to pick up the older two from school because Dylan was napping and Josh didn't want to wake him.

"Susanne can bring them," Josh told her, "but we like to keep a little distance between the kids' security and our normal lives whenever possible. We try to just use Dan and Susanne for rides when we're desperate."

In truth, it was mostly a ploy to get Kayla out of her funk and out of her pjs. The workshops would not be starting up again for a few more weeks and Josh, her concerned older brother, felt she needed a purpose.

"Jessie's not here," he added warily. "She's on her shoot. You won't run into her."

"Fine," Kayla answered with a grunt. "But you should know I haven't showered in three days."

"And you think I'm the one who is making the wrong choice? Kayla, if you love Paul, go get him back. Love is worth hanging on to."

She jumped in with the first voice of reason Josh had heard from her since she and Paul split. "Big brother, I've been on the blogs. Most writers argue that one partner cheating on the other is a symptom of larger problems. I, personally, acknowledge that Paul and I lost our magic somewhere along the line. The guy's a lawyer and I'm a dancer. We probably did good staying together as long as we did."

"What happened with Jessie and Jacob was completely different, Kay.

It was motivated by tragedy." Wandering up the stairs as he talked, Josh peeked in on Dylan. Moving into the semi-dark bedroom, he ran a finger over the child's curls. What would life be like for Dylan as he grew older and fans forgot to filter their comments about his parentage? At least in Josh's childhood experience with Wes, Jonathon was a closely guarded secret.

I'm here for you, buddy, he said inwardly as he listened to his sister.

"Don't kid yourself. Talia was still alive at La Casa on Boxing Day, Josh." The silence on Josh's end of the line threw her. Despite her own issues, Kayla couldn't stand the thought of her big brother going down another dark road. She threw out a lifeline. "Look, I'm sorry, I'll go get the kids and check in with you to see if you're still in your pajamas. I hope you've showered since Jessie left, though, because the two of us stinking up your house would not be pretty."

Laughing, Josh ended with, "You've got an hour. Shower first. I'll call the school and Susanne as well to tell them you're coming."

Later, Kayla bounced into Josh's home with more zest and smelling much better than he anticipated. Emily-Grace's fingers were wrapped in hers, and the little girl was skipping. Raising his eyebrows in curiosity, Josh smiled at the sight of the child who, it was obvious, was clearly relieved to have her much adored cool aunt around.

Kayla propped her niece up on a chair at the kitchen island while Josh puttered around and made snacks. Apple slices and yogurt were today's choices, with chocolate almond milk as a treat.

After Susanne lifted him into a chair, David added ice cream with chocolate sauce drizzled overtop to his order. She took the now awake but grumpy Dylan into her arms so Josh could have both hands free for food prep.

Emily-Grace was rambling on about Kayla's hair that, Josh noticed, now had large swaths of cranberry through it.

"I colored it again," the dancer said proudly. "New digs, new clothes, new tattoo, new hair. New everything."

"You're more like Jessie than you think, Kayla," Josh chuckled. "I seem to recall that coloring her hair was the first thing she did when she took off years ago."

"When she vanished and left everyone hanging for a year and a half, you mean? I'm nothing like her. I simply changed my hair color. I didn't cruelly disappear."

"Ouch. Thanks for that."

"Jessie does what Jessie wants to do, Josh. Always. She's a major star with a huge ego, and she's used to people catering to her. I'm just surprised Jacob is the only guy she's—" Covering Emily-Grace's ears, she gestured to Susanne to cover David's. "Slept with over the years. Maybe he isn't, in fact. Seems like you guys hardly ever see each other."

Susanne jumped in. "Josh has the same opportunities, Kayla. We all do, in relationships. Cheating isn't reserved for celebrities."

"Do you worry?" Kayla asked her as Emily-Grace tried to figure out what the adults were discussing and while David dipped his apple slices in the ice cream Josh slid before him.

"My guy's a good looking NHL hockey player. These days, he's down south soaking up the sun while I wilt up here in the rain or freeze in the snow. Of course I worry. Actually, while we're on that subject…" Susanne looked up at Josh. "Can we talk over here for a sec?"

Josh nodded. "Sure. Yeah. Um, Kayla can you—"

"Yeah, yeah," his sister interjected with a wave of an arm. "I got it. I'm all over these munchkins."

Susanne handed Dylan to her, and Kayla immediately lifted him and blew a great big raspberry into his belly, which instantly bent him over in a fit of two-year-old giggles, his 'I just woke up' crankiness quickly becoming eradicated with the arrival of his loving aunt.

"You are adorable," she giggled, not realizing that Josh was still within earshot. "You look just like your handsome daddy."

Unbeknownst to Kayla, Josh stopped in his tracks and stared.

Emily-Grace's spoon was suspended as she tried to sort out the hurt in her father's eyes. Over Kayla's shoulder she met his despondent gaze. "It's okay, Daddy," she told Josh. "Momma always says David looks just like you, and there's a lot of love in her eyes when she says it." She turned to Kayla, who had gone white when she realized her faux pas in front of both Josh and his kids. "Dylan's so lucky. He has two daddies."

"Not anymore he doesn't," Josh grumbled as he followed Susanne into the living room. Pushing aside the shock of hearing Kayla voice a truth he didn't care to hear, he dropped down onto the leather couch and, with a gesture, invited Susanne to sit. "Why do I feel a little sick right now?" he asked her, wondering what was on her mind.

She didn't keep him waiting. "I'm sorry, Josh. I don't suppose I have great news for you, but I know you'll understand. Saving a marriage takes work. Running between Tampa and Vancouver, not to mention all over the place with you and Jessie and the kids, is not leaving me a lot of time to give my husband the attention he deserves. I need to move on."

"Really, Susanne? I honestly didn't see this coming." His heart sinking, Josh instantly felt an icy chill travel up his spine. Replacing Susanne was a terrifying thought. Morgan's treachery crossed his mind.

"I've been thinking about it for a while. My man's got needs." A half-smile crossed her lips. "And a lot of options, if you know what I mean."

"Must be that Florida sunshine," Josh frowned. Leaning forward and resting his elbows on his knees, he ran his fingers through his hair and sighed. "I'm terrified to see you go. The kids love you. They know you. We know you, and trust you. I honestly don't know what to say."

Sympathetic, sorry to be the cause of what she knew would cause a certain amount of grief for the Keating / Sawyer camp, Susanne lightly touched his arm. "Josh, I'll stay in touch with the kids. Maybe they can have Arnie or Matt for a while, until they get to know my replacement."

"The last time we hired someone new it didn't go so well, Susanne." Josh stared at a toy on the floor at his feet. It was a plastic fire engine. The memories suddenly attached to it were sickening.

"There are more good people than bad out there, Josh. All of you will do your due diligence. There won't be another Morgan."

"I know, I'm..." His heart racing, Josh picked up the fire engine and regarded its hoses and ladders. "I'm being selfish. Of course you need to be with your husband. It's the worst, being separated all the time." Forcing a small smile, he looked up at her.

"I know it is," she agreed. "Sometimes reality sucks."

"Have you already told Charles? And Ulysses, I gather, since Matt's with Jessie?"

"Charles and Ulysses know. They'll let Matt know. I assume whichever of you gets to Jessie first will tell her."

"She'd probably want to hear this directly from you, Susanne."

At that, Susanne hesitated. "Josh, I'm sorry, but…when all was said and done, when all the pros and cons were weighed out, Jessie was the final reason I decided to go."

"Oh. OH. Because she…"

"It scares the hell out of me to leave my guy alone as much as I do. I always figured if he wanted to cheat there wouldn't be a damn thing I could do to stop him. So why worry, you know? But when you love someone as much as I love him…I've started to think that I'd be cutting the chances of him cheating on me down a lot if I was actually in his company."

"So like…he gets what he needs at home, he doesn't go looking, is that it?"

"That's not what I'm saying, Josh. Not everything in relationships is about sex."

Crestfallen, Josh ignored her and went down that road anyway. "Did Jessie ever say anything to you? About us? I thought she was happy with me. With…sex. You know."

"She's blissfully happy with you, Josh. That was never an issue, as far as she's spoken to me, at least. I've never seen her more happy than over the past few years, with these children, and with you."

"Let's be honest, Susanne. The occasional sadness still sneaks through."

"Not very often, honey. Mostly only in her music. That woman is desperately in love with you. And by the way, the entire time she was living in New York with Jacob she was on her knees for love of you, for how much she was missing you. If there's sadness here, it's nothing like it was then."

She tapped Josh on the knee, and rose. "I'm going. I'll give you some time to digest this and figure out whether you want me to tell Emily-Grace and David, or whether you want to tell them yourself. I've given Ulysses two weeks' notice but I told him I can stay longer if you're still searching for a replacement. I understand the need to find the right person."

Susanne left Josh sitting quietly in the living room while she went to hug and kiss the kids before leaving for the day.

Setting Dylan on the floor and handing him a bucket of large, colorful

Lego blocks, Kayla wandered over to Josh and plopped down next to him. In the kitchen, Emily-Grace and David had their stuffed toys on the island and were ungracefully smashing them into each other as they finished their snacks.

"What was that all about?" Kayla asked. "It seemed rather serious."

"Susanne's leaving us." The news was still sinking in. This would devastate Emily-Grace, and the idea of finding someone new that they would all have to get to know was more than disconcerting. Plus what if another Morgan… the thought was unthinkable. Josh had more to say. "Don't gloat, but it would appear Jessie's nefarious actions left an even larger trail of destruction than she obviously ever anticipated."

"Susanne's leaving because of Jessie?"

"It would seem leaving your partner alone is no longer a good idea." Setting down the fire truck and giving it a light kick with his toe, Josh filled Kayla in on Matt's situation.

"It's an epidemic," Kayla mumbled.

"We need to find someone new, who we can trust." Thoughtfully, Josh scratched his jaw. "I wonder if Matt's brother Michael has anyone on his and Kelly's team who might want to relocate to the cool Canadian north?"

"This isn't the north, bro. People golf here in January. They sail all year round." Kayla sat back and mused over this new Sawyer family dilemma.

"Yeah, but Florida it ain't. Thank God," Josh added with more than a touch of sarcasm.

"Hmmm."

"What?"

"I was just thinking. Talia had a large security team, many of whom were at the workshops the days she was there with Jacob. They were fairly formal, but they were approachable. Sadly, some of 'em might also need work."

"I guess." Josh frowned. "I'll call Charles and see if he can reach Talia's manager, Richard. He'll know who to talk to."

"No need, Josh. I can contact Jacob."

"What?" Josh pounced on her declaration, which instantly alarmed and upset him. "I don't think so, Kayla. If someone decides they need to talk to Jacob, it will be Charles, Ulysses or Matt. For a name that is no longer supposed to be spoken in this household, I sure hear it a lot. That'll be twenty bucks for the swear jar, sis."

"Josh, Jacob has a vested interest in the security of at least one of your children. As your children's aunt, so do I. He knows Talia's team, so he'll know who might be best suited to working with children. Let me ask him."

"And you know how to reach him how?" Sitting back, Josh glared at his sister. "Are you in touch with Jacob? I would think he's the last person you'd want to talk to!"

"No, no! Relax, bro. I have his email from the workshops. I don't know where he is, but I would assume he checks his messages. I'll just drop him a note."

"So Jessie's on your shit list and not worthy of forgiveness but for some reason Jacob's just fine. He's, uh, what's the word? Absolved of guilt for fucking my wife?"

Rising, Kayla shrugged. "Jessie went to Florida, Josh, when Jacob made it quite clear he didn't want her there. Your wife went after him when he was vulnerable and alone, and apparently she got what she wanted. She treats Jacob like a treat to pull out when she wants him. And don't get me started on my feelings for how that means she treats you."

Stunned, Josh stood and watched Kayla wander back out to the kitchen, where Emily-Grace had just calmly taken charge and wiped up the remains of David's melted, spilled ice cream. Dylan was singing to himself—*no surprise,* Josh thought, smiling sadly at the little guy, who was piling up blocks and knocking them over as he sang.

Grabbing his phone from the arm of a chair where he'd set it earlier, Josh tapped on his messages to see if anything new had come in since he last checked it an hour ago. Jessie's name was at the top of the list. With a grudging finger, Josh selected her message. He couldn't help but smile when he read it. It came with a picture.

Wandering into the kitchen, Josh grinned and sidled over to his daughter. "Emily-Grace," he chuckled, "you're going to want to see this." Holding the phone in front of her, Josh was tickled to see a wide smile spread across his usually quiet daughter's face. "Momma got a haircut, baby girl," Josh said. "How do you like it?"

Emily-Grace grabbed the phone. "Is it for the movie, Daddy?"

"Yep, I would say so." Admiring the photo of Jessie with her hair about ten inches shorter than she usually wore it, the flecks in Josh's eyes danced happily.

"It's pretty," Emily-Grace sighed wistfully. "I like the way it's curled."

Unable to help herself, Kayla wandered over and peeked at the screen. "She kept her long layers, I see. It's lighter, too," she announced, before looking up to meet her brother's warning eyes. "Okay, okay," she acquiesced. "I won't hate her forever." She was whispering behind her hand so small ears wouldn't hear this time. "She is Jessie, after all. She's always been a mixed-up kinda kid."

"Yep," Josh agreed. "That'd be one way of portraying her. I can think of a few more rather colorful descriptions too. But I won't bother getting into those in mixed company." Lifting David at the waist and placing him on the floor, Josh let a full-fledged smile break out. "Come on, kids. There's a rare Vancouver dusting of snow outdoors. Let's go see if we can conjure up enough to make a snowman with Auntie Kayla. What do you say, Emily-Grace?"

"Can we FaceTime Momma later?"

"We'll try. She's hard to reach way over there. If we can't get her tonight because of the time difference, we'll call her in the morning, okay?"

Moving to the back door, Josh reached towards a wooden hook and tossed a small snow jacket and pants over to his sister. "Start with the littlest and work your way up," he grinned. "Grab Jessie's black North Face jacket for yourself. Her boots should fit you too. It's snowman-making time for the Sawyer household! Maybe later we can rig up a puppet show. Whaddaya say, kids?"

Rousing cheers and lots of jumping up and down were Emily-Grace and David's thrilled responses. Taking his cue from his older siblings, Dylan clapped his hands and yelled.

Nudging Josh as she passed to grab mittens and boots for Dylan, Kayla leaned into her brother and, as the children hollered behind them, she whispered, "You're way too happy with Jessie gone. It's like the grey clouds have disappeared."

"Emily-Grace is talking to me, David looks like me, and Dylan's no longer cranky. Jessie is beautiful, mostly happy I think and, I hope, sending pictures just to me. Matt's with her, so she's safe, and there's fresh snow outside. What's there to be sad about, Kayla? The world is full of hope."

A wild whoop was Kayla's response. Half of her newfound joy was seeing the light in her brother's eyes. As she turned and bent to help Dylan, who was not easy to dress while jumping up and down alongside his siblings, a sentence formed in her mind. It was the first line of the email she would send to Jacob, and it would be accompanied by a photo of Dylan's new snowman.

Hey there. I hope my note finds you okay, wherever you are. I have a question to ask you...it concerns your son.

That night, after helping Josh bathe and feed the kids, and after tucking them into bed with stories and hugs, Kayla cruised back to her new place and waded through unopened packing boxes to prop herself up in front of her laptop. It only took her a few minutes to compose the email, and a split second to hit *send*.

On Jacob's end, it took three days to check messages, one day to digest Kayla's email, and half a day to decide what to write back. When Kayla saw his note in her inbox, her heart rate picked up and the eyes Josh was tired of seeing filled with sadness, lit up brightly.

I might know someone, the email from Jacob started. Kayla was surprised and touched to see how it ended: *Charles messaged me about Paul. I'm really sorry. Hey, if you ever need to get away, I know a weird, sad guy with a cool guitar and a leaky boat.*

And I know a weird, sad girl with a leaky heart, Kayla mused inwardly. *I just may take you up on that, Jacob Ryan.*

As she closed the screen of her laptop and plodded down the hall of her new condo towards the bedroom, Kayla couldn't help but smile. *Jacob.* A thrill started at her toes and worked its way up her body, leaving electric tingles in every important nook and cranny.

Wouldn't Jessie love seeing the two of us together?

Sleep was elusive for Kayla that night, for all the right reasons. When she roused herself for a six a.m. run, her mind was in overdrive, and her body was pumped.

Chapter Five

*W*hile Kayla was jogging the Stanley Park seawall and fantasizing about the sexy way Jacob moved on stage, Jessie was hurriedly FaceTiming with Josh and the kids. Jessie could hear Matt in the shower next door, and she had yet to shower for the dinner she and Matt were attending as guests of the film's producers.

Tonight she would stand before her bosses in a private, intimate space filled with selected invited guests to perform songs from the film's soundtrack with her co-star. It would undoubtedly be an emotional experience. This would be her first public performance with a singer other than Jacob at her side singing harmonies. The male star of the film was a few years older than Jessie. Bearded, with haunted eyes, sensitive and kind but somewhat distant in what Jessie assessed as his need to keep an emotional distance for the purpose of their characters in the movie, John was an intuitive and capable singer. Their voices melded beautifully together, and the songs—classic gospel and blue-grass, mostly—were poignant and memorable. This would be a special night.

Now, Jessie cocked an ear. Matt had just turned off the shower's faucet. She turned back to the screen and blew kisses to her children, who scattered off to play while Josh filled Jessie in on Susanne's decision to leave.

"I know," she admitted. "Matt spilled the beans this morning. I'm devastated."

"Charles has a few ideas where to look for a replacement. We'll find someone we can trust," Josh ascertained, wisely deciding not to tell Jessie exactly why Susanne decided to bail, and that Kayla was making inquiries too, that Josh didn't necessarily sanction.

"Matt's got his thinking cap on too," Jessie said, twisting a ringlet and absently hoping she could manage walking on her high heels tonight. *Thank God for Matt,* she thought. *I'll lean on him. As always.* Aloud she said, "Dee's flying over this weekend. Can you send my moleskin journal? I've got some lyrics in it I need."

"I can, or I can scan and email them if you need them right away."

"No, I…no, just send the whole book, if you don't mind. Scanning would take you forever."

"All right." Something about the request bothered Josh but he didn't have to dig far to know what it was. The book contained lyrics. Jessie was writing a song for Jacob. He looked away, sighed, and when his eyes met Jessie's again, they were liquid where before they were solid.

"Josh, it's nothing," Jessie said softly. "It's just a few words, that's all. The song's mostly worked out, I'm work-shopping it tonight in fact, but I made a few notes a while ago that I want to review."

Licking his lips nervously, Josh shrugged. "Whatever," he replied, his knuckles white on the edges of the iPad he was using to FaceTime her. "I'll send it with Dee."

"Christian's coming with her. We need to fine-tune that song so we can send the arrangement off to the other musicians who will be playing with us at the Grammys. I'm hiring a cellist. It's going to be beautiful." *If I can get through it.*

"I bet."

Inhaling, she changed tack. "So you guys are coming next weekend?"

"Yeah, I guess." Josh paused. "Do you want us there?"

"Heck, yeah."

The next question was harder. "All of us, Jess? I haven't exactly been great company lately."

"You more than anyone," she murmured. "I miss you, Josh."

There it was again, that old small but genuine smile Jessie loved. A happy light settled in her eyes. "Get here sooner rather than later, okay babe?"

"All right. I'm glad."

"Yeah. Me too. Look Josh, I'm gonna tell Matt he should ask Julie and Katy to come over next weekend too. I don't think they've even talked since we got here. Katy could help with the kids."

"There's lots of room on the jet. Will she need some convincing? Do you want me to call her?"

"Sure. You can try." Jessie's voice was strained.

"What?"

"Oh, you know. Everyone knows my dirty laundry. I'd try calling her myself but I don't think she'll take my call."

A hard twist seized Josh's gut. It seemed everyone was blaming Jessie for his or her own woes. How did she stand it? *Maybe Kayla's right,* he thought. *Maybe I am too soft.*

"I'll call her," he managed, as a knock came at Jessie's door.

"Shit, that's Matt. I've really gotta go. I'm not even dressed."

"So is he, like, your date as well as your security these days?" Josh asked amicably.

"Yep, pretty much. It would be Dee actually, if she was here but since she's been fighting this flu, Matt's been a great standby. He doesn't seem to mind."

"And you wonder why Julie worries?"

"Are you worried?"

"Should I be?"

Frustration tinged Jessie's voice. "Is this going to be our future now, Josh? This is Matt we're talking about, for God's sake."

"The guy's a snappy dresser, Jess. He doesn't have any trouble attracting women."

"Yeah and those spikes in his hair are downright adorable, but I want my husband, okay? Get your sexy butt over here. Now if you don't mind, I've really got to run. This shindig tonight is kind of a big deal."

"Okay, Jessie. I love you. Have fun tonight."

"Love you back, Josh. So much." A wistful longing was the last image she telegraphed to Josh, who sat back with a grin at the good natured teasing about Matt who, he knew, was Jessie's rock.

In Brussels, Jessie jumped up and whipped open the door to her large suite. Contrary to what she said to her husband, her heart actually lurched when she saw Matt. "Damn," she whistled, as she backed up and let him in. "You clean up nice."

The usual embarrassed pink flush arced across his cheeks. He was wearing a vintage black tux, with a white silk scarf tossed around his shoulders for effect.

"Dapper," Jessie added.

"Too bad I can't say the same about you," Matt chided her, eyeing her black yoga pants and white tank top. "Go. Get dressed. We're already late."

"Ahhhhh," was Jessie's frustrated response as she moved towards the shower. "I was FaceTiming with Josh and the kids. It's always hard to say goodbye."

On her way to the washroom, Jessie pulled her tank top over her head and tossed it on a lime green sofa. She wheeled around to Matt, who had seen her do this many times, but for some reason this time it bothered him. *Julie,* he cursed under his breath. His wife's accusations about Jessie had changed the dynamic in their little camp. He wondered if Jessie got the same vibe. She didn't seem to. She was speaking to him while she casually hauled off her pants.

"I was thinking you should invite Julie and Katy to hop on the jet and come to Brussels next weekend, Matt. With Josh and the kids."

The invitation took him by surprise. "I don't know, Jessie. I'm not sure that would be a good idea."

"You haven't talked to her since you left, have you, Matt?" Jessie was standing at the entrance to the washroom now in only her bra and panties.

Her careless manner and the memory of his wife's accusatory remarks had Matt steaming. Uncomfortable, he frowned. "Can we talk about this later?"

Jessie's light smile flipped over.

Moving towards the washroom, Matt strode past Jessie, stormed inside, and cranked on the shower's elegant gold faucet. Holding open the glass door, he moved aside and waved her in.

Grumbling, Jessie sidled arrogantly towards him, hauling off her bra and panties as she walked.

He averted his eyes.

"What, you've never seen a woman before, Matt?" She stopped in front of him but realized, as she did so, that he was actually pissed.

Matt angled his head around to face her, but kept his eyes solidly on Jessie's. "Your snarky little game is crossing a line, Jessie. Get in the shower."

There was something erotic in the way she was studying him, though, through

the beautiful, sparkling pale eyes that were once featured in suggestive photos and adult films. With her new curls just brushing her bare shoulders, and
the way Jessie was petulantly standing with her feet apart, it almost seemed
like she was daring him to touch her. Clearly uneasy, Matt swallowed. But he
didn't look away.

Josh's teasing reverberated in Jessie's mind. The way Matt was looking
at her now…there were flashes of anger in his eyes, yes, but there was something else there too.

Suddenly there were sticks in Jessie's throat. This was not a moment she
wanted to experience with Matt—her friend, her protector, her employee.
Inadvertently, she shook her head and let her eyes narrow a little as she ques-
tioned the way her body was suddenly reacting to him.

"I'm sorry, Matt," she managed as she brushed by him and entered the
shower, letting her fingers linger in his as she passed.

Pushing the glass shower door to a gentle close behind her, Matt left the
washroom, shutting its door as well. In the living area of the suite, he collapsed onto the sofa and hung his head in his hands. "I can't do this," he
mumbled to himself. "Not alone with her. I can't."

Deirdre would be arriving in a few days. Tonight there would be other
people around to take the pressure off. Reprimanding himself, Matt tried to
maintain his dignity and self-control. *I'm not Jacob and, if it counts, I'm not
Jessie either,* he told himself. *I know where I stand and where I need to be. I know
where the line in the sand is.*

Resolving to back off and be super professional in Jessie's company, Matt
left the lavish suite when he heard the shower grind to a stop, and he waited
in an uncomfortable overstuffed wingback chair down the hall.

After a bit, Jessie made her way to him and turned slowly so he could rise
and zip up her black cocktail dress.

When his hand on the zipper touched her neck, she turned back around
and faced him. Confused, she asked, "What the hell happened back there,
Matt?"

"Nothing happened, Jessie," was his gruff answer. "It was just a moment
between two lonely people who spend far too much time alone together,
that's all."

He started to move away but she tugged on his sleeve. "Matt?" she asked, turning one high heeled ankle over in her childish way.

Against his better judgment, he turned.

With pure, innocent naiveté in the diaphanous eyes, and all of Jessie's tender fingers clinging to his sleeve, she peeked up at him. "It was a good moment. Wasn't it?"

He paused before answering. Then Matt said, "You're killing me, kid," bent forward, and brushed his lips against her forehead. "Now push that moment somewhere far, far away. Make it a memory. Let's go."

The elevator door opened, but Jessie hesitated before entering. Matt did what he always did—he took Jessie's hand in his and led her inside.

But for some reason, this time it felt different. His hand over hers felt safe—on a whole new level. For both of them.

And for some reason, it felt damn good.

Chapter Six

The Sofitel Brussels Le Louise, on the prestigious Avenue Louise, was a five star luxury hotel nestled amongst quaint chestnut trees and stately art deco mansions. But tonight, neither Jessie nor Matt would walk under the pretty trees or regard the mansions in wonder—the film's producers had chosen, as the evening's venue, a grand half-ballroom just downstairs from Jessie and Matt's floor in the luxe hotel.

All eyes turned to Jessie when she entered the sumptuous space. The hem of the midnight black cocktail dress—which was trimmed with French lace at its low moon neckline and therefore righteously teasing men with what lay barely hidden underneath—clung to the tops of her muscular thighs. With Matt's strong arm gracing her waist as they were led to their table, none of the assembled cast, crew, film executives and invited Brussels elite noticed Jessie cursing under her breath at the impossibly sky high heels Dee had insisted she pack for evenings such as this.

Matt knew she was cursing, he could hear her, but his mind was a jumbled mess so he ignored the exasperated anti-heel tirade being played out for his ears only. Jessie's little game before she got in the shower was costing him dearly. Always the gentleman, he had in his opinion avoided looking at what really mattered, but still…Julie's accusations rang in his head like bells before Sunday mass. Thoughts had been planted that Matt quite simply didn't welcome, yet seemed helpless to push away.

Unaccustomed to being Jessie's 'date' at events like this, Matt's discomfort was increased a thousand-fold. He fidgeted until Jessie, in mid-conversation with the elegant female producer to her right, discerned his misery and slipped her left hand onto his thigh and twisted her fingers around his. This was not a surprise to Matt. Jessie had a knack for recognizing the distress of others; this was simply her way of offering comfort.

The affectionate touch settled him immediately. However, until the first course was served, Matt couldn't help but turn his palm around to tenderly brush his thumb against her fingers. She didn't seem to notice. Jessie carried on her conversation with ease. Recalling the days when she could barely breathe at an event as formal as this, Matt looked over at her with a reserved smile. In those early days, he could usually be found standing statue-still in a corner with his arms clasped at his groin, feet apart, as he scanned the room.

Old habits die hard. Examining the room now, Matt focused on a six-foot high stage in the center of the space, designed for viewing from all angles. Tonight was a forum to show off the songs forming the heart of the film, which had finally officially been called *If I Needed You* for one of the featured bluegrass tunes. On the stage, Matt spied Jessie's Gibson perched on a stand, waiting patiently. He straightened in eager anticipation; he would hear her sing later.

There would be one special number played tonight that was not a part of the film's soundtrack. Jessie wanted to workshop the song she was writing for the Grammys. Accompanying herself, she would play the song from a high stool.

Hearing his name called, Matt turned to its source. "Sorry," he mumbled to Jessie, jiggling a little in his seat, letting go of her hand at the same time since their first course was arriving.

Contented eyes shining, she was smiling brightly at him. "I'm glad you're here, Matt. I can't picture Arnie sitting at this table."

"I'm not loving it," Matt admitted.

"I know. Your hand is all sweaty. Alice asked me if I was stepping out on Josh. I think she wants to know if you're single."

Leaning forward, Matt glanced at the woman on Jessie's right. Sitting back again, he exhaled nervously and said, "Despite the fact that I might actually be single and just not really know it yet, she looks like a tougher version of Deirdre. I think I will pass."

Throwing back her head to laugh, Jessie had to add an addendum to his comment. "I think Deirdre, and possibly Charles, would take offense to that remark." She softened. "I'm sorry you're so worried about Julie, though. I can see how much this is hurting you." Indeed, upon close inspection of her good friend, Jessie was dismayed to see dark circles shadowing his wise and gentle eyes. "I wonder if you shouldn't go home, Matt. Switch off with Arnie. Go see what's really up with your marriage."

Matt nodded, and told her he'd think about it, but inside he wondered if Jessie's suggestion wasn't somehow wrapped up in their earlier 'moment.' That started a whole new parade of unwelcome thoughts rambling around Matt's tired brain. How upset was Jessie, really, over it? Why was she upset? She had acknowledged feeling something too, but both knew where the vibe was coming from. Matt and Jessie shared a secret related to Jacob's assault, and both were fighting with their partners about a singular topic that had the power to destroy what took years to build.

Jessie watched the tough emotions flit around Matt's mind. The earlier electricity had jarred her—it sent her reeling with its surprise intensity. It shook the ground beneath her feet. No doubt Matt was thrown, too. They would have to talk about this later. Maybe it would be best if he went home for a while, until more people would be around as distractions to prevent such a thing from ever happening again.

The remainder of the meal was uneventful. Eventually an artsy man to Matt's left, the film's director, started up a conversation with him.

"I think he likes you," Jessie bent and whispered in Matt's ear at one point. "Why don't you have some fun while we're here?" She winked, but without breaking stride in the conversation with the director, Matt grabbed her hand and squeezed it until she yelped.

After dinner, when the time came to showcase the songs, he turned to his charge with a twinkle in his eye. "Nervous?" This would be Jessie's favorite part of the night. It was common knowledge that Jessie Wheeler-Sawyer was always most comfortable on stage, when she could be lost in the power of music to take her away.

"Yes," she replied with a vehemence that surprised him. "If I trip in these fucking heels it'll be all over Twitter in seconds."

Matt roared at that one. Three glasses of bourbon had relaxed him quite sufficiently. Someone at the on-stage microphone was saying Jessie's name now, introducing her to the excited crowd, so he shoved his chair back and gently pulled out Jessie's. With a warm glow lighting up his smile, he held an arm out to her.

Ducking her head, delighted but somewhat embarrassed, Jessie turned an interesting shade of pink as she accepted the gesture. Escorting her around their table to the steps leading to the stage, Matt handed Jessie off to her co-star, waited til she was safely positioned, and made his way back towards his seat.

He settled in to watch magic happen.

Taking the microphone between her fingers, Jessie treated the elite audience to a wide smile. "I hate these shoes," she admitted honestly. "Is there a woman in here who actually likes high heels?"

A vociferous cheer broke out in the room, accompanied by vigorous clapping and whistles. Laughing, Jessie caught Matt's eye. "Matt Kelly, everyone," she said tenderly, lifting an arm towards him. "The incredibly handsome man who watches over me."

Her arm floated there, and sent forth an invisible silver-blue thread linking Matt and Jessie. Over the heads of the entitled that were assembled in the grand high-ceilinged room, the glittery thread hung suspended, fueled by alcohol, loneliness, and the heady spell of an exotic city.

The room swirled. The universe was off its axis. Bourbon for Matt and wine for Jessie had elevated the evening to a whole new level, which had already catapulted itself to a rare, special place via that moment of connection by the shower.

Matt braced himself as Jessie held his gaze. In the exquisite, sensuous lacy cocktail dress—the center of everyone's attention, the object of many male and female fantasies—she was a vision.

He knew what was coming.

The thing about Jessie's music, whether it was her own creation or a cover of another artist's song, was that it was a true and beautiful heavenly gift. Like any piece of music offered up to the Gods on a voice of pure silken honey, as was hers, it had the power to heal. It had the power to bring peace to a broken and scarred world, and it most certainly had an equal power to bring the same restorative amity to any individual hurting the way Matt was in this chic space this evening.

Many times over the years, Matt was witness to the way Jessie's music commanded a room, a theater stage, an arena. Always, she had an audience's attention from the moment she stepped to the mic and started to sing; or earlier, if she was strumming on her guitar. The magic always went the same way, even at the big shows where thousands of people screamed her name, where expensive production numbers involving complicated dance sequences and costume changes were too numerous to count.

Now, people quieted. Hearts swelled with love for their beloved singer. They listened.

The smaller intimate venues were Matt's favorite. Leaning back, he soaked up the extraordinary essence of the woman in his care. He held his breath as she turned to her right and nodded with a small smile at her co-star, John, so he could signal the small back-up band and count them in.

With the first strains of a familiar old gospel tune, the room came to life. The music had a vibrancy to it, an energy that encircled everyone in the space with promise.

But, Matt soon realized, it also had an ache.

～ ～

A half hour later, by the end of the gospel infused bluegrass numbers, Matt was lost in more than Jessie's power to lift an entire room and, as well, to bring it to its knees. He had read the script for this film. He knew the music had to support the heartrending story. What he hadn't counted on was anyone, besides Jacob Ryan, ever having the power to sing in and around Jessie's soul again the way her scraggly co-star did. The film was about the loss of a child and the breakdown of a marriage. The music laid it all out bare. Sinking into character, Jessie and John melded their voices in perfect harmony. The performance was captivating and emotional, and when the last note of the last song faded into some distant, murky corner, the audience was metaphorically on its knees.

Jessie hadn't looked at Matt again as she sang. She didn't look at anyone; she generally never did. On this dreamlike evening, she had become someone else, as per her role in the film. She had become a woman with nothing left—no child, no connection to her husband. Lost and alone, Jessie found a place inside herself where she could connect with her character, where she could disappear.

Matt was speechless. Enthralled by the beloved voice, lost in Jessie's mesmerizing aura and in the melancholy sadness of the lyrics, the music, and the complete breakdown of his marriage, he felt like he was in the presence of God. Plain as day, there was a spiritual message in the music, and it had to do with Julie.

As clearly as he discerned Jessie's sentences beside him at dinner earlier, a voice entered Matt's heart and mind.

Let go, it said. It's over. Let her be.

The directive was numbing.

There was a problem. Matt knew if he let himself 'feel' the way the music seemed to want to make him feel, he would lie on the floor, curl up into a ball, close his eyes, and fade off into some distant never-land.

The music was that powerful. Jessie…and her co-star…were that powerful.

With the exception of Matt, everyone in the grand ballroom was standing now, and many were unashamedly crying as they clapped and cheered. As he regained focus, and the blood came back to Matt's drawn face, the smoky mist in front of his eyes cleared and he saw that Jessie's eyes were fixed on him. She was worried, he knew. About Julie, about Katy, about his marriage.

About him.

He, Matt, was worried about Jessie and her soul-bond to Jacob, her angry shouting matches with Josh, her fallout with Kayla, and—above all, now— this deep, new, elevated connection with him.

She held his gaze as he rose, finally, and started to clap. Then, as if in slow motion, Jessie turned her lips back to the mic and softly told the room she had one more song to sing. Behind her, the other musicians exited via a back set of stairs, and Jessie bent and grasped the neck of the Gibson. She couldn't quite sit on the stool, her dress was too short, but she leaned her butt against it and waited while a sound tech adjusted a mic in front of the guitar, and lowered the vocal mic to her new position.

"This is a song I'm work-shopping for all of you," she said as Matt stilled, afraid the dam would totally break if he had to hear her sing one more sad song. "It's for a friend who I feel I've hurt deeply. Who hurt me too. Take it and use it for yourself if you need it."

One more wistful smile in Matt's direction, and Jessie started to play.

The song rose above them as if it was created for the space they were in. It dipped and soared and dove as it was meant to, all around and inside each and every soul present. But the one it got to the most was Matt.

When Jessie looked for him at the end of her song, he was no longer seated. She didn't find him until she went upstairs to her suite, accompanied as far as the elevator by the kind director, the uncomfortable heels dangling from one hand by the time the elevator deposited her on her floor.

There was no one else staying on the floor. For security purposes, Jessie and Matt had it all to themselves for the duration of the shoot. As Jessie moved towards her door at the far end, confused and concerned for the man responsible for her safety, she saw him, seated on the carpet part way down the hall, knees drawn up to his chest, elbows folded over his knees.

He didn't look up at her until she knelt before him and tipped his chin up with her thumb and forefinger.

"I think…was it the music that got to you, Matt? It seemed to get to a lot of people tonight. Our heartbreaking film has a very powerful soundtrack."

"It was perfect," he told her in a whisper. "I didn't expect to see you sing like that again, without…without Jacob by your side."

"He was," Jessie murmured, her eyes clouding over. "In my heart he will always be there. I pictured him there."

"Ah. Figures." Matt allowed a small smile, but he was half-drunk and completely empty.

Jessie extended a hand to him and he took it. "Thank you for being there for me, Matt. I'm grateful."

As he stood, Matt found himself feeling more lost than ever. "I thought about what you said. About going home to see what's up with Julie. But I'm afraid, Jessie. I'm scared of what I might find. It's over. I feel like it's over."

"Then don't let it be. Don't let it be over."

"Do you think it's that simple? Because I don't. Look at Kayla."

"Kayla and Paul were very different right from the start, Matt. I think she's changed. The workshops have changed Kayla. They've given her a new purpose. Paul is and always will be a Vancouver boy. Kayla's meant to see the world. They were bound to grind to a halt."

"And what about you? You and Josh haven't stopped sniping at each other since Boxing Day. What if he decides to let go?"

"He won't. He promised me. But if he tries, first I'll nail his balls to the wall and then I'll tie him to our bed and feed him nothing but crackers and rice. He'll grow so weak he'll have to stay."

Matt's wry smile took Jessie by surprise. As they walked hand in hand down to the end of the hall, where their suites were, he said, "It amazes me how you can poke fun at things that, not all that long ago, were pretty darn serious, Jessie."

"If you're referring to me and the kids being trapped in the Langley house, we had more than crackers and rice to eat, Matt. If you're referencing Josh and me splitting up for a while afterwards, keep this in mind. It taught us to fight for each other, no matter how bad things get." Tucking her arm into Matt's as she walked, Jessie leaned her head on his shoulder. "God, I love you," she murmured. "I really do."

She turned when she realized Matt had stopped walking. He was still holding her hand, but his expression was drained and piqued, and a somber lackluster light had settled into his eyes. "I mean it," he said quietly. "It amazes me how you poke fun at serious stuff."

Jessie swallowed. This was not her Matt. This was not the man who was always hollering at her to move her butt, who placed himself in front of her in Paris with no regard for his own safety. Who took a bullet for her in New York.

Taking a step towards him, she reached up and undid the black tie he was wearing around his neck. Anything to keep her fingers busy, to keep herself from looking into those suffering eyes and melting, like she thought she might. Or worse, feeling that erotic electric charge zip up her legs again and land in places unsavory to a married woman who was in the company of another woman's man.

Matt lifted his hand and touched her chin, though, forcing Jessie to look at him. "I'm sorry," he whispered. "I hope you can forgive me." And he bent forward, just a bit because she was close to him anyway. And he kissed her.

Jessie's lips tasted like wine and felt like silk. He heard her suck in a breath, but she didn't pull away. *Maybe she was afraid to,* he thought many times later. *Or maybe she liked it.* At the time, lost in the intoxicating emotion of the past few weeks, which was brought to a head by a fairy-tale night with soul-changing music and a beautiful woman by his side whom Matt had cared for, worried over, and adored for many years, he thought she wanted the kiss.

It seemed she did, because Jessie moved into him and let her tongue touch his. She parted her lips so he could run his tongue over her teeth; he pressed her body to him when he heard her breath catch and felt her body cave. The hungry, passionate kiss lasted long enough for both Matt and Jessie to feel suspended and heightened by the promise of ecstasy, but all things considered, it was fleeting.

In the end it was Matt who pushed Jessie away, and not Jessie herself who backed off.

Looking at her from beneath his misty eyes, Matt saw and felt only tragedy in Jessie's stare. She was still hanging onto him, onto his elbows now, but she slipped both hands up to his white shirt, and laid her palms flat against his chest.

"The thing is, Matt," she started as choking sobs took root somewhere deep inside her, "this would be too easy for me. You know that about me. Don't," she shook her head at him as he opened his mouth to speak, "tell me that's not true. Because it is. I can invite you into my bed and I can make you very happy. But it won't last. It'll be like one of those mirages in the desert that disappear when you try to reach out to touch them. It'll be a bubble that bursts and leaves you soaking wet. This—you and me—can't happen. But dear sweet Jesus, right now I want it to."

His words were spoken haltingly. They were apologetic, but laced with dismay. "I needed to know," he told her. "That's all. I just needed to know."

She nodded, moved her hands to his waist, and scrunched up her fingers so she could hold onto him tighter, as if she was afraid her good friend was going to turn and bolt. "I get that, Matt. I know that what Julie said to you threw you for a loop, not just about her and…well, her thing, but also what she said about me."

"She thinks I'm in love with you." A strangled sound escaped his throat with the admission.

"I'm not all that interested in what Julie thinks," Jessie replied, her heart rate picking up. "I'm more interested in what you think."

He shook his head. "It doesn't matter."

"I know," she moaned, and laid her head on Matt's chest. "You're going to go away again, aren't you? I'm getting low on people who still like me, Matt. I'm like that end of the magnet that repels people. Everybody leaves me."

The way the light caught Matt then, from a golden wall sconce a ways down the hall behind him, made him appear like he was standing in front of a sunset. "No," he told her. "I'm not going. I'm not leaving you."

"Yeah," Jessie whispered. "Actually you are, Matt. You're going home to make things right with Julie. Arnie can fly over here to be with me."

"No," he demanded gruffly. "I won't overstep my boundaries with you again, Jessie. You have my word."

"Well," she answered honestly. "I appreciate your gallant attempt, sweet Matt, but I've got news for you." Her eyes grew small and she swiped the back of one hand against them. "It's not you I'm worried about."

His knees melted then, and if Jessie hadn't been holding him up, Matt would have sank to the floor.

"Go home," she told him, firmly now. "Go home and don't come back. You're fired from my immediate service."

"Arnie's not available. He's going south to locate Jacob."

"Well then, now I guess that will be you who goes south. I hope you and Jacob don't kill each other. Just what I need, by the way. The two of you down there feeling sorry for yourselves and me up here wishing to hell I could fall into a great big sinkhole and die. Jesus Christ, Matt! What'd you go and do that for? I need you!"

There was nothing he could say at that point. Matt just raised his arms and started to back away. "I'm a fucking mess, Jessie. I'm so, so sorry."

Reaching his door, he inserted his key card, which took him three tries because he was trembling so badly. When the door opened, Matt leaned his back against it and watched Jessie, waiting to see her go into her own suite, because some half-assed part of him knew he was still responsible for her safety.

Shock and surprise almost gutted him when she moved towards him instead, took him in her arms, and held on tight. "You stupid, stupid man," she growled at him, as his body shivered in her arms.

Matt placed both hands behind her head, then, and grabbed handfuls of the new shorter hair. Tilting Jessie's head backwards, he took what he knew he would never get again—hungry mouthfuls of the perfect lips, the cheeks, the sweet place at the corners of her eyes, the long, graceful neck. The kisses were urgent and they were reciprocated, but when Jessie whimpered and reached for his belt, Matt stopped her. She touched him anyway, without looking into his eyes, with her lips buried in his neck as she stroked him on the outside of his pants.

He moaned, and pressed her closer to him before he gradually pushed her away. "I'll call the production and arrange a secure escort for you in the morning, Jessie," he managed, his voice thick and hurting, his eyes electric and pained with thwarted desire. "I'll catch a flight out and get Arnie over here as quickly as I can." With a gentle push, he forced her to take two steps backwards.

Just before he moved indoors and let go of the door, he called to her over his shoulder. "If you really need to know," he said, "I think I've probably always loved you."

The door clicked shut.

An image of Josh passed through Jessie's mind as she stood there shaking and shuddering, still wanting what she knew she absolutely could not have, should not have. There was no way Jessie could go into Matt's suite and think there would be any way in hell Josh would want to preserve their marriage if he found out and, when all was said and done it was, and always would be, Josh who Jessie wanted. Right now things were just messed up, that was all. One crazy night with Matt, even if it could remain their secret, would only serve to dig Jessie a deeper hole.

All that long night, after she twisted around and somehow made her way back to her suite through reams of tears and choking sobs, Jessie ached for Matt, who she knew was likely beating himself up big time just past the wall at her back. She stayed there, against that wall, sobbing until she had nothing left, until she sank to the floor and, curled up into a ball, cried herself to sleep.

Just beyond her, sitting on his bed with his back to the wall, Matt forced himself to listen to Jessie's cries. He'd been cruel, he knew, to kiss her in the first place, because there was no question that once that line was crossed, there would be no going back. Matt was Jessie's friend, yes, and family of a sort, but he was also her employee. He would hope to stay in Charles' employ, at least for a time, but would have to come off his detail with Jessie. Unsure just what the future held, Matt considered Josh's position in all of this.

"You bastard," he said idly to the air, picturing Josh quietly listening, "don't even think about leaving her."

Jessie may think of herself as a whore, but Matt didn't doubt that she had some feelings for him. She hadn't pushed things further than he allowed them tonight. She walked away when he asked her to. And, as she said herself, it would have been so easy not to.

What would tomorrow bring? A trip down south, Matt thought as he swiped at his own incessant tears.

A trip down south, and one less spoiled and lonely female superstar ass to watch over, and to try to keep safe.

Chapter Seven

*J*osh landed at La Casa with Dylan in tow exactly five minutes after Arnie, who was responding to a request from Charles that he drop by immediately.

Dee was rushing around, packing, and Josh held out Jessie's moleskin journal as the older woman zipped by with a shiny pair of Christian Louboutin heels in one hand. Taking the journal from Josh, she paused just long enough to brush her lips against Dylan's soft little boy cheek. Unable to resist, she held out her arms and Dylan dropped into them.

"Come with Grammie," she said with a smile. "I bet your pretty momma wishes I'd just pack you in my suitcase and bring you along with me!" Aiming a narrowed eye at Josh, her expression became serious. "Charles is down the hall, Josh. I should warn you, he's on the warpath."

"Why?" Josh asked, but Deirdre was already halfway up the stairs, crooning to her grandson, who was holding the shoes against his belly and making silly faces at his grandmother at the same time.

Wandering down the hall, Josh found both Arnie and Charles in the media room. Both fell silent when Josh stepped in. "I would think there's something badly wrong except that Dee seems okay, for the most part," Josh started, planting his feet on the Turkish rug and hooking his thumbs over his pockets. "If this doesn't concern my family, I'll go, but judging by the way the two of you are looking at me right now, I'm going to make the assumption that it does."

Nervously fingering his tie, Charles broke in. "Arnie's to go home and pack. He's agreed to go to Brussels with Deirdre for the remainder of Jessie's shoot."

65

"Oh. Okay. Uh, why?" Suddenly a light illuminated Josh's muzzy brain. "Matt's been dealing with some marriage crap, Jessie says. I gather he's coming home?"

"He left Brussels before eight this morning Belgium time, Josh. On a commercial flight."

"Oh. Jesus, is everything okay with Julie and Katy? I talked to Jessie yesterday. She was on her way to some big music showcase the production company was hosting. Matt was her escort."

"As far as we know, Katy and Julie are fine. I talked to Jessie. All she said was that she and Matt had some kind of falling out."

"What? That's weird." A gnawing, aching feeling started in Josh's gut. "What kind of falling out?"

Ignoring him, Charles glanced over at Arnie, who was shuffling his feet and shaking his head as he tried to put two and two together. "Arnie, if you're up for switching gears this quickly, go pack. The jet's fueled and ready. Christian's meeting Deirdre at the airport at noon. She'll see you there."

Arnie spoke to Josh. "Go to meetings, okay? I'll get Ulysses on your back if I hear you're not going."

"Sure. Yeah. Thanks, Arnie. For caring, you know?"

"Just go."

At that brief directive, Arnie nodded brusquely at Josh, who called out a hasty, "Give Jess a hug for me, will ya?" at his back as he walked away.

Josh turned back to Charles. "Jessie's pretty attached to Matt, Charles. This is not likely going to go down well with her, if you think she and Matt had words. She sounded fine yesterday."

"I don't know for certain what happened between them, Josh." Charles' voice was sober. "I can guess, but I hope it's nothing, and I hope Matt feels free to illuminate me when he gets home. I know how close he and Jessie have become over the years. And I also know that you and she have been at each other's throats since Christmas. Throw a man in the mix whose marriage is on the rocks, and you've got a volatile combination."

"They fight, but they always make up, Charles. It would have to be pretty bad for Matt to choose to come home."

"Matt didn't choose to come home, Josh. Jessie fired him. And I likely should too, except that with Susanne leaving, I'm a mite shorthanded."

"What? She would have called me. Why wouldn't she call me?"

"You haven't exactly been on Jessie's side lately, Josh. Besides Dee and I, Matt is likely the only person who has been accessible to her lately, since Steve and Charlie are busy with their own families these days. Matt is who she feels safe to confide in. Unless you count Arnie, and he hasn't been around much lately. They've been spending a lot of time together. They likely just got on each other's nerves and need a break."

"I don't know, Charles." Josh swallowed. The ache in his gut was twisting now. "When they get on each other's nerves, they just take walks or go running. Jessie would never fire Matt unless he really stepped over the line."

"Then, Josh, I hate to say this, but I would expect that Matt stepped over the line. Jessie's tears over the phone today pretty much confirmed that. She didn't have to voice it any other way."

"We're talking about Matt here. Dependable old Matt!"

"Dependable old Matt is your wife's best friend. Dependable old Matt is going to get his ass kicked when he gets back if my instincts are right. And you, Josh, might want to call our girl. In the space of a few short weeks she lost a new friend in Talia, and Jacob, a musical soul mate we both admit she loves dearly, a good friend in your sister, and now someone very close to her who she generally loves and trusts. She's going to need a friendly ear."

Josh was reeling. "What if—what if—"

Charles interjected by air palming Josh. "Don't go there, Josh. Even if something happened between Jessie and Matt, it's not a complete surprise. They're attractive people, they were out drinking, and they've both been feeling vulnerable. Doesn't mean I won't kick Matt's ass if that's the case, and I can't tell you how to deal with your obstinate wife, but there's no point in surmising anything or jumping to any conclusions. Deirdre will be with Jessie soon, and she'll see what kind of shape she's in."

Charles clapped a hand on Josh's back and started moving down the hall. He had a little more to say as they strode towards his home office. "You're taking the kids over next weekend, right?"

Josh's answer was a quiet, "Yeah, that's the plan," but his mind was whirling around and around; it kept landing on Jessie and Matt.

"That'll give things some time to cool down," Charles continued. "For now, Josh, just come with me and grab the latest episode one script revision for our series."

Carlotta, who was dusting nearby, perked up as they walked by. Josh was white and Charles' lips were pressed together in a thin line. "Would you boys like some coffee and something to snack on while you meet? I just made a batch of carrot muffins. They're still warm from the oven."

"Not hungry," Josh mumbled, his eyes darkening. "But thanks anyway, Carlotta."

After they passed by, the friendly maid wandered down to the kitchen and prepared a plate of muffins anyway. On her tray she placed two mugs of steaming coffee, a tiny pitcher of milk, and two serviettes. "You say you're not hungry," she smiled to herself as she picked up the tray, "but I know my boys. Days like today, food is sometimes the only comfort."

She received grateful half-smiles from both Charles and Josh when she placed the tray on a corner of Charles' big desk. She handed each man a mug and a muffin, and closed the door behind her when she left the room.

~ ~

The production design team for the Brussels film had built a hospital set for the scenes with the dying child. It was so realistic, especially when extras costumed as nurses and doctors walked the long hall, that it gave Jessie the creeps. Sterile and filled with set dec pieces like hazardous waste bins and emergency medical gear, it made her shiver, and intensified the loneliness of an already imposing and difficult shoot day.

They were filming all of the hospital scenes together over a three-day period. With Matt's sudden departure hanging over her head and heart like an anvil, Jessie's mood was already dark. Matt's tormented eyes, and the licks of desire that flickered back and forth over them as he touched her, as he kissed her, were haunting Jessie. That night, lust had cascaded over her eyes, too, and flushed both cheeks before landing in the more delicate parts of Jessie's body and tormenting her with unfulfilled promise.

In counterpoint to the heavy ache of remorse was an image of Josh, trusting her, already at a loss concerning her overtures towards Jacob.

For the thousandth time in the already new day, Jessie leaned back in her cast chair, threw back her head, and moaned.

The First A.D. wandered by. She was checking out the electricians and gaffers to see how close they were to being ready to shoot. Upon hearing Jessie's angst for about the fourth time already, she pulled up an empty chair and spoke in a thick accent Jessie figured was some kind of European cross.

"I jus' hear on walkie your manager jus' arrive. She here soon. Maybe that make you feel better, no?"

"Nothing will make me feel better today," Jessie grumbled miserably.

The older woman's voice was tender and understanding. "It's hard scene you shoot today, no? Your little girl die? Yes?"

The statement sent a chill through Jessie's heart. "Yes," she answered. "We're shooting the toughest one today. It's going to be a long day."

The A.D. touched Jessie's knee, and listened to a voice coming through her walkie. Nodding her head as she focused on the French words sent her way, she stood. "She here now, your manager. I go get her. You stay."

Tears were pricking at Jessie's eyes as she said, "Thank you." Leveraging herself upright, she sighed heavily and dropped the script she'd been trying to study on the canvas chair. Seeing Deirdre stride around the corner a moment later, all concern and business, with Arnie at her side, was both a tremendous relief as well as a stark reminder of the latest loss. Launching herself into Dee's arms, Jessie forced her tears to remain at bay. She had to maintain some semblance of control over her emotions today, both to navigate the tough shoot day, as well as to not let on to Dee just how serious things had become as far as Matt was concerned.

Dee knew her girl, though. And she knew Matt. "Sit," she ordered, as Arnie encircled Jessie in a hug before letting her go and sidling over to the craft table.

"Where's Christian?" Jessie asked, peering behind her and swiping at an eye.

"I left him at the hotel. At the moment, I expect he's in the ballroom bossing around the piano tuner."

"Good on him. I'm going to need some music after this day." Glancing towards the set, Jessie sighed deeply. "They're almost ready to go."

"We'll talk about Matt later then."

"There's nothing to talk about. I sent him home. He was a mess." The half-truth slid out easily. Jessie hoped it would be enough to satisfy Deirdre and, by extension, Charles. She wasn't so sure about Josh.

"You fired him."

"I did, yes."

"Why?"

"So much for talking about this later. Jesus, Dee."

"The two of you are inseparable. This is serious, Jessie."

"Ahhh! I know it's fucking serious, Dee." Closing her eyes, Jessie apologized. "I'm sorry." Slinking deeply into the chair, she dug one set of fingernails into the back of the opposite hand.

Deirdre casually removed the anxious hand. She wouldn't have bothered, except there would likely be close-ups on the day's shot list and half-moon rings in the back of Jessie's hand weren't likely to go over well.

Exasperated, Jessie let her. She sat on her hands. "I shouldn't swear, I know," she continued. "Emily-Grace would have a fit. She and David eat a lot of pizza funded by the good 'ole Sawyer swear jar."

Dee pressed on. "Jessie, honey. Matt is dear to all of us. You letting him go like this is cause for concern."

"Is Charles going to fire him altogether? Or just keep him away from me?"

"What? No, he's...well, with Susanne leaving..."

"Yeah, I know. We need him. For now." Like a fresh breeze in spring, relief flooded Jessie's soul. She mouthed a silent prayer of thanks.

Deirdre softened her tone. "Did he do something? Did Matt hurt you?"

"No more than I hurt him, Dee." The response was subdued, and spoken without meeting Deirdre's eyes. Finally, Jessie looked up, but she wished she hadn't. Her manager's concern was heartfelt and sincere, and made Jessie want to fold herself into her arms and have a good cry. "We were spending too much time together. We were enjoying each other's company too much, in a way...in a way we shouldn't have been."

"You were sleeping with Matt."

A vigorous shake of Jessie's head dispelled that notion. "No," she said vehemently. "No, I wasn't. But, Dee…I thought about it. I would have if Matt hadn't put the kibosh on us. I was past the point of no return."

"I know things have been tough with Josh lately, Jessie. I'm not sure if the two of you ever really put Jacob behind you, and all that hopeless Nadia and Morgan stuff, either. I want you to know that neither Charles nor myself blame you or Matt for anything that did or did not transpire between you." Searching Jessie's face for signs of an imminent meltdown, Dee smiled tenderly. "He's a very special man."

"I know that, Dee. Don't you think I know that? This sucks. I need Matt in my life."

"When it comes to men, Jessie, and a marriage that's suffering, it's easy to give in to desire. To be honest, I'm guessing you and Matt are the only two who are genuinely surprised at the attraction between you."

"Seriously? Really?"

"We should have known better than to send the two of you over here alone, with things not being so good at home for you right now."

"Julie knew better," Jessie said glumly. "She asked him not to come." Looking up, she twisted a ringlet before asking, "If you figured this out, then I bet Josh has too. Dee, he's a hair's breadth from jumping ship right now, thanks to Kayla and her current bitter influence."

"Oh, honey," Dee sighed. "Josh was at the house when I left. Charles was on the warpath wondering what the hell Matt did to get himself sent home, so yes, Josh knows something's up." A wide yawn almost cracked her jaw in two. "I'd suggest you call him but us Vancouverites are generally in bed at this hour."

"We're ready to go, anyway," Jessie said, standing as the First A.D. signaled to her. "I need to just try to get through this hellish day first. I'll call him at wrap." A few steps towards the set, and she stopped and turned. "Dee? Can you call Charles? Tell him…tell him I was every bit as much to blame as Matt for what happened. Tell him not to fire him altogether, okay?"

"He won't," Dee assured her, settling into the cast chair to watch the shooting. "He's sending him Jacob hunting in Arnie's place."

"Ah. I thought he might. Great. Matt and Jacob together. I'd like to be a fly on the wall for that one. Or a water bug on a sailboat."

Wheeling around, she wandered onto the set and shook the director's hand as various crew started appearing from the various corners of the large indoor studio. The child playing Jessie's little girl bounced up beside her, and Jessie bent and lifted her. "Hello, sweetheart," Deirdre heard her say as Jessie hugged the child tight. "Are you ready for some silly playacting today?"

"I'm supposed to die," the seven year old said. "I'll probably just pretend I'm sleeping, but my mother said you are supposed to cry."

"I just might," Jessie was telling her as Dee cringed. "Today, sweet girl, I just might."

At that, the A.D. called, "Rehearsal's up! Places, please," and shooting started in earnest.

⌒⌒ ⌒⌒

After wrap, many hours and multiple heart wrenching shots and takes later, it was Deirdre who ended up calling Josh instead of Jessie. At eleven a.m. Vancouver time, Josh pulled himself up to a sitting position in bed and wiped his forearm over sleepy eyes in an attempt to wake himself up enough to focus on what Dee had to say. Dylan was fussy, up half the night before, and they were napping.

"I left her in her suite," Jessie's manager was informing him as Josh leaned sideways and tucked the duvet up over Dylan's shoulders. The littlest Sawyer was missing his mother more than the others these days, and had become a constant nighttime companion. "Today was the toughest day of the entire shoot, emotionally, Josh. She couldn't even speak at the end of the day. You know Jessie, she just goes somewhere deep inside when the world gets to be too much. She collapsed on her bed and I expect she'll sleep right through to morning."

"Is she okay, though, Dee?" *Damn, I wish I was there,* Josh thought inwardly.

There was a slight pause from Brussels. "Not really, honey. But I'm sure she will be."

"The Matt thing?"

"The Matt thing is over and done, Josh. I'd prefer you didn't bring that up to Jessie until you can speak to her about it in person."

A quick rise in blood pressure flushed itself across Josh's cheeks. "She slept with Matt? Jesus Christ, Dee! She's trying damn hard to kill me!"

"She didn't sleep with Matt, honey. They got a little too close and both were wise enough to know that their working relationship had come to a close. That's all. You need to be grateful for both of them to have known when to call it quits."

"Dylan was up all night, Dee, I think he's sick, and I feel like I haven't slept in days. I'm not going to be feeling very damn grateful any time soon."

Deirdre cut in. "Don't do anything rash, Josh. Jessie and you are living very demanding lives. It's common for people who work as closely together as Matt and Jessie do—did—to rely on each other when things get tough at home. Just relax, bring your babies over here next weekend, and talk to Jessie then."

By the time Josh disconnected, he was wishing he was heading to Brussels now, although he strongly considered putting the pedal to the metal and swinging by Matt's place to land a few well-placed punches.

Instead, Josh got up and called Dylan's pediatrician, and if it hadn't been for a newly scheduled mid-afternoon trip to the doctor's office for a possible ear infection, which explained the other reason Dylan was missing his momma, Josh would have pointed the King Ranch towards Matt's home.

Carrying Dylan out of the doctor's office later, unaccompanied by security and simply ignoring the usual stares and whispers, Josh held his son tight as he strode to the big truck, a prescription in his hand. Dylan was feverish and whimpering in pain.

"You and me, buddy," Josh said to him, "need to see our girl. We need some Momma hugs, don't we?"

In response, Dylan wrapped both arms around his father's neck, buried his face in Josh's long layered chestnut hair, and cried from the heart. "Hurts, Daddy," he said over and over.

"I know, buddy," Josh told him, his own heart breaking as he buckled the little guy into his car seat. "I'm the king of hurts. Trust me. I know what I'm talking about. You and me gotta stick together."

He pointed the pickup east, drove to a pharmacy, and filled a prescription for Dylan, hoping the infection would clear up in plenty of time to give them permission to fly to Europe the next weekend.

By the time Dylan was more up to travelling, Matt was gone.

Matt didn't have a choice. He had to drop in to La Casa to talk to Charles and, in his experience, it would be better to do the dirty deed sooner rather than later. After a cold chill from Julie upon returning home with his tail between his legs, there was a part of Matt that figured he would welcome the rant he expected to receive from Charles. At least his boss' thoughts would be out in the open, whereas Julie's feelings were non-verbal and disturbing.

What Matt didn't expect, and what he got, was the older man's understanding.

"I thought you'd fire me," he said to Charles as he sat opposite him, beyond Charles' large desk. "I came here half-expecting to be fired."

"Jessie's request, Matt," Charles confessed. "I admit, I wanted to kick your ass from here to Timbuktu. But my wife has a way with words. She's not even remotely surprised that this happened. Part of me thinks she figured it would happen sooner, to be frank, but I would suggest that Jessie had her hands full with her other two delinquents."

He moved forward in his wide chair and leaned both elbows on the desk, then lifted a mug Carlotta left earlier, and took a sip. "Matt," he started, "the truth is, we put you in an awkward position. We left you with Jessie for far too long. After Morgan…" He sighed. "After Morgan she wanted you with her as much as possible." Pondering Matt, he added, "You look like shit. But I think you should forgive yourself. Jessie's always been crazy about you. This is not, by her admission to Deirdre, entirely a one way thing, apparently."

There was a blunt pencil on the desk. Idly, Matt reached for it and rolled it around between his fingers. "I don't know how to respond to that, Charles. I was drinking. The music got to me. She got to me. None of this is Jessie's fault."

"Well, it's my understanding that some of it is. She's been having a few very tough days over there, reeling with this new indiscretion or whatever the hell you choose to call it, and reeling with her loss of you. On top of that, she filmed the death scene yesterday. Or today. Whatever the hell day it is over there." In a softer voice, Charles added, "Deirdre said she was uncommunicative afterwards. She went straight to bed."

The pencil froze in Matt's hand. Closing his eyes, he exhaled slowly and turned his head to the left.

"After all this time, Matt...why now? Why now."

Shaking his head slowly from side to side, Matt couldn't bring himself to immediately answer. Eventually he had to deal with the overwhelming silence in the room, though, so he did finally meet Charles' kind but steady gaze. "I think my marriage is over." A choking sound startled him when he realized it came from himself, and he cleared his throat while he tried to get a grip. "Julie's been having an affair. I think I just needed a friend."

"I think maybe you both did, Matt. And I'm truly sorry to hear about Julie."

Matt was silent so Charles idly tapped a finger lightly on the desk and studied him. He filled in the heavy gap. "I'm also sorry that you and Jessie had to let each other go this way. Knowing both of you as well as I do, I can see why you were wise enough to call a halt before you started a deception that would have hurt a hell of a lot more than just the two of you."

"The kids." Groaning, Matt placed a thumb and forefinger on his forehead and pressed hard. "Jesus, Charles, what the hell was I thinking? I'm going to find myself at the end of Josh's fists for this." Looking up, he added, "He doesn't deserve this."

"You didn't sleep with her, Matt. According to Jessie, you didn't go that far."

Matt's voice was gravel on a country road. "Do you really think that matters, Charles? I'm not sure it makes one bit of difference. All the way home, given the way I feel right now, that my world is crashing down around me... I wish we had. I wish to hell I had one damn night to hold on to." Scraping back his chair, Matt rose. "I don't know what the hell I'm doing, or where I'm supposed to go. I think I wish you would fire me."

"Why?" Charles stood as well. "So you can pull a Jessie and run away? No. You're a responsible grown man, Matt. And you're a very important part of this family. Family helps each other through the bad things life throws at us. I'm sorry to hear about your marriage, but I'm not surprised about that either. As for what you need to do now, I need you to jump aboard what was supposed to be Arnie's little mission."

"I was afraid of that."

"Go home, shave. The jet's on its way back from Brussels. It'll need a few hours to refuel and re-crew, then it's filing a flight plan for the Caribbean. I expect you to be on it."

"Where in the Caribbean exactly, and what the hell am I supposed to tell Jacob when I find him?"

Charles pushed a printed email across the desk towards Matt, who picked it up and studied it thoughtfully. "His last known port. I'm sure if you start there someone will know which direction he's travelling, and how far he could have possibly gotten to. As far as what to tell him? I just want to know how he's doing. I need to know that he's okay. Jessie…needs to know that he's okay."

A second groan, albeit a little weaker than the first, escaped from between Matt's lips.

Charles added, "I'd like to know his plans, and whether or not he intends to play at the Grammys. And Matt?"

"Yep. Still here."

"I need to know if he's coming home. Stay for a while. Take a little holiday. But don't go buying yourself a sailboat. Until we find a replacement for Susanne, the Keating camp is a few men short of an army."

"I can't do Josh and the kids, Charles. I can't look those kids in the eye right now."

"You'll switch off with Ulysses, then. For now. Coordinating and driving Deirdre and I when we need you. But someday, Matt, you're going to need to make peace with Josh and Jessie."

"I think for now, Charles, I'd just rather set a date and plan to retire from your service. You'd better extend your recruitment ad to two people. In the meantime, please know how sorry I am. Please…tell Jessie how sorry I am."

Reaching for the door handle, Matt turned to Charles one last time. "I'll be in touch as soon as I can. I won't stay long. Although she hasn't come out and said it, Julie seems to want me out of the house, and I'd just as soon not come home to all of my things fueling a big bonfire in the front yard."

"Do what you need to, Matt. Jacob will not be that hard to find."

Ten minutes later, Carlotta swept in and gathered up the tray of treats she left the men, zucchini muffins this time. To her dismay, Matt hadn't touched his muffin, nor did it appear he took even a drink of coffee. Perplexed, worried, she stared at the tray before lifting it. A voice from behind the desk offered what comfort it could.

"It wasn't you, Carlotta," Charles said kindly. "Matt's not himself today."

"Nobody is ever themselves when love goes bad," the maid said, as she headed across the large office to the open doorway. "I hope Jessie is doing okay."

Disconcerted by the offhand remark, Charles' fingers poised over his keyboard. He looked up in time to see Carlotta's back pass through the doorway. "Carlotta, you're wiser than the rest of us," he muttered. "How is it you and Deirdre saw this coming, and I really didn't have a sweet clue?"

Sighing heavily, he opened his email, and got back to work.

Chapter Eight

*L*aughing, Jacob was answering an email from Kayla when he saw Matt's familiar sturdy shoulders and spiked hair down in the harbor where Sarah May was docked. With his laptop leaning against his knees, bare feet up on a deck rail, Jacob was lounging around an outdoor bar so he could access the spotty public wireless. Pausing, then hitting send and closing his laptop, he straightened and focused his gaze on the man who had often watched over he and Jessie in the New York days, and in the Miami days before that.

"Hmmm," he pondered, talking to himself as he scratched his five-day beard, "are you here to pound the shit out of me or are you here to—" A sudden knifelike thrust in his stomach bent him in two. Vaulting up, Jacob froze and wondered whether something was wrong back home, or…or maybe in Brussels. Why the hell would Matt be here? As far as Jacob knew, Jessie was on the Belgian shoot. Her protector, Matt, was always by her side.

Matt caught Jacob's movement the same time the grizzled old sailor he was querying about Jacob pointed out the young newbie mariner. Wandering up the ramp, he crossed the small clearing, leaned on the rail opposite the singer, and gestured behind himself.

"Which one's yours?" As he asked, he removed his sunglasses and propped them up on his head.

Visibly, Jacob relaxed. Matt looked like shit. He was pale and unshaven, which was odd for him, since he was usually impeccably dressed, and today although he was wearing some expensive nautical brand sunglasses, his sea-blue v-neck T-shirt was untucked and his tartan scotch shorts were wrinkled. But at least he didn't seem upset. Fists weren't flying and the man's eyes weren't raging, as they were the last time Jacob laid his cobalt blues on Matt. Nor were Matt's eyes steady and focused, hawk-like and businesslike as always. Instead, they seemed kind of sad.

"She's the faded green one," Jacob replied, his curiosity rising. "Sarah May."

"Do you actually sail her or do you just live on her? Do you just sit up here, drink beer and watch porn all day?"

"I've been sailin' her."

"Get the shit scared out of you yet?"

"Once or twice. I got over it." Jacob set the laptop back down on the table and squared his body to his old bodyguard. "What the hell are you doing here, Matt? Isn't Jessie still in Brussels?"

Something untoward sputtered across Matt's eyes at that, and Jacob felt his defenses rise. Matt looked down and then away, across the small marina restaurant and bar towards the open sea, which beckoned him with its promise of aquamarine peace and healing. "Yes, Jessie's still in Brussels," he said quietly, refocusing on Jacob. "Arnie's with her."

"She's okay?"

"Not entirely. But you know Jessie. She always rebounds."

"What, did her and Josh—"

"Don't get excited, Jacob, they're working through the shit storm you created." *That I took advantage of and have no idea how they're handling,* Matt thought as his stomach wrenched.

Jacob settled, relaxed his body, and grabbed the rail with one hand. Placing the other on his hip and hoisting a foot up on the bottom rail, he said simply, "Good. I'm glad," but he couldn't help but wonder what the hell Matt wasn't telling him.

Grabbing his sunglasses and dangling them from one hand before he put them back over his eyes to cut the glare from the hot tropical sun, Matt studied Jacob. The guy looked a helluva lot better than the last time they laid eyes on each other. He was tanned, more muscled under the black tank he wore over a pair of faded cut off jean shorts, and there was a quiet peace about him. It encircled him with an unseen glow. A loosely wound red bandana tied around his neck gave him a rebellious air; worn leather flip flops on his feet topped off his summer vibe, striking Matt as almost odd since he was accustomed to seeing Jacob in jeans and one form of boots or another.

"Doin' the hippy thing, are you?" Matt asked, attempting to inject some lightness into the conversation. "Living on a boat, letting your hair grow long. I suppose you can do handstands on a paddleboard by now. And the Yoga tree pose? Although I have no idea how the hell you can do that in waves."

As if in protest, a gust of warm wind picked up Jacob's curls and gave them a swirl. Absently, he swiped one rogue strand out of his eyes and shoved it behind his ear. A pair of aviator sunglasses sat on the table next to the laptop. He picked them up and placed them on top of his head to keep the rest of his hair in line. "Life makes a lot more sense down here, Matt," he said simply. "A man can just be who he needs to be, and forget about all the worldly shit that makes people crazy."

A small smile turned up on Matt's face, and his eyes regained a sparkle of light. "If there's beer to go along with that, I'm in."

Jacob grinned and waved an arm. "C'mon over to my side of the fence. As long as you promise not to get rowdy again, that is, cuz I got me a nasty hangover and I ain't too keen on fightin' back."

"I'm all outta fight, Jacob." True enough, Matt looked pretty done in.

Regarding him closely, Jacob cocked his head to add, "You runnin' away too?"

"Something like that," Matt answered honestly as he swung a leg up over the rail, leapt over it, and landed next to Jacob, who faced him, eyes somber.

"Jessie?" he asked.

Feeling completely exposed in front of a man who Jessie had loved intimately, Matt shrugged. "What about her?" It was a weird way to answer the simple query, but hearing her name voiced in that questioning way had caught Matt off guard.

"What'd she do to you? Because somehow I don't think Jessie sent you down here to look for me. Although I admit a part of me wishes she had."

"Jessie's Jessie. That's all I have to say on the subject until I get really drunk and say far too much."

"You fuck her, Matt?" Jacob wasn't asking in an accusatory fashion. Instead, the question was handed off to Matt in a very casual manner.

80

Growling, Matt took a step back. "Why is it nobody seems surprised that Jessie and I might have hooked up? And no, for Christ's sake, Jacob, I didn't."

"But you wanted to." Raising an arm, Jacob signaled the server. "Two beers, man," he called. He shoved a plastic deck chair in Matt's general direction.

"Like some rebel musician types I know, there may have been a moment when I wanted to—or three moments, maybe—but I didn't. I might have kissed her, but I didn't take her to my bed. Or to hers. And I sure as hell didn't force Jessie to do anything she didn't want to do."

Jacob's voice grew quiet. "I was a mess that day, Matt. I've been punishing myself for my actions every day since." He grinned as his voice took on a lighter tone. "Matt finally goes for Jessie. I've been wondering when that would happen. It just kinda seems right, in some ways. She fucking adores you."

"Jesus Christ." Matt wrapped his fingers around his newly arrived beer bottle and started picking at the label. "Apart from the age difference, there are a thousand reasons why me being with Jessie seems anything but right, Jacob. You might recall that she's so lost in Josh she once took off in order to protect him."

Ignoring that hurtful truth, Jacob pushed Matt for more. "Must have gotten a little hot and heavy, since you're here and she's there, eh Matt?" Jacob thrust out a hand and seized Matt's arm. Raising it, he studied it until Matt roughly yanked it away.

"Do you mind?" Matt asked gruffly.

"I don't see any bruises." Sitting back, Jacob lifted his feet to a nearby chair and crossed his ankles. "I can't imagine Josh is thrilled."

"I left Vancouver before he found out, I think."

"Got the hell outta Dodge, you mean. Before Josh came after you with guns blazing." Grabbing his own beer bottle, Jacob raised it and clinked the neck against Matt's. "The guy does know how to handle a shootout. Apparently there were many on *Drifters* back in the day."

"As do you know how to handle a shootout, I recall," Matt replied wryly. "Yes, I'm in good company, apparently." Grumbling, he lifted the cool beer to his lips.

"So…is she okay?"

Averting Jacob's close scrutiny, Matt paused before taking a long pull on his drink. "I doubt it."

Licking his lips nervously, Jacob studied Matt. "I've never seen you like this, Matt, all out of sorts," he decided, announcing the fact in a rather subdued tone. "She must have really done a number on you."

Rolling his eyes, Matt didn't answer.

Jacob answered for him. "She has that effect on men. It's not her fault, it's just part of the Jessie Wheeler charm."

"Part of the mystique, huh, Jacob? Can we stop mouthing off about Jessie now and just get drunk? I'm ready for some good old fashioned mindless puking in the hot Tropicana sun."

"It's early, but hell, I'm up for it. Glad to have you aboard, Matt. Drink first, business later." Conspiratorially, he dug out his wallet, opened it, and tossed Matt a couple of condoms. "You'll need these, buddy. The women here are young, sweet and willing. And they're not expensive."

Raising his eyebrows, Matt pocketed the condoms. "And by not expensive, you mean—"

"What I mean, Matt, is that they won't break your heart. Seeing as that's a price both of us have already paid dearly for the sake of love." Holding his beer up high, a wide smile broke out across Jacob's face. "It's good to see you, old boy. Here's to getting wasted, here's to anonymous sex, and here's to a complete disregard for our beautiful, tragic Vancouver girl. Plant your dick in one of these honeys and you'll forget about Jessie forever."

"Uh huh." Dryly, Matt raised his beer and mumbled, "Cheers."

"Well," Jacob added in a slightly more restrained tone as flecks of dark blue danced across his eyes, "one can always dream. Right?"

A slow chuckle made its way up Matt's throat, so he shook his head and let it come. It was the first time he felt any release of the burden from that amazing, troubled night with Jessie.

He held up his bottle and tipped it towards Jacob's so they clinked. "Cheers," he said again, and settled in under the midday heat to get roaring drunk with a man who, a few days earlier, he would have gladly choked with his bare hands.

"This jet lag's gonna be tough on the kids," Josh was yawning to Big Dan as they carried two of the sleeping Sawyer children down the steps of the jet. "We left at seven last night, flew for ten hours, and it's now two in the afternoon Belgian time, but only four in the morning Vancouver time. This is going to mess them up entirely."

"Once they see their mother, they'll be just fine," Dan assured Josh. "Trust me. And as far as waking and sleeping goes, just roll with the punches. They're small. They'll adapt."

"Well, it's not like we haven't done it before," Josh replied as a large black SUV pulled up. Apprehensive, he stopped at the bottom of the steps, Emily-Grace clinging like a monkey in his arms, and waited.

The passenger door swung open, and Jessie hopped down onto the tarmac. Even from twenty feet away, Josh could see the toll this tough film was having on her. Or was it all the other shit that was coloring her life these days? As she approached, he remained unmoving, and swallowed uncomfortably as his eyes drifted over her body. The way she was slowly walking as if she was tired and unsure of him, of them…the way her eyes were radiating hurt…the way her fingers were twisting in and around each other…It was all there—nerves, physical and emotional fatigue, perhaps even exhaustion.

When she drew close enough, Jessie touched her daughter's hair, which stirred Emily-Grace a little but not quite enough to wake the sleeping child. Then she tried to smile up at her husband, but couldn't seem to quite manage it. The pearlescent blues landed on David next, in Dan's arms. Jessie bent forward and kissed him, lingering for an extra moment to inhale his sweet little boy scent of shampoo mixed with caramel from an earlier apple dip snack.

Victoria navigated the steps carefully with Dylan in her arms, and handed him over to Jessie, who took him, turned away from Josh, and pressed his small body to hers.

Unlike the other two, Dylan awoke and recognized his mother, wrapped his small arms around her, and sleepily whimpered, "Momma," over and over.

This is not a good sign, Josh caught himself thinking. *She hasn't even said hello.* Quietly, he followed Dan's lead and placed his daughter on a booster seat in the big SUV, trying not to wake her, and soothing her back into sleep when she did stir by placing singer-dolly in her arms and a blanket over her slumbering body. Arnie was along too, in a second vehicle to accommodate all of them, and it struck Josh as odd to see him there instead of Matt.

David was soon secured, but Jessie seemed reluctant to let Dylan go. He was nestled securely into her now, and was blinking hard trying to stay awake.

Josh reached for him, but Jessie turned sideways and held on. "Just one more minute," she pleaded. "I need this."

"All right." Standing back, Josh watched her while the local crew as well as Dan supervised the transfer of luggage. "Are you okay, Jessie? You look kind of tired out."

"This film was tougher than I thought it would be, Josh," she admitted without meeting his eye. "I just…there were things I didn't expect, that's all."

"Like…the whole Matt thing," he said, deciding to hit the bull head on.

She stilled. It hurt to even say Matt's name at this point. Jessie missed her old friend so much that she had started to smoke weed again. Anything to lessen the pain of loss, to help her through the rest of this difficult time. "Yeah. There was that," she said finally.

"Are we gonna talk about it?"

"It was nothing, Josh. Just a moment, that's all."

"Enough of a moment for you to send him packing."

"Julie hurt him," she replied, turning to Josh and meeting his eye for the first time. "He leaned on me. We realized it wasn't a good idea. I sent him home. Okay?"

"Okay." But for some reason, Josh still felt a wary vibe about the whole thing, partly, he realized, because his wife had yet to touch him. She certainly hadn't kissed him.

"Come see this beautiful historic city," she was saying to him now, though. "The art deco mansions around the hotel are something else."

Arnie approached and reached for Dylan, who protested vociferously but went along okay after Jessie whispered a hushed, "Momma loves you," in his ear. Soothing the little guy as he moved, Arnie walked him to the second vehicle. Jessie's arms were free.

Regarding her carefully, Josh just stood in silence, trying not to look as glum and disappointed as he felt. He knew his wife like the back of his hand, and something about the way she was receiving him today was off. It was upsetting. The two of them would have to find time for a real heart to heart over this quick trip to Brussels. They needed to find time to mend the hurts that had been circling over their heads like hawks since the Christmas holidays.

She was watching him too, shoving both hands in her jeans pockets, facing Josh with her feet apart and her head tilted nervously to one side.

Eventually he asked quietly, "Do I get a kiss?" realizing he was speaking softly in case someone overheard and she turned him down.

He got more than a kiss. Jessie stepped forward, pressed her lips to his, melted into his arms, and buried her face in the familiar chest she loved, that she ached for. Her body trembled as she clutched Josh to her, as all the fears, the pain from both life and the hard topics characterizing her film work over the past few weeks, and the losses of both Jacob and Matt, caught up to her.

"I can't stand it," Josh heard her say. "I can't stand it. It hurts."

Stroking the unfamiliar shorter hair, Josh tilted Jessie's face up so he could see her more clearly, so he could look into the eyes he cherished and try to get a reading from her, of what was troubling her soul.

In the end, though, he had to ask. He did so by scrunching up his eyes and holding a palm against her cheek. "What can't you stand, Jessie?" he asked, praying and hoping she wasn't referencing him.

"Everything," was her downhearted answer. "Missing everybody."

"I wish," he told her as he let her go and started to back away, "that for once you would just say me. That you were just missing me."

Leaving her standing there, Josh climbed into the second vehicle next to Arnie.

After a shocked moment to sniffle and wipe her nose on the sleeve of her tight denim jacket, Jessie peeked at her sleeping children, and then slid into the passenger seat of the first car. In separate vehicles, Josh and Jessie were driven into the city in silence, lost in thought, wondering how to fix something they both desperately wanted, but which was starting to feel like it was beyond repair.

Chapter Nine

A few days later, Kayla dropped by to see Josh and Dylan before pointing her pink scooter north to the Deacon space on East Hastings. Now, as she drove, avoiding cool, slushy puddles, she considered what her big brother told her.

"It was a quick trip. Jessie had to shoot part of the day Saturday, so we checked out the soundstage and some of the exterior locations while she was working. On Sunday she and I mostly just hung out in the hotel and played with the kids. Took them to the pool, snuggled up and watched cartoons, that kind of thing. It was okay."

Josh filled Kayla in on the latest development with Matt and, listening, Kayla just shook her head. "None of this is good, Josh. What's been happening with her—these are signs you have to stop ignoring. What did she have to say for herself?"

"Not a lot. She hardly spoke to me."

"Great. That's awesome."

"Easy, Kayla. We had two and a half days together, and believe me, I didn't mind that the kids were all over her. They needed her, and she needed them. Leaving sucked. For all of us. Dylan was inconsolable."

Kayla nodded towards Dylan, who was snuggled up in Josh's arms as they sat on the couch and chatted. "He might love his momma, but he's become a real daddy's boy."

"He is. He's my kid." Josh's hard stare was a warning Kayla wisely heeded.

However, the new direction she took caught Josh off guard. "You're doing fine raising these kids on your own, Josh."

His glare was ice. "I am not raising these kids on my own. Jessie's coming back."

"Bro, I hate to break it to you, but she's messing around with other men. In case you haven't noticed."

Josh's voice had a quiet desperation to it. "She loves me, Kayla. She's not going anywhere. And not that it's any of your business, but we had some pretty damn good sex in Brussels. She may not have spoken in words, but her actions were pretty damn clear."

Kayla harrumphed loudly. "Yeah, Jessie speaking in 'sex' is such a stretch. For her. The slut. Were her eyes open or closed?"

"Seriously. Seriously?"

"You can have sex with one person but be thinking about another. Hell, I had to do it all the time with Paul, or I never would have climaxed." *And I am not telling you who I was thinking about,* Kayla added, unable to prevent her cheeks from cresting pink.

"You're pushing it, Kayla. Watch yourself. Jesus." Pissed, Josh bit off, "Jessie will be okay. And I sure as hell don't appreciate my sister calling my wife a slut."

"I hope so, Josh. I hope she'll be okay. For your sake." Kayla ignored the slut comment altogether and reached out for Dylan. "Hey, little guy. Come see Auntie Kayla before I have to go." Dylan was only too happy to snuggle with his beloved aunt, who couldn't resist losing herself in his innocent miniature Jacob-eyes.

Josh took advantage of free arms to start prepping some espresso for cappuccinos. From the kitchen, forcing his blood pressure down, he tried to take the high road by changing the conversation to something that felt safe. "You're going down to the Deacon space today?"

"Yes, I am," Kayla answered, fingering Dylan's Jacob-curls and wondering how the hell Josh could stand raising Jessie and Jacob's love-child. Shaking her head to dispel the nefarious thought, she said, "I wish you could come with me and hold my hand."

"Charlie said Jack fired Mandy." Opening the fridge, Josh swifted out a carton of milk and poured some into a metal pitcher so he could steam it.

"He did. She's supposed to have cleared out her office. But her grimy fingerprints are all over the place. Not to mention her and Paul's—"

"Too much information, Kayla." Josh was quiet for a minute as the noisy steamer did its thing. A few minutes later, he sauntered into the living room and set her cinnamon-sprinkled drink on the ottoman. "I'd go with you if I could but this little guy's got a re-check on his ear today. You'll be fine. Call me if you need me."

Now, as Kayla zipped the scooter into a tiny parking spot, she eyed the Deacon space with disdain. All the hard work, all the hours she put into teaching the Downtown Eastside youth to dance…it was tainted now. Her stomach clenched at the thought of shoving the key in the lock and walking inside. She was, simply put, quite disgusted with all the breakdowns that seemed to be happening around her.

"Stars, I wish you would all just realign yourselves," she muttered as she looked both ways before crossing the street.

Inside, she flipped on the light switch, punched in the alarm code, and stepped into the dim space. A bright floral fragrance caught her nose. *Talia.* It struck her as odd, to still sense Talia's favorite perfume all these weeks later, but she supposed it was possible for the scent to linger. A sorry twinge seized her belly.

"Talia, silly girl. I really liked you. You were a breath of fresh air, country girl."

Crossing the floor to her office, Kayla dropped down behind her computer and flipped it on. Moments later, she was laughing at an email from Jacob. There was, apparently, company staying on his boat—Matt.

We're figuring out this sailing thing together, the short note read. *Matt sailed some when he was a kid, and some of it's coming back to him. We're actually pretty good together. You should come down. I can teach you a few things.*

"I'll bet. Ha." Her body tingled at the thought of Jacob's warm breath on her skin, and Kayla hoped his touch was what he was referring to in the email. Pushing the thought away before she got too crazy thinking about Jacob's tight black jeans and sad, sexy eyes, she considered his current company. "Matt and Jacob together," she slurred in curious wonderment. "Jessie's little throwaways. Use 'em and lose 'em. The bitch."

Sitting back now, she reflected on her choice not to tell her brother she was in touch with Jacob. Their correspondence had begun over the need to find new security to replace Susanne, but it had grown over the last few weeks to an almost daily news feed. They shared songs and videos, and gossip and tidbits of their daily lives. Once, Kayla got up the nerve to ask him how he was doing, or how he was coping, more like it, over the loss of the woman he was supposed to marry.

To her surprise, he had written a long and poignant letter back. It was as if Jacob needed and cherished the outlet Kayla gave him to reflect on Talia. By writing to someone who knew her, from behind a computer screen instead of looking into compassionate eyes, Jacob had obviously found it easy to let go. And it appeared he needed to. Kayla had cried over his obvious love for the woman he lost, and then immediately reprimanded herself for the ache in her heart she felt when picturing Jacob alone down south, trying to find his way in a world that had suddenly, overnight almost, turned dark and ugly.

She blamed Jessie, and had told Jacob that. He wrote back, scolding her for being too harsh and quick to judge. *I already went down that road,* he had disclosed. *But if there's anything Jessie taught me, it was to forgive others. I'm trying to let go of her. Forgiveness is a part of that process. Letting go of my anger towards her is a part of that process.*

"You will defend her to the day you die, won't you, Jacob?" Kayla had growled to the screen before slamming it shut without answering his email. An hour later, though, she couldn't resist. This secret—writing to Jacob on the down low—was quickly becoming an addiction.

Now, Kayla had some fun typing out a long email to her new pen pal. Merciless, she referred to he and Matt as some kind of broken heart club, and asked permission to let Josh know where the guys were—*in case he needs to join you.* In the last paragraph, she took back her earlier jibes and admitted that Josh did not seem angry, that he was as committed as ever to making things work with Jessie, and that apparently he and Jessie had great sex while he was in Brussels.

"Stew on that, you two losers," Kayla said in earnest as she mouse-clicked on 'send.' Immediately she was hit with a quick pang of 'sender's remorse,' but she shrugged it away. Inherent in the overt message was a simple statement—*Josh is not giving up on Jessie.*

Kayla hung out at the rehearsal space, answering emails and sorting out admin details for the upcoming workshop session until her belly started to protest. Locking the door behind her, she wandered happily down the block towards Revolver, where she knew she would find a home-baked muffin and superior drip coffee with which to wash it down.

Inside, she grabbed a metal chair by the main window, and struck up a conversation with a social worker from the Downtown Eastside who she'd met through the workshops. As with most people who discovered Kayla's work—namely being one of Jessie Wheeler's regular dancers—the woman's dialogue was peppered with questions about Jessie (What's she like? Is she as sweet as everyone says she is?), Josh (You're his sister? You've got to be kidding me, what I would give to meet that man in person...do you think you could arrange that?), and Jacob (What a tragedy, losing Talia. After all he went through losing Jessie, my heart just breaks for him). After twenty minutes of desperately trying to be civil and not resort to eyeball rolling, Kayla finally swallowed the last bit of her muffin and smiled her goodbye to the well-meaning but distressingly annoying woman.

On the street again, she was about a block from the Deacon space when she spotted Paul's jeep, which was parked outside a trendy interior design shop. Hesitating, because she had to pass it in order to get back to the workshop space, Kayla finally decided to tough it out, and she started to wander by. At that moment, fate intervened and the door of the design shop flew open, to the soundtrack of high-pitched female giggles and the low hum of a man's voice—Paul's.

Kayla went rigid. It was too late to go back, and impossible to consider moving forward. They were suddenly in front of her, her ex and Mandy, and they were lost in each other's eyes. Worse, they were obviously joking about sex—past, present, future, it was irrelevant which—and were suddenly engaged in an intense, lustful kissing session just in front of Kayla.

When they finally started to move, Kayla found herself locked in Mandy's glare and Paul's deer-in-the-headlights stare.

"You said it meant nothing," she wailed to Paul. "You said it was over."

In front of her, Paul held tight to Mandy's hand and raised his chin. "You kicked me out," he chastised her. "You never gave me a chance."

As the impact of that sank in, Kayla found her feet moving forward, but she had no memory of jumping on her scooter and piloting it to her new condo. At home, she buried her face under her pillow and sobbed until she was dry.

At midnight, soaked in moonlight, she pulled out the chair to her small desk and re-read Jacob's earlier email. *You should come down.*

"The broken heart club," she thought. "I'd fit right in." Poising her fingers over the keyboard, she thought for a minute before typing a note to Jacob.

I hope you meant that, because I'm coming down. I won't cramp your style. I just need a break. I'll find a place to stay.

A second email she typed out to Benjie, her good friend from Jessie's dance troupe. Kayla asked him to take charge of starting the workshops up again until she got back. *Sharlyne and Cheyenne can help,* she wrote. Benjie called her immediately and accepted.

A third email went to Jack Deacon to explain that Benjie would be taking over. A fourth was sent to both of her brothers.

Zach and Josh—I'm taking a little trip. I need the break before the workshops start up full time again. I'll be in touch.

She did not say where she was going, or with whom she planned to meet up. Josh, in particular, would lose his mind if he knew she was writing almost daily to Jacob, much less about to go in search of him in some random Caribbean port.

Pondering her choice of travel destination, Kayla wondered if she was making a mistake. Jessie crossed her mind—Jessie and Jacob, in fact. In the old days, at concerts or festivals, Kayla had often seen them together backstage, lusting after each other in the way only couples who really enjoyed each other's bodies did—Jessie sitting on Jacob's lap covering him with passionate public kisses; even the occasional little moans had slipped out here and there.

Once, Kayla had walked in on them—it wasn't her fault, Jessie had always told her dancers that her dressing room was always open to them. But this time, Jessie had been straddling Jacob, her arms around his neck. His hands were high on her sides, his thumbs brushing against Jessie's half-exposed breasts in the loose halter top she was wearing.

When Kayla had bounced in, Jacob was bent forward, his lips pressed to the base of Jessie's neck. That was all well and good; what really burned on Kayla's retinas was the memory of Jessie moaning and rocking herself on him, and Jacob's slight rhythmic movements back. There was a second when Kayla thought they were actually having sex then, but they'd both just looked up at her when she entered, their eyes dusky with desire, and Jessie had lain her cheek down against Jacob's shoulder as he wrapped his arms possessively around her.

At the time, Kayla had been angry, pissed at Jessie for hooking up with Jacob while Josh was struggling with addictions. But, too, there was something erotic in Jessie and Jacob's interactions then and always; now, remembering, Kayla wanted what Jessie had.

Please, Jacob, she intoned now as she stared at the pale moon outside her window. *Please.*

As she drifted off to sleep, the last person to cross her mind was Jessie, and the last image was Kayla's middle finger, raised in smug satisfaction.

In the vision before that was Jacob, rocking underneath Kayla as she straddled him.

Uhhhhh, she had moaned as she thought about him, as she lay on her belly aching for his touch. Raising her hips just high enough to slip a finger underneath, Kayla had moved a finger down between her legs so she could deal with the desire consuming her, wishing the whole time that the finger was Jacob's. She brought herself to climax with a half-satisfied cry, and settled into sleep with a small smile.

The next day she dug out her summer clothes and packed a suitcase. As she zipped the bag shut over sexy sundresses and ultra-short bleached denim shorts, over cotton halter tops and bikinis, she gloated.

Fuck you, Paul, she thought as she headed out the door. *Fuck you Mandy, and...* she couldn't help but add... *Fuck you, Jessie. I'll see you on the flip side.*

There was no room to consider Jacob not wanting her. Why wouldn't he? Kayla was a fit, gorgeous blonde (at least partly—now, her hair had cheerful cranberry waves throughout) who danced her way around the world for more than just Jessie Wheeler. She was financially independent, sunny (well, maybe not so much lately) and kind.

But most of all, she was single, lonely, and hurt. She and Jacob had a lot in common. To him she could offer solace and a willing, sensual body.

And, if he would have her, she could also offer love.

~ ~

Soon, Kayla was standing on the dock in the small marina where Sarah May was docked. Jacob was on the cabin scrubbing the old boat up in preparation for Kayla's imminent arrival, and Matt had two foresails spread out on the wooden dock and was taking lessons about their purpose and how to care for them from the grizzled old skipper he met on his first day in the marina.

Jacob caught his breath when he saw Kayla meander slowly towards the boat. It was not a stretch for him to gauge just how nervous she was. In denim shorts and a blue dotted top she'd tied up past her belly button, and wide aviator sunglasses, she was showing off her lithe dancer's body to its best effect. Jacob whistled under his breath, and stood.

"Matt," he called, as he dropped the rag he was using to clean with and hopped down to the open cockpit and then on to the dock. "Our company's here."

"Hey," Kayla said, chiding herself for the slight tremor in her voice, "sorry for the short notice. I sure as hell hope you were serious about inviting me, because there ain't nowhere to stay here. I asked around."

The old skipper hauled an unlit cigar from between his teeth. "You can stay on my boat."

A wide grin spread across Jacob's face. A few steps forward, and he had Kayla's small suitcase in his hand. "You travel light," he declared.

"I've travelled a lot," she smiled. "I'm always following crazy musicians around. I'm a girl who knows how to pack."

"Good thing," Jacob teased, "because the old girl here doesn't have a ton of space. But she's cozy and comfortable, so you're in good hands."

"I hope so," she sighed, hoping he literally meant his hands. "I won't stay long, Jacob, I swear. I just needed to get away for a bit."

"Well," he answered, as Matt launched himself forward for a nervous hug, given that Kayla was Josh's sister, and Jessie's dancer, "I totally accept that. Sometimes, my friend, we just need a break from the heartache. Isn't that right, Matt?"

Saluting Kayla, Matt's eyes danced gladly. "Welcome to the broken heart club, Kayla."

Jacob tossed in, "I think we should celebrate. Who's up for a brew?"

Matt had another thought as he watched the nervous tension pass between Jacob and his new guest. *I think it's time for me to go home.*

But for now, there was booze, there was weed, and there would be music later, when Jacob got his guitar out and opened his soul to the moon and the stars.

And there was, for a time, three broken hearts aligned as one, far from the pressures of the world, and far, far, far from the people who broke those hearts in the first place.

Chapter Ten

*J*essie pulled Josh to her on a dark, stormy night two weeks later, during a five-day break from shooting. She had hopped aboard the Keating jet with Deirdre and flown to L.A. for the Grammys and was now comfortably ensconced in a king-sized bed with the man she loved most in the world. The only thing missing was their children, but Jessie and Josh would fly up to Vancouver after the awards show so Jessie could hold them for at least a day before flying back to Brussels. One last week of shooting remained, to be followed by a week of recording the film's poignant soundtrack.

Now, though, she held her man tight and breathed in his essence. There was no feeling like it, holding him after making love, and being held in return.

The afterglow was short lived. The Red Hot Chili Peppers' lonesome tune *Under the Bridge* started playing, its hollow lilt emerging from Josh's iPhone on the bedside table. The forlorn song sliced the night in two, and struck a desolate tone in the semi-darkness.

Grunting, Josh twisted his torso around and grabbed it. Scanning the call display, he looked at Jessie and mouthed, "Charles." Into the phone he said, "Yeah, hey Charles. What's up?"

Charles' words, barked into a phone just down the hall in the luxury hotel, were urgent. "Josh, Ulysses just called. There's some kind of flu going around La Casa. He's sick as a dog, Dan's down for the count, Carlotta's been in bed all day, and Susanne needs to leave for Tampa. Emily-Grace has that field trip to Science World tomorrow that she's been looking forward to all week. Deirdre will stay in L.A. but I'm going to commission Arnie and head home with him so he can eyeball Emily-Grace on her field trip and I can help with David and Dylan."

Josh was already out of bed. "No, Charles, listen, I'll go. They're my kids."

Behind him, Jessie was propping a pillow up against the headboard, a curious scowl on her face. Leaning back, she eavesdropped as a growing apprehension started in her gut.

"Josh, this is one of those times I'm going to insist that you stay. Jessie's not doing well on the Brussels shoot. She's drained. She only has a few days with her husband, and I intend for her to get them."

"Oh, shit. I know." Josh glanced over at Jessie. Clearly, she had lost weight, and she was still rather uncommunicative. He was worried. He wanted the difficult film shoot to end, and now. A thought passed through his mind. "She's going to need Arnie, Charles, or somebody. She's got that interview with NBC, and it's going to be a madhouse. Can you get someone? Can Michael and Kelly loan us someone in a hurry?"

"I've got someone," Charles communicated with a calm he didn't feel. "Matt will be here by morning."

A silent fear worked its way up Josh's body. Even his toes tingled with dread. "I don't think so, Charles. I don't think that's a good idea."

Jessie was watching him with the eyes of a hawk now, sharp and focused. Knees drawn up, she had the covers pulled up to her chest and her arms wrapped around Josh's pillow, clutching it tightly to her body.

"We need someone we know and trust, Josh. Someone who knows the ropes here. It's two days. I don't see any other way around this."

"I can't imagine Matt's thrilled at the idea of being here with us." Josh eyed Jessie to see how she would react to this news. His heart sank when he saw her bite hard on her bottom lip and turn her head away from him.

"He's not. But he's a professional and he's had some time to process what happened in Brussels. I expect the two of you to act like the professionals you are as well. Put it behind you, Josh. Deirdre will be along to mediate any discomfort."

"Lovely. Hugs to the kids, okay? I hope they don't catch this bug."

"I'll cuddle up with them. They'll be fine. Tell Jessie I'll call her tomorrow and wish her a good show, okay?"

Josh was silent after he disconnected. When he set down the phone, finally, and lay down beside his wife, who was back on her side on her pillow, he brushed back a strand of hair and ached for her to let him back inside those beautiful pale eyes.

"Jessie," he pleaded, "whatever happened between you and Matt, or if it's this film that's got you hiding back inside yourself, you need to let it go. You need to let me back in."

"I don't want to see Matt," she whispered. "Please, Josh. Get someone else."

"Did he hurt you?" Josh asked, alarm coloring his tone. "What exactly happened in Brussels?"

"It's not that. It was just rough, that's all, having to let him go like that. And I'm singing this song…"

"I know about the song. I heard you working it out, remember?" Tenderly, Josh continued to brush his fingers against his wife's cheeks. "I know it's a sad one, and I know it's for Jacob."

"He won't even hear it. He's not here."

"He'll hear it. Your performance will be up on YouTube before you're off the stage."

"Josh…in Brussels…Matt lost it when I work-shopped that song. His marriage was ending. He left the room, I…I found him all curled up into himself upstairs in the hallway of the hotel, by our suites. He won't do well standing in the wings of the stage while I sing it."

"Jessie, I don't know what I'm supposed to say when you tell me Matt will likely lose it while you sing for Jacob, but not once have you mentioned any kind of concern for me." Josh wasn't accusing or expressing anger; he was just confused.

Jessie alleviated his fears with the first genuine smile he saw pass through her eyes on this trip, and with one simple statement.

"Babe," she said with a tenderness Josh hadn't seen in a while, and which he greatly missed, "I'm not worried about you. You are everything to me, and you know it. Through all of this, the crazy Jacob shit and then Matt's breakdown and my part in it…" She sighed, "You've told me you're sticking by me. And so far, you have been. I love you more than I could possibly ever communicate to you in a song, even though I've tried, many times. There are no melodies and no words big enough for the love I have for you. That's never going to change. So I know, Josh, that even though this song will hurt you, you will also understand that it's my final goodbye to someone I loved for a while when things went sour for you and me. After I pour my heart out I will leave that stage and you will take me in your arms and love me the way you always have, with all of your heart and all of your soul. And I will love you back."

True, sometimes there simply were no words. With one small *ahhhh* in his throat, Josh moved on top of his wife and took her once more, with the confidence that her deep abiding love gifted him. She was right. Unlike Kayla had with Paul, and unlike Josh's ability to do in the past, he had hung on through the tough times life had thrown he and Jessie since Christmas. There were a few short weeks left of her time in Brussels. He needed to be patient and understanding just a little while longer. With Matt back around, tomorrow and the next day would be tough on all of them, but optimistically Josh hoped they could all somehow make up and put the weirdness behind them.

What he didn't, and couldn't possibly know, was just how deeply Matt and Jessie had come to care for each other, and how much Josh's anger and fear of losing her would impact their next few days.

⌒⌒

Since Jessie was nominated for three Grammys, including two against crossover artist Talia, the next day was a mass of interviews and meet and greets, capped off in the evening with the formal televised and live-streamed Grammy awards show.

She was expected at NBC Universal Studios at 8:30. When she blinked her eyes open at five, Jessie gave up on sleep and nudged Josh awake for a cuddle, in which he was only too happy to partake. Before she awoke him, however, she lay on one elbow and watched him sleep. The easy rise and fall of his chest, and the long, layered hair fanned out on the pillow, made up a priceless image that Jessie wanted to package and take back to Brussels with her. Waking him was equally priceless. Burying her nose in his neck, she inhaled his musky essence and, as he stirred, she let her hand move down between his legs. Slowly, as if deep in some sweet dream, he came awake with a mischievous smile and rolled a little on his side towards her while she played. Soon, Josh was actively kissing his wife, loving her with the freedom granted to husbands and wives who cherished and trusted each other and who craved the pleasures their bodies offered. This trip to L.A. was business, but it was also an opportunity to reconnect, to try to put the difficult past behind them.

After a room service breakfast of eggs and bacon for Josh, and yogurt and granola for Jessie, she took his hand and led him into the adjoining washroom. Steam rose off their satisfied bodies in a cleansing shower.

Afterwards, as he dried her off, Josh wrapped an arm around the small of his wife's back and pressed her in close. He tipped her chin up to face him. "Today's going to be crazy busy," he asserted, "but I'll be beside you all the way, okay little one?"

She frowned. "Dee the lion lady will have me ten paces in front of you all day. Don't forget that I'm with you while you're signing autographs for all your adoring fans."

He laughed. "This is your weekend, Jessie. It's all about you."

Jessie sobered. She searched his eyes. "Josh, are you…are you going to be okay with having Matt around?"

Just like that, the needle zipped across the record of their sacred time together, and Josh's warm smile flipped upside down. "I'll have to be, won't I, Jessie?"

"It's going to be just as hard on him as it will be on us."

"I have to be honest, I'm still out in left field on that one, Jess. I don't get it. I don't get what really happened between the two of you. I think I'm scared to know."

"And this is not the time to talk about it," she replied, reaching for the casual dress she was wearing to the NBC interview, a pearl blue silk slip dress that just brushed the tops of her thighs.

Muttering under his breath that there never seemed to be a time to really talk about what happened with Matt, Josh fastened it at the neck for her, and stood back to admire his wife.

"Stunning," he murmured, his eyes lighting up. "You are so beautiful." Swallowing, eyes suddenly a serious shade of deep brown, he watched Jessie adjust her dress over her hips.

"What?" she asked him, before catching his eye in the mirror and tossing him his pants. "Get dressed, cowboy, before my hair and makeup team arrive. I don't need them drooling all over you."

"I just...you wonder why I worry."

Smiling, Jessie twisted at the waist while she ran a wide comb through her damp hair, and she watched Josh start to dress. "I just had three orgasms courtesy of People's Sexiest Man of the Year and you're the one who's worried? I don't think so, Romeo." Appraising him, Jessie's blue eyes drifted up his body, admiring the black dress pants as he zipped them, the strong hands as he fastened his belt, and the chiseled biceps as Josh reached for a white undershirt to wear underneath his dress shirt. "Fuuucckkk," she whistled. "Can we just skip all this Grammy shit and go back to bed?"

Josh sidled forward and, from behind, wrapped both arms around his wife's body. The two of them took a moment to study their reflections in the mirror before Jessie squirmed around to face him. A few long luxurious kisses later, Josh pulled away. "Okay, little one," he teased, "any more of this and I'll have blue balls all day."

With a diabolical wink, Jessie grabbed his crotch. "Oh, Lordy. It's going to be a long day."

She wasn't kidding. It did end up being a long day, and it didn't conclude with the lovemaking both were hoping for at the start of the day. Instead, the interminable day ended in a rip-roaring fight.

It started out okay. Despite the nervous anticipation surrounding Matt's arrival, when he did show up at their door all three pushed their fears aside and tried to recall the years they'd spent together at events like the Grammys. Some hangover from the Brussels weirdness was to be expected, but it had to be pushed aside in order to get through the day.

Matt's knock was timid, but Josh swung open the door and welcomed him as warmly as he could muster. Jessie's hair and make-up team had arrived, and they were just finishing up in the expansive washroom. Dee had yet to grace them with her presence.

"Matt," Josh said in welcome, his voice a little gruff. Clearing his throat, he gestured for their old security to make his way inside the suite.

Inhaling carefully, Matt, who had chosen a stylish new black leather dress jacket for the occasion, wandered in. "Josh," he responded in quiet greeting, averting his eyes.

"Been south, I hear?" Josh asked, biting back the urge to grab his old friend by the scruff of the neck and pound the shit out of him.

"Yeah, yeah, actually. Charles sent me off in search of Jacob. We did some sailing."

"Sailing. Jacob. Oh." *First nail in the coffin.* Josh tried again. "Got some shit out of your system, did you?"

Matt, who had done a quick scan of the suite in search of Jessie, faced Josh head on. "Yeah. I guess you could say that." He noticed that the nerve on Josh's cheek was twitching. Not a good sign this early in the day. Deciding to clear the air before the public scrutiny they would soon be faced with, he sucked in a breath and said, "Look Josh, I fucked up, okay? In Brussels. I know that. I let a few drinks and what was happening at home color my judgment."

"Uh huh. *You* fucked up. Good to know."

"It cost me a lot, okay? It's changed everything."

"I see that."

"It was stupid. It won't happen again."

Just as Josh was about to open his mouth and get Matt's opinion on exactly what happened, Jessie made a subdued entrance.

"H-hey, Matt," she said, completely thrown by the strong feelings that suddenly assaulted her upon seeing him in person for the first time since Brussels. She avoided Josh's gaze, but he saw the pink flicker of—what, desire? Lust? Love?—that dusted her cheeks when her eyes landed on a man she cherished and missed.

For his part, Matt's lips opened but no words emerged. Jessie, in the filmy blue silk dress, which complemented the thoughtful, sad gaze she was aiming at him now, took his breath away.

Moving towards him, almost forgetting that her husband was in the room, Jessie shoved aside the discomfort and nerves all three were struggling with, and took her friend in her arms.

Turning his face away from Josh, Matt couldn't help the small strangling sound that crept up in his throat as he held her, but he had enough decorum not to hold on for too long, and not to press his body tightly into her or bury his face in her neck the way he damn well wished he could. He let go first and took a step back as Josh bristled nearby.

This was more than Josh expected. Something he didn't like was at play between his wife and their old security—and good friend—and it sent blood rushing into his brain suddenly and without hesitation.

Another knock came at the door. Deirdre. She danced in the way she always did, taking immediate command of the room and the three uncomfortable people in it. In the washroom, the hair and makeup team gossiped quietly as they packed up.

Grasping Jessie's hands, Dee took a good scan of the dress, the hair, and the makeup, and then she lifted the guitar-callused fingers and studied Jessie's nails.

"You had some time at the hotel spa yesterday?" she asked.

"Yes, ma'am." Jessie smiled agreeably.

"Did you eat?"

"Worms and dirt."

Raising her eyebrows, Dee frowned. "I see. We're in that kind of mood this morning, are we?"

"Dee," Jessie offered with a toss of the newly styled hair and eyes that suddenly sparkled, "it's Grammy day. It's going to be long and arduous. Let me have a little fun."

An accompanying twinkle in Deirdre's eyes gave her away despite the *harrumph* she mouthed as she pivoted around on one fancy cream heel and took in the two moping men. Her glossed lips were happily upturned. Grammy day. The powerful woman was in her element.

"Is the car here, Matt?" she asked, revving them into high gear, and they were off, with Deirdre assuring Jessie during the walk down the hall that her usual back line band was already waiting at the studio so they could accompany her as she sang.

Once they were seated in the day's sleek limo, Jessie asked Dee to call Charles so she could check on the kids. The call broke up the uncomfortable silence but did nothing to quell Jessie's increasing nerves. She was seated next to Josh but Matt was just across from her, and she was dying to have some time alone with him to see how he was adjusting to the whole post-Brussels thing.

There was also the question of that tan—she knew he'd been sent down south to hunt up Jacob. So how was that? How, for that matter, was Jacob, who was supposed to be here at the Grammys but who had cancelled his appearance?

After disconnecting from Emily-Grace, who was more interested in her school's field trip than in her mother's big day, Jessie ignored her anxious, tumbling belly and somewhat morose husband, and she fixed her gaze on Matt, who couldn't help himself and studied Jessie back.

"Nice tan," she started tentatively, as Josh perked up and placed an arm proprietarily around her shoulders.

"Thanks," Matt mumbled as a quick flash of desire nipped across his groin, unwanted but unavoidable as he looked into those beautiful eyes he missed, and as he remembered their last few minutes together. A slight flush rose in his cheeks and he shifted positions on the leather seat. Jessie felt Josh straighten and tense beside her. She laced her fingers through his and squeezed, but continued speaking to Matt.

"How's Jacob?" *That ought to settle both men,* she mused, but was slightly disconcerted when Matt chuckled at her.

"You were right about him. He's quite the man whore. Not that a single pretty lady down there knows a damn thing about what a big star he is in the rest of the world. To them he's just a source of steady income."

He's trying to hurt me. Jessie swallowed past the sticks in her throat. Josh's fingers tightened around hers.

She hit below the belt. "So...were you his pimp or were you just supplementary income for the girls?"

Matt's lips parted but his eyes kept up a steady gaze. *Fuck you,* he was thinking while, next to Jessie, Josh stilled.

What the hell, was passing through Josh's mind. This was a standoff. Jessie and Matt were purposely slinging arrows at each other. As the lavish limo floated them towards NBC Universal, Josh realized that a serious passive-aggressive battle was heating up inside, and it stank of a lover's rejection. His eyes narrowed at Matt as their old friend spoke to Jessie.

"It was a very liberating trip." Matt's tone was distinctly crusty and edged with something bordering on revenge. Jessie raised her chin and sent him a silent *fuck you.*

"Lovely," she managed to whisper as the car pulled up to the studio.

"Well hell," Josh cursed as he escorted her through a large crowd of fans into the building, "maybe I should switch rooms with Matt tonight so the two of you can fuck yourselves out of this funk."

Jessie stopped moving and stared at him, shock and a cool hurt lining her face.

"You leaned on each other, huh?" Josh's body was rigid, his eyes flashing. "How fucking hard? Where were his hands and where was his dick? Jesus Christ, Jessie."

"I don't need this childish crap today, Josh," Jessie bit off. "Drop it. Now."

The look he sent her was barely disguised disgust. It covered a heartache and a growing, nagging worry that ate at Josh all through Jessie's attempt at carrying on a happy social concourse with the touch-up TV makeup and hair team, her NBC hosts, and throughout the duration of the sad song she had been asked to sing which was, of course, her 'sorry song' for Jacob.

Somehow, though, they got through the bulk of the day. Matt was busy enough coordinating and organizing Jessie's movement through the crowds that he sank into his usual bossy security mode, which enabled him to temporarily push the hurt aside. Jessie, too, was busy and so by association was Josh. They ended up signing a ton of autographs and posing for a lot of what felt like very stilted iPhone pics throughout the day.

There were moments, though, when the crowd got a little too rambunctious and hairy, and Matt had no choice but to wrap an arm tightly around Jessie's shoulders the way he used to, and navigate her through the craziness. That happened more than once, and each time Jessie turned her face into his neck and inhaled deeply as he moved her along. It wasn't so much desire she was feeling then, instead it was simply a craving for Matt's presence, his essence. She memorized the way he so coolly moved, the way he took charge and brusquely called out to the local security, snapping his fingers towards Josh and Deirdre so the team would tail them.

At one point, as Jessie and Josh took a few minutes to sign autographs on their way back into the hotel to rest and then dress for the evening's awards show, a hyper-excited teen grabbed Jessie's arm and pulled her back towards him, then an older man did the same so that she lost her footing. Matt was at her side, though. Josh was down the line a ways posing for a selfie with a fan, and so it was Matt who rescued Jessie and pressed her close to him, and who wrapped an arm around her shoulders to keep the fans from having any physical contact with her.

"I hate this stuff," Jessie mouthed into his neck, and although he couldn't make out what she was saying, Matt felt the ticklish vibration of her lips on his skin, and he closed his eyes just for a split second, relishing the feel of her body against his.

A second later he passed her off to local security with the hoarse words, "Get her the hell inside," and, with one eye on Josh, he walked behind Jessie.

Josh, who was now making his way towards them, was witness to the brief intimacy.

Deirdre was already indoors at that point, saying, "Goodness," over and over and attempting to sort out her windblown hair.

"What the hell, Matt," Josh demanded as, heart racing, he drew near. He gave Matt an incensed shove, which did not go unnoticed by the fans.

"Easy, Josh," Matt growled, a quick anger sparking across his eyes. "These fans will ignite. They've been standing out here for hours."

A loud cry rose up behind them. "Josh, you suck! Jacob, Jacob, Jacob! We want Jacob!"

Josh turned, and Jessie halted and glanced behind her.

The fans continued their insistent chant as one screamed at Jessie and pitched a full water bottle towards her. It bounced off her bicep, but was soon followed by a second.

"Bitch!" she heard, which completely floored her.

"Matt," she moaned, gesturing nervously towards her husband who, according to the quickly twitching nerve on Josh's cheek and his clenched fists, was losing it.

Matt got to Josh the second the actor reached a man who raised his arm and pitched a small glass bottle at Jessie. This one hit her on the forehead and immediately opened a wide gash, from which blood started to seep as she cried out.

Josh had the angry fan by the scruff of his neck and was about to haul him over the metal railing that stood between them, when Matt grasped his shoulder and hollered at him.

"Leave him, Josh. Let's go!"

But the chanting had gotten to Josh. This wasn't the first time throughout the day that fans expressed their outrage at Jacob's decision not to appear at the Grammys, and they didn't refrain from blaming Jessie for it. Josh was still, in the eyes of many, a quick tempered hothead as well as a drunk who spent time in rehab more than once, and who may have possibly, at least in their muzzy memories, have beat his wife and put her in the hospital.

Their rising anger towards both Jessie and him hurt. He lost it. It took three of the local hired security to pull him off the fan, but Josh landed a few well-placed punches first. The worst, though, was after he was hauled backwards and shoved up against the brick of the hotel, and had Matt in his face, yelling at him to calm down and get a grip.

A white-hot rage exploded in Josh's brain then, and he grabbed Matt with both fists, spun around, and shoved him up against the rough brick. By then, Josh had spied Jessie, bent over with blood running down her face, as Dee hurried towards her. "Get your hands off me, you fucking man-whore!" he was screaming to Matt as he repeatedly shoved him up against the hotel.

Jessie was there then, bloody but incensed and well aware of the copious amount of not just smartphones, but also media cameras, present and pointed in their direction. Her stomach sank like a stone as Josh started pounding Matt.

She tried to get in between them, but Matt freed an arm and, in an attempt to keep her from getting hurt, he used it to keep her at bay. Furious, Jessie twisted her torso around and grabbed Josh's bicep, then swung underneath his arm and tried to get his attention by facing him, but he was single-mindedly focused on swinging at Matt and didn't quit throwing punches until his fist connected with her head.

Immediately realizing in the chaos and confusion that he'd hit Jessie instead of Matt, Josh grabbed her, and kept her from sinking to her knees.

Matt, still in security mode and now super pissed at Josh's quick tempered actions, quickly wrapped both arms around Jessie's waist from behind, and hauled her upright as she clutched at the side of her face and tried to keep the world from spinning. Moving to shield her from Josh with his body, Matt swept her into the hotel.

She sank into his side and let him scoop her along as, behind them, local security finally got their hands on Josh who, by virtue of social media and rapid-fire worldwide news releases, immediately reclaimed his title as the world's bad boy. He, as an individual, was also further cemented as Jessie Wheeler's worst decision ever, in that the musical magic Jacob and Jessie once made had been singularly destroyed by her choice of spitfire Josh over dreamy Jacob.

Neither Deirdre nor Matt gave a sweet care by then what was happening with Josh. Inside, Matt lifted the faltering Jessie into his arms and, followed by Dee, carried her into an elevator being held open by the hotel's concierge, to whom Matt brusquely demanded find them a doctor. When the door closed behind them, Jessie was sobbing into Matt's neck while she leaked blood all over his new leather jacket and onto her beautiful gauzy blue dress.

"You can't leave him out there," she was crying. "Matt, please, go back."

"There's other security with him," Matt fumed. "They'll deal with your reckless husband."

Moments later, the door slid open and he carried Jessie, her body quaking, to her suite. Deirdre was uncharacteristically quiet as Matt set Jessie down on a contemporary white leather sofa and knelt before her. The older woman rushed into the washroom and soaked a soft cream-colored facecloth in cold water as he spoke to Jessie, lifting her chin so he could make out the damage.

Stripping off his jacket, his lips pressed together, he used the sleeve of his white shirt to wipe away the trail of blood oozing down the side of her face. Jessie tried to push him away but Matt grabbed her wrist and held her still.

"Easy," he said softly. "Look at me, Jessie. Look at me. Let me see."

He felt her body relax when she met his eyes, and Matt would have crumbled then and there if the adrenaline coursing through his body had called a halt. But as it was, he simply sent her a silent *it's okay, you're safe,* and continued to wipe the blood from her face.

"He hit you," he murmured.

"He didn't mean to. He was aiming for you."

"Yeah, he's got quite the punch. He landed a few on me too. Which makes me concerned about you. How bad is it?"

"I'm fine," she lied, as a nasty headache bloomed. "Matt, leave me be and go get him. For God's sake, please. He's already going to be all over the news." Devastated, she sank back against the couch and curled up into a ball. Covering her face with her palms, Jessie gasped as great lurching sobs overtook her.

The door to the suite opened then, just as Deirdre came back with the cloth and tried to sponge up Jessie's cut, but it was Josh at the door, escorted by security, and so Jessie vaulted up and launched herself at him. As she clutched his jacket and gave him a hard shove backwards, Matt signaled to the two brawly security attending Josh to leave the suite, which they did. They did not need to witness this marital dispute, which was about to get ugly.

"You stupid bastard!" Jessie was crying as she pushed her husband again and again. "You attacked a fan! And your own security! On camera, for God's sake!"

Sinking back against the wall, Josh almost collapsed. The sight of his wife, bloody and enraged beyond sense, was bringing him back to reality real quick.

"Your children!" she was screaming now, eyes wide with fright and anger, "your children will see those videos, Josh! Emily-Grace, who has just started to relax around you again, will see those clips! What the hell were you thinking?"

"I don't know, Jessie, I...I just lost it. That guy...he called you a bitch..."

"Like I have never been called a bitch before? I've been called a helluva lot worse, Josh, occasionally by you!" Backing up, she collapsed onto the sofa again, as Matt placed his hands on his hips and eyed Jessie from underneath moist eyelashes.

Deirdre sat gently next to her girl and started mopping at her face again. At first, Jessie resisted, but then Matt knelt before her again and took the cloth out of Dee's hands.

"Listen, Jessie. We've got less than two hours to get some food into you and get you dressed for the Grammys, if you're even up for singing now. But I think we need to fit in a visit to the hospital. You're in need of some stitches to close that cut."

"Make Josh do it," she bit off. "He stitched folks up with rusty needles on *Drifters* a dozen times. Just find me a twig to bite down on."

"Those are for bullet wounds," Matt managed to smile. "Twigs, I mean. With booze."

"The booze I can do. Dump it straight down my gullet. How about some good old Jim Beam?" Both hands lying weakly in her lap, she glared at her husband, who was sinking to the floor, his back against the wall, as she fumed. "What do you think, Josh, should you and I just get roaring drunk together? We're gonna need lots of insulation to deal with all those videos your children are going to see tomorrow. How about I go get some and pour it down your throat for you? All you have to do is swallow."

"Jessie," Dee chided quietly. "Honey, that's enough. Josh is going to suffer enough over this."

"Our whole fucking family's going to suffer over this, Dee," Jessie wailed as more sobs overtook her. "Jesus, Josh. You couldn't get through this one stupid weekend with me without losing it, could you? One weekend? It's barely been twenty-four hours!"

Exhaling slowly, Matt grabbed one of Jessie's trembling hands and pulled it away from her face.

Numb, Josh watched as Matt spoke to her in the gentle tone he always used with her when she was upset. "You need to calm down, Jessie. When the doctor gets here, we'll arrange through him to get you some stitches or glue or whatever the hell it is they use these days for cuts like this one. He may even want to get you a scan to be sure you're okay from that punch of your husband's." Josh winced as Matt continued. "In the meantime, let me clean this up. Dee will find you something temporary to wear." He nodded at Deirdre, who immediately rose and went to root through Jessie's clothes. "We'll wait an hour or so before we decide if you'll be doing the show tonight."

"Matt, I'm supposed to do my sound check at five."

"Christian and the band will be there. They can get it started. I'm not putting you on that stage tonight until I know you're okay."

"Matt, I'm not okay, and I'm not going to be okay anytime soon." Jessie stood and faced her husband, who was sitting on the floor by the door with his head bowed into his hands. "I just want to go back to Brussels," she said to the room in general, while looking at Josh.

Matt eased himself up and watched her as she turned slowly back around towards him. "I just want to go back to Brussels," she said again directly to him, aching to fold herself into his arms so he could help sort this new mess out.

Knowing Josh was now watching him, Matt nodded slowly. "So do I," he whispered, and watched the fear and worry on her face dissipate into more of a calm wishful acceptance. A small smile curved up on his lips, and Jessie's worried eyes remained locked securely into his until a quiet knock came at the door and the doctor entered.

Chapter Eleven

"You know the only way to neutralize this at all is to take Josh's hand and go public," Deirdre was saying to Jessie. "The press needs to see you with him."

They were at the hospital, where Jessie had been rushed into a scan to ensure the knock she took from Josh was no more serious than a facial bruise, and where she had to sit patiently and endure six stitches to close the seeping wound on her forehead.

"If they think I'm a battered wife they'll have a field day," she replied dryly to Dee as an escalating headache brought on a searing grimace while a young female doctor worked her magic on the cut.

"Good thing you're not. Him hitting you was an accident, right?" Dee paused. "Has he ever lifted a finger to you in private?"

A weird choking sound escaped Jessie's throat. "Josh? Are you kidding? He's the biggest softie on the planet. That's why this is so hard. Dee...I'm the only one who knows that about him."

"Then let it go. Hold his hand and support him. You and I both know why he lost it today."

"Yes, because I was with Jacob. Because I got too close to Matt."

"Because, sweetheart, two mentally ill people who lost their child sent your family spinning into a very dark hole that the two of you are still trying to climb out of."

"That a lot of us are still trying to climb out of, Dee. Don't forget how much Jacob is suffering right now."

"He had two beautiful years with Talia, and he got a lot of love from you

111

before that. Matt says he is really doing okay. He is finding some peace within himself down south on his sailboat."

"I wish he would share that with his fans," Jessie grumbled.

Later, standing next to Matt at the side of the stage, Jessie was slightly nauseous but, upon her insistence, drug free, which was facilitating no relief from the agonizing headache she was suffering. She sighed, laid her head on Matt's shoulder, and took his hand.

Numb, Josh stood behind them and watched Jessie take solace in Matt's company. Her behavior was no surprise to him. After his appalling conduct earlier in the day, he felt a small sense of relief that Jessie at least had someone by her side that she trusted the way she trusted Matt. She sure as hell wanted nothing to do with him at the present time.

Jessie had a question for Matt. Over the music of the band on stage he barely heard it, and had to ask her to say it twice.

Repeating it, Jessie's voice was thick with fear. "Is he going to be charged?"

They were standing in the wings where Matt, as was his usual custom before a big show, had walked Jessie to await her cue to perform. Josh and Deirdre were close by; neither had felt comfortable taking their seats in the audience, although after Jessie's performance the four would sit in solidarity amongst the other celebrities and their entourages.

Matt answered Jessie's question. He had to turn his head and put his lips to her ear because the band was loud enough to shake the rafters of the Staples Center. "No," he replied cautiously, "I was told there will be no charges if you don't press charges against the fan for throwing the bottle in the first place."

"And you?" she asked him. "Will you be pressing charges?"

"Of course not. I'm not that guy, Jessie. I know what fueled Josh's meltdown today."

"It didn't help my mood that you filled me in on yours and Jacob's nocturnal activities down south."

"Who said they were nocturnal?" Matt's pretty boy dimples came into play as he chuckled. "I won't lie to you. After Brussels I...I needed to let off some steam, Jessie."

"Is that what they call it these days?" Jessie was wearing a low cut gown for the occasion. Marilyn Monroe red, it was clingy and sensual, slit high

112

up the side of one leg. Wheeling around to face Matt now, just as the band on stage was wrapping up, she caught his eye and held it.

"What?" he asked, trying to keep his gaze on her eyes but desperate to step back so he could let his eyes drift all over her.

"I was just thinking."

"About?"

"Matt…" Her voice got dusky, sad. "I don't know where, or when…but I have this feeling. I feel like someday…you and me are going to finish what we started in Brussels."

His lips parted and Matt swallowed. Placing a hand behind Jessie's head, remembering her old tradition with Jacob, he kissed her in a very gentle, non-threatening way. A kiss for a friend. "In the meantime," he joked, the delicious sweet taste of her hastily consumed dinner of two strawberries on his tongue, "I might have to go back down south." Closing his eyes, he let his forehead lean against hers. Then, as she was cued to move on stage, Matt wished Jessie well and let her go.

In his heart, though, he knew he would not put himself in such a position of temptation again. Divorce was in his future, but he had been with Jessie for many years since she'd met Josh. And he had no desire to see the two parted again, even for his own sweet pleasure, because Matt had lived that sorrow through with the two of them. No, if anything, he would try to help them heal. It was the least he felt he could do.

For the next few moments, though, he felt like she was his. There was nobody between Matt and Jessie at this time, no other body, as she took her place in the semi-darkness before a live audience of thousands, and a TV audience of millions, and waited for Christian's musical touch on the keys to set her free. As the lights came up, Jessie was caught nervously fingering the white bandage on her forehead, and Matt cringed, hoping the fan that hit her with the pitched bottle was spending the night in jail.

The piano was perfect. The first notes were at once gentle and powerful; they took Jessie inside their flawless bubbles and let her float up and away from the harsh reality of the world today, away from her husband's savage public outcry against those who continuously wanted to hurt them.

Matt watched the peace he expected come over her body. Jessie's hands, the fingers of which he felt wanted to reach up and start twisting a ringlet, fell to her sides as if the strings of anxiety attached to them, holding them up, melted away instantly, like wax against the heat of the sun. Her lily-white shoulders eased slightly downwards, her lips opened where before they were pressed tightly together, and her eyes closed.

Matt knew that in her mind, Jessie was not on stage at this moment, very publicly broadcasting the hurts from the day's unfortunate events in front of millions. No way was she the object of everyone's derision and pity for choosing to deeply love a volatile man. No way was she in full public view of anyone but one person now. One person who would see this performance and know it was about him, that it was a message to him. Yet, even though beneath Jessie's closed eyelids would play a slideshow of Jacob and their hard goodbye as she sang, to Matt the lyrics once again played out for him, and for Josh as well.

The song was classic Jessie Wheeler. It topped everything she'd written before, including *Josh's Song*, and here on this difficult day, in haute couture, heels, and hair and makeup that were still being touched up while she was walked to the stage, Matt watched her lose herself in it, and in the memories and hard truths of love.

Supporting the piano was a cello, played by a woman who urged the bass notes forth with an otherworldly grace. There were kettle drums to give the song life with a 'barely there' heartbeat; violinists drew upon their bows with a painful restraint Matt felt in his body even now, as the memory of Jessie's touch in Brussels ignited an electric desire that caused him to suck in his breath. He wanted to scream at the violinists to just let go, to reach the perfect high notes, damn it; to let out the beauty their instruments were capable of. He ached for them to set upon their violins with *all* of the skill and mastery they'd learned over time so they could set the captive notes explosively free.

So they could set him free.

Soon, she was there, in the song.

At its climax.

With Christian's help, Jessie had crafted the piece to rise and fall in small crescendos and decrescendos until it was time to let go. Through all of it, throughout the entire piece, Jessie's journey with Jacob came to life, starting with a tender but lonely opening. The climax was sexual, to Matt. Fierce in its intensity, it was driven and desperate. Lyrically and musically, the song told the story of two people who clung to each other in a desperate time; who loved as hard and fast as life permitted, and who eventually had to let go.

Why can there be only one? Matt begged the universe now. *Why can she love only one? There are more for her. There is Jacob, and there is me.*

He knew the answer. It came to him in the awed, hushed wonder that followed the final notes.

The audience, transfixed and mesmerized by Jessie's passion, which she'd laid completely bare on the stage, was momentarily sucked into a whirlpool of dreamlike silence. There were many who loved this sad girl with the tragic past. And suddenly, in the extraordinary poignancy of the fleeting calm, Matt knew he was one of the lucky ones because he was close enough to Jessie for her to love him deeply back. For her to lean on him, for him to feel her touch, even if only in the small hands digging themselves deeper into his; even if only for the pearlescent blues to lose themselves in his soul for one small moment, for the head to lay on his shoulder for a second and the warm breaths to breathe life into his body for an instant.

I have always loved you, he told her silently now as he watched her take a step back, as her shoulders shook and tears started to fall, one by one. It didn't cross Matt's mind that behind him, the man Jessie truly loved back— would always love back the best—was standing in spellbound wonder and thinking the very same thing.

At La Casa, Charles, Jonathon, Charlie, Jack and Steve had gathered to watch the Grammys. They were sitting in subdued silence because, earlier, they'd heard newscasters slam Josh back into the ground. Now all, without exception, were trying to stifle hard emotions.

Before them, live on screen in front of millions, Jessie, with trembling fingers now touching the bandage again, was taking her rousing standing ovation with tears flowing profusely from her tragic blue eyes. She'd just said her final goodbye to Jacob through song while at the same time she apologized for breaking his heart, on a day when misinformed fans and a wretched past had catapulted her husband back into a world of shame.

The broadcasters knew a powerful moment when they had one. They waited, and let the audience have its time with this special woman before they called for a commercial break. What they got in the end was Jessie quaking so hard she couldn't move.

At La Casa, there was a collective intake of breath after Charles muttered, "Jesus, go to commercial and help her off the stage."

In the wings there was movement. Unconcerned with how anyone felt about his unscripted actions except him, Matt pressed his lips together, fixed his gaze on the woman in his care, and strode forward with confidence.

Shaking with sobs now as the music released her and shot her back into a harsh reality she was very, very tired of, Jessie didn't notice him until he grasped her fingers. There, center stage, with Matt in his tux and Jessie in her gown, she turned, melted into him, and let him hold her while she cried. It wasn't long, just a few seconds really, before he lifted her chin and calmed her, a steady light burning in his gentle eyes.

"I know how bad it hurts," he whispered, and her knees went weak because Jessie suddenly felt understood, felt real, after what seemed like an interminably long stretch of *lonely*. After an extended time of feeling invisible, of living her life behind a wall that, since Jacob's admission on Boxing Day and his angry actions in Florida afterwards, had shielded her from real connections. That left her feeling lost and adrift as she played a character in a Brussels film whose marriage was eroding past the point of no return, whose child died while, inside, Jessie felt like she was dying too.

Matt's hand was firm on hers. "You ready?" he asked her, and waited until a slight tilt of her chin signaled that she was—that her feet and legs were stable enough now to move her off the stage—before he turned, placed an arm around her waist, and led her to the relief of the wing's semi-darkness, to a sobbing Deirdre, to a stunned and frightened Josh.

There, Matt watched as, over the shoulder of Dee's tight hug, Jessie's eyes landed on her husband. Matt saw her hesitate before she went to him, and although it hurt, he knew what drew her to him.

Apparent on Josh's face was the struggle to realign himself with Jessie after the tough day, and to realign his soul as well. This song, this performance—Josh had been dreading it long before the day arrived and went completely sideways. It was about Jacob, there was no secret in that; it was a goodbye song Josh secretly called a good riddance song.

But now there was a whole new truth washing over Josh's eyes. The song? Josh felt that all it really served to do was destroy Jessie all over again. Always, there was an inherent guilt in that she had chosen him over Jacob back when it really counted, when she was pregnant with Jacob's child. And today Josh had blown Jessie's trust and faith in him all to hell.

He didn't deserve her.

Matt? Thank God for Matt, and damn, it sucked that all of a sudden Matt was a casualty too, a whole new loss to have to consider.

To consider if Jessie and Josh chose to stay together, that is. If they chose to fight for each other. Because there had to be a breaking point. This latest hell was going to have to go one way or the other, either up like the climax of the song, or down to its lowest note. And right now, after hearing that song loosed from the soul of this woman Josh loved from the moment he met her, all of these emotions and more were playing across his face. Licking his lips in nervous frustration, fighting the heady emotion the song wrought, hands shoved deeply in his pockets, he waited for Jessie to let go of Dee.

Matt knew there was no question she would go to him.

In Jessie's mind, Josh was back in the garbage, lost and alone. Earlier today, when he collapsed on the floor of their hotel suite and shoved the heels of his palms into his eyes as if he was trying to press the agony out of his skull, he became that lonely boy again. They'd all heard his great hulking struggle to breathe, to catch his breath, while she screamed at him, an alcoholic, to get drunk on Jim Beam with her. But now, watching the ragged emotions criss-cross those liquid brown eyes, Jessie saw not what the world was now seeing as millions went to YouTube and damned him again. Instead she was seeing the man she knew, the soul for whom she ached, the body she deeply loved.

And so she let go of Dee and went to Josh. She wrapped her arms around him and pressed his body to hers. Their embrace was long and lingering, and Matt had to look away, but some small part of him was glad for it, because the day had been damn long enough.

Soon, though, he had to touch Jessie's back and urge her to let go, to move forward. An aide was waiting to lead them to their seats for the remainder of the awards show, which would make the day even harder by including a video tribute to Talia, and which would also include the awarding of the Grammys for which Jessie was nominated.

To her credit, she joked on the way down the hall. Clutching her husband's hand, she paused to let the makeup guy dry her tears and cluck affectionately at the mascara trails on her cheeks, and she tossed off to no one in particular, "How bad do I have to pee right now?"

It worked. The tension eased enough for them to carry on and, in silence, the weary foursome made their way to their seats and settled in for the rest of the evening.

Chapter Twelve

There was a clear directive from Charles, communicated via Deirdre's cell phone, that they were not to attend any of the usual Grammy after-parties. Not one of the four disputed his orders. All were more than happy to go back to the hotel and skip the interminable questions and curiosity they knew would face them if they showed up in public. Besides, Jessie's headache was ghastly. She wanted to go home, drink some Baileys, chain smoke for an hour, and sink into oblivion in bed.

Matt came to Jessie while she was changing. He unzipped her dress and turned away while she pulled on jeans and a v-necked grey T-shirt. Following her to the washroom, where she started to strip away the night's glamorous make-up, he asked how she was feeling.

"Nasty," she admitted honestly as she scrubbed at her face. "This was the suckiest night ever. And I've had a lot of those."

"Deirdre asked me to tell you to pack, Jessie. I know you're tired and want to sleep but Charles has had the jet fueled. Our driver has a few other folks to run around first but he will be back in an hour to drive us to the airport."

"We're running away," she sighed. "So the media can't ambush us in the morning."

"Yes. We need to get out of here before things get crazy."

Dropping the facecloth to her thigh, where she grasped one wrist and forgot about it, Jessie asked Matt where Josh was now. The police were talking to him again so they could complete their report and put it to rest, and Dee was with him.

"He's just down the hall," Matt told her, "in Deirdre's suite. He won't be long."

"All right." Jessie tossed the cloth in the sink and marched back into the bedroom part of the suite. She dug around in her suitcase and pulled out a pack of cigarettes, which she held up to Matt with thinly disguised glee. "Oh, looky what I found here."

"Thought you quit."

"Could be worse," she said, sarcasm tingeing her voice, "could be weed." She paused, a lighter poised over the end of a cigarette. "Or should I say it could be better? Huh. Not sure."

Lighting up, Jessie wandered out to the deck and eased her exhausted body onto a chaise.

Matt sat on the side of the one opposite her and watched as she inhaled deeply before blowing wispy smoke rings into the still night air. "Will you call me if things get out of hand?" he asked her, his voice subdued.

Looking over at him, Jessie took a breath before answering. "What's gonna get out of hand, Matt? You mean like if I leave Josh or something?"

"You won't. That's not what I meant."

"What if I do?"

"You won't. You'd be miserable."

"Maybe it was a mistake. Coming back to him, I mean. Maybe Jacob was right and Josh is always going to be a guy with a quick trigger finger. How might that translate to our kids as they get older and start talking back to us?"

"I don't know what to tell you, Jessie. I know Josh very well and I've rarely seen him this angry. It's this pressure cooker that broke him today. I guess the answer is to try to avoid pressure cookers."

"Jacob's no longer an issue. I banished him tonight."

"Nice try." A small smile curved up Matt's lips as he reached for the smoke and took a puff. "Good luck with that."

A tiny surprised chuckle from between her own lips caught Jessie off guard. "Okay," she said, taking back her smoke. "I tried." She tossed him the pack of cigarettes and he leaned back on his chaise and lit one up. "I suppose you've now become one of our pressure cookers."

A slow exhale followed Matt's long, leisurely drag. The smoke curls disappeared into the atmosphere. "Charles told me tonight that I am back on Sawyer family duty. He wanted me to go back to Brussels with you."

"So Arnie can stay with Josh and guide him through this new madness. With AA and stuff." She looked over at Matt. Softly Jessie asked, "Are you coming?"

A head shake preceded his response. "No," he declared. "No fucking way."

"Please, Matt. Come."

A quick smile in her direction was enough to almost sink the two of them. "Do you want to know what Deirdre said about it?" he asked.

Jessie's words were so quiet he barely heard them. "I don't know. Do I?"

"She said, 'Matt, go. You would have two weeks. Bring peace to our girl during this tough time. She's going to need somebody. Go and have your two weeks with Jessie.'" His fingers shook as he emphasized the blanket statement by pointing his lit smoke at Jessie. Quieter, he added, "I thought about it. I pictured what it would be like...with you."

Frowning, Jessie squirmed slightly. "I know what it would be like. I'd be late for call every day, sleepy on set, missing cues, forgetting lines, and then for the last week when we're recording all those sad songs I'd be a mushy mess. That's what it'd be like." Taking another pull on her smoke, she aimed her gaze at the smoky sky and added, "But sex with you would be amazing. It'd all be worth it."

"No," he admonished with a small smile, "it wouldn't be. You'd be cheating on your husband and I'd be beating myself up for hurting someone I used to consider a good friend. Sex under those conditions would only start us on a new downward spiral."

"Have you forgotten what it was like that night, Matt? By your door? God, I wanted you. I wanted to put my hand down your pants and hear you moan when I wrapped my fingers around you. I wanted to grab your hand and shove it up under my dress. Fuuuccckk." She shrank back in the chaise and moaned.

"Okay, Jessie, enough. Jesus. God, you realize you've pretty much destroyed me for any other woman now, right?"

She laughed. "Talk about pressure cookers. Maybe we should just get it over with. Um, how much time do we have?" A twinkle in her eyes gave her away, and despite the new discomfort he felt between his legs, Matt was relieved to see her smile.

"I would do anything for you, Jessie. Anything but destroy further what I think I've already had a hand in destroying."

"That's because you, Matt Kelly, are a good man. You are a very good man and I love you deeply. You constantly remind me why."

Matt blushed and looked down so he could take one last big haul on the smoke. He extinguished the cigarette in a ceramic dish that Jessie borrowed from beside the soaking tub in the bathroom after emptying its decoratively shaped little soaps on the counter.

"My family, though," Jessie sighed as she took her final drag too. "How are we going to protect the kids through this, Matt? I have no clue if Josh will go off the rails more or not. And I won't be there to help him, to keep an eye on him or pick up the pieces. He needs Arnie." She looked back over at Matt and had a hard time not climbing onto his chaise and snuggling up in his arms. Matt just seemed so calm. So sure of himself. So…welcoming. And Jessie wanted a hug. She needed one. Again, she squirmed and sat on her hands.

Matt spoke with the quiet wisdom the entire Keating camp had come to count on over the years.

"Jessie, this is what's going to happen. Arnie will go back with you to Belgium. Dan and I will do some 24-7s with Josh and the kids. Ulysses will be around to spell us off and help until things settle down." He raised a hand to air palm her and stop her from trying to speak until he was ready. "I know everyone is concerned because we have yet to find a replacement for Susanne, and now things are even more messed up. I'm here and I can help. But it's the lesser of two evils for me. Partly because of what you said by the stage earlier tonight, I can't be alone with you right now. What you just said to me about…" He gestured to himself. "Didn't help. Not at all."

"Blue balls, huh?" she teased. Releasing one hand, reaching across the small space between them, Jessie tucked her fingers into Matt's. "You know something, Matt? I won three Grammys tonight and I performed a beautiful song that is going to become everyone's 'I'm sorry I hurt you' anthem for the next number of years. It was a liberating, magical experience. Yet it was the loneliest night of my life. I was going to add 'until now,' because I am glad you are here. But hearing you tell me you still need to walk away just made me feel more lonely."

"You are the one who said it the first time," Matt answered honestly. "I was going to try…"

"I know," she cut him off. "You needed to go. But now I just don't know anymore. Nothing's clear. The whole damn world around me just exploded again. Nothing makes sense. It's not just me, and how I feel, is the thing. It's the kids now too. What if he does lose it again?"

"Then you deal with that when the time comes."

"My kids, Matt."

"Jessie, do you honestly think Josh would do anything to hurt your children? Ever?"

"Not intentionally. No."

"Then relax."

The door of the suite opened, and they heard footsteps behind them. Jessie tensed.

"I'll take him to meetings myself," Matt told her as he kissed the back of her hand and let her go before leveraging himself upwards. "I could likely use a few of those myself after…well, after you. The whole beautiful, sensuous, gorgeous, childlike you. Don't smoke the whole pack. I'll see you in an hour, kid."

He paused at the deck's sliding glass door. "Jessie, there's one more thing."

She waited.

"It's about Kayla. Have you been in touch?"

"N-no. Is she okay?"

"Jessie, she showed up in the Caribbean. You should know that she's with Jacob."

Letting the shock of that sink in, Matt propelled himself forward and moved inside.

Immediately, Jessie lit another cigarette. "Jesus, Kayla. What have you done?" she muttered. The news threw her for a loop. She didn't want to ponder how Josh would take it.

She could hear Matt talking to Josh behind her, and could only assume the men were having a similar discussion to the one she just had with Matt, perhaps minus the sexual innuendos peppering the difficult chat.

Then, the main door to the suite opened again and Matt was gone.

Jessie had a glass of Baileys at her side. She took a big gulp before Josh's shadow diluted the light from the doorway. He stepped over to her, straddled the chaise she was sitting on, and faced her.

"Here we go," she mumbled. "This should be one for the record books."

Josh started by touching the bandage on her forehead and then running his fingers over the bruise on her face.

"You could have at least nailed me on the opposite side to Jacob's fist," she said hotly. "I wonder who will hit me the next time. Three times a charm... oh, I forgot about Deuce. I guess he was officially number one."

"Jessie..." Josh's eyes were swimming.

Jessie eased off and remained quiet, biting hard on her lip as she watched him struggle with what to say and how to say it. She took a drag of her new cigarette and turned her head sideways to eradicate the smoke, hoping that the exhalation would cleanse the ache in her soul as well.

In the end, Josh went with the simplest thing possible. "I'm sorry."

"You," she said, pointing her cigarette at him, "keep digging your own holes."

Josh spoke slowly, his voice husky, as if the heavy emotions of the day had left him drugged and barely capable of speech. "I know, I know, I...I just lost it. I feel like I'm in another dimension here. Like I don't know what the fuck is going on around me anymore. I feel like...you want me to pull the trigger. Like you're purposely giving me reasons...to pull the trigger."

The image chilled Jessie. She swallowed, extinguished her smoke, and pretty much inhaled half of her drink in one large gulp.

Josh went on with, "I feel like you are pushing me away. But I don't know why. I don't know what I did...or what I can do to make things better. Jessie... why are you trying so hard to push me away? What do you need me to do? Who do you need me to be? You're asking me to hang on but you're not giving me anything to hang on to."

Going quiet, Jessie blinked back tears and waited for him to say more, to explain away his disgraceful actions on this horrible day.

Watching her finish her drink, Josh wished he could have one sip, one taste to dull the searing pain in his gut. Where was all of this going to land?

"What'd you say to Matt by the stage tonight?" he asked. He was fairly certain, judging by the way Matt looked at her at the time, that he would not be a fan of Jessie's answer.

She caught her breath, and debated whether or not to tell him. But Josh had pretty much singlehandedly destroyed a night that should have been very special. "What, no congratulations for the three Grammys?" she started. "No, let me see, wow that was some song."

"The song was for Jacob. It's beautiful, Jessie, it's a stunning song, but it's meant for Jacob."

"I told Matt that some day..." She hesitated, then fixed him with a hard stare. "That some day he and I are going to finish what we started."

Josh chewed on his lip before answering. He started slow, but could feel the pressure building again. The words emerged imbued with hurt. "I'm not drinking, Jess. I'm not under a bridge shooting up, I'm not sleeping around. But I want you to know that I sure as hell feel like I could do all of those things right now."

"Um, yes, and beat up a few good people while you're at it, I suppose. Who's next, the Paparazzi?"

"Ha-uh," he let a strange twisted laugh escape, and gave her a look that said *you're nuts*. "Is that what you think? That I'm just going to lose it?"

"I'm just worried about our kids, Josh. Their future. Tomorrow the entire world is going to have a field day with us."

"You want me to pull the plug on us. You're practically begging me."

"That's not what I am saying."

"Then why? Why Jacob and why Matt?"

"Jacob is off the table. It's over, it's done. Tonight was the end. He's gone. I promise you."

"And Matt?"

"Because he was my rock and I was his. Everyone else is off their fucking rocker right now! Including your crazy sister, who's got you over-analyzing shit that, when all is said and done, really doesn't have a goddamn thing to do with you."

"How does my wife sleeping with other men have nothing to do with me?"

"May I remind you that I did not sleep with Matt, Josh. So enough about him, okay?" Jessie gave her husband's chest a light shove. "You think I'm testing you? Is that what you think this is about? I'm testing you to see how much you can take? So I can watch you break? Again?"

"No, I think you're self-sabotaging us because you don't think you're worth loving."

"Got it all figured out, do you, bad boy?" Looking into his eyes was killing her. The deep brown was a velvety soft now, a troubled russet-running river that entered her body and crushed her soul with its power to know the real truths about her, Jessie Wheeler.

"I've got some of it figured out. The more men you love, who love you back, the easier it is to tell yourself you're worthy."

"Jacob was about music. He was about sharing a part of my soul that I miss. Matt is about being someone I can depend on. Who I have always depended on while everyone else around me blew up."

"Is, huh? Present tense? Have you been sleeping with him all along, Jessie?"

"Duh, are you even listening? I've never slept with him. But you know that ache you have right now for alcohol? For drugs? For anything to ease the pain you caused today? I feel it too. But it's for Matt. It's a deep, deep longing and it fucking hurts."

Silence.

Josh's voice returned in a surprised whisper. "We're not going to get past this."

There, Jessie caught herself thinking. *This is my chance. He's already detonated. Come clean. Tell him what hurt you the most and sent you off the rails. Tell him what Jacob did. Tell him what Jacob did so he will understand why Matt's arms feel so fucking good. So…safe.*

But she couldn't. Josh seemed okay now, quieter, calmer, but it was almost in an eerie way. Jessie was afraid to take the chance, to reveal the truths she held so close to her chest. What good would telling him solve, anyway? Would it solve anything? The only power she figured it might have was to maybe—a big maybe—help Josh understand that she never meant to hurt him in the first place.

Josh could read her like a book. He could enter her soul through those pale, scared eyes and almost tell her what she was thinking. "Have you lied to me, Jessie? Is there more that I don't know?" he asked.

She blinked, and chose not to answer. Instead, Jessie looked away.

"What? What have you lied to me about?"

Countering, Jessie said, "I just won three Grammys. I would have preferred to remember this night fondly, instead of the same way I remember winning my Oscars which, I recall telling you, was the loneliest night of my life, Josh."

"I told you I was sorry."

"And then you said you don't think we are going to get past this."

"It's pretty damn hard to see any kind of future when you close up like a clamshell, Jess."

"Fine, then."

"Fine what?"

"Fine, I'll tell you what I think this is all about. Where it started. Since…" She swallowed. "Since Jacob, I mean. Since we were together in New York."

This was something. Josh straightened, took her hand in his, and listened.

Jessie inhaled deeply, and dove in. "It's about you. It's all about you and how you feel, and how you're letting Kayla make you feel. What you've failed to consider since Christmas—no, since I left Jacob in New York to come back to you—is how I feel!" Tears pricked at the corners of Jessie's eyes. The admission hurt. It felt selfish.

"I'm raising yours and Jacob's kid! How can I not be considering how you feel?"

"Josh," she said wildly, "you just fucking said it. Jacob's kid. At some point Dylan's going to wake up and realize that's how you see him, no matter how great you are with him. And it hurts me. The guilt I carry about taking that child away from a man who took care of our two when neither you nor I could…it's eating me alive! I thought that by going to Jacob when he lost Talia I could at least hold him and help him the way he helped me when I needed someone. But Jacob fucked me and pushed me away. So I leaned on Matt and now he's, for the most part, gone. You've been threatening to leave since Boxing Day. You haven't said it, you keep saying you will never let me go, but thanks to Kayla's influence you've been hanging it over my head like a curse instead of holding me and helping me process all this shit that's running around in my head and breaking my heart."

"I've been trying to process this too, Jessie. I'm still trying to figure this out too!"

"Why don't you just go, Josh? Why don't you just call it quits now and save us all a lot of grief?"

He choked on the words as he spoke. "I might be messed up but I'm trying here, Jessie. And I've told you, I am never letting you go."

"You're never letting me go, but you'll carry all this anger around inside of you while you try to figure out what the hell's going on, and the next time another fan pushes the wrong button, you'll beat the shit out of him. Somehow that doesn't feel like a really great solution, as far as I'm concerned!"

"I can't...I'll go see Trudy. We promised each other. We said vows, for better or for worse, we said, and I'm holding us to that."

"Well, Josh," Jessie said, unfolding her legs from underneath her and standing, "I've got news for you. In the end? It might not be up to you."

While he sat, stunned, and considered what she might mean by that, Jessie started towards the patio door leading into the hotel suite.

At the entrance, she turned back to him. "Yeah. With one breath you tell me you're not giving up, and with the other you make threats. I'm working on this film right now where a relationship is breaking down. Everybody is exploding around me and I'm just trying to find a goddamned rock to hang on to. Tomorrow my husband is going to be all over the news again as a guy who likes to beat the shit out of people, and I won't be here to make sure you don't go off the rails and forget to feed our kids while you go have a good drunk! I have to go back and finish this film. And I can see it in your eyes that in your heart you don't know if I am worth hanging on to."

"That's the film talking. It's your character, it's not you. You're taking it too personally."

"That last bit was Kayla talking. It's Kayla's broken heart. You can't see past her pain to see mine. You know how my film ends, Josh? You read the script, right?"

"No," he said softly, rising and approaching her. "I mean, yes I read the script but no, Jessie. Don't do anything stupid." He took hold of her elbows and tried to read, in the sad downturn of her quivering lips, just how desperately she was hurting.

"She takes a bottle of pills. The pain is so bad she wants to die."

"No," he said more adamantly. "We have children, people who love you..."

"I'm not talking about me! I'm not the one who was so completely lost that I got drunk and passed out, and forgot I had kids in the house!"

"No, you just ran away and hid. First to the playroom and then to New York."

"I wouldn't hurt myself, Josh. But I'm scared for you. I'm so damn scared that you might. I'm always watching you for cues, d'you know that? To see what your breaking point is? In some ways, today was a relief. But now it'll start again, the whole 'walking on eggshells so Josh doesn't lose it' crap. And I won't be the only one watching. Once again, thanks to you, the whole goddamn world will be waiting for you to crack."

Josh had no good answer for that. He tried a small, "I go to meetings, Jessie. I'll go to more."

"I've got two more bullets to fire at you and then I'm done. We're pulling out of here in half an hour and I can't wait. But here you go. One, you're going to get pulled off of Charles' series. Jonathon's on board now, remember? Your father? Whose show got screwed real good the last time you fucked up? And two, I know you've been wondering where Kayla took off to. You're gonna love this one. Guess where she is."

Slowly, Josh shook his head from side to side. "I have no clue." Dread started in his belly and squeezed his innards til they hurt.

"She went south. She's with Jacob, and she's living on his boat."

"Wh-what? No."

"Oh, yeah. Your hypocrite sister is fucking the one man in this world you utterly despise. And I've got news for you. He's likely only doing it to get back at me. At us. At you."

Silence. Josh sank back down onto the chaise.

Jessie paused before moving away. Her final words were said in a softer tone, although the anger hangover from the day was still staunchly in place.

"Come on, Josh. We have to pack."

Outside, the smog over L.A. hung thick and heavy. It hurt Josh to breathe and he wondered why Jessie smoked when she was hurt and angry. It seemed to him that there was enough crap clogging up his throat to make breathing hard. There was enough crap already burning up his lungs.

He sat for a full ten minutes before joining Jessie, packing, and like a bandit on the run, sneaking out of the luxury hotel for a moonlit flight out of L.A.

Chapter Thirteen

Josh paused in the aisle by Jessie's wide leather seat on the Keating jet. Clearly she wouldn't want him in the seat next to her, not tonight. Clearly she was still super pissed at him, judging by the fresh Baileys Victoria had set down for her and the final cigarette she'd inhaled outside.

But she surprised him. Jessie's hand swept down and she moved her phone from its perch on Josh's usual seat when the two of them were flying without the kids.

Wordlessly, Josh eased his tired body down next to her. Before long, he felt her fingers wrap around his, and the relieved sigh that escaped from between his lips took with it some of the sick stomach he'd been contending with since the second she'd uttered the words *it might not be up to you.*

Moving onto her side, resting her leg over Josh's like she always did, Jessie coiled one arm around his waist, buried her face in his neck, and held on tight. Soon her regular breathing telegraphed that she was asleep.

Matt was kitty corner across the aisle from Josh. When it came to his feelings for Jessie, there were never any illusions about where her heart was firmly and securely anchored. Really, it killed him to see the two fighting and now, as he watched her cuddle into her husband and sink into sleep, relief washed over him. Maybe they would be okay. Maybe they could hang on. Certainly all indications since they got back together after New York were that they could get past all the hurts that Morgan and Nadia caused. Now, watching Josh bend his head to his wife and tenderly run his fingers through her hair, Matt wondered where this latest fallout would land. Jessie and Josh loved each other and wanted to be together—that was evident in the way

131

they moved around each other, in the way they touched or looked at each other, even when they were fighting.

Jacob...they needed to be apart from him. They needed separation from him. Unfortunately, if the rape ever became public knowledge, Matt surmised that the tenuous hold Josh and Jessie had on each other these days would disintegrate. That knowledge would be disastrous. Jessie protecting Jacob from Josh's fists, from prosecution? No way would Josh buy into that. Even though, after this crazy day, Matt understood very clearly that by not telling Josh what actually transpired in Florida was really her desperate ploy to protect him—and their family—from himself. But Josh would never see it that way. No way.

Might a public admission bring Jacob's golden aura down in the eyes of the fans who, like the bottle thrower today, despised Josh and had a lower regard for Jessie because she went back to Josh? Maybe. But Jessie would never, could never hurt Jacob that way. She was a classic victim, a woman who once sang with Jacob at a series of Domestic Violence awareness concerts, who was protecting him because she loved him. What Jacob did to her could, if word got out, destroy his career entirely.

Kayla...she was a hotheaded little problem. Showing up in the Caribbean was gutsy but it was also careless. Jacob had only lost Talia six weeks earlier. The boy had a long ways to go towards healing. In Matt's opinion, he didn't need a wild card like Kayla throwing off his newfound equilibrium. And he sure as hell didn't need that wild card to be Josh's sister.

The first night after her arrival, Matt had bunked in with a sweet girl less than half his age that was working from her father's boat. Everything about the liaison screamed *wrong*, especially given Jessie's history, but the girl had seemed quite content and at peace with her profession, and Matt paid her for an entire night so financially she was doing okay, at least. It had just seemed awkward to him to bunk in with Jacob and Kayla.

The next day, after one last sail, Matt had said his goodbyes and pulled out. *How are you two doing now?* he wondered of Jacob and Kayla, as he watched Josh close his eyes and move his lips in what seemed like a whispered prayer.

Matt couldn't look away. Jessie was asleep, and her husband seemed to be praying. There was a touching tenderness in the way he moved his hand gently over her; it was completely at odds with the incensed rage that darkened his eyes hours earlier.

Please be okay, Matt pleaded, letting his eyes drift down to Jessie's arm around Josh's waist. She'd won three Grammys that night, but Matt knew they were inconsequential to her. What mattered to Jessie was the man whose body she was half-laying on, as if by absorption she could save him—them.

When he looked back up, Matt was startled to see Josh's eyes on him. Blinking, he remained quiet, and didn't look away.

Josh let out a breath, turned his attention back to his wife, gathered her in as close to his body as he possibly could, and closed his eyes.

I get it, Matt breathed inwardly as, across from him, Josh's lips moved once more in silent prayer.

Contrary to what Matt figured was transpiring down south, though, Jacob was not actually sleeping with Kayla. He was doing quite the opposite. They sailed together, had lunch together, and made coffee for each other. But in the evenings, after dinner, while Kayla sucked on a straw dunked into a layered Spanish coffee (or three), and after Jacob downed a few beers, he generally hooked up with one of the local ladies.

It pissed Kayla off to no end, but she had some understanding of this boy's soul—who didn't, he bled all over his music—and right now, only a short time after the loss of the woman he was supposed to marry, plainly he was insulating himself with whoever would take him, Kayla not included. She figured it was because she knew him too well. She understood his past, his hurts, his history. Jacob needed superficial layers, not someone he might let inside his blistered soul.

Not to mention that she, Josh Sawyer's little sister, would be a whole new hot blister. Add that Kayla had been a good friend to Jessie, and no way would a sexual or romantic liaison with Jacob go over well in Vancouver.

This night, as Josh held his wife on the jet and, with a quiet and fearful awe, watched her sleep, Jacob and Kayla were sharing a high pub table at the marina bar. Both had tried and failed to get drunk. Jacob had turned down every young hottie who approached him tonight, so after a while they let him be, figuring he'd finally hooked up with the blonde who was living on his boat, who was always watching him with quiet reverence and thinly disguised desire.

Jacob and Kayla had eaten a late dinner at the bar tonight, in almost complete silence apart from the occasional, "Pass the pepper."

Only one conversation lasted more than a few sentences. Munching on a French fry, Kayla had tossed in, "D'ya see that new boat? The 32 Hunter? That skipper looks ready to call it a day. I heard they caught a storm a few days ago and his wife said she was done. I heard she's flying home tomorrow."

Jacob's response was a grunt. Kayla was well aware that the demons bothering him today were Grammy related, for tons of reasons. One, he was supposed to be performing. Two, Jessie would be there. Three, Talia was supposed to be there. Instead, only her likeness would appear, in a video and in a live tribute to her music.

Around two a.m., she slipped off her tall chair, reached down to a canvas bag at her feet, and pulled out her iPad. Grabbing the chair and sliding it across the floor so it landed beside Jacob, she laid the iPad on the table before them and climbed back up into her seat.

"I can go away," she declared, "but I'd prefer to keep you company in case you decide to take a midnight swim with concrete blocks tied around your ankles."

Jacob fisted his hands into his forehead. "I don't want to do this, Kayla."

"Yeah, you do," she said quietly. "In your heart, you need to see this so you can let it rest. Otherwise you'll just let it eat you up inside." Poking the power button, she added, "Besides, the tribute they're supposed to be doing for Talia will be beautiful, Jacob. She would want you to see it."

He didn't answer, but removed his hands from over his eyes and sucked in a breath.

Carefully, Kayla watched him for signs of disintegrating or bolting, but he stayed put, and locked his eyes on the small screen.

"Okay, here goes," she mumbled, and typed *Grammys* in the search bar.

The screen filled with links. To the shock and surprise of both Jacob and Kayla, at least half a dozen were worded *Josh Sawyer viciously attacks fan and security.*

"What the hell?" Jacob watched as Kayla narrowed her eyes and clicked on the first link. Inadvertently, his hand grabbed hers as they watched her brother attack the bottle-thrower and then nail Matt up against the brick of the hotel. In the melee too was Jessie, bleeding from a cut on her forehead before becoming the victim of a misplaced punch.

"Unbelievable," Kayla breathed as her eyes started to swim. "They wanted you. Josh went after them because they wanted you."

"Your crazy brother going after a fan, and Matt of all people, has shit all to do with me, Kayla," Jacob bit off. "He's a fucking loose cannon. And one of these days Jessie will finally see that and walk away from him for good."

"Oh, give me a break, Jacob," Kayla fired back. "Josh has had to deal with more shit in his lifetime than a lot of people, a lot of it in a very public way and most of it because of Jessie. And it started when he was conceived, by the way, when his biological father walked away from him."

"Ouch."

"Josh is amazing with your kid. And he's amazing with Jessie, who I've started to think doesn't deserve my adorable brother. So ease up on him, will you?"

Stunned at another video of the incident that Jacob was replaying in front of them, she hit *pause* when the camera picked up Jessie's bleeding forehead as she moved towards Josh and Matt by the hotel.

Jacob waited a moment before he spoke. "All hell's breaking loose, Kayla. I can't see Jessie handling this very well."

"You're hoping she'll leave him once and for all." In her heart, Kayla felt sick at the thought of it. If there was leaving to be done, she wanted it to be powered by Josh so he wouldn't be completely destroyed.

Waving an arm at the screen, Jacob hit *play* and they watched as Josh threw Matt up against the wall. "I don't want a man with a temper like that raising my kid. Do you want him raising your niece and nephews?"

"Don't you even think about going after full custody of Dylan, Jacob. You've hardly been around him at all."

"Like I had much of a fucking choice. That's not what I mean, anyway. I don't want that. Not on my own, not without Talia or—" He bit back the word. It tasted foul in his mouth, like long spoiled milk.

"Jessie," Kayla filled in the blank for him. "The two of you are perfect for each other. She's a whore and you're a man-whore."

"Let's get one thing straight, Sawyer." Jacob emphasized the name, almost spitting it out as it slipped between his lips. "I may have invited you down here, but there were no ulterior motives. I just lost Talia. I'm still messed up over Jessie. Trust me, you don't want this." Gesturing to himself, Kayla was saddened to see a sheen of moisture cross his blue eyes.

"I never said I did," she muttered quietly. "I lost someone too. And I'm not saying it sucks about losing Talia the way you did, Jacob, but sometimes I think it would have been easier if Paul had died."

"Nah," he countered softly, "it wouldn't have been. Trust me. And just for the record, I kinda lost both ways. She called off the wedding the minute before our car was hit by that drunk."

"Oh. Jacob, I…I didn't know that. I'm sorry. Really." Confused thoughts flittered across Kayla's sunburned face. She fixed her gaze on him. "Jessie," she said finally. "Because of Jessie."

"Yeah, of course. You were there on Boxing Day. Look Kayla, you need to chill about Jessie. She's not the ogre you think she is."

"I used to adore her Jacob, I really did, but I feel like she's let me down big time."

"She's had a rough go of it too, kiddo. And maybe you don't know the whole story."

"She took advantage of you when you were down. And all it did was create a brand new big old whirlpool of chaos."

"Like I said, Kayla, you don't know the whole story. And I don't feel like getting into it right now, okay?"

"Oooo-kaaayyyy… fine." Puzzled, Kayla refocused on the iPad. "Enough of this bullshit," she said firmly. "I'll call Josh tomorrow and see how he's doing." Softer, she added, "Do you think you can handle the tribute to Talia?"

A heavy exhalation was Jacob's first response. How could he tell Kayla that what he really wanted to see was Jessie's performance? Did she even sing? Was she even okay? Mouthing a silent *I'm so sorry* to Talia, he let Kayla select a YouTube clip featuring Talia's tribute, and nodded when Josh's sister poised a finger over the *play* button.

They watched in silence. Kayla was right, it was beautiful. Jacob himself was featured in a lot of the clips. More than once, he had to look away. When it was over, he found his fingers securely locked in Kayla's, surprised to realize that he was trembling, but that her grip was strong and secure on his.

"Thank you," he whispered to her when it was over.

"Again?" she murmured with a poised but sorrowful air.

Shaking his head from side to side, Jacob signaled *no*. "Jessie," he breathed, without looking at Kayla.

Against her better judgment, Kayla scrolled to a video announcing Jessie's Grammy appearance and hit *play*. In all of its magical bittersweet splendor, Jessie's painful apology to Jacob played out in front of them.

Spellbound, breath held, Jacob watched her sing. He saw it all—the close-ups of the bandage on her forehead, the lost way she melted into the music, and the way she tried to stay buried in the song until reality called by way of a standing ovation racked with obtrusive applause. When Jessie's tears fell, even Kayla cursed under her breath and silently ordered a commercial break, but then Matt was there and Jessie was rescued.

Kayla could feel Jacob quaking beside her. A little afraid to look over, she finally sucked up her courage and peeked at him. His shoulders were hunched over. He was sobbing in silence.

"Okay," she murmured softly, letting go of his fingers as her own tears started to trickle down her cheeks. "We go now. To boat. We go." She grabbed the iPad but his hand shot out.

"Once more," he croaked.

It took her a few seconds to decide whether or not to follow his wishes. But the look on his face—that quiet desperation—was killing her. She hit refresh and the video started again.

This time, with a keen attention to the lyrics, both Kayla and Jacob watched Jessie sing her song for a man she'd so badly hurt. At the end, Jacob had two things to say as he swiped the back of his arm across his eyes.

"Thank God for Matt," was the first. The second was, "It was a goodbye song, Kayla. She was saying goodbye. It's over. It's over for good."

"Honey…I'm sorry. I don't know what else to say."

Ordering another beer from the server, Jacob slid off his chair when the cool beverage arrived. Kayla had already packed up the iPad and was fingering a new drink herself. Now, about to climb back into her seat after putting the bag at her feet, she paused. The way Jacob was looking at her—chin raised, jaw set, eyes painfully wet but devoid of light—frightened her. Her shoulders sank.

"First," he said, "you need to go back to Vancouver tomorrow. Second, I'll see you in the morning."

"Jacob!" she called hopelessly as he brushed by her and made his way over to a cute little honey he'd hooked up with before. The girl was the same one Matt had spent his last night south with. "He'll be okay," Kayla mumbled under her breath. "He just needs a little insulation tonight." Inside, she wished to hell he'd chosen her. Inside, she ached for more from this man whose touch she craved, whose eyes she got lost in every time he set them on her. Inside, the ache of losing Paul was starting to fill in. But it was starting to fill in with a whole new ache that hurt even more as, now, Kayla watched Jacob put on a fake smile, whisper to the girl at his side, and drape one sexy arm around her shoulders.

Moving towards the open latticed entry of the small bar, Kayla hung her head. Between this new acute longing, the sorrow in Jacob's eyes, and Josh's new hell, she bitterly joked to herself that she was ready to find some concrete herself to tie around her ankles. But nobody seemed concerned about her. Nobody seemed to care that Kayla, too, was afloat in her very own fishbowl of disappointment and grief.

Stepping onto the dock, she strode to Sarah May, hopped up and into the sailboat's cockpit, undid the hatch's lock, and climbed down the short ship's ladder into the cabin. Collapsing onto the V-berth under the bow, where Matt had previously slept because Jacob refused it on account of it was a double bed, she dropped the canvas bag to her side and wept.

Chapter Fourteen

The next day, Jacob dropped heavily into a plastic chair next to Kayla in the outdoor deck area of the marina restaurant/bar. One hand clutched a rolled, damp towel. Hanging out over the ends of it, coiled inside its soft cocoon, were last night's clothes.

Kayla eyed him critically. "You realize it's noon," she admonished. "Did you have to pay extra last night? Does she triple charge after sunrise?"

"The showers up here suck," he replied, ignoring her dig as he stretched both arms above his head and yelped adorably. "Ouch. I gotta get back to the gym."

"Aren't you going to ask me why I'm still here?" she pouted. Sitting with one leg crossed underneath her butt, Kayla was poking away at her iPad.

Jacob yawned, and lifted his feet up to rest on the chair kitty corner to him. "I can't be with you, Kayla," he said with a dull-edged bluntness that surprised her. "If that's why you're here. If that's what you're hoping for."

She left the iPad alone and sat back. "Why? Because you don't want to be with me? Or because of who I am."

A sad gaze aimed in her direction was his only response.

A frustrated *ppfffttt* snuck out before she threw at him, "Because of Josh and Jessie, right? A man you hate and a woman you love. Who just happen to be my brother and sister-in-law. Jacob…" She wiggled her butt up higher in the chair and faced him square on. "Shitty things happen to people in life. They lose people they love, whether through death or through choices made for them by other people. It doesn't mean they have to stop living."

"Look, Kayla," Jacob started. "I'm sorry. I like that you're here. I really

139

do. Having crew makes sailing a helluva lot easier. And in case you haven't noticed, I *am* living my life down here, more than most people, I'd say. I'm just choosing a world I prefer, and," he pointed a finger at her, "you're too close to the world I'm trying to outrun."

"What'd you tell Matt about getting back to work? I assume that's why he was here."

"Partly," Jacob snorted, to Kayla's perked up nose and sudden curiosity. Jacob fidgeted, and took his feet down off the chair opposite him. "I told him to give me a little more time. That's what I told him."

"How much time?"

"Hell, I don't know, Kayla! A month, six months, a year, I don't know. I really don't." Tossing his towel and clothes onto the tabletop, Jacob leaned one elbow on the arm of his chair and pinched his bottom lip. Reflecting on her frown and her focused attention on the iPad, he nodded towards it. "What's today's news from the real world?"

She sighed and shoved the laptop away. "It's bad. And that's why I haven't found a flight out yet. Matt sent me an email and suggested I stay away until things settle a bit. He said Jack had to hire security for the workshops because there are reporters stalking the place, hoping for my take on why Josh flipped out. Apparently Benjie told them I'm away indefinitely." As an afterthought, she grumbled and added, "Jessie is supposedly going to help Benjie out when she gets back from Belgium. She's got another couple of weeks left there."

"So she's…"

"Still with Josh, yes, at least if I read between the lines, that's what it looks like. She flew out to Belgium with Arnie, and left Matt with Josh, though. Which strikes me as really sad. Jessie must have done a helluva number on poor Matt."

"She did. You saw the heartbreak in his eyes. What's Josh say about it?"

Subdued, she replied, "He hasn't written back. The doofus."

"All right, then. Stay another few days if you want, but clear out by the weekend, okay? You're starting to cramp my style. All the girls are jealous."

"You're kinda gross, Jacob. You make me a little sick to my stomach." Kayla went back to her iPad.

Without responding, Jacob shoved back his chair and stood. Since he didn't seem to be walking away, Kayla looked away from the depressing reports about her brother's latest bad behavior, and glanced up at him. Jacob was suddenly downright pensive.

"What?" she asked, annoyed.

"I didn't have sex with that girl last night. Or with the one the night before, Kayla. Not that it's really any of your business."

"I've seen you go off with them, Jacob. I don't really care, anyway."

"I just…sometimes it's nice just to have someone to hold, you know?"

"As if you could not have sex lying next to one of those girls," she intoned casually. "The way Jessie tells it, the two of you were always at it."

"Yeah, you know what, Kayla?" Jacob's voice got hard, but it had a soft edge to it. He had grabbed his rolled towel and was slapping it against his thigh as he spoke. "When it feels like your world might come to a crashing halt any day, you ignite that fire as often as you can. You want to keep it burning, you know?" Starting to move away, he added, "What I had with Jessie? It was never enough. Sex, I mean. Holding her. Making that intense soul connection we had into a physical thing. It was never enough and no woman will ever replace her. Talia…didn't replace her. I'll never connect with anyone again the way I connected with Jessie. The music…you know…?"

Kayla stood too. She grabbed her iPad and tucked it under her arm as she started to walk away alongside Jacob. "I know," she said. "Music was always yours and Jessie's thing. I don't know why everyone manages to see that except Jessie. Josh has never had that glue with her, if that's what you want to call it, and he never will."

"You're a little wrong there, Kayla."

"How's that, Casanova?"

"Josh doesn't write or play music, but he sure as hell gets it. Have you ever been around him when he's watching her sing?"

"Y-yeah. I guess." She hooked her arm in Jacob's and almost started skipping as they walked.

"Like I said," Jacob lowered his voice respectfully, "you're too hard on Jessie. She knows what she has and I expect she intends to fight for him."

"And you're all of a sudden defending her why?"

"I have my reasons. Maybe some day I'll share them with you. Although

I will add that it goes without saying that I would take her back in an instant. But I know now, Kayla, after her song last night, that it's not ever going to be an option."

"You think she was saying goodbye. For Josh's benefit."

"And for mine. I know her. I know her music and the way her mind works. I don't *think* she was saying goodbye. I know she was."

"Doesn't matter, for Josh at least. I can't imagine how they'll get past this one."

"Kayla?"

"Yep?"

"It's not really our problem. They're not our problem."

"Ah. You're moving on, Jacob," Kayla smiled at him. "Take whatever time you need down here to set your spirit free, and let them go. All of them, all of your ghosts. And call me when you need a friend, okay? You're not alone."

Jacob had to pause and swallow the lump in his throat before he trusted himself to speak. Kayla's eyes were Josh's eyes, sometimes, liquid brown and sad, yet kind and tender. She was looking at him through those eyes now, but for once Jacob didn't see Josh there. He was seeing Kayla, clearly, for the first time. He was seeing a friend.

"You're not alone either, Kayla," he finally said, in a husky voice that was a little less pouty than usual. Arm in arm, he led her back towards the boat. "What do you say we grill up some bacon and eggs and then hoist the sails for the afternoon? Feel that sea breeze in your hair. Look at this sky. It's perfection."

Indeed, the tropical sky was an indigo blue, a canvas free of clouds and torment and angst. Perfection indeed. Kayla's smile got wider and, despite herself, she did start to skip.

⌒﹏⌒

Much later, after a relaxing sail and a rejuvenating swim, Jacob lay back on Sarah May's deck, crossed his ankles and his arms, and drifted off to sleep in the late afternoon warmth. When he awoke, Kayla was nowhere in sight, and the sun was going down. His belly was growling, so he decided to head up to the restaurant to see if she was around. On the walk up it occurred to Jacob that, upon waking, the first person he'd thought of was Kayla, instead of the usual Talia or Jessie. And for once, his stomach didn't clench as his eyes blinked open. For once, the anxious urge to puke or weep was non-existent.

Whistling, when he hit the top of the ramp that extended up from the docks and set his feet on solid earth, Jacob noticed a dim light in a small building used for classes like Yoga and Zumba, and for the occasional club movie night. Supported high on the wall at the far end was an 80-inch monitor, which Jacob noticed was playing, as it often was, an American music video channel. Right now, his image was up on the screen. After all this time in the limelight, it still struck him as surreal and a little bit strange. Oddly enough, someone was moving around in the space below. *Dancing,* he thought, as he watched the person's silhouette move gracefully to the beat of the tune.

"Hmmm," he thought, and sidled casually over, both hands in his shorts pockets and his leather flip flops grating on gravel as he reached a small path that led to the wide barnlike opening of the activity space. It crossed his mind that the dancer was likely Kayla, but what Jacob didn't expect was how her interpretation of his song would affect him.

The song was a ballad, a 'Jacob special,' the kind of tune that had women cranking up their stereos and sobbing all the way to work. It was not a song he wrote with Jessie; this one was new and had garnered him a 'Song of the Year' Grammy nomination (a category Jessie won). It was fluid, sad, pretty and heartfelt. Jacob counted it as one of his favorites. To him, it spoke legions about how he felt when Jessie left him for Josh. It spoke legions about how much he still hurt.

Now, there was Kayla—indeed, it was her—moving her body to his music in a way that blew Jacob's mind. Yeah, sure, he knew she was a dancer. She'd danced for him and Jessie, the odd time, and Jacob had certainly seen her on stage during Jessie's shows when she was on tour. Those high level production numbers were always choreographed by someone else—Priya, usually, Jessie's standby choreographer. The dance numbers in the B boyz workshops were Kayla's work, but they were ensemble pieces. Here, in front of Jacob now, was Kayla dancing free and unencumbered. Here, she was dancing from her soul.

She didn't see him watching. Jacob, somewhat subconsciously in his rather surprised frame of mind, had chosen to remain outside of the building. With one hand resting on the doorframe of the entrance, he was not visible to Kayla unless she completely turned and caught him standing there. So he was a quiet, invisible fan for the most part, and she was a lithe, graceful star.

Denim shorts were Kayla's staple that day, short but not uncomfortably short for the old skipper down the dock from Sarah May, who liked to start each day with coffee on the deck of his boat and see what Kayla would emerge wearing. Her top was a halter that fastened mid-back; blue, with small white polka dots, it left her belly and back exposed but allowed ease of movement for her covert dance.

There was ink on her body, which Jacob thought echoed Kayla's independent spirit.

If music be the food of love, play on

A tramp stamp, scripted across her lower back. It was accented with delicate eighth and quarter notes. He'd seen it before, it wasn't hidden, but for some reason tonight, watching her dance, Jacob wanted to run his fingers over it. There was a newer one, too, that Jacob hadn't eyeballed until Kayla arrived on his dock. Inked inside a wrist, it was a scripted K for Kayla, in a circular pattern into which was drawn a musical staff, complete with quarter notes. This was Kayla's ode to herself after Paul's treachery.

Her feet were bare, which was okay on the tile floor; to his song, they touched down with the grace of a dove, and pirouetted with the beauty and ease of a classical ballerina. Kayla's hands floated and moved in complement to her body. Rising above her head, they arched and dipped in perfect time; they gave her balance and earned her hope.

Eyes half-closed, Kayla wasn't watching the video monitor where some director's visual interpretation of Jacob's song was screening. Instead, she was lost in some inner dream-state that fed her spirit and motivated her movements, which were carefree and weighted and poised and melty all at once.

She was sublime. From the perimeter, Jacob felt his breath catch from the first moment his cobalt blues captured her essence, dipping and soaring and swooping and diving like a hawk, floating like a hummingbird, lit only from small sconces on the walls, soulful and perfect in his sight. Most stunning of all was not that she was free in her interpretation of his song. Most stunning of all was the peaceful half-smile on her face, the pure joy radiating from her body, the light clearly emerging from within as she danced.

The poise of her movements, the poetry of her body—all of it was conjoined with perfect passion.

Kayla goes somewhere else when she dances, Jacob caught himself thinking. *Kayla is as lost in the music as I was when I wrote it. As I am when I sing it.*

As all beautiful music does, the song came to an end. A lovely, sweet last few chords brought it to rest with a flawless grace. Jacob held his breath and watched as, before him, Kayla did a Jessie move. It took her a moment to come out of the song, the dance. It took her a few seconds to find the world again.

She looked around, almost confused, and Jacob saw reality play out on her face. Paul hurting her, Jessie hurting her by way of hurting her brother, a life adrift, a lack of energy and interest in the workshops she created, running away, hiding, wondering what to do next, where to go. She was wringing her hands now, swallowing, looking around her at the floor, instead of rising up with a peaceful countenance and exuding pure joy as she had moments before.

He stepped into the space.

Kayla heard his footsteps. Startled, she looked up. "Oh," she managed, embarrassed to be caught dancing to Jacob's song. "I'm sorry. I was walking by and I heard the first few chords. I couldn't help myself."

Beyond the dance itself, Jacob saw Kayla herself now, alone and scared, vulnerable, tired. Like him.

Like me, he thought. No longer was she Josh's sister, Jessie's sister-in-law. No longer was she a drifter hanging out on Jacob's boat, eating his food and drinking his wine. She was just a sweet girl who had fallen on some hard times and who was looking for a safe place to land. For a soft place to fall.

In a few short steps, Jacob was by her side. Nervous now, he took her hand, this new, odd friend of his, and he gave it a gentle squeeze. In front of him, Kayla swallowed and held her breath. Would he be mad? She had become his shadow, a clingy grey thing Jacob didn't need harping at his feet down here where he craved peace and solitude. She felt like a stalker of sorts, by virtue of being here, and by virtue of interpreting his song, that she was well aware was some kind of sacred ode to Jessie.

"It's okay," he whispered to her, raising his left hand and laying a palm against her cheek. "Don't look so scared."

"Please," she murmured, her knees melting in the loving way he was looking at her, in the tender way he was touching her. "Please, Jacob."

She didn't need to add more. Jacob could read Kayla now. He could see in her posture that the way she'd carried herself around him this last week or so was one big hulking false bravado. She was as damn hurt and scared as he was. Lonely. Kayla was lonely. She needed to be touched; she needed to be loved, by someone who could connect with her on a soul level.

Music. That was the key; that was the entry to this girl's soul. Kayla was no fool, she long knew that Jacob's soul could be opened the exact same way. But it wasn't until Jacob saw her dance that he unlocked his door and let her in.

Standing there before her, Jacob let his lips brush hers, and waited for her response. With the women he chose to have sex with down south, he was always rough and a little bit desperate. Often with Jessie, their sex was the very same way. But this girl needed something different; she was already crumbling underneath him here, now, after the emotional journey of her dance. She would require tenderness, a sweet tender, loving touch, a slow lovemaking that would start to heal the wounds Paul left raw and bleeding. Kayla would need love.

He felt her swallow again, before Kayla finally lifted her hand and grasped Jacob's elbow. It felt like neither of them were even breathing, but Jacob could see Kayla's chest rise and fall; she was still coming down off her dance. His right hand lifted and caressed the few cranberry-blonde wisps of hair that had escaped her ponytail, and then Jacob let the hand fall to her belly, which she sucked in at his touch. He let the backs of his fingers play there while he kissed her, and she gasped at the hot white trail they left as they moved over her body.

"Come," he said gently, lifting her wrist to move his tongue over the new tattoo. "Be with me."

"Don't break my heart, Jacob," she begged before she moved. "Please."

He smiled. "Not tonight," he murmured. "Not tonight."

But on the way out of the building, as Jacob held Kayla's fingers tightly in his own, his body already tingling with the sweet pleasure he knew awaited them, a brisk cool wind came up and whisked over him. He shivered, as did the woman by his side and so, protectively, Jacob wrapped an arm around Kayla's shoulders and held her close.

It hit him then that this beautiful, sweet, sad girl affected him deeply. Even when they'd met at her workshops in the fall there was some intrigue about her, that encircled her like a halo. She was captivating, funny, and she liked spontaneous adventure. Music was sacred to her. She was a wonderful aunt to Dylan.

The future unfolded before Jacob like a rose in bloom, expanding and stretching out its arms, creating beauty where before there was only a deep, barren loss.

And it hit him too, that Kayla…was Josh Sawyer's sister. She was Jessie's sister-in-law. There would be Christmases and birthday parties and, if Kayla and Jessie reconciled, Kayla would likely continue to dance in Jessie's big shows.

"Fuuuuccckkkk," Jacob breathed as he led Kayla down to Sarah May, hoping he said it quietly enough that she wouldn't hear him. "Just fuck."

But he smiled, despite himself, and laughed.

And held his new girl close.

Chapter Fifteen

A gentle lapping woke Kayla the next morning. Sarah May was rocking just slightly, creaking in the way that old wooden boats do. Above, she heard the main line slap against the mast, and on the dock somewhere nearby water was rushing from a hose as some sailor washed footprints off his sailboat's deck. Greasy bacon was frying up close by, and its salty smell along with the more welcome heady scent of someone's morning coffee was heaven to her nostrils.

Like a baby in its cradle, she smiled, letting her gaze rest on Jacob's naked body as he slumbered next to her in the gently rocking cabin's wide forward berth. Sunlight poured onto his butt and lower back through the hatch that, in their haste to make love last night, they'd left open.

Unable to resist, Kayla touched his bicep, which jarred him slightly awake. Nervous, she waited to see how he would react to this new reality in daylight, without the magic of her starlight dance to his song playing havoc with his overheated, tingling senses.

She needn't have worried. Jacob's lips spread in a wide, contented smile.

"You sure are pretty to wake up to," he told her in his dusky half-asleep voice. "Unless...am I still dreaming?"

"I think I might be," Kayla whispered. "Is this for real?"

"Felt pretty real for most of the night," he teased. "You dancers have a lot of stamina."

"Ah," she said, rolling over onto her back and wiping loose hair back from her forehead. "So it begins. You're gonna have to try not to compare me to Jessie, Jacob. Unless you've had more dancers I'm not aware of."

148

"By definition Jessie is not a dancer. That's, like, her third occupation. After singing and acting, of course."

"Jessie could dance rings around any of us. And she didn't start training until after her first film in her early twenties. She's like Madonna. A friggin' powerhouse. Her dance company? We have to beg for breaks."

"You ever gonna start talking to her again?"

Kayla was silent for a few seconds before answering. She looked back at Jacob, who seemed quite content as he lay there and casually ran a finger around and around one of her nipples as they talked. "I guess so. One of these days, if I want to keep up a good relationship with Emily-Grace and the boys."

"How's that going to work? With us?" Jacob nudged closer to Kayla so he could plant kisses against her neck while he played with her body.

"Oh," she breathed, as the backs of his fingers languished against her skin on their way down her abdomen. She laid her hand gently over his and guided him lower, then spread her legs a little and turned her face into his so she could enjoy a few little kisses while he pleasured her. "Not sure," she gasped. "Maybe we could...not talk about Jessie...while you and I are...Oh. Oh, fuck. That's a good spot."

Lifting his head up slightly, Jacob murmured seductively into Kayla's ear. "Little wider...for me," he pleaded. "Please."

"Oh...manners...always nice...in bed...Okay, Jacob, glad I don't have to...train you. Oh, Jesus."

Soon the boat was rocking even more as Jacob made love again to the woman that, less than twenty-four hours earlier, he'd told could never be his. He was gentle and sweet, and respected her boundaries but was glad to see signs that showed him she would be a good match for him in bed, slightly adventurous and willing to play. She, like Jessie, respected and loved her body, and knew how to use it for her own and for her partner's pleasure.

Jacob got up after and used the head, then came back to bed to let Kayla have a few moments of privacy too, but they both collapsed back in bed afterwards, silly grins on their faces and an apple in Kayla's hand.

"Do I still have to go?" Kayla goaded him. "Like, tomorrow or the day after?"

"No hurry," he whispered adoringly. A thought struck him. "Your workshops,

149

though, Kayla. You worked so hard to make them happen. Those youth love you. The tour…"

"I know." She frowned as she munched on her apple and ran her fingers through Jacob's long curls. "I'll go back. I swear." Doubt ran through her veins as she said so and, as she studied his eyes, she saw by the disappearing flecks in the beautiful blue depths that he was feeling it too, that nascent surprise ambush of new love.

"I don't want you to go at all now." Smiling seductively, he lifted his head so he could place his mouth over a nipple and suck lightly.

She moaned, and arched her back, and after a bit he settled happily beside her.

Things settled into serious mode quickly then. Kayla started them on the direction but Jacob, perhaps in some way needing the release—to let go—kept on track until it got too tough.

"It's soon," Kayla said softly. "After Talia."

"Yeah," he sighed. "But you know something, Kayla? I loved Talia, I really did, but she was already spreading her wings beyond me. She was rushing headlong into this fame thing and I was pulling back. It was already starting to tear at us."

"I think Jessie was what was starting to tear at you."

"Yes, but it was easy to push her aside and pretend she didn't matter as long as we were nowhere near her. I thought…well, we only went to the La Casa Christmas thing because I thought I was okay. I thought I could handle it. I have no fucking clue how you and I are going to be able to…" He drifted off.

"Yeah," she admitted, offering him a bite of her apple, which he took with gusto, his large, luminous eyes peering at her from atop the apple. "And that's after Josh and Jessie get over the shock of finding out we're together."

"You already hate her. Talia was amazing, she could handle being in Jessie's presence when we were at the same show together, or in the same room, until the end, really. Until she saw me kiss Jessie at La Casa. I guess that made it real."

"And…you're thinking I won't be able to keep it together."

He raised his eyebrows at her.

"Yeah. You're right. I'm toast." Moaning, Kayla tossed her apple core in the nearby garbage.

"The thing is, Kayla," Jacob said. "I wasn't kidding when I said Jessie's Grammy song was goodbye. There's…" He swallowed. "There's a pretty good reason for that."

"Meaning? You've got me wondering, Jacob. Did something happen between you and Jessie that finally burst your sizzling bubble?"

"I guess you could say that. Look, if I tell you this, you have to swear it won't go anywhere. This is not something that needs to be out in the public eye, or something your brother needs to hear, for that matter. If Jessie hasn't already told him, I mean, and I doubt she has, unless that's what set him off last night."

"Okay." Kayla raised herself up on an elbow, and Jacob did the same. "I'm listening."

"All right. Well…it's like this…when Jessie came to Florida to see me I wasn't in a good place. Emily-Grace was sweet. It helped to have her around, it really did, but…" He shook his head. "With Jessie, there's always so much emotion. There's hurt, there's rejection, there's loneliness…and there's anger."

"Ah. I think I see where this is going. I know you hit her." Kayla's voice was soft and tender. It was understanding, despite the foul taste in her mouth about the idea of this adorable man losing it enough to hit a woman he loved. Josh crossed her mind. Had he ever hit Jessie? On purpose? She couldn't picture it.

"Kayla, it was more than that." Jacob exhaled slowly, his nerves exposed as a long whistle filled the otherwise quiet air. He laid back and stared at the sunlight and blue sky beyond the hatch. *I just have to tell her,* he told himself. *I need to say it and then let it go.*

"Whenever you're ready," Kayla encouraged, laying a hand on his stomach as she furrowed her brow and watched him struggle with whatever it was he needed to say.

Little beads of sweat were breaking out on his forehead. Jacob wiped an arm over them and jumped in deeper. "There's always been, and there will always be, a strong attraction to her for me. Sexually, you know?"

A slow grin widened on Kayla's face and her cheeks flamed pink. "Yes, well, I see where that comes from."

"No, Kayla, look…" Jacob was getting frustrated. Kayla stilled, and waited. "I couldn't even see straight. Before Talia…well, before the car hit us, I told you she called off the wedding. It wasn't just because of Jessie. We were fighting…in the car…about Jessie. That's why Talia pulled over."

"Oh." That was a shock, on so many levels. "Oh." Kayla, too, laid back and stared at the open world beyond the creaky wooden boat.

"So when Jessie showed up at my door…"

"Hence your anger at the funeral."

"In Florida? I didn't just hit her. Kayla, I…well, I guess what I did was rape her. She was saying no. She was going along with me, but only to a point. I could see the fear on her face. I could see she knew what this would do to Josh, if she and I went there, you know. I can't imagine how he felt about her coming down to see me at all. I think he likely just went along with it because I took care of his kids when things were so bad. Kind of like a thank you. And then what do I do? I force myself on his wife."

The last words were uttered so quietly Kayla hardly heard them. She'd gone a deathly shade of white.

Slapping a palm on her forehead, she groaned. "Sweet Jesus, Jacob. I've pretty much condemned Jessie for…" Whipping onto her side to face him she said, "She hasn't told anyone. Did she charge you?"

"No. You know Jessie. She wouldn't want that kind of publicity for either of us. Plus I'm pretty sure she chalked it up to my insanity that day."

"But Josh…he thinks…"

"Yeah, you saw him on those videos. You think Jessie wants him unleashed on me? Somehow I doubt it."

"She's protecting you…at the risk of losing her marriage. She's…choosing you. Again. Jacob, if Josh finds out about this—"

"He won't. Right, Kayla? You can't tell him."

"Who else knows?"

"I would assume just Matt. If Charles knew he would have cut me loose. And Deirdre would have my balls cut off."

"Ah. That explains Matt going after you at Talia's manager's home."

"Yep."

Another thought crossed Kayla's mind. She felt a slow nausea work its way up to her throat. "At what point did you hit her?" she asked softly.

It took Jacob a while to answer. "I hit her to get her to stop fighting me."

A quiet chill filled the warm tropical air. After a while Jacob managed, "I'm not proud of myself, Kayla."

"You've done concerts to support fundraising and awareness about violence against women."

"I've never…it was a one time thing. Jessie's not afraid of me. She knows it won't happen again, not like…"

"You're going to say not like Josh. His temper is pretty much unpredictable."

"I guess if we're going to hang out I'll have to watch what I say about him, huh? That is…if you still want to take a chance on me, Kayla."

Sighing, she snuggled in under his arm. "I do, Jacob. I just won't ever make you mad."

"That's no excuse, Kayla. Being out of my mind was no excuse. I can't tell you how sorry I am that I lost it with her. But you should know that it's also why I know things are truly over with Jessie now. There's no coming back from that shit."

"I just…I feel bad for being so hard on her."

"I'm not in any way blaming her, or excusing my actions, Kayla. But Jessie was right there with me. She was grinding up against me, Kayla, with her tongue down my throat. So she's not entirely off the hook, in my books. At least not in the wanting it part. You still have the right to be pissed at her for hurting your brother."

"This is a lot to handle."

"Yeah. I'm sorry. But if you and I are going to hang out, I needed you to know. Not that it in any way cleans my slate, Kayla. You just needed to know, that's all."

"Okay. God."

"Yeah."

After a while of watching the clouds float by outside, Jacob kissed Kayla's forehead and eased himself off the low berth. After a great catlike stretch, he stood and extended a hand to her. "Come on, dancer girl. This man's stomach requires more sustenance than a healthy apple. I need grease."

"Yeah," she agreed quietly, still lost in the visual imagery and unbelievable violent actions of the man she was starting to seriously care for. Wondering whether this new news was something she could handle, and worse…whether it was a secret she could keep. Josh…her brother…didn't he deserve to know? His marriage was suffering as a result of a line he thought his wife had chosen to cross. What was Jessie thinking, keeping this big a secret?

Protection. For both Josh and Jacob, in her weird, twisted way. That's what she was thinking, yet as a result the sinister secret was eating away at her relationship with Josh. Confused, Kayla shook her head as if the action could clear her muzzied thoughts, and as she wrapped a ponytail elastic around her hair, Jacob saw the struggle crisscross her pretty face.

After pulling on a pair of old baggy faded jeans and a grey T-shirt, and grabbing a towel and bar of soap for the marina shower, he turned back to face her.

"Kayla," he tried slowly, "I get it if this is suddenly all too much for you. I get it if you want to go."

"I don't," she said, scrunching up her shoulders and raising her chin, which made the corners of his lips turn up and brought a new twinkle to his eyes. "I want you, Jacob. I've wanted you since you were at the workshops. Am I afraid you're going to hurt me? No," she decreed. "No, I'm not. But if you try, I should warn you that I used to do karate."

"Ah," he said, sobered but trying, as she was, to lighten things up. He moved aside so she could climb the small ladder to the deck ahead of him and so he could admire the way her dancer's butt looked in her short shorts. The skipper down the dock would be impressed today. "So what belt did you get to?"

"Brown." Kayla reached a hand down to Jacob and grinned.

Emerging into the bright sunshine, he pinched her bicep and she yelped. "And how old were you?"

"Fifteen. I quit because dance started to take up too much time."

"You shoulda stuck with it."

"Um…I was hoping I would never need it."

154

"Kayla, I'm hoping you'll never need it too. And I want you to know that I promise you that it will never be an issue with me. I'm very, very sorry for what I did to Jessie, and that kind of violence will never happen with any woman I'm ever involved with again."

A tiny pang clutched at her heart. Kayla hooked her fingers in Jacob's droopy belt loops and searched his eyes. "I was really hoping I'd be your last woman."

Taking her elbows in his hands, Jacob spoke over the lump in his throat. "Optimistic much?"

"You bet."

His smile warmed her heart. "I'll try to do right by you, Kayla," he murmured and pressed her body against his. "You are a sweet, kind, talented woman. Good at sex too," he added, and she swatted him playfully.

They hopped off the boat together and, hand in hand, made their way up the dock towards the clubhouse for showers and sustenance.

The old skipper down the dock sipped on his third coffee of the day, and raised his mug to them.

"About time," he cheered inwardly, a fleet of his own long lost loves sliding across the picture gallery in his mind. "Don't mess it up, boy. She's one of the good ones."

At the top of the ramp, Jacob pulled Kayla to him again and kissed her pink lips. "Too bad we can't shower together," he teased.

"We can in Vancouver," she hinted, watching him to see how he would react. It took a bit, but then a slow smile widened across his face.

"That we can," he replied, before swinging around on one flip flop and walking backwards towards his shower, the usual rolled towel dangling from his grip. He saluted her, and grinned until he had to turn around so he could see where he was going.

"That we can," Kayla repeated happily, watching him saunter away. "That we can."

Chapter Sixteen

Josh held on for as long as he could, but once he and Jessie were safely whisked to La Casa—because their home was already a campground for media—he made his way up the mahogany staircase and walked down the hall to the bedroom Jessie once occupied when she lived at the cozy Spanish style home. He had taken a few moments to hug his children, but all three of them were trying to get their mother's attention, asking about her bandage and crawling all over her since they hadn't seen her in a few weeks, and so Josh snuck away unnoticed except by Matt and Carlotta, and headed for sanctuary.

The ache he held inside since the incident at the Grammys was numb now, as if it was a fire that hadn't quite gone out; the ache was red-hot coals burning through his gut from the inside out. Placing a hand over his stomach at the entrance to the bedroom, Josh could feel his shoulders caving and his emotional state quickly deteriorating. It was hard, holding these raw feelings in at the hotel, at the Grammys, on the jet, in the car on the ride from the airport. Holding Jessie in his arms and praying she would stay there forever had helped, she was like a balm for his soul, but now they had one day—less than a day, really—to try to make sense of their worlds again before Jessie lit back out for Belgium.

Once inside the large room, which Deirdre had updated with a new four-poster bed and tasteful but feminine bed coverings, Josh didn't hesitate. He went straight to the ensuite washroom at the south end, stepped inside, gripped the edges of the sink, and shook.

More than anything, he longed for a drink to numb the ache, but Josh was keenly aware that he and Jessie were already skating on thin ice. No way was that an option. Not even close. It was like the time he broke his wrist—well, Wes broke it for him—and because of Josh's addictions history he wasn't given meds to ease the pain. This new-old pain, too, would have to be suffered naked and bare, so that Josh was exposed and vulnerable instead of insulated and protected.

By the time Jessie made it upstairs ten minutes later, Josh was a puddle on the floor. He couldn't hold it in any longer. The hotel, the plane, the car—they were interminable. Trying to maintain a brave face at the Grammys, on the jet—in front of the Keatings, their security, his children—had been damn near impossible. Josh needed to let go, and so he did.

Standing just inside the bedroom, Jessie heard him sobbing—great, gasping sobs that tore at her heart. Reaching behind her, where Matt was following with her bag, she met his eye and whispered, "Thank you," before closing the door on him.

He nodded at her, his way of saying *It's okay, I understand,* and although Matt was glad Josh would have Jessie next to him now, quieter, calmer, still head over heels in love, he couldn't help but wish that he could take *her* in his arms and soothe her great hurts too.

Inside, the door now closed, Jessie let out a long breath and tiptoed over to the washroom door. Carefully, she depressed the handle and, with two fingers, pushed the door enough so that it opened and she could move inside. Bending before her husband, who was sitting against the shower with both knees drawn up and his fists in his eyes, she grasped his wrists.

Embarrassed but unable to stop the great cries that insisted on cleansing him, Josh twisted his head away from her and tried to remove her grip from his wrists.

"Josh," Jessie started, "we can work through this. We can, and we will."

"I'm such a fuck up, Jessie," he told her through a clenched jaw. "How am I any good for you or the kids? We can't even go home."

"They'll get tired of us eventually. Some other poor bugger will make a mistake and become their next victim."

After shoving the bathroom door shut in case Dee or Carlotta or one of the kids, who were now entertaining their grandmother in the playroom, decided to stroll in and accidentally see Josh in such rough shape, Jessie twisted her body around and settled next to him. "I can send you a yellow card if that helps."

"I have one," he managed. "But thanks."

"You still have it?"

"You bet," he sniffled, his voice raspy. "I'm never giving that away."

Leaning her head on his shoulder, wrapping her arm around his and taking his fingers in hers, Jessie smiled. "Seems like so long ago now."

"Like a lifetime," he said, sobered at the highs and lows of the last many years.

"Are you going to be okay, Josh? Can I go to Brussels and finish this film and know that you'll be okay? Deirdre's already managing the shit out of the whole Grammy thing."

"I don't care about the outside world," he breathed. "I need your help with Emily-Grace, that's all. And David too, I guess, at least as much as we can tell a four year old."

"Almost five," Jessie smiled. "I'll be home on time for his birthday. And yes, I'll corner our daughter at bedtime and try to help her understand why we're not at home, and why the next little bit might be a little tough at school."

"You know Jess, no matter how I try to package this in my head it still comes out all messed up. Losing you...the kids when they're older, hating their father..."

"When they're older they will understand better how tough you had it."

"So you're not still mad."

"Of course I am. I'm pissed. But I look into those sad eyes of yours and I melt, still, Josh." Reaching for his chin, Jessie turned his face towards hers. She was right. The liquid chocolate sadness crushed her. "See?" she whispered. "Look at me. I'm a mushy mess."

The corner of one of his lips turned up, just a tiny bit. "Will you be okay in Brussels?"

"I don't intend to go there and worry the last two weeks away, if that's what you mean. I'm sure the producers are already concerned about whether I'll be distracted. But I do need to know you will be okay here."

"I will be," Josh answered honestly. "I promise you that."

"For the kids."

"Yes. You have my word."

"Charles said he's not worried about the series, Josh. He knows what you were up against in L.A."

"And Jonathon?"

She shrugged. "He's your dad. Stay sober and he'll be fine. Charlie will be there to help you through any tough days. And once we get the songs recorded here, the kids and I will ride your ass too."

"All right. Okay." A deep inhalation followed by a slow exhale did wonders for Josh's emotional state. "We'll be okay, then, you and me."

"Always," Jessie said.

"And forever," Josh added, settling lower against the wall and leaning his head against hers. He couldn't help but add, in a subdued tone, "Has Matt changed his mind? Is he going with you?"

Jessie paused. It had physically hurt to shut Matt out of their bedroom earlier. Loyal, dependable Matt. "No," she said quietly. "He is staying here to keep an eye on you and the kids."

"Jesus, Jessie, is it that serious with him? That he can't be with you?"

"I trust him with our lives, Josh. And right now there are four of you and one of me. That's why he's staying," she half-lied. "Please don't start anything with him."

Josh was silent. After bit, he lifted his wife's hand and brushed his lips against it.

She let out a slow breath. "Dee is putting a movie on for the kids. I told her I was coming upstairs for a nap but she knew better. Come on. Let's grab one last snuggle before the craziness of dinner and bedtime. You know we'll both pass out when we hit the sheets tonight."

It didn't take any more convincing than that. Jessie pulled Josh to her on the bed where she used to make love with Jacob when they spent time at La Casa. "I love you so much," she murmured as she felt his body sigh into hers. "So much, Josh. Please be okay."

He didn't answer, and pushed up her top instead.

Soon her breasts were free and Jessie's breath was ragged and hurried. Even after all this time, she still cherished making love with him, and now they had even more reason to connect, so as Josh moved down her body, taking her jeans with him, Jessie closed her eyes and focused on his touch. They didn't take long. With three small children, they had learned to make love efficiently and with a few laughs tossed in.

It wasn't a problem for either to reach climax—with serious intent on pushing the intensity of the last few days away, and another ending during the grey light of dawn tomorrow morning, Josh and Jessie needed this. They needed to part as friends and as a loving husband and wife. With those roots securely in place to anchor them, they could figure out the rest later.

"You are not alone, Josh Sawyer," Jessie told him afterwards, as he lay his head on her chest and waited for his heart rate to return to normal. "You are not alone because no matter where I am in the world, I am with you. Always."

Too emotional to answer, Josh reached for her hand and held it. There would never be a substitute for the love of this woman. Ever. If she left, if they decided they couldn't hang on after the chaos Morgan and Nadia left for them to muddle through, a messed up Jacob included, there would only be a new black hole, an endless vortex of misery.

That night, with the house in darkness and most of the household asleep, a quiet cry from the nursery down the hall awoke the very tired sleeping parents. Josh kissed Jessie softly. "I'll get him, you need to get up early," he said, and slipped out of bed.

"Josh," Jessie mumbled, still half-asleep, "I can sleep on the jet. You have to be awake for these rug rats all day." But she didn't move, and Josh shook his head with a chuckle as he heard Jessie start to snore.

"Coming, little guy," he murmured as he pulled on pajama pants and padded quietly down the hallway.

A quick scan and Josh saw that Emily-Grace and David were off in what appeared to be contented sleepyland slumber. Dylan was the culprit, which Josh knew he would be, based on the child's low whimper. "Hey," he said, as Dylan's cries grew more tragic with the approach of his father. "What's the matter, buddy?"

Picking him up, he frowned. "Ah. Somebody else in our family is feeling the stress. Either that or potty training is over rated, isn't it, Dylan?"

"Daddy, I peed," Dylan moaned, his big Jacob-eyes wide and worried.

"I see that," Josh smiled. He kissed the boy he considered his son on the forehead. "Don't you worry," he told him. "Daddy will fix that right up and then I'll bring you in bed with me and Momma, okay?"

His little body shaking, Dylan nodded. "Daddy fix me up," he repeated, his entire body trusting Josh to do what was right by him, his soul feeling safe and loved.

"How about we run a warm bath?" Josh suggested. "And we'll get some fresh jammies."

When Jessie awoke again ten minutes later, Josh still wasn't back in bed. Yawning, she sat on the end of the bed and stretched, then headed down the hall towards the nursery. What she saw before her was an incredible husband and father, whistling quietly as he removed Dylan's soiled sheets. Staying back so he wouldn't see her, Jessie watched as Josh disappeared inside the small bathroom attached to the room and emerged with their youngest son wrapped in a big white fluffy towel.

Her heart almost stopped when Dylan said, "Sing me, Daddy."

"Ah. Okay," Josh agreed as he set Dylan on the bed and proceeded to dry him and dress him in fresh pajamas. A few months earlier Josh would have said, "You know, your other daddy is a much better singer," but tonight he just paused and then started in on *You Are My Sunshine*, which Dylan loved, judging by the sweet smile lighting up his eyes as he gazed at Josh with unequalled adoration. Josh got half the words wrong and, watching, Jessie had to stifle her laughter with the sleeve of the hoodie she'd tossed on before leaving the bedroom.

Never thought I would see Josh sing to Dylan, she thought inwardly, *but I would pay millions to repeat this concert forever.*

Against her will, because she wanted to spy longer and watch this father and son bond more, Jessie snuck back into her bedroom and feigned sleep when Josh padded in a few minutes later with a sleepy, contented Dylan in his arms.

Josh laid their son in the bed facing his mother, and crawled in behind him. Jessie blinked open her eyes and smiled at Dylan, wrapped an arm around his small body as he cuddled into her, and kissed him lightly on one pink cheek. Then she looked over at Josh as he settled on his pillow, and she winked mischievously.

"We'll have to work on that second verse," she joked.

"I think I need to learn some new songs," Josh grinned. *I draw the line at Jacob's,* he thought, but wisely kept it to himself.

"I think you do too." She laid a palm against his cheek before returning it to Dylan's already slumbering body. "When I get back, okay?"

"Promises, promises," Josh challenged with a light chuckle. "Just come back," he added. "Just come back, Jessie."

"I will," she said. "As long as you want me back."

"Always and forever," he whispered, and kept his gaze tenderly on the diaphanous blue eyes he loved until fatigue won the battle, and Jessie drifted off to sleep.

Chapter Seventeen

The chaos outside the UBC home settled when it became clear that the Sawyer family wasn't going to make an appearance. One by one the television media packed up their video cameras, and the paparazzi their long lenses. Josh moved the children home three days before Jessie was due home from Brussels. With Charles' advice he still had not spent any time on the Internet, so the transition into the world's 'bad boy' again was less painful for him than it might have been. The hardest part to deal with was the children, namely Emily-Grace although David was starting to understand as well that there was something different about his father that people did not always respond well to.

Matt helped. Despite himself, Josh found himself ducking his head and keeping his cool when Matt was around, mostly for the sake of the kids. Discussions often centered around Jessie, and Matt was often a quiet part of them. Part of the reason to keep cool, too, was that Matt's daughter Katy often babysat the kids, usually with Dan around although sometimes with her own father present to keep a watchful security-focused eye.

Against Matt's better judgment, Josh went out alone to pick Jessie up at the airport. Josh had taken to avoiding public stops apart from getting gas, picking up or dropping off the kids at school, and dropping by ROAM, where he felt he had been a regular for so long that judgment might be a little slower in coming. But even at ROAM, things were tense. It seemed everybody had seen the videos of his rampage in L.A. and so Josh was on many radars. The day Jessie came home, he planned to stop at ROAM just briefly and then go to the gate at the airport, although he was considering taking Jessie for a

163

drive up Cypress Mountain to their favorite overlook, just to reconnect and snuggle, and maybe even make love if she was up for it.

Matt let him go without a word. They'd managed to get through the two weeks without a single harsh word or look between them, and today was not the day to start bossing Josh around. If anything, Matt was grateful for some quiet time with the children who felt like his own.

When Josh stepped out onto the deck, he looked back to close the sliding door and saw Matt framed there, Dylan in his arms and the other two at his feet, coloring. He seemed so natural there that it gave Josh a start.

Glancing up, Matt caught the look. "It's okay," he said, slightly startled at the fear in Josh's eyes. "It's okay."

One nod, a nervous swallow, and Josh strode down the back deck towards the flagstones, truck keys dangling from one hand.

At the airport, he sipped on a coffee from ROAM and watched the jet taxi in for a landing. What would Jessie's arrival home bring? More tension? The Grammys fallout was easing off although, like anything on the Internet, Josh knew he could never eradicate the incident entirely. The past few weeks were extremely lonely. Matt was around, yes, but he was no longer a trusted confidante. Their friendship was warped, different, if Josh could even still consider it a friendship, which he kind of didn't anymore. Charles and Dee were back to playing it cool. Charlie and Steve were the old standbys, and Josh did manage to spend some time with Charlie, but Steve was working on a film in California now, so he wasn't around, although he called when he could.

Now, Josh took stock of the fallout and realized he'd come out not too badly, considering. Charles and Jonathon were keeping him on the series, although Josh was apprehensive about how well that would go, and he credited Jessie for likely sticking up for him. Charles Keating would do anything for his girl, even if it meant retaining her husband in a part that he could easily handle, but which he might screw up by virtue of relapsing into substance abuse or by losing his temper.

This rankled on Josh too, Jessie's influence. Was he grateful for her? Hell, yeah! But Josh knew in his heart that he now had this part only because of his association with Jessie, and that if it weren't for her, it would have skidded out from under him quicker than a young child's blade on ice for the first time. Charlie knew this too. So Josh's visits to the Southlands ranch, where he spent more and more time in the quiet, accepting company of the troubled horse, Blue, were often fairly silent. For certain, any conversation deeper than a generic 'hello,' and 'how's she doing,' and 'goodbye,' were readily avoided by both men.

Blue...the horse. She was Josh's closest confidante and connection during the troubled first few weeks after the Grammys. She was a steady, reliable, non-judgmental trusted friend who accepted Josh for who he was, who didn't ask questions, and who let him rub her and run his hands through her mane and over her body without fear of reprisal.

Sitting in the pickup watching the jet land, Josh took a sip of his drip coffee. After his initial breakdown at La Casa, he had settled into a low depression, a new numbness, and today was no better than the last. It was like he had given the dark night at the Grammys all the fight he had left.

In the mug holder in the center console sat a mocha for Jessie, always a part of their homecoming routine of late. He would swing back by ROAM and get her another if she found this one too cold, but Josh wasn't anxious to go back there. The baristas tried, he knew, but the stares from the patrons— some downright hostile—made him miserably uncomfortable.

The worst part? Josh was well aware that his hotheaded actions had caused this paradigm shift in his world, in his family's world. Maybe there just was no real coming back from the Morgan and Nadia days, from Jacob's involvement in their lives. Even if Jacob didn't stay involved with Dylan, the guy was like a tumor in a kidney, impossible to remove unless the whole kidney went with him.

The door to the jet swung open and the stairs folded down and settled on the tarmac. Moments later, a tired Jessie stepped out and stopped at the top. A cool breeze picked up and swooshed her hair around but she ignored it. Her eyes were on the metallic grey King Ranch parked at the edge of the lot by the fence, and its driver, who was watching her from inside the safety of his vehicle.

Quietly, Josh set his coffee into the vacant cup holder where it snuggled next to Jessie's mocha, and he levered open the big door. By the time he was outside and had slammed the door behind him, Jessie was walking carefully towards him, a computer bag slung over her shoulder and both thumbs tucked into her jeans' pockets. If Josh was hoping to assess her mood, he was shit out of luck because his wife was wearing an implacable expression. It seemed she was too busy studying him and trying to read his mood to relax and let her own show.

They met halfway between the jet and his truck, and stopped six feet away from each other. Josh was wearing his security jacket—the vintage dark green leather one with sleeves that fell over his knuckles. Underneath was a simple zip-up black hoodie. Jessie found her eyes immediately landing on it, and something akin to desire flashed across them, alighting the sea-pearl blues in a way that Josh loved and missed. He exhaled, and let his shoulders droop.

A slight upturn of Jessie's lips telegraphed that she was relaxing too. Shifting her weight to one foot, she said simply, "Coffee?"

"Mocha," he answered, and let a tiny grin escape. Josh licked his lips nervously and watched her for cues.

"How long?"

"Half hour."

"Will do."

"Good."

A pregnant pause stayed their movement temporarily. Then Jessie blushed, ducked her head, and moved towards her husband, who took a half step forward and, with a deep exhale and a low contented *ahhhh,* gathered her into his arms.

"Drive?" he asked.

"Kids okay?"

"Matt and Katy are making them pizza."

"Okay. Good."

Josh looked behind Jessie. Arnie was making his way towards them, his boxer's physique easily handling her large suitcase as well as his own bag, which he'd hoisted up onto one shoulder. Letting go of his wife, Josh strode forward to help.

"Good trip?" Josh asked him.

"Too many sad songs," Arnie replied. "Take her home and give her some cuddles, will you, Josh?"

"It's going to be an amazing film, Josh," Jessie said, picking up the pace to walk beside Arnie and Josh, "but Arnie couldn't handle the sadness."

"And you could?" Arnie asked, biting his tongue the second the words were out.

She didn't miss a beat, but her voice quaked a little with the response. "Oh, it wasn't a problem for me, Arnie. I'm used to it."

The words choked Josh, and he looked to his right to gauge how much of the comment was in jest. By her somber expression, it didn't seem any of it was. He swallowed uncomfortably, waved 'so long' to Arnie, and lifted Jessie's large bag into the bed of the truck.

Jessie sensed his sadness too, and she was emotionally and physically drained after the long shoot and the inherent drama that seemed to dog the whole thing. But after saying goodbye to Arnie, she walked around to the front of the truck, where Josh was leaning against the grill waiting for her, and she placed her feet in a wide stance, hooked both sets of fingers over his belt, and faced him.

He couldn't help but smile, just a bit. With the shorter hair and large curls, a tight tan leather jacket, and a low cut floral top, she was, in Josh's opinion, adorable. Allowing a hand to rise up and brush a wisp of hair off her cheek, he waited to see what she had to say.

"I was…talking to Charlie," she started.

Josh's smile did a flip.

"He said you've been pretty quiet. Except as far as Blue is concerned. Apparently she got a lot of your attention while I was gone."

Josh was silent. Jessie melted as his tender gaze drifted over her body and ended locked in her eyes. His hair, too, was blowing in the breeze. Lifting a hand, he sighed tiredly and rifled his fingers through the long layers.

"Okay," Jessie started again, her heart picking up its pace. "I so want to go to bed with you right now."

The comment resulted in a parting of his lips, but Josh didn't speak. The lips closed again and he shifted his stance. And waited.

As if she needed to clear some cobwebs, Jessie shook her head and refocused. "So. Back to Charlie. He was worried but he said you had a good few weeks."

"Meaning I didn't get drunk or get into any bad shit. Considering the hell of the media circus currently around our family thanks to me."

Jessie chose to wisely skirt the subject. "Emily-Grace had a good few weeks in school?"

"She did fine. Matt had to tune her teacher in, though. That woman shouldn't be teaching."

"What did she do?"

"She showed the kids the video of me losing it."

"They're in grade two!"

Josh cleared his throat. "Emily-Grace wasn't there at the time. That was the first day, and if you recall, we kept the kids at La Casa until we had a chance to talk to the school."

Jessie's voice got small. Tears pricked her eyes. "She's okay, though?"

"Meaning with me, you mean?"

"Yeah. With you."

"She stuck pretty close to Matt while you were away. When he was around."

"Ah. I see. So the horse became your best friend."

"She reminds me of you. Troubled eyes." Josh used two fingers to gesture to his own eyes.

"Troubled eyes. You think I have troubled eyes?"

"The way you are looking at me right now, yes. I do."

"Because I'm worried about the man I love more than life itself. I want to disappear inside you and just curl up there." The tears were tough to beat, but Jessie stirred up her courage and shoved them away. She was home now. Things were settling. Josh needed her, and she needed him.

"Okay," Josh said, not moving, just watching, studying. "C'mere."

They didn't know it, but there was a smart paparazzo that snuck his long lens into the secure compound where everyone knew the Keating jet usually landed. He did it via a cousin who loaned him an orange vest and an ID badge. Now, the guy lowered his camera. He'd expected to see Josh and Jessie fighting, but it was clear, in his vision, that they were still crazy in love. Raising the camera again, he snapped a few photos of them kissing tenderly, amazed at how long they stood in each other's arms just holding on tight, Jessie's face buried in the familiar curve of her husband's neck.

When they finally separated and the King Ranch pulled out, the paparazzo knew he could make a killing on photos of where they went. But he was a good guy, and chose not to follow. It was obvious the Sawyers wanted—and needed—some time alone. They sure as hell deserved it.

Josh didn't even ask. He pointed the truck north on the 99 and cruised over to North Van, stopping for Nanaimo bars at Lansdowne Quay on the way. They ate them on the way up Cypress Mountain, not speaking, just listening to the radio and holding hands when they could. When a Jacob Ryan tune came on, Jessie steeled herself and switched the station, although Josh had a tense moment wondering if she was about to turn up the volume.

They made the overlook on Cypress in good time. There were a few tourists around, but Josh knew where the best place to park was, so he maneuvered the truck to a private area, and switched off the ignition.

Smiling now, licking her fingers and taking one last sip of the now cool mocha, Jessie looked admirably at the view—the sprawling, mountain hugged, hippie city of Vancouver, spread below them—then set down her cup and wiped her sticky fingers on her jeans.

"Push back your seat," she ordered her husband and, after he obliged, she climbed onto his lap and undid his belt. "I love you," she whispered, straddling him. "I'm home. Let's just love each other, okay Josh? No more stress. No more worries and no more jealousies. Just you and me, in love like always, raising our three children and making love as often as we can."

Undoing her jeans for her, Josh slipped a hand inside her panties and sucked in a breath when she gasped, spread her legs wider, and buried her face in his chest.

"Oh fuck, I missed this," she moaned as he started to move his fingers in the sweet dampness he found there, for him. Riding him as much as she could with her jeans on and his fingers pleasuring her, Jessie bent to Josh's lips and bit the bottom one. Their lovemaking increased in intensity until her jeans had to come off and she eased down onto him. The outside world disappeared as they built to a satisfying climax, regardless of the fact that some tourists were now wandering around wondering what the two folks in the big truck were up to.

When they were done, Jessie collapsed against Josh and laid her head against his shoulder. "Your heart is racing," she murmured, and only then, in the silence that followed, did she realize that he hadn't spoken the entire time they made love, nor did he now. His eyes were damp, but he was under control, she could see. He was just quiet, holding her against him and staring out of the windshield at the city below them, which was now dotted with lights, until she disturbed him by needing to pee.

Jessie slipped out of the passenger side door, peed behind its shelter, and put her jeans back on while she was outside. Josh banana'd around the front of the truck and found a tree to empty his bladder under.

He gathered her to him one more time, kissed the top of her head, and dreaded the day he would go to Alberta to shoot the series. Jessie was Josh's rock, and he needed to be hers. Separations sucked, period.

"C'mon little one," he finally said. "Let's go see your babies."

And Matt, Jessie caught herself thinking. She chided herself for thinking it and then added, for good measure, *my best friend, apart from this quiet man at my side.*

But Josh knew. He knew Jessie and Matt had been joined at the hip much of the time over the last many years, and he wasn't soon to forget her comment about him at their hotel after the Grammys, the one where she referred to Matt as a drug she craved.

*Jacob, Matt, Dylan...Jacob's music on the radio...Kayla disappearing down south to be with Jacob...*Josh didn't relax into the drive back home until a single image flitted across his mind, that of a troubled horse with a white blaze and the saddest eyes he'd ever seen, apart from Jessie's.

Blue was her name, and at the time, she felt like the only woman Josh could truly trust.

Chapter Eighteen

𝒜 pale rose hue flowing into an inky sky backlit the Keating Building on Robson when Matt pulled in a few weeks later. He was a break-of-dawn riser most days, and since there were a lot of details to sort today with Charles' imminent regular travels to Calgary for the series, *Sacred Peace*, and an upcoming Sawyer family household move to the Alberta ranch, Matt had a lot on his plate. The best time to catch Charles was always early morning. Usually La Casa was the chosen spot for a breakfast meeting, but today there were files they needed to access at the downtown office. Magda, too, had come in early to help out. The dark beauty was a whiz at locating 'lost' files and managing the frustrating high-tech photocopier.

Whistling, Matt punched the '31' button in the elevator and leaned against the back wall for the ride upstairs. He was carrying a tray of hot coffee from Elysian on West Broadway; decent coffee from freshly roasted beans was worth driving out of the way for. Plus Elysian had the best and biggest lemon-cranberry muffins in the city. Holding a paper bag in one hand, Matt could feel the warmth of the moist muffins soaking through—comfort personified. Joking with himself, he compared the anticipation of sitting down with his breakfast with the anticipation haloing Jessie's comment at the Grammys that someday he and she would finish what they started.

Immediately, Matt chided himself. For one, the thought caused instant discomfort in the groin region that he had no desire to carry around with him all day. For two, since she'd been home from Brussels, she and Josh seemed dedicated to trying to work through their issues. The only hindrance seemed to be the increased time she was spending at the downtown workshops, working with Benjie and the twins to fulfill Kayla's dream while Kayla remained conspicuously absent. Matt had stopped in a few times to see how things were going. However, Jessie was adamant about decreasing his time in her company—she preferred to see him with the kids at school, or on their outings. Part of this was her middle finger sticking it to the media after the Grammys disaster—keeping her kids protected from photo ops— and part of it was her need to keep some distance between herself and Matt as she tried to sort things out with her husband.

The few times he did drop in to the workshops, Matt found Jessie exhausted but happy. The film in Brussels had become very personal, and he could see the darkness starting to dissipate the more she spent time in the company of the excited Downtown Eastside gang who, in a few short weeks, would embark on their first big cross-country tour. For Jessie, dancing was key, and music was key. Both the physical exertion and the creative outlet were bringing Jessie back to herself. No more forlorn bluegrass / gospel music about the loss of a child and the breakdown of a marriage. Now she danced to upbeat, happy tunes, and it showed in Jessie's everyday relationships.

Josh was another matter. He hadn't yet come out of the funk from the weekend at the Grammys. More and more, he seemed to be quietly disappearing inside himself, although he spent a lot of time with the children, especially Dylan, whom he catered to during the days when the older two were at school and Jessie was at the workshops. This worked well because Josh was still doing character research for his new modern gunslinger part in Charles' and Charlie's series, and there were lines to learn and the household move to coordinate. He was bringing Blue with him, so that was taking some forward thinking too. Josh hoped to trailer the troubled horse and drive her to the Alberta ranch the same day the workshop tour hit the road.

The observations about Josh were Matt's own. He did not speak to Charles or Deirdre about increased concerns for Jessie's husband, nor did he have any desire to bring his worries up to Jessie. But he was well aware that she was watching Josh like a hawk when she was home. Her voice was always low and tender around him, and her hand was always touching a shoulder, an elbow, his fingers. The way Jessie moved around Josh reminded Matt of a mother with a child. Josh needed forgiveness, love and understanding if he was to remain sober, if he was to regain the already fragile self-esteem he lost with his temper on that fateful day. What he didn't need was Jessie losing it with him again; avoiding him and judging him with threats and snide remarks.

So far it seemed to be working. Despite Matt's own deep love for Jessie, earned over many years of watching the way she carried herself through life—with love and kindness, despite tragedy—he was humbled as he watched her care for her husband.

Josh was completely capable of fulfilling any and every need the children had, and he participated fully in parenting them. When Jessie—usually tailed by Big Dan, and sometimes tailed by their finally newfound security, Sam, a young, fit ex-U.S. Olympian (cycling)—took Emily-Grace and David to school, she always kissed Josh and Dylan goodbye and left them to fill their days until she returned with the kids when school let out. She called and texted during the day, usually finding Josh home, but sometimes she would locate him at the Southlands ranch, where he and Dylan often hung out with Charlie, Jack or Lydia, whoever happened to be around, and where he visited Blue.

Jessie had remarked to Matt one day at a La Casa Sunday dinner, "Josh and Dylan are attached at the hip."

True, their bond, with Jessie away for six weeks and now at the workshops most days, had grown and strengthened. Dylan adored his mother but it was Josh he wanted at bath time, to rock him to sleep, to cuddle or to play with him. And after Josh returned from solo drives or solitary meetings about the series at La Casa, Josh migrated to Dylan the second he was in the door.

"I don't know what it is about the two of them," Deirdre remarked to Jessie that same Sunday night. "They have a secret language."

"I know what it is," Jessie had told both her and Matt at the time. "It's loneliness. Dylan knows something—someone's—missing from his life, and Josh is still just feeling lost and scared after…well…after everything."

She'd been almost too scared to look at him after saying that, Matt recalled. And when Jessie had finally met his eyes, he saw a flicker of sorrow there. For what, he wasn't sure, but he knew it had to do with him. Josh was, and always would be, Jessie's heart, however unreachable or sad or hurt. And Matt was Jessie's anchor, her safe place, a steady voice in her ear, her protector.

Apples and oranges.

Now, Matt stopped whistling long enough to give Magda her coffee and a warm muffin. Continuing down the hall towards Charles' office, he picked up a new tune and tried to push Jessie from his mind. Never in a million years, until Julie's jealous speculation, had he seriously considered any kind of physical relationship with Jessie. She was everything to him, he had figured that out very early on when the Keatings first brought him on board to watch over their sweet waif, but in the early days Matt found himself simply captivated by her, by Jessie's endless capacity to swath those around her in love and light, even though she barely spoke in those early days. It was her music, but it was also her essence—scared, sad, lonely, even in Charlie's company back then.

Over the years Matt found her an easy celebrity to watch over, until she started rebelling against her fame somewhat and taking off on her own. He and Charles and Dee had no choice but to let her do her own thing in those days. Then when she started working with Josh on *Drifters*, something changed within her. A new light came from deep in her soul, and it attached itself to the sad guy with full-blown love and acceptance. When Deuce McCall came to town and things went awry, and Jessie disappeared, Matt felt like his soul had caved in and gone missing too. The others did too, they all mourned her loss with an intensity borne of deep love and friendship, but it was only then that Matt had begun to realize what Jessie meant to him, and to him alone.

Still, it wasn't a physical desire, even then. It was a soul kind of love.

Afterwards, with the ups and downs in Jessie and Josh's relationship, and the birth of their first child, Matt had felt like a parent and grandparent. When he left the Keating employ out of fear of not being able to protect the Sawyer family because of Jessie's insistence on continuously going rogue, his heart broke anew. Jessie was a light in his life and, by then, Julie was clearly seeing this. Julie was the one who put her finger on the truth—that her husband adored this singer and actor in a way that left him bereft and hurting when not in her company.

Matt…loved her.

It was in Florida that the truth really hit Matt. Lying behind her, spooning

Jessie and her daughter, keeping them safe on a night when her visit to Jacob had gone totally haywire, had confused him, although he still didn't consider it a desire for physical love at the time. Instead, he had on his hands a broken woman who Matt found in equal parts absorbing, rebellious, spiteful, loving and...beautiful. Jessie was a beautiful woman, and the older she got, the more stunning she became. It came from that light she carried within, the one that always tried to believe in hope when things got bad. It came from her music. It came from her spirit.

Now? After what happened in Brussels, how did Matt feel about her? Did he have hope that the night she intimated might happen between them would ever come to fruition? No. Not seriously.

Matt was almost to Charles' door now. He tried to push the unacceptable thought away. Josh's fear of losing Jessie was always palpable, even though Matt was aware that some of that fear was because Josh's sister Kayla was telling him he needed to be the one to leave.

It had occurred to Matt more than once that maybe, just maybe, he and Jessie could have just one night...or maybe two...He refused to tell himself he deserved it after all the years of grief she gave him. He buried that notion in some deep, dark place. Matt would take what the universe gave him, and right now he was just relieved to have her nearby again, for hugs or for the occasional light touch and, of course, for that light again. But...sometimes the way she looked at him...like that Sunday night at La Casa when she was talking about Josh...it was like she was telling him that she loved him too, but she had this broken man to cherish and care for, who needed her more. The look was in some ways apologetic. It was truth. Matt had simply swallowed, gripped the edge of the kitchen island, and nodded.

I get it, he had said in silence to her. *I can wait.*

Outside Charles' door now, Matt paused and knocked.

"Come in, Matt," a gruff voice welcomed him.

Charles. He may as well have been Jessie's father, both for their history and for the way Matt looked up to and respected him. Rather imposing at the best of times, he was sitting behind his big desk with reading glasses perched on his nose and the usual impeccable cranberry silk tie—this one with tiny gray stripes—over an expensively cut white dress shirt.

Charles was looking down, studying something on the desk in front of him as Matt set down the remaining two coffees and the muffins, dropped into a wide chair, and inserted his hand into the muffin bag, which crackled contentedly at his motion.

"Here," he said to his boss, retrieving his breakfast and pushing the noisy bag towards Charles. "Eat something."

"Not hungry," Charles replied, and reached a hand up to his neck to loosen his tie. "We have to get through this anyway, Matt. No time to eat."

"You need to slow down, Charles." Matt raised his eyebrows. Charles had yet to look up at him. "You need fuel. Eat something or your wife will rap my knuckles."

"Yes, yes, I will, I..." Charles finally raised his head. A damp sheen of sweat lined his forehead and lay across his upper lip. Matt's heart rate picked up. "I've got some kind of bug," he said. "Feeling a little nauseous today, Matt."

"You're burning the candle at both ends with this new series, Charles. Why don't you let me see what I can sort out today, while you go home and take a day off?"

Brushing a hand over his mostly balding head, Charles let out a quick breath. "Let's see...this thing with Josh has really set us back. Let's talk about that for a bit and I'll see if I can't sneak home for a nap this afternoon. Or maybe this morning," he added, as a wave of nausea crumpled him over.

Matt tensed. Setting his coffee down, he pulled his chair in closer. "We'll be in Calgary, Charles, not in L.A. The media has, for the most part, let up on Josh, I think largely thanks in part to that paparazzo at the airport who got the shots of Josh and Jessie the day she got home. Our biggest issue with *Sacred Peace* will likely be supervising the movement of Jessie and the kids when they arrive."

"How is Sam doing? In your opinion?"

"He's great. The kids love their new 'friend.'" Matt raised his hands in finger quotes. "He tosses them around like footballs."

"So he's a great babysitter. What about the school? Is he bored out of his tree?"

"He's making it work. Takes the time to stroll the grounds and stays out of the kids' way at recess and lunch. We had one incident with Emily-Grace and that same kid that likes to get a rise out of her, and it drove Sam nuts not to be able to help her, but he gets why things need to be that way."

"So he's already attached to one of the Sawyer women." Despite his discomfort, Charles managed a wry grin in Matt's direction.

"Likely to both," Matt groaned. "Keep him away from Jessie."

Sitting back, Charles studied his old friend. "I need to ask you something, Matt, and I want you to be honest with me."

Matt poked the last mouthful of muffin into his mouth and grabbed his coffee cup. "Why don't I like the sound of this?" he asked after chewing, swallowing, and biting one corner of his lip.

"Look, Matt, we're doing okay here. You and Josh and Jessie seem to be on some kind of even keel again, at least. And your personal life is none of my business, but where Jessie is concerned, well, she's not really personal, is she? For you? She's business."

"That's a departure from the 'just go to Brussels and have your two weeks' shtick I got from Deirdre, Charles."

"Look, I know how deep your feelings for her run. And they are clearly reciprocated. But I'm going into this series with Josh, who we all know is still really struggling to figure out where he and Jessie fit, and I can't help but picture a bomb about to go off."

The image chilled Matt. "No, look, Charles, you don't need to worry about me and Jessie. We know our boundaries. She's crazy in love with her husband—"

"Matt, I'm not talking about love here. Okay?" The man's voice was hard now, and his hand slammed onto the desk as if he was desperate for Matt to understand what he needed to say. "I'm talking about sex."

"What? Charles, I—"

"Listen, goddamnit. Matt, we all know Jessie's background. We know now that she worked for that black box studio, doing those erotic photos and films. We've seen the photos, we don't know what the hell ever happened to the films and we hope they never see the light of day. But Matt...even though apart from Jacob we think she's been faithful to Josh, I don't think she's had the temptation apart from, well, apart from you. In a while. I don't think she cheated on Charlie, either, although why the hell not I sometimes wonder. I just..."

Straightening, Matt interjected. He raised a palm and held it out to face his boss. "Charles…are you saying what I think you're saying?" He, too, felt sickened all of a sudden.

"I'm saying that given Jessie's background on the Downtown Eastside, three small children, and the strain between her and Josh since Christmas, and really, since long before that, that I can see where your obvious mutual feelings could easily end up in an ongoing sexual relationship."

"A sexual relationship. Jesus, Charles. She's not a—"

"I'm not calling her a whore, Matt."

"Actually, you pretty much just did, Charles, by virtue of including her time on the Downtown Eastside. I have to tell you, I'm rather disgusted." Matt's ire was rising but he immediately felt terrible, because it was obvious Charles really wasn't feeling well. He was now an odd shade of green and seemed to be leaning uncomfortably on one folded arm on his desk.

Charles sighed heavily, the weight of the world on his shoulders. "Maybe what I am saying is that it likely wouldn't be a big stretch for her to take that leap. That's all."

"Jesus Christ." Shoving back his chair, Matt stood. "First of all, give me some credit, Charles. I haven't pushed her, nor will I." Jessie in Brussels, at his door, crossed his mind, and he looked away, hoping that Charles wouldn't see the sheer lust at the memory cross over his face. Matt clearly recalled being the one to push her away that time, even though earlier she had told him 'they' couldn't happen. "I respect her. She's trying to reconnect with Josh."

"Matt, Jessie is going to be here for two weeks while Josh is in Alberta. You and her will no longer be separated as much, because we are going to need you here. *I'm* going to need you *here*," he said again. "What I don't need is my actor imploding just as we get this series going."

"I thought I was going to Calgary with you, Charles," Matt started, curious, and now growing increasingly anxious. "Charles, I think we should take a trip to the emergency room. I've never seen you like this."

"That's what I'm saying, Matt," Charles growled. "I don't think I'm going to be going to Calgary to supervise the series, at least not right away, if I get there at all. Matt, I think I'm having a heart attack."

"Jesus Christ!" Matt exclaimed for the second time in just a few minutes.

Charles was now almost lying on the desk. "I'm calling an ambulance." Yanking out his phone, he sprinted to the door of the expansive office. "Magda! Magda!"

She appeared at the end of the long hallway just as the 911 operator answered. "I need you!" he cried, and at the urgency in his voice she came running.

He whipped back around in time to see his boss try to rise, and instead start to collapse. Catching him just on time, Matt laid him on the floor.

"Charles. Charles!" he yelled to no avail.

Magda rushed in with an anguished cry, and bent by Charles and Matt. "I've called 911," he said, his voice earnest and strained. "Let building security know to escort the EMTs up here." As he was barking orders, Matt felt for a pulse. What weak bit fluttered beneath his fingers was quickly fading away. "Hurry!" he demanded. "I'm starting chest compressions and I need you to do mouth-to-mouth. Do you keep any baby aspirins around the office?"

"No," Magda wailed. "Nothing like that." She made her call downstairs to alert security, and took over mouth-to-mouth while Matt counted.

By the time the EMTs arrived ten minutes later with meds and a defibrillator, Charles was still not breathing. Matt and Magda stood back to watch, and prayed.

It took four tries. "I'm not giving up on you, you old bastard," Matt muttered in between prayers where he found himself literally begging God not to take this deeply loved and respected man.

Finally…a ragged breath…Matt almost fell to his knees in gratitude. As it was, he bent over and clutched the arm of the couch against the far wall. Magda grabbed his hand and silently thanked whatever energy the universe had provided that granted a lifesaving heartbeat back to her boss.

As he followed the gurney towards the elevator, Matt spoke quickly to Magda. "Keep this quiet until I get a chance to call Deirdre," he ordered. *And Jessie*, he thought. *Oh Lord. Another downward spiral. Jacob…*The singer, too, was an adopted son of the Keating power couple. Looking upwards, Matt sent another silent prayer forth.

A last look at the stricken Magda, and he disappeared into the elevator. The doors slid shut with an echoing *whoosh*, and Matt and Charles were gone.

Chapter Nineteen

"Ulysses," Matt started, trying to keep the fear out of his voice, "bring Deirdre to the hospital right away. Charles is being transported by ambulance. He's had a heart attack."

"What? Oh, Jesus." Ulysses shoved a palm against his forehead and tried to keep his voice cool. "Matt, I'm at Josh and Jessie's. I'm on school duty today. Sam flew to Houston for two days and Dan just called in sick."

Behind him, Jessie was grabbing the kids' schoolbags. They hovered in mid-flight at the sudden panic in Ulysses' voice as Josh, too, who was helping David zip up his coat, looked up. Catching their eyes each in turn, Ulysses turned his back to them. Stepping outside onto the deck, he spoke more quietly into the phone.

"We don't want to frighten the kids by changing things up," he said to Matt. "But Jessie will want to go to the hospital. We'll leave them at home with Josh for the day."

"Jessie will want Josh with her. Bring the kids to school and I'll hire local security for them. I've got some connections I trust that will do in a pinch. I'll go get Dee. Send Jessie and Josh to emerge right away."

After he disconnected, Ulysses swept back into the home, where Jessie and Josh were frozen, waiting for this new force of nature to be thrown into their path. Taking her husband's hand, Jessie faced Ulysses with stoic reserve.

"It's Charles," Ulysses told them. "He's on his way to the hospital. Heart attack."

Jessie gasped and almost collapsed. Josh wrapped an arm around her shoulders and hugged her to him.

Ulysses quickly changed his stance and jumped in further. "This is what needs to happen."

At the mention of local security to watch the kids at school, both Josh and Jessie panicked. "No," Jessie said. "Only people we know. We can't take a chance, Ulysses. Not after…" She swallowed, remembering that horrid time in the Langley basement. "Someone will get wind of the change. This would be the perfect time for them to swoop in."

"Matt seems to think he can find someone trustworthy."

"Matt's off his rocker. No." Jessie was already on the move. "They're coming with us. Josh, grab Dylan."

They were at the hospital in twenty minutes, not far behind the ambulance. Cursing under his breath, Ulysses scooped David up from his car seat while Jessie grabbed Emily-Grace's hand and Josh picked up Dylan. At the last second, Jessie hooked her fingers over loops on the two older kids' knapsacks. This could be a long day, and they had snacks, lunches and workbooks already packed for the school day that might help keep them occupied.

Inside, Ulysses made some quick enquiries, and insisted on a private room for the celebrity family to cut out the likelihood of gawkers and curious fans. An administrator was called in and the Sawyers were ushered into a vacant boardroom. In time, Matt arrived with one arm around Deirdre's waist, and Carlotta trotting close behind. One look at the terror on Jessie's face and he pivoted back around and went stomping through the halls in search of an update on his boss' condition.

Jessie took the quaking Deirdre in her arms. "He'll be fine," she croaked. "He's a tough old coot."

Josh was supervising all three children, helping them find stuff to do, and trying to keep them from seeing the fear on their mother's and grandmother's faces, but now he looked over at his wife. She met his eyes. A silent cable flitted between them.

Years of marriage and one day we will be separated. It's inevitable.

Jessie closed her eyes as the horrific thought gutted her. With one hand on his hip, and the fingers of the other pinching his lip, Josh crossed the room and grasped his wife's elbow. He pulled her to him and brushed his lips against her neck as she let her body sigh into his.

"One day at a time," he whispered as she trembled. "Hell, one breath at a time, little one."

He hadn't called her little one since the day she came home from Brussels. Jessie wrapped her arms around him and held on for dear life.

Matt had found someone to talk to, who could inform them as a group. The boardroom had walls of glass, with blinds for privacy, but as yet the blinds were pulled up and the family was as exposed as fish in a fishbowl. With one hand on the outside of the door, Matt stopped and watched great love pass between Josh and Jessie.

When she finally let go and stepped back from her husband, over Josh's shoulder Jessie met Matt's eyes. Matt let his hand drop from the handle of the glass door, and he wheeled slowly back around so he could get a grip.

"They'll be okay," he told himself inwardly. "I'm glad."

Unfortunately, Josh caught the tormented expression on Jessie's face and he twisted around to see what—who—she was looking at. He caught sight of Matt just as the man glanced away from Jessie and spun around.

"It's nothing," he heard Jessie murmur as she grasped his hand. "He saw us, that's all. He knows, Josh. Really. He knows what we mean to each other. You don't need to be afraid."

Her much-silent husband studied her. Without speaking, he leaned forward and brushed his lips against her cheek, turned to Deirdre and did the same, and then moved quietly back to the kids at the table, where his first job was to immediately referee a fight between Emily-Grace and David over a dull crayon.

Matt regained control of his emotions, and led a physician into the room. As the grey-haired male doctor started to speak, Matt found himself trying to stay focused on what he was saying, but his worried eyes kept drifting between Jessie and Josh. At the end of the short explanation, which granted them the good news that Charles was conscious and responding, the doctor credited Matt's quick actions for saving Charles' life.

"You and Mr. Keating's assistant, I understand, did CPR and mouth-to-mouth for an extended time."

Hands on his hips, choking on emotion, Matt just nodded. Beside him, Jessie crumpled and Deirdre let out an anguished, relieved cry.

"You saved Mr. Keating's life today, Mr. Kelly. Well done." With that, the physician wheeled around with a promise of hourly updates, and family visits with his patient after tests, when Charles was considered more stable.

Matt didn't dwell on his actions. There would be time later to sink onto the floor on his hands and knees and thank God again for helping him have the sense to act when he needed to.

For now, he had another person on his mind.

He didn't voice the name, Jessie did, and she said it with her gaze fixed on Matt. "Jacob." That was all, just a name, spoken with a voice swollen with barely contained emotion.

This was a bad scare, and Charles still had a fight on his hands. If Jacob cared about the man he considered a second father, he would want to be notified, and he would want to come to Vancouver to see him, to offer what support he could to Deirdre who, pale and wan, had just collapsed into a chair with Carlotta next to her, holding her hand.

"I'll see if I can reach him," Matt muttered to Jessie, touched and troubled at the way she was looking at him now.

You need a hug from me, she seemed to be saying and, by her posture, she appeared almost ready to leap into his arms. *You saved Charles' life.*

He was about to turn to go when he felt her touch his sleeve. Watched by everyone in the room, including a nervous Josh, Matt let Jessie pull him close and hold him as tight as she could, her eyes closed and tiny sobs coming from somewhere deep inside that frightened her, and which hurt him. Slowly, Matt let his arms encircle her waist, and he pressed the much longed-for body against him.

His body was shaking then too, but just a little, because he had to be strong for all of them. He was their unspoken leader, even though technically Ulysses had held the top job since Matt left the Keating camp in Peterborough years earlier. So Matt couldn't let loose and cry the way he felt like crying, even though a small voice he loved was now moaning into his neck, "Thank you, thank you, thank you."

It sure as hell felt good to be held by the one person in the room who recognized that he, Matt Kelly, was also very, very worried about Charles Keating, the man whose life he had just saved, who was, overall, his very good friend.

Kayla and Jacob were just starting to make love in Sarah May's sweet comfort when footsteps rushing down the dock outside stopped and hopped onto their boat.

A face appeared in the open hatchway just as Jacob was shoving Kayla's tank top upwards and burying his lips in her pierced navel. She cried out, and not from ecstasy.

The face belonged to one of the bar servers at the marina's club. "Jacob, phone call for you," the guy, an American ex-pat of many years, called down, letting his gaze linger until Kayla frowned and yanked her top back down over her small breasts.

"That's odd," Jacob remarked, rolling off the berth as the boat rocked from the force of the guy's quick hop back onto terra firma. "Nobody ever calls me. We either email or FaceTime." He glanced over at his dead cell phone, which he'd long ago shoved into a side pocket on the sailboat and forgotten about.

Like an obedient puppy, Kayla followed him up to the club, where the ex-pat tossed him a handset.

"Yeah," Jacob barked into the mouthpiece, his pulse quickening. Something was obviously not right in the 'real world.'

"Jacob, it's Matt. Put the boat away for a bit. Time to come home, buddy."

A few minutes later, Jacob let the phone fall to his lap. He met Kayla's frightened eyes and let his gaze drift over her body. Inhaling slowly, he took her hand.

"What?" she asked, taking a step backwards so she could better study the sudden fear in his eyes.

"Vancouver," Jacob managed. "Matt's sending the jet."

"Oh, God! Jacob, who—?"

Uncertain, a thousand confused thoughts running through his mind, he shook his head. "Charles," he told her. "He had a heart attack."

"What? Charles? Is he—"

"He's stable. But I need to go. I need to be there."

"For yourself? Or for Jessie?" she asked hotly.

Jacob's eyes sparked. "Not going there with you, Kayla. And I suggest you don't, either."

Dropping her hand, he strode over to the bar, handed the server the phone, and headed back through the gate and down the ramp towards the boat. Jogging in quick time, he was at Sarah May's side in a minute, and did not look back.

Chapter Twenty

$\mathcal{B}$y the time the jet was crewed, fueled, and made the trip south to pick them up, it didn't get Jacob and Kayla to Vancouver until two days after Charles' heart attack.

While they were in the air, Kayla dug out something in her arsenal that had been on her mind since she and Jacob hooked up. She broached it to him moments before Victoria told them they would soon be landing.

"I'm going back to the workshops," she announced. "I always planned to do a solo in the show. Jacob...do you think you could arrange for me to have permission to dance to your new ballad?"

It was the first time Jacob looked at Kayla during the entire flight. "S-sure," he stammered, fighting the urge to vomit as he worried about what they would discover when they landed in Vancouver. "I don't see why not."

Although the response wasn't the romantic gratitude she expected, Kayla was happy for something, anything, to use to hang onto her new man. The dance to the ballad had won Jacob over in the first place, so it seemed a sure thing. Settling deeper into her seat in preparation for landing, she reached up and removed his hand from his face. Jacob was repeatedly wiping it over his light beard, and the anxious movements were driving Kayla around the bend.

Finally, she had his attention.

"Kayla," he said, twisting slightly so as to better face her. "I have to tell you, I don't know what to expect in Vancouver."

"About Charles, you mean."

"Yeah, but...not just Charles, you know?"

Thinking about it, she blew out a *pffft* sound. "I guess. Yeah. About us."

"Look," he tried, fidgeting. "Don't take this the wrong way, but—"

"Telling your new girlfriend not to take something the wrong way is not a good way to preface a discussion, Jacob."

"No, look, don't get upset. I just mean that we need to keep us on the down low for a while first. I just…it hasn't been that long since Talia…" Bending forward over his legs, staring at the floor, Jacob rested his elbows on his knees and started twisting his fingers around and around.

"And Jessie," Kayla finished for him. "Whose fans are already incensed at the two of you for splitting up so she could go back to, may I add, my brother. So they're going to have a real hate-on for me." Sitting back, she moaned. "I don't have a fucking chance with you."

"You're jumping to conclusions," Jacob tried, but he didn't reach for her. "Time," he added dully. "We just need a little bit of time for people to get used to the idea."

"So what, we break up before we land, in like, two minutes?"

"No. No! That's not what I'm saying. I'm just saying that we don't need to make overt public appearances, that's what I'm saying."

"Lovely." Turning her back to him, Kayla tried not to let her emotions get the best of her, but she couldn't help swiping at a tear that leaked out from her right eye. She stared out of a small window. "It's so cold," she declared bleakly as the jet landed and slowed. "Look at the big jackets those guys are wearing."

Sure enough, when Jacob peeked past her to peer outside, he shivered at the apparent coolness of this west coast Canadian city in early March. And Vancouver was one of Canada's warmer cities.

Yet, his and Kayla's worlds were about to get a whole lot colder.

Matt picked them up. He gave them good news right away.

"Charles is out of intensive care," he said. "The heart attack was just a ploy to get one of his favorite singers to come home."

"Ah. Producers and their ploys," Jacob declared as relief washed over him. "Charles is always up to something." Grabbing Matt, he gathered him into a bro-hug. "That's such great news, Matt. You just don't know."

"Yes I do, actually, Jacob," Matt smiled, patting him on the back and then moving to Kayla to give her a big hug. To her he said, "I know a certain brother who is going to be very glad to see his sister back in the city."

"Or not," she declared staunchly with a sideways glance to Jacob as Matt moved away to open the Audi's trunk so they could drop their bags in. "Brrr."

All the way to the hospital, Matt wondered whether or not to warn them that Jessie would be there. She'd been there almost twenty-four/seven. In the end, Matt let it go. There would be time enough for stress and worry and uncomfortable meetings between all of them.

On Charles' floor, Kayla took Jacob's hand and entwined her fingers through his. Together, with Matt alongside them pointing out the way, they walked quietly, unsure just what they would face.

Kayla and Jacob spied Jessie before she saw them, and Jacob groaned inwardly when he felt Kayla's fingers tighten around his.

When Jessie felt the light source at the door shift, she looked up from the iPad she was studying, and watched Jacob sidle into the room. She swallowed uncomfortably as her eyes glided over to Kayla. Jacob felt the familiar old electric shiver pass through him when Jessie's eyes drifted lower on his body and landed on his fingers intertwined with her sister-in-law's.

"Won't Josh be thrilled?" Jessie tossed in sarcastically before anyone else had a chance to say anything.

The spiteful pronouncement was fired at Jacob, and he raised his chin in unified defiance with Kayla. Jessie ignored Matt altogether, but she bristled under the scrutiny she knew she was under.

Jacob put on his usual sad pout as he staunchly set his puppy dog eyes on Jessie, who stood. At the same time, he quite noticeably yanked his fingers out of Kayla's grasp. She stiffened, and Jessie moaned under her breath. Matt's shoulders sank.

Jacob moved forward and gathered Jessie to him. Her body became rigid, but his usual green apple aura softened her. She hugged him back, intentionally not looking at either Kayla or Matt as she did so.

"Good to see you," he mumbled as, behind him, Kayla seethed.

A tired, gruff voice from the bed interrupted the fiery stares that were heating up the room with unspoken threats as they flew back and forth. "Glad to see someone's got some color to them," Charles said. "Come here, Jacob."

A slow grin spread over Jacob's face, and he wandered to Charles' bedside. "Hey, old man," he said, bending over for a gentle hug. "Glad to see you haven't shuffled off this mortal coil. I've had enough of that for this year, okay?"

Jessie chided herself at that. *God, I'm a selfish bitch,* she thought, recalling the sweet Talia and missing her vibrancy and light. Peeking over at Kayla, though, as Jacob and Charles talked, she saw someone else she missed greatly. Praying Kayla was not just a hole Jacob was filling, Jessie decided to suss out the situation.

"Come, Kayla," she sighed, extending an arm. "Jacob and Charles have a lot to talk about. Let's go grab a coffee."

Hesitant, but remembering what Jacob told her about the night with Jessie in Florida, Kayla accepted the outstretched arm. It actually felt pretty damn good to slide underneath.

"Matt," Jessie said, catching his eye. "Go home. We'll be fine."

"Emily-Grace has ballet," he reminded her. "I'll text Josh and Dan and see if I can help."

"I'm sure you have a life outside of us," Jessie tried softly. "If not, you need one. Walk down to Elysian on West Broadway and have a coffee or something. Meet some nice young doctor. I hear that's where they all hang out."

Ouch, Matt thought, unimpressed. *Jacob comes home and suddenly I'm no longer needed.*

"All right," he agreed less than amicably, his voice hard-edged. Swinging around on one heel, he left the younger crowd to sort out their tough issues. "I'm just a text away."

Jessie moved to Charles and kissed his forehead. "Kayla and I will leave you two boys to talk shop," she said. "Back in a bit."

"Go home, Jessie," Charles smiled wanly. "Deirdre will be back after dinner. Go see your family."

"I'll go when Dee gets here," Jessie replied, all businesslike and in control. "I'm not leaving you alone for a minute. If I leave you unsupervised, you're likely to start pinching the nurses' butts or something."

"Not the male ones," Charles teased.

"Ha ha, Charles Keating made a funny." Swatting him lightly, Jessie sent Jacob a cool look and sidled away.

As the girls left the room, Jacob settled into a low, comfy chair at Charles' bedside. "You must be doing okay," he started. "Little Miss Sorrow seems fairly chill."

"She's putting on a good face," Charles answered, keeping an eye on Jacob to scan for signs of his emotional state. "She knows I'm okay but I guess I threw her for a loop." In a softer tone he added, "She had quite a time on the Belgian film."

Jacob squirmed. He knew about Matt's dalliance with her and, thanks to Kayla, the struggles Jessie was having in her marriage. Then there was that Florida thing...

Charles was saying more. "Jessie's beat. She was down at those work-shops every day until this happened, trying to choreograph and teach and get those dancers ready for the tour. Kayla needs to stay in Vancouver and finish what she started."

"Aren't you supposed to be resting? Take that producer cap off."

"This one's the father cap." Charles smiled. "I worry about her. I worry about all of my kids."

A pink flush spread across Jacob's cheeks. He had a father he'd recon-nected with, the singer Tom Ryan, but he rarely saw the man, and Charles had stepped in and filled the father gap quite beautifully over the last many years. "Yeah, us kids worry about our dad too," he grinned. The grin eased off, though, when he brought up Josh. "This Grammy bullshit," he started. "How's Josh doing?"

Sobering, Charles shrugged. "Josh is Josh. He tries and tries. It just kills me to watch him. With those kids? With troubled horses? He's magic. It's like he speaks their language, but he can't quite figure out grown-ups in the real world. Mostly he stands in a corner and watches, like he's on the outside looking in. I suppose that's part of what makes him such a good actor."

"I suppose that's why Jessie is so drawn to him."

"Sure. She loves to wrap her arms around people who are hurting. That's her specialty."

Choosing to ignore the pointed comment, but shifting awkwardly in his chair, Jacob grunted. "Is he okay at home, then?"

"More than okay with the kids, I gather," Charles replied casually. He paused. "I hope you don't mind me saying this, Jacob, but...Dylan worships him."

"Slice me right open, why don't you, Charles?" Jacob sulked, drooping lower into the big chair and resting his elbows on the arms.

"Look, I'm not sure how Josh and Jessie are doing, Jacob. As a couple, if that's what you really want to know. Am I worried? Yes. Josh is starting on my series in a few weeks and sometimes lately it seems like he is barely even on the planet."

"I suppose I'm partly to blame for that."

"You and Jessie sleeping together in Florida? Yes. You should have kept your dick in your pants."

"Easy. Rest." Jacob let his gaze drift sideways. He found a crack on the floor to stare at.

"Between you and Matt now," Charles grumbled, "Jessie's a wreck. And people wonder why my heart attacked me?"

"You don't need to worry, Charles. I'm..." Jacob sighed and leaned forward. "I'm seeing Kayla now. We've agreed...I think...to keep it quiet for a bit. Since Talia..." He shrugged.

"Good idea, son. Talia's fans will be watching you with their little eagle eyes. They'll want approval power, and they'll have it, between Instagram and Twitter and all those anonymous soul-destroying social media things you kids like."

"Grrreat." Jacob frowned. Shuffling, he took a new tack. "Charles, in the interest of healing and moving on, um...I need your help with something."

Raising his eyebrows, Charles said, "Um? What?"

"A song." Jacob inhaled and raised his shoulders. "Maybe a video."

"Oh. I see. In response to what Jessie sang at the Grammys, is that it?"

"Yes." Swallowing, Jacob blinked at Charles. "Yep."

"What about Kayla?" Charles' words took on a subdued tone. "Are you serious about her? Because, and don't get me wrong, I'm happy for you if you love her, Jacob, but I can see potential for all kinds of conflict here."

Running his tongue over his lips as he pondered what to say, Jacob, in the end, didn't have to say a damn thing. Charles could clearly read the boy's thoughts, and his heart as well.

A wide smile almost cracked his jaw in two. "You love her," he said quietly.

"Talia was a dream, Charles, but…" Jacob's jaw worked as he sorted what to say. "Kayla…I saw her dance to one of my songs. She has a lot of Jessie in her."

A quizzical expression settled into Charles' eyes. "I don't think you should be looking at her quite that way, son. Pardon me for being blunt, but it's never been my strong suit not to be. You shouldn't be looking for a substitute for Jessie."

"No, that's not what I meant," Jacob broke in immediately, his voice rising in pitch. "I didn't mean that. What I mean is that she has music in her in a way I can relate to. Geez Charles, when she was dancing, it was surreal. And she's sweet, and funny, and into sex…oops, should I have said that?"

He grinned at Charles, who was smiling wholeheartedly back, and who nodded happily. "I don't mean any disrespect to Talia, Charles, but Talia sang country. I just couldn't always *get* country, you know? But Kayla, she's a dancer mostly for, well, you know, Jessie. So she and I are already tuned in."

"Just be careful, Jacob," Charles advised wisely. "Kayla is Josh's sister. She is not going to be a popular choice amongst your fans, and she is awfully closely connected to Jessie. Just be careful. With your heart as well as hers."

"I just need to record the song," Jacob said softly. "Jessie let me go. I know that's what she was doing, with her *I'm sorry I broke your heart* bullshit lyrics. Now it's my time to say goodbye. Once and for all. And I'm moving on."

"With Josh's sister. Jessie's dancer. That's your way of moving on."

"Hey. You're not my real dad, you know."

Charles was instantly remorseful for his comment, but when he looked at Jacob, there was a big ole twinkle in the singer's eye. Charles laughed outright.

"I love you, kid," he said. "Thank you for coming home."

It was a rare thing for the great Charles Keating to publicly say that he loved anyone. Jacob grinned stupidly at him. "I'd say," he started, "that I have no words. But I do." Standing, he leaned over Charles for another small hug. "I love you back, you old bastard. Now get the hell out of this hospital bed so you and I can go make some musical magic together."

"So you can say goodbye to Jessie," Charles countered, his voice thick with emotion.

"So I can say goodbye," Jacob confirmed.

And he smiled.

~ ~

While Jacob and Charles were having a real solid heart to heart, the girls found they had little to say to each other. It saddened Jessie, but Kayla was a real Sawyer. She was as reticent to speak to Jessie as Josh was, these days. Mostly she just stared at her coffee cup and twisted it around and around in her fingers while Jessie tried to loosen her up.

Finally Jessie had enough. After the trials of the last few months, not to mention the sheer emotional exhaustion of the Brussels film, and now the hours and hours she was putting in at the workshops to help Benjie—in Kayla's place—her patience was running thin.

"Listen," she said brusquely, "if this little princess act of yours is because you're worried that I'm going to swoop back in and gather poor little Jacob up in my arms, you're dead wrong. I have nothing left for the little prick."

Shocked at Jessie's choice of descriptive, Kayla sat up and took notice. "That's cruel," she said.

"That's generous," Jessie replied. Sighing, she placed both elbows on the small round café table and leaned on folded hands. "Look Kayla, I love Jacob, I do. I always will. But he's done a few things—"

Interjecting, Kayla quite succinctly cut her off. "I know about what he did to you."

Now it was Jessie's turn to look surprised. "You mean?"

"What he did. That he…raped you." The violent word, the way it slipped from between Kayla's pink lips like water, with no vicious undertone, shocked Jessie. Kayla's eyes were cool, slightly narrowed, focused.

"Oh. Oh, fuck. He told you?"

"Obviously. We're dating, Jessie." Again, so cavalier. Jessie instantly recognized this Sawyer trait. Kayla was on the warpath.

"You can't say anything," Jessie gulped. "You can't tell Josh. He can't ever know."

"We thought maybe he knew. The whole Grammy thing..." Kayla leaned back and narrowed her eyes. "Okay, so he doesn't know. I thought you two told each other everything. Isn't that where things start to go off kilter in marriages, when husbands and wives start lying to each other?"

Jessie's voice was a whisper. "We're already off kilter," she admitted sadly. "We've been off kilter for years. We can't take any more off kilter." The blue eyes started to swim as Jessie slumped over the table.

A twinge of remorse crossed Kayla's heart. "I'm sorry," she softened, just slightly. "But Jessie, I can't for the life of me figure out why you would choose to protect Jacob over deciding to tell the truth about something that's eating away at your marriage. That could stop the bleeding."

"Kayla, that's not what...Jesus. I'm not doing this to protect Jacob. I'm doing it to keep Josh from going nuts again and killing the guy! And destroying our sweet little family in the process!"

"Jessie, Jacob and I talked about this. It's killing him, what happened. What he...did to you. But you never charged him. You never held him accountable in any way, and I'm glad you didn't, because I completely understand what drove him over the edge, but how do you think Josh will see this?"

Jessie winced. "Kayla, whether or not he sees it the way I do is not worth the discussion. Because he will never find out. Will he." She watched Kayla process the notion of keeping that big a secret. "Jesus, Kayla. It'll be the end of Josh and me," she pleaded, begging. "We're barely hanging on as it is." With the small vestige of pride she had left, she sat back and raised her chin. "And just how much do you care about Jacob?"

"What?" Kayla was transfixed. She raised a hand in frustration. "Are you asking me not to tell my brother, by holding Jacob over my head? So like, if you and Josh break up, you and Jacob will start jumping each other's bones again?"

"Hell, Kayla, no! What I'm trying to tell you is that a helluva lot more than Josh and I will be destroyed if Jacob's actions become known. On the home front, we're talking Dylan, for one. This is not something that child needs to stumble upon when he's old enough to understand, whether or not

Jacob ever comes back into his life. And if it goes public, Jacob will find him-self largely condemned!"

"Ha. Not entirely. He can still play the sympathy card for what you did to him, and for losing Talia a few days before he was supposed to marry her. And by the way, you were right about that guy—he's unreal in bed. That man really knows how to fuck."

Running a finger over her top lip, Jessie narrowed her eyes. "That's not a discussion I want to ever have with you, Kayla. Not you."

"I saw it in your face upstairs, Jessie." Kayla swooped a finger in Jessie's direction. "That hungry 'fuck me' look. Your type doesn't hide it very well. You'd take Jacob back in a second if you and Josh split."

"I said my goodbye to Jacob," Jessie snarled. "He got violent, and we're done."

A loud screech telegraphed the backwards motion of Kayla's chair. She stood. The women were being stared at now, and a few daring folks were even snapping less than discreet iPhone pics of the two, but neither Jessie nor Kayla noticed.

"Well, Jessie," Kayla preened unkindly, "the way I heard it, you were right there with him. Jacob told me you were grinding up against him with your tongue stuck down his throat. I felt bad for the way I treated you for, hmmm, maybe about a minute when he told me. In my books you pretty much still cheated on Josh."

Jessie closed her eyes and moaned. *Fuck, Jacob. Seriously? You told Kayla everything?*

Kayla continued throwing her knives. "The only thing you didn't do was let Jacob finish the way a man needs to finish when things get to that point. I'm sorry Josh thinks you went for the whole she-bang with eyes open and all systems go, because it hurts me when he's hurting. But overall? I seriously still wish he would just dump your selfish ass." Despite the steady fear gripping her belly at the idea of losing Jacob now, especially to Jessie, Kayla added, "You know why I still want him to dump you? Because, Jess, you're as much to blame as Jacob is for crossing some imaginary line in the first place. You're the whore, remember?" She paused. "The name Matt mean anything to you?"

Jessie closed her eyes.

Kayla continued her rampage. "You fucking slut. I won't tell Josh the truth about Jacob, because I don't want to see the pain in his eyes when he thinks you're risking your marriage to him to protect Jacob." Kayla's bottom lip was trembling as she backed away. "And I don't want you pulling your 'I'm so lonely' crap and jumping back into Jacob's bed. But I gotta tell you. I'm some fucking sick of you constantly crushing my adorable big brother."

And Kayla walked away—sweet, kind, loving, vibrant Kayla. Jessie buried her head in her arms and moaned again.

A light touch on her shoulder made her look up, wiping her eyes at the same time so some fan wanting an autograph wouldn't see her crying and tweet a pic or something.

Matt.

"Jesus, Matt," she begged, "put me out of my misery, will you?"

A slow smile spread across his face.

"No," she wailed. "Not you too. Doesn't anyone care if my marriage survives this hell?"

"Come on," Matt said, laughing. "Deirdre's on her way to sit with Charles, and I know a little girl at a ballet class who would love for her momma to see her dance."

"Not that I'm a fan of dancers right now," Jessie grimaced, grabbing her bag from its place on the floor, "but I can make an exception for my own daughter. Let's roll, Matt."

Kayla, at the elevator, frowned as she watched Matt and Jessie leave the hospital together, their arms cozily wrapped around each other's waists.

Sinking back against the wall, she closed her eyes and said a silent prayer.

Please God, let me have this. Let me have Jacob. Please.

Confused thoughts floated around her brain like tufts of cotton in the wind.

Poking the button for Charles' floor, the door closed in her face, and Kayla was swifted away.

Chapter Twenty-one

$\mathcal{J}$acob went home alone to his old Southwest Marine Drive basement apartment, stood in the doorway, and stared. He'd spent so many days, weeks and months on the road, and hanging with Talia in Nashville, that he rarely entered this dim space. Now, in rushed a ton of memories from the old days—the newness of his fame in the music biz, working with Jessie on *Mystic Nights*...and the months spent in New York, back when he dared hope he and Jessie might grow old together.

Kayla was not on Jacob's arm tonight. She went home after Jacob suggested they cool down for a night or two. But already he missed her—the bouncy ponytail, the sexy tattoos inked on her body, her tight dancer's butt and her willingness to snuggle when he wanted to which, let's face it, was most of the time in this new relationship. Was she happy about going home without him? No. But Jacob needed time to regroup, to figure things out. The last thing he desired was a nasty fan-driven media storm like Josh was recently victim to.

Pulling his iPhone out of his pocket, Jacob did a search for a local Domino's Pizza joint and ordered a pizza with the works. He'd asked Ulysses to drop by a liquor store on the way home. Now, he shoved twenty-three bottles of Granville Island Pale Ale in the fridge and took one into the small living room with him. Collapsing on the couch, he fired up his old TV—it worked just fine. Placing his booted feet up on a dusty antique trunk, he selected a movie on Netflix—not one of Josh's or Jessie's—and sucked away at the cool beer. Soon, though, his eyelids grew heavy and Jacob dozed off until a knock at the door announcing the pizza's arrival jarred him awake.

He ate alone, while all the time he wondered what Kayla was doing, and he ached to be curled into her sensuous body, entertained by her cheery laughter.

⁓ ⁓

Later that night, after falling asleep with Dylan, Josh wandered the house and found Jessie downstairs in the media room, lying in semi-darkness on the black leather couch. She had a tune playing—it filled the room. Josh stopped just beyond the door when he realized which song it was, which artist—it was Jacob's latest ballad.

It was no secret that Jacob was back in town, with Kayla in tow. It was also clear, by the rare snipes Jessie made at Josh when they got home after Emily-Grace's ballet class, that she was in a foul mood. After Jessie got the two oldest Sawyer children bathed and put to bed with hastily read bedtime stories, she had banished herself to this dark room.

Josh was about to back away and leave her alone when his heart took another beating. Jessie's hips were moving slightly and he could hear the occasional moan. Her belt was undone and her fingers were down her jeans. Stunned, wondering exactly what she was remembering as she listened to Jacob's song, Josh braced himself against the doorframe and remained statue still. Undetected, his throat tightened and his knees weakened as his wife brought herself to climax alone.

Cursing under his breath, Josh swung around and went upstairs to bed.

⁓ ⁓

A few days later, life was back on some sort of even keel. Kayla returned to the workshops, kindly thanked Benjie for his hard work, asked him to stay on, and released Jessie from helping.

Josh dropped into the workshops to see his sister, since she didn't seem to be interested in coming out to the UBC house. In the meantime, he could barely look at Jessie, and spent very little time at home, to Dylan's and to Jessie's utter dismay. The weather was warming up—he started taking the Harley, which Jessie also hated. One, because he was sexy as hell on that bike, and it attracted women like flies, and two, because she worried about his safety on the busy, fast moving Vancouver streets.

When Josh dropped in to see Kayla, she was dancing, but she took a break and let the twins and Benjie carry on while she closed the door of her small office behind Josh.

Dropping into her office chair, she anchored both feet on the top of the desk and crossed her arms.

"Go ahead," she dared him. "Make my day."

Coolly, Josh laid his half-helmet next to the computer and eased himself down opposite her, unzipping his heavy leather motorcycle jacket as he did so.

He shrugged. "I'm not your keeper, Kayla."

"Doesn't matter anyway," she declared. "The second he got the call he fucked off back into himself. He makes me sick."

"But it was good down south." To Josh, she looked about ready to cry.

"Fucking perfect," she confessed. Kayla studied her fingernails, two of which were now cracked from all the floor-based B boyz numbers in their show. "He is so goddamned amazing." Eyes darting up, she yanked her feet off the desk and sucked in a breath. "Oh shit, Josh. I'm sorry. Obviously you're amazing too."

"You know, as far as sisters go, you really suck, Kayla."

A weak smile landed in his direction. "I try, don't I?"

Josh looked away.

Kayla kept going. "Zach called me. He's super pissed. He yelled for a while at the sheer stupidity and lack of brains his younger siblings apparently have." Watching Josh stare at the wall, and wondering what he was thinking, Kayla added a gentle postscript. "Are you okay, honey?"

The tenderness in his sister's voice almost did Josh in. He shifted his weight and looked back over at her. "I don't think you should get involved with Jacob, Kayla. Jessie's never going to be over him. And he'll never be over her."

Lightning. It sliced through Kayla's heart and sucked the life out of her. "I think I'm in love with him," she whispered.

"For fuck's sake," Josh muttered, looking away again. "Fucking Jacob. I wish he had just pulled the goddamned trigger on me when he had the chance. I thought we were done with him in this family. In this town!"

"He's a good guy, Josh. You know that. Mostly," she added wanly.

A new thought struck Josh. "What about Dylan?" he asked in a gruff voice.

"I don't know. He doesn't seem to have any interest in trying for custody, that's for sure."

"He'd probably get it, you know." Josh absently tapped his fingers on a thigh as he considered why. "After what I did at the Grammys, Jacob would have no trouble getting custody of Dylan."

"He's not going to go there, Josh. It sucks for everyone, but he says he could never do that to Jessie. He won't try to take Dylan away from you guys."

"Yet she did it to him. That makes me feel so much better."

"Y-yeah. Josh, are you finally starting to see Jessie the way I've been seeing her since Christmas?"

Picturing his wife pleasuring herself a few nights before, alone, to Jacob's music, Josh considered his feelings. He shook his head. "I don't know what to do, Kayla. I don't know what to do or where to go or how to feel…about anything."

Her voice was soft and encouraging. "You're not drinking though, right Josh? You're staying away from dirty shit?"

Frustrated that everyone seemed to think he could so easily go back down that dark road, Josh cursed again. "Jesus, Kayla, no. I'm doing my best here."

"Do you think…about leaving her?"

A long pause preceded his answer. Josh picked at a hole in his jeans as he thought about what to say. "I won't leave her," he said after a minute. "I just need to find a way to bring her back to me. So she doesn't leave me. So she never looks at another man."

"She's Jessie Wheeler, Josh. She can have any man on the planet."

It remained unspoken that there was also a time when Josh could have any woman, but likely that field was a little smaller these days.

Kayla had another thought to add. "Josh, do you want to be one of those men whose wife constantly cheats on him? Wouldn't you rather have someone who loves you the most?"

Josh slid back his chair and leveraged his tired spirit upwards. "She does love me the most, Kayla. I know that. I trust that about Jessie."

"Then why…?"

"I don't need to question the thing with Jacob. Lingering feelings, a lot of pain, I know where that came from."

"And what about Matt?" Again, Kayla's voice got soft and tender.

Josh groaned and anxiously ran long fingers through his hair. "Apparently it was a thing that never fully happened." Finding a modicum of self-respect, he tossed his hair and looked at her. "At least I think it never fully happened." He paused. "Do you know something I don't?"

Kayla blinked and averted her gaze. Steeling her nerves as she pondered Jacob's shocking admission the first morning the two of them were together, she just shrugged, dropped Jacob's violence from her mind, and forced her voice to stay casual. "Matt hid out on Jacob's sailboat for a while. They talked."

A weird choking sound escaped from Josh's throat. "I heard. That must have been some shit storm of a conversation. So…?" Settling into a quiet stillness, Josh held his breath and waited.

"Honey, it's going to happen, Jessie and Matt. The way things are with the two of you right now…"

Josh exhaled in a sort of beleaguered relief. "You're wrong. It's not Matt she's fantasizing about." Josh grabbed his helmet and pointed it at his sister. "It's Jacob. Stay the hell away from that loser." As Josh moved towards the main room, he had one final dart to throw. "I can't believe us, sitting here discussing Jessie like she's already on her way out of the door. She's not, Kayla. She makes love to me the way she always has. She looks at me the same way. She tells me she loves me—every day she tells me. We're just having some trouble communicating in ways other than with our bodies right now. There's just been too much shit thrown at us lately. Things will get better. I know they will."

"I hope so, Josh, I really do. For your sake, not for hers. I'm no longer a Jessie Wheeler fan."

"You're going to burn a few career bridges with that attitude, Kayla."

"I don't trust her."

"Good thing it's not your job to, then."

After Josh left, Kayla sat quietly alone until she heard the Harley start up outside, then cruise on down the street. Rising with a heavy sigh, she was about to rejoin the dancers when a new shadow darkened her doorway.

Jacob.

She straightened. They hadn't seen each other since the night at the hospital. "H-hey," she said.

Leaning against the doorframe, Jacob stuck his hands in his jeans pockets and gestured with his head towards the fading sound of the Harley. "He okay?"

"With us? With you and me? Or just in general?"

"All of the above."

Slowly, Kayla shook her head from side to side. "In general? Not really. And in terms of referencing us, the answer is also no. If there's still an us, I mean. I'm not sure there is."

Chewing on his bottom lip, Jacob chose to skirt over the thought for now. "Josh is still messed up, isn't he, Kayla? Charles thinks he is."

Her sisterly defenses rose quicker than a three a.m. nightmare. "He says he's not into the dirt."

"Not that. I don't mean drugs, or drinking. I just think...I think...a man can never really get over the agony of losing his family in one fell swoop, can he?"

"How could he?" Sitting back against the desk, Kayla thoughtfully regarded him. "Wow, Jacob. Why is it you understand Josh in a way most people never even consider? And why do you care?"

Raising a thumb to his teeth, Jacob chewed on the nail for a few seconds. "I think your brother wants to be a good guy, Kayla. He's just been pushed down a lotta dark alleys. That scares me." He hesitated. "You know why I care. He has intimate access to people who mean something to me."

Her eyes faded.

"Including you, dancer girl."

Brightening, she offered him a tiny wisp of a smile.

"Charles says Josh has been pretty distant lately."

"It's not helping that you're back in town."

Jacob scrunched up his nose. "Why? Jessie and me are done. I mean that, Kayla. Even if they split up, there's too much water under the proverbial bridge now. As you know."

"Is there."

"So he warned you against me, I take it."

Kayla's heart rate picked up. "Everybody has warned me against you, Jacob."

"Everybody doesn't know my heart."

"You're killing me here." Her gaze hadn't left the puppy dog eyes since Jacob sauntered into the office.

Now, he dropped into the chair closest to her. "Can we go somewhere and talk?"

"I wish. I have to stay. I need to try to finalize this number so we can get it fine-tuned and nailed before tech night at the Orpheum." She winced and grabbed a pencil to chew on. Her mind and body were crying *go!* "What is it you need to say?"

"I want to try with you. That's what I want to say." Lowering his thumbnail from his teeth, Jacob studied her.

Flickers of hope cascaded across Kayla's cheeks, her eyes. "Okay," she whispered. "Hell, yeah. But Jacob…you're sure about Jessie? I don't know if her and Josh…what if they split up?"

"Jessie and I are done, Kayla. I promise you. My heart can't go there anymore. Look, there's just one thing…one final loose end with her." He debated how to tell her.

"What? What's the one thing?"

"That song she sang at the Grammys."

"What about it?" *Why am I scared again?*

"I need to do one too. A sorry song. A goodbye song."

Kayla could barely breathe. "Why?"

"I can't give her the last word," he tried to joke.

It worked. Kayla smiled. "What about Talia's fans? About me being Josh's sister? About it being too soon?"

"We'll keep the public stuff on the down low. Like we said. Just for now."

"I'm going on tour for a few months anyway."

"It'll be a long few months," Jacob complained. He pointed to himself. "This boy needs sex."

"Then meet me here and there. In every redneck town if you want."

"I will." He stood and stretched, complementing the adorable movement with a wide yawn. Kayla let her vision land on Jacob's exposed belly as he raised his arms above his head.

"I want that," she told him, then pushed herself away from the desk and faced him. "I want that belly."

Laughing, Jacob took her hands and placed them under his T-shirt. She sighed and pressed herself against him.

"I missed you," she breathed. "Lots. Longest days of my life."

"Missed you too," he replied rather wistfully. "How's my dance coming along?"

"It's nice. I love it."

"Can't wait to see it, Kayla."

"You'll have to wait until opening night at the Orpheum."

"Can't wait," he repeated, and took her chin in his fingers. Lifting her face to his, Jacob kissed her, and teased her with his tongue. "Can I see you tonight?" he asked dreamily.

"Twist my arm," she answered, reaching between his legs for a little over-the-pants rub.

Grabbing her arm, Jacob twisted it lightly behind her back, then pulled the other arm back too, and held her wrists. "Okay," he teased. "Twisting." Bending closer, he murmured in her ear. "Like that? I've got a nice grey silk tie in a drawer somewhere."

"Ha!" Flushing pink, Kayla considered throwing the dance she needed to finish out of the window. "Little 'Fifty Shades' action, Jacob Ryan? God, your fans would die if they knew."

Sobering, a serious overture colored Jacob's next words. "Only if you're up for it, Kayla. I would never ask you to do anything you're not comfortable doing."

"I know," she smiled. "I trust you. Implicitly."

Stepping backwards, he grinned and let her go. "Text me when you're done here, Kay. I'll dig out that tie."

"Okay. Coupla hours."

When he was gone, Kayla sat quietly and waited until her breathing went back to normal before she rejoined the dancers. She didn't notice, but Casey was watching her with barely disguised jealousy. The rest of the tour group was all over her.

"We saw him kiss you! Jacob Ryan kissed you!"

"Shh," Kayla said, using her hands, palms towards the floor, to motion to the group to settle down and lower their voices. "Can't let this go public, gang. Not yet." But her eyes were twinkling and Kayla felt joyous, albeit she could also sense her world spinning totally out of control.

I'm already in love with him, she said to herself with an equal mixture of dismay and joy.

This is gonna hurt.

Closing her eyes, she relished the memory of the feel of Jacob's body against hers, of his tongue sliding erotically across her lips, then down her abdomen to land between her legs. Almost sinking to the floor in weak-kneed ecstasy at the thought of being with him again tonight, with maybe a grey silk tie involved in the action, an unbidden image of Jessie floated across her brain. Jessie, who had so quickly become someone to fear.

"I'll never give up," she said to herself as Benjie called "Places" to the dancers. "I love him."

With a perma-smile on her face, she surrendered her body to the music, and her heart to the man.

~ ~

Eventually Charles was released from the hospital with strict orders to take it easy. He had a new diet, a new exercise regimen, and a new lease on life. The first thing he did was book Jacob into the studio to record his song for Jessie.

Deirdre rather uncharacteristically cursed him when he told her he was going out one day. In a huff, she called Matt, who laughed.

"I'll accompany him to the studio, Deirdre, since Ulysses needs to be with you today," he promised. "You know your husband. When he stops making music, he will lose the will to live altogether, and I don't think you want that."

"Keep him off the series, at least. Jonathon and Charlie are picking up the slack for him. Or Jonathon's minions are, at least."

With her blessing, finally, Charles let Matt drive him to the studio. Jacob was already there, huffing and shifting his weight nervously.

"I need your magic," he told his producer. "I've got most of it worked out but I'm not sure how to create and capture some of the sounds I'm hearing in my head."

Recording ended up being a two-day job. It was a great distraction for Charles, who sat in the sound booth and bossed the recording engineer around. On day two, studio musicians joined them to lay the other music tracks, like percussion and keys, and backup singers came on board in the evening. They added a third day to bring the entire ensemble together with a small film crew to record a simple live performance music video.

Matt sat with Charles and munched on an apple after the first take of the video recording. "You better follow your doctor's orders, Charles," he said, pointing the apple at Jacob. "That kid's about to make you another cool million or five."

Charles sat back and smiled widely. "That kid's some find," he said. "And you wanted me to release him? I can't imagine why."

Matt stilled. Yes, he had wanted that back after the Florida thing. But now things were different. Everything where Jessie was concerned was different. Life had changed in an instant, and again in another instant, and again in yet another instant. And now, Jacob was in love with Kayla Sawyer, happy, it seemed, and Matt understood how the guy's temptation on that awful Florida day had turned violent. He didn't forgive it in any way...but he understood how it had happened.

Now, before him, Jacob's agonized heartfelt apology to Jessie was unfolding. It was his healing song, his goodbye song, the kind of ballad a listener could disappear inside.

No doubt. It would make millions.

On his way out of the door, Jacob stopped by Charles and Matt to say goodnight before he went off to meet Kayla for a quiet dinner at her place. "Oh, Charles?" he said. "That song? Can you make sure all the profits go to some organization that raises money for women who have been, uh," he avoided Matt's eyes, "victims of violence? You know, like, uh, rape...and that kind of thing." He blinked and swallowed.

Charles paused and stared at him. "All right," he said in a confused stupor as Jacob nodded his thanks and left.

Matt was quiet as he waited for Charles to say something, but Charles just fixed a concerned gaze on Jacob's back as, guitar in hand, the singer sauntered off down the hallway.

"They came and they went. My new millions," he finally mumbled as Matt dropped a hand on his good friend's shoulder and grinned.

Chapter Twenty-Two

$\mathcal{I}$n mid-march, the workshops wrapped up. The participants, all of whom stayed successfully in the program, and all of whom became reasonably skilled dancers and musicians in the intense short time they were together, were scheduled to present an opening show at the Orpheum Theater in Vancouver the night before they were to leave by bus for a comprehensive tour.

Jack Deacon bought a number of tickets for his friends and family. When he handed Jessie hers in the lobby before the show, she paused and fingered it tenderly. Looking up at Jack, she raised a finger to push a loose curl back behind one ear and aimed a sweet, sad smile in his direction.

"These youth were me," she said simply, suddenly overcome with emotion as he moved forward and hugged her.

"And look what you've done for the world since," Jack replied, his voice also choking on the emotional memory of finding the scared, skinny musician on the streets of the Downtown Eastside, and inviting her to his acting workshops. "You're a blessing, Jessie. I knew it the first time I walked by and heard you sing."

"You walked by me a lot before you finally spoke to me," she winked.

Sobering, he agreed. "A lot of us walk by the homeless without a second thought," he admitted. "We fail to consider there are actual people with real stories behind those timid faces."

"Well, I'm glad you stopped to consider there might be something in me worth saving," Jessie said softly, in the innocent childlike way everyone adored about her. "I'm sure all of these youth will forge careers out of Kayla's workshops. Maybe not all in dance or music, but the confidence they've built and the connections they made are priceless."

"Casey's really something," Charlie said, overhearing as he wandered over with Jane on his arm, before sweeping Jessie up in a big hug. "I dropped in to the rehearsal yesterday. You need to get her some more training on drums and give her a shot."

"That would be easier to do if she didn't hate me," Jessie moped. "She's, like, the poster child for the Jacob Ryan fans who've banished me."

Josh was on Jessie's right. He scuffed the toe of his boot on the floor and avoided everyone's eyes, but Charlie noticed his discomfort immediately and tactfully changed the subject.

"You ready to roll out tomorrow, old boy?" he asked. "Blue's trailer is geared up and set to go, thanks to the new groom Jack here hired."

"Thanks, Jack," Josh mumbled to Charlie's dad, who gave him a salute and wandered off to chat with Charles and Dee. To Charlie, Josh said, "The truck is packed. I'll drive up to Southlands after Jessie and I stop by the tour bus in the morning to see Kayla off."

"And when are you and the kids moving to the ranch, Jess?" Charlie asked.

Pixie-haired Jane piped up. "Soon, I hope. I'll be a wreck until you get there."

Charlie was renting a mountainside chateau in the town of Canmore, not far from where Jessie and Josh would be living during the *Sacred Peace* shoot. He and Josh would share condo digs in Calgary as well for the days when they would be shooting late at night or super early in the mornings. Jane would be spending a fair amount of time alone with their daughter Stella and the new baby, Lucas, although Stella, Emily-Grace and David would share tutored classroom time on set and at home as often as possible once Jessie arrived in Alberta with the kids.

"Give me a few weeks to get your soundtrack recorded," Jessie said to Charlie and added, to Jane, "I've got to get into the kids' school to sort out their tutoring. Then I think we'll be ready to make the move."

"The sooner the better," provoked Charlie, lightly punching the quiet Josh's arm in jest but not hiding anything from Josh, Jessie or Jane. His message was a serious one. "This guy's a mess when you're not around."

"I'll get there as soon as I can," Jessie said quietly, telegraphing to Charlie with a 'look' that he better keep an eye on her husband in her absence.

Unable to help himself, Charlie allowed a small nod in her direction, which Josh caught. Josh had been mostly staring at the floor during this discourse, now he glanced between Charlie and Jessie and wished he could sink into a giant hole. Most times these days he felt completely useless, except with the kids and with Blue, as if he were the poor cousin everybody else needed to care for. Josh was the messed up guy, the black sheep, the loser in the group.

He couldn't wait to get to work on the series. Josh needed to feel useful, and good at something again; he needed to bury himself in a character he liked and who he looked forward to exploring.

Jessie slipped her fingers in his. She knew exactly how her husband was feeling, and she felt powerless to help him. Just then, the Orpheum's 'front of house' manager dimmed the lobby lights, signaling that it was time to go in and take their seats.

"We'll be right there," Jessie said to their friends, as she turned towards her husband. "Hey," she said to him as Charlie and Jane wandered off, "are you okay tonight, Josh? You've hardly said a word since we left the kids."

Looking into Jessie's eyes before an impending separation was always tough for Josh. This time there was such a vortex of chaos around them, it seemed, that his emotions were intensified. Laying a hand on her cheek, and using his thumb to brush her skin, he searched those blue eyes now and wondered what secrets they still held captive. Was she close to running? Was she even going to come to the ranch? He'd asked her twice already about getting the kids' personalized education plans sorted out. Josh was seriously starting to wonder.

Now, he simply said, "I hate leaving you. I hate it when we're apart."

"Me too," she whispered, closing her eyes, laying a hand over his on her cheek and angling her head to more closely feel his warm skin press against her face. Jessie stepped closer to him and leaned in for a lingering kiss. She shivered in anticipation of what she hoped would transpire in their bedroom later that night.

Josh felt her desire transmit to him. Closing his eyes too, he relished the moment, the feel of her, the way she seemed to honestly want him—not

Jacob, not…Matt. When he reopened his eyes and fixed her in his gaze, he soaked her up. Jessie was stunning in a new Zuhair Murad outfit for Kayla's opening—a cream lace-trimmed silk dress with long lace sleeves and a revealing short hemline, plunging neckline and matching wrap heels. With the shorter hair styled into large curls, and evening makeup, she was anything but the woman Josh carted kids around with, the one who wore endless Lululemons or faded jeans, her hair often swept up into a messy ponytail.

Her eyes flitted open and Jessie trembled at the way Josh was looking at her, with a slight downturn to his lips and *worry, worry, worry* sinking into his eyes the closer he got to leaving for Alberta.

"You're too serious," she murmured in his general direction. "You're scaring me."

"I don't know if I can do it, Jessie," he said suddenly, inhaling deeply and surprising the hell out of her. "You, the kids…I want to get to work but I want you with me. The thought of—"

"Shhh." With a manicured fingertip to his lips, she cut him off. "Babe, no. We said we were moving forward. Giving Morgan and Nadia—"

Josh blanched at their names and shuffled his feet.

For strength, Jessie took in a breath and continued, "Giving over to our fear is like giving them power over us still. We can't go back there."

"It's just…everything is still so fucked up, Jessie. I thought everything was going to be okay but now I really don't know. I'm so fucked up."

The admission chilled her. This was more than Jessie had heard from Josh in a while, in terms of communicating how he was feeling these days.

"You're scared," she said quietly. "It's a big change, moving our household for an extended period and taking on this new role with mostly new crew who don't know the Josh Sawyer I'm head over heels in love with."

His head snapped up. "Still?" he asked, almost begging for her to fall on her knees for love of him. He needed to know. "Still in love?"

"Oh God, Josh," was Jessie's response, as a hand tenderly moved that favorite rogue piece of hair back, and new tears pricked her eyes. "How can you even ask that? I am, and always will be, absolutely crazy in love with you. You know that, babe."

"I saw you one night," he said in such a quiet tone she had to ask him to repeat himself.

"What?"

"In the media room," he told her. "I saw you touching yourself. To Jacob's music. You're not done with him. Singing a sad song to the whole world does not make you done with him."

The lobby was almost empty now and, inside, Charlie and Jane were quiet as they waited for Josh and Jessie to take their seats next to them. Something was up, still, between their good friends, and Charlie did not have a good feeling about it. Glancing towards the aisle, he held Jane's hand and waited.

In the lobby, Jessie groaned. "It wasn't...it wasn't Jacob I was...Oh, Jesus." Jessie closed her eyes. "It was just a stupid moment. I was feeling relaxed, the music was perfect, I...It was a rush of hormones, Josh, it meant nothing. I would have saved it for you but I thought you were asleep with Dylan and I didn't want to wake you."

The young house manager touched Jessie's elbow then. "Mr. and Mrs. Sawyer, I'm sorry, but I'll have to ask you to take your seats. We need to start the show."

"Sorry," Josh mumbled to him. "We're coming. Some of us more often than others."

"Oh, for heaven's sake." Jessie grabbed his sleeve to prevent him from moving just yet. "Next time I'll wake you, you big sulk. You're making a big deal out of nothing."

"Am I."

Jessie's eyes flickered over to Matt, who was conferring with Ulysses in a corner, likely well aware that something had transpired between the Sawyers that didn't bode well for the remainder of the evening. Matt caught her eye and straightened as Josh motioned for Jessie to move forward. Wiping a sweaty palm on the hip of the delicate dress, Jessie sent Matt a silent pout and held his curious gaze until he was out of sight. Ignoring Matt altogether, Josh followed his wife into the theater with a light hand at her waist and a heavy stone in his heart.

Inside, they were barely seated when the house lights went to half and then, thirty seconds later, to full black. Charlie bent over to Jessie.

"Everything okay?" he asked. Jane peeked over her husband at Jessie and raised her eyebrows.

"Ha," Jessie harrumphed. "This is Josh and Jessie you're talking about. Is everything ever okay?"

"Shoulda married me."

The comment earned Charlie a playful punch but he put on a smile and wrapped an arm around Jessie's shoulders. "Luv ya." He threw her a lifeline. "He'll be okay. I'll make sure of it."

"He better," Jessie replied, aching and seriously embarrassed at the idea of Josh watching her have her private moment downstairs in the media room that night. It sucked to think of him standing there thinking she was fantasizing about Jacob again, because it wasn't the case. She'd been thinking about well-dressed, good-looking Matt. Her sweet best friend. Which also sucked. For all kinds of reasons.

Just…the man tantalized her. For whatever reason, Jessie wasn't sure. The newness of the admitted attraction, maybe, and Josh's distance…In the media room, her mind had wandered back to that perfect Brussels night, and what Jessie considered unfinished business with Matt. In her mind as she lay on the black leather couch was the fantasy conclusion…

I would be on top. My hands would roam over his body, over that hard stomach of his, and I would pull his shirt out from beneath the waist of his pants… my lips would find a place to land, and I would trail whispery kisses down his stomach to his belt…I'd unfasten the belt and lower his zipper, then give him a nice little suck, if he would let me (and why wouldn't he?); Then I would slip off and lie on my back…my back would arch and I would moan when he slips a hand up underneath my dress for the first time…he would watch me cry out when he removes my panties and puts two fingers inside me and uses his thumb to stroke me, because my pleasure increases his pleasure…I would hear his sounds, I can imagine what sounds he would make, like, when he first touches me and sees how wet I am…for him…how bad I want him…before he starts to move his hips, as his breathing grows ragged and his eyes flicker with desire… before he puts his lips on me and I gasp with pleasure…before he begs me to let go, to come just for him; before he goes inside and takes what I know he wants from me, from my body.

The visual images Jessie placed in her mind that night only ended up reminding her of how desperately she had wanted Matt in Brussels.

It's okay, it's totally normal to have sexual fantasies, she had told herself in the media room, and again now, as Josh pretty much settled into a whole new funk next to her. *One just…probably shouldn't be having them about one's bodyguard and, well, best friend. Oh Jesus. I suck.*

Laying a hand over Josh's fingers, which were resting on his leg, she squeezed them in an attempt to offer reassurance.

But he wasn't buying it. Josh let her touch remain, but he locked his eyes on the stage and tried to lose himself in Kayla's show.

⌒～ ～⌒

There was one more moment during the show that further ate at Josh's insecurity in regards to Jacob, but it soon turned to more of a simple curiosity. It was during Kayla's solo dance, which opened the second half. Jessie, who was growing more apprehensive about Josh's mood and their impending separation the next day, especially with Josh's awareness that Jacob would be in Vancouver while Josh would be in Alberta, was settling in to watch the second half when the first strains of Jacob's latest hit ballad filled the beautiful, historic theater.

Jacob himself, who they hadn't yet spoken with tonight, was sitting a row ahead of them in Jack Deacon's block of tickets, about ten seats to the right in the center section of the Orpheum. He straightened when the song started.

Despite Josh's freeze-out because of his insecurities about Jacob, Jessie's eyes lit up. Kayla, a stunning, skilled, original dancer, was on stage interpreting a ballad her new love had written and recorded. Magic was happening, illuminated by a perfect symphony of crimson, indigo and white stage lights and held up by the already lofty spell the evening's performances had generated amongst an audience thrilled to be celebrating the success of the workshops.

"Beautiful," Jessie whispered to no one in particular as, completely captivated, she held her breath.

Even Josh seemed taken in by his enchanting sister as she easily thrilled the mesmerized audience with her movements, which seemed to be a combination of classical ballet, contemporary dance, and B boyz dance. She was wearing a halter and baggy jeans as she danced, and had her hair tied up in its usual loose ponytail.

The thing that really got Jessie, though, and Josh when he glanced at his wife and saw wonder in her eyes as she turned her head and sought Jacob's reaction was, well, Jacob's reaction.

He was close enough for them to see, and there was enough light bleeding from the stage to capture his utter loss in the music, in the dance. Jacob was rigid and still, and completely overtaken by this exquisite girl's feelings about his song, which she was conveying through her body's movements. The expression lining his face, highlighting his cheeks, was pure peace, joy, surprise to an extent, and—love.

He's crazy in love with her, Jessie thought, surprisingly relieved.

Almost afraid, Josh peeked back over at Jessie. He expected to see dismay in the pretty blue eyes. Instead he spied amazed, blissful goodwill, all aimed in Jacob's general direction. Catching her husband's eye, Jessie's smile widened, and she shrugged. In her opinion, if Jacob could let the past go, and if all of them could find some way to be in each other's company without poor feelings and old jealousies, Kayla would be a good match for him. Her interpretation of his music confirmed it. She *got* him, and he obviously had discovered, somewhere along the line, that he *got* her too.

I don't know how this is going to work, Jessie thought, as the song came to a peaceful end and the audience rose as one to award Kayla a standing ovation, *but I know two very lonely people who could build something wonderful here.*

Beside her, Josh stood and reached a hand down to Jessie to help her rise. Instead of clapping, Jessie leaned into him and wrapped both arms around his waist. Josh bent his head to her and pulled her close.

"She was incredible up there," he murmured. "My baby sister. Coulda picked a better song, though."

"She's pretty special, Josh." Jessie soaked up the warmth of his embrace, relieved that her husband's silent treatment seemed to be ending. "I hope she'll let me back into her life."

"Only if she doesn't bring Jacob around," Josh agreed, planting a gentle kiss on the top of his wife's head.

Okay, she thought, *so that's how it's going to work.*

215

Chuckling, she loosed herself from Josh's grip and whistled loudly. She wasn't the only one. The theater was filled to the rafters with an appreciative audience, most of whom were very generous with their praise.

A last peek to Jacob had Jessie completely humbled. Her ex was standing like everybody else but his stance was wide, quiet, and fearful. Both hands were shoved in his pockets, as usual, and he was dressed to the nines as were most of the Deacon guests, but his head was lowered and he wasn't clapping.

Oh baby, Jessie thought sadly. *You're terrified.* Her heart melted for him, this young man who had already lost so much—a woman who rejected him, a woman who passed away just after letting him go, and a child, who a man Jacob had a hard time accepting, was raising.

As if he could sense her thoughts, Jacob twisted around at the waist and looked back at Jessie. His eyes were tragic, the earlier peace destroyed. *Help me,* he seemed to be pleading.

Jessie was still clapping, but she touched her fingers to her lips and kissed them, then moved her hand outward. *I love you* floated over the heads of Charles and Deirdre and Jack and Lydia, and a few more Deacon friends, and landed in Jacob's terrified heart. *It will be okay,* she was telling him. *This is good.*

Jacob's eyes flitted over to Josh before he looked back to the stage to see the next number start. Josh, Kayla's brother, Jessie's man. Josh would be key in making this new relationship work. His approval wasn't just hoped for. It was absolutely crucial.

Josh caught Jessie's air-kiss to Jacob, but he chose to interpret it as it was meant, kind of as a *you done good* and *good luck* supportive gesture. Now, meeting the guy's scared gaze, Josh stopped clapping and dropped his hands to his hips. Chewing on one corner of his lip, he watched Jacob for cues, and saw a silent request for approval pass over the heads of those between them.

Josh raised his palms just slightly then, as if to say *I just don't know, Jacob,* but that was enough at the time. The movement was accompanied by a glow for Kayla that Josh telegraphed clearly, so as far as Jacob was concerned— and Jessie too, who was watching the little interplay between the men with interest—it meant half the battle was won, at the very least. Now to sort out the rest...

The next number was already a few bars in before the audience settled, spellbound and lifted high into the graceful Orpheum's lovely rafters by the magic of Kayla's dance and Jacob's music. Jessie eased down into her seat to watch as Casey, in a featured drum solo accompanied by dancers, blew the rest of the incredible night into the stratosphere.

It was a treat to witness such talent and know that a new generation was coming forth to share their gifts of music and dance, and to realize that this would mean more workshops and more young men and women saved from destitute lives on the streets. For Jessie, Josh, and those in Jessie's inner circle, the show was even more humbling.

For Jacob, and for Kayla too, it was downright surreal.

Chapter Twenty-three

While he was waiting for Kayla to accept her praise from well wishers at the Orpheum and make an appearance at the after party, where he was waiting and which was being held at a hotel a few blocks away from the Orpheum, Jacob got up the nerve to approach Josh and Jessie, who were chatting with Charlie, Jane, and Steve and Sophie, who flew in for the show.

"Hey, guys," he managed, unsure of the reception he would face after he slouched over to them.

Charlie, being the wise big brother type, took the high road and addressed Jacob's loss. "You doing okay these days, buddy?" he asked kindly, taking note of Jacob's tan and rare clean shave. "You look a little thin."

"I'm all right," Jacob answered honestly. "I'm doing okay."

Sophie, bless her heart, moved to him and hugged him generously. "We're glad you're here, Jacob," she said. "Not that we're happy about why you're here, but now that Charles is doing okay, I think it's okay to say we're glad you're back in Vancouver. You're amongst friends, you know that, right?"

Jessie's cheeks turned pink. She avoided Josh's sudden rigid posture and the shuffling of his feet, but she couldn't help hearing him clear his throat. Nor could anyone else, but Sophie had a heart of gold. She hugged Jacob a second time and he, too, blushed.

"Thanks, Soph," he mumbled as she let him go. "That means a lot."

After some idle chit chat, Steve and Charlie and the girls surreptitiously moved away when Jacob tossed in a careful, "I guess I should ask how Dylan's doing." He said it while looking at Josh, not Jessie, and immediately Jessie

218

sent a disparaging stare to Charles across the room, which the older man thankfully didn't happen to notice.

Josh narrowed his eyes and gave Jacob a hard look. He didn't answer.

Jacob waited.

Jessie jumped in, inwardly worrying for Josh, who she knew was head over heels in love with their littlest Sawyer and who was, since Christmas, terrified of sharing him with Jacob in any way. Or, really, even acknowledging that Jacob was the child's biological father. Josh used to play Jacob's songs for Dylan, he used to tell him stories about his 'other daddy,' but now Jacob's name was no longer mentioned in their household unless Emily-Grace happened to bring him up, which was happening less and less these days.

"He's fine," Jessie illuminated Jacob. "Growing like a bad weed."

"Okay," Jacob said. "Maybe I can see him while I'm in Van."

Silence. In the far corner, Matt's head perked up. Josh was usually quiet and somewhat despondent these days. But now, too, his face was flushed and he kept shifting his feet while he regarded Jacob.

Matt watched Josh speak to Jacob. He tensed, and waited for all hell to break loose. He could see it coming as easily as new snow on a cool grey day.

"That won't be happening, Jacob," Josh said evenly. Too evenly.

"He's my kid, Josh."

"Like hell he is. We agreed. You wanted space, you got it. You took it, actually," Josh drawled slowly, his brown eyes darkening.

"Oh fuck, you two," Jessie breathed, clenching her hands into fists. "This is not the time."

"He was really sick while Jessie was in Brussels," Josh declared, to the sound of Jacob's breaking heart. "Ear infection. Little kids don't do so well with those. He was inconsolable." The memory of holding the child, rocking him, cuddling him, soothing him, tore at Josh. Dylan was still little enough that if Jacob wanted him—and he could likely sue for custody and win, given Josh's messed up escapade at the Grammys, although the possibility was never discussed—Dylan would likely forget about him.

"He's okay now?" Jacob was trying.

Jessie held her breath and wondered where this stilted conversation would land.

"Y-yep," Josh said, wary. "We had a few all-nighters."

We.

Jessie made a fatal error. "Look, Josh," she said, trying to make the peace, "there's no reason why Jacob can't see Dylan some afternoon."

Josh was picturing his wife masturbating to Jacob's song. "We talked about this." His voice was dangerously low.

"For Christ's sake, Josh, Jessie can be there if you want since you'll be in Alberta. With supervision by one of the Sawyer minions, I don't care who."

"How about *Matt*," Josh spit back at him, emphasizing Matt's name. "When Dylan takes a nap you can all hop in bed and have a threesome."

The shock of the statement sucked the color out of Jessie's face. She whipped around to Josh. "You really want to do this at your sister's party the night before you leave?"

Neither Josh nor Jacob heard her. Jacob couldn't help but wonder how much Josh really knew about the night in Florida. He was downright hostile, but likely if that button were pushed Jacob would be on the floor and Josh would be hauled off to jail for assault.

Jessie grabbed Josh's arm but he shook her off. Matt started walking towards them as Charlie sent Steve a warning look.

"Come on, Josh. No more of this bullshit, okay? We can't do this any more!" Jessie was beside herself. She started pulling at her husband but Josh wasn't budging.

"He's my kid," he said to Jacob, pointing at himself. "You didn't want him and then you fucked up by sleeping with my wife in Florida. I don't want you around my house, my wife, or my kids. Especially Dylan."

To Jacob's credit but Jessie's dismay, Jacob's eyes misted over but he was too stubborn to swipe at them with a fist and let anyone see how quickly his evening was deteriorating. Choking back the heavy emotion, he hooked his thumbs in his pockets and tried to make Josh see the light. "I screwed up," he said, the words emerging gruff and big. "I messed up. I'm just asking to see him, that's all. That's all, man."

Heartless, Josh threw in, "Did I add my sister in there? She's off limits to you too."

There was noise in the room—people talking, music playing—and somewhere off in the distance was a huge happy whoosh as the night's entertainers were finally making their entrance. But to Jacob the sound left the room at Josh's final declaration. The happy sounds were sucked out, all of them, to leave the room devoid of light, to leave him bereft and wanting.

Matt was close by then, but he stood back, although Jessie met his eyes and silently begged him for help.

Jacob almost lost it. Raising one hand slowly, he held his fingers up and showed them to Josh. He spoke so slowly and quietly that Jessie had to really focus in order to hear him, but when she did, tears leaked unencumbered from the corners of her eyes.

"First Jessie," Jacob said darkly, hoarsely, counting on one finger, "then *my* son," finger number two, "then Talia. I have nothing more to give the world, Josh. Meanwhile," his voice shook as he said it, "you have it all. You have everything. And you continue to try to piss it all away."

Kayla, her arm around Casey, who, like the rest of their group, was dressed exquisitely in a gown Jack Deacon purchased for the after party, entered then, and met Jessie's eyes. Jacob's back was to her, but Kayla's exuberant expression immediately changed when the commotion their entrance created caught Jacob's attention and he turned and gazed sadly at her. Kayla's knees melted as she realized Jacob was talking to Josh, and from thirty feet across the room, clearly the conversation was not going in Jacob's favor.

Before Jacob turned away, his breath caught when his gaze drifted over to Casey—Casey, the eighteen-year-old whiz on the drums that was usually dressed so casually...and now was incredibly stunning and feminine in a low cut indigo blue Vera Wang party minidress.

Jacob's heart was empty. He was done. He looked back at Josh, and Jessie was witness to the beautiful puppy dog cobalt blues fading into dust.

"You don't want me to have Kayla either? Well then, she's all yours. Have fun picking up the pieces while you're in Alberta and she's on the road, Josh. Watch me destroy her. It'll be easy. She's one of those weak, goddamned Sawyers. The Sawyer spirit? It's easy to kill. All it takes is one—good—fuck."

Gasping, Jessie watched as Jacob made his way across the room to the group of newly arrived dancers and musicians. And she watched as he ignored Kayla entirely, took Casey in his arms, and evidently said something flattering.

"She worships him," Jessie exhaled. "Josh...what have you done?"

Letting go of his arm, Jessie backed away. She had to turn away from watching Kayla process what was happening to her. In a pretty yellow silk dress, the girl who danced so exquisitely earlier to Jacob's ballad, was stunned, silent, and shocked as, nearby, the man she'd fallen in love with took Casey's hand and offered to buy her a drink.

Kayla's gaze flashed over to her brother, and landed there for an extended moment. She swallowed, gave him an upside down third finger salute, wheeled around, and left the room.

Josh felt the glares of his friends around him. He felt Jessie's icy, judgmental stare knifing into his back when she dared turn around again. But most of all, when Kayla stormed out and all that really remained in his direct vision was Matt, Josh felt fear creep up his body. *What have I done?* he asked himself. *What—have—I—done?*

To the uninitiated, Matt was regarding Josh with his usual cool non-judgmental gaze. But to Josh, who knew Matt well, there was a flicker of something dangerous dancing across his eyes. It started at Josh's frozen stare, drifted to the right, and landed on Jessie.

～～～

It didn't take Jacob long to get drunk. Within the hour he was plastered and begging Casey to take him home. She was young and enraptured by this sexy international singing star. She couldn't wait. They left by a side door.

Kayla was back at the party. She watched them go, and turned to her friend Benjie, who was whispering seductively in the ears of the twins, Sharlyne and Cheyenne. Raising her eyebrows, she said, "Can I get in on this action?"

Benjie high-fived her while the girls laughed.

Inside, Kayla cried.

Jessie avoided Josh with everything she had in her. She steamed and seethed at a separate table while he sat in silence with Charlie and Steve, and she went to the washroom any time he tried to approach her. Her fury was not well disguised, and Deirdre, who spent most of the night with her, laid a hand on her arm and tried to calm her to no avail.

Matt had enough. Just as the party was slowing down, he approached Jessie and asked her for a dance. She was so upset with Josh that she accepted, and let Matt lead her onto the small dance floor. Once there, he held her a little aloft so as not to alarm Josh and, in front of everyone, hiding nothing, he, her best friend, let her have it.

Matt started with, "What the hell are you doing? You have it. You have it, the magic. Your husband is leaving tomorrow and you are throwing that magic away because of Jacob," he leaned forward so he wouldn't share Jacob's violence with the tired partygoers in the rest of the room, who were almost all without exception watching Jessie Wheeler's bodyguard give her hell, "who fucked you over real good in Florida."

Trying to pull away, Jessie physically fought him when Matt refused to let her go. "Jacob's breaking Kayla's heart, Matt. Because of Josh being a total and complete douchebag!"

"Her heart, Jessie, not yours! If you expect me to stand by and watch you suffer again because you're putting Jacob ahead of the man you love the most, you've got another think coming. I won't stand by and watch the two of you destroy one of the greatest gifts mankind has to give. Do you know how rare that is, what you and Josh have? Josh, who said what he did to Jacob tonight because he's terrified—terrified, Jessie—of losing you or Dylan or both, and likely Emily-Grace and maybe even David in the meantime!"

Mid-song, Matt dropped his arms from Jessie, and wiped his nose. His eyes were red and bloodshot, and he was shaking. "You know how rare it is, Jessie," he said with an intensity that surprised her. "And how hard that kind of love is to come by. Get your shit together, the two of you. Stop fucking it up!"

Backing away, he threw his hands out to the sides.

Behind him, Josh stood, unsure of what to do or what to say to either him or to Jessie who, now, was standing alone on an almost empty dance floor, big fat tears trickling down her stricken face.

Matt had one last thing to say. "I'm with Jacob on this one, Jessie. You and Josh have it all, but you act like you have nothing, like you're still lost in that basement apartment in Langley and he's still buried in booze and coke and Nadia in Toronto. Get your shit together. You have everything! The rest of us are the ones with nothing."

Wheeling around, he stormed away.

"Oh, hell," Jessie breathed, fighting for control, fisting and unfisting both hands at her sides as she watched him struggle with his own losses. "Jesus, Matt," she said to his disappearing back. "I'm sorry. I'm so fucking sorry."

Around her, the world seemed to move into slow motion. Swaying, Jessie glanced left and then right. She was almost alone on the dance floor. "Well," she said to the last few people around her as she quaked in a very unsophisticated way on much despised sky-high heels in the very sophisticated Zuhair Murad, "this has suddenly become a rather epic night."

Her eyes landed on Josh. Standing before her, apologetic and scared, it was obvious he didn't have a clue what she expected of him now. Jessie exhaled loudly with blowfish cheeks and opened her arms to him. Moving into them, he buried his face in her neck.

"We suck," she managed as her shoulders shook. "You and me as a couple. We suck."

"No," Josh told her, for the first time in ages feeling a sense of calm overtake him, "we don't suck. We just have a lot to learn about how to love one another. We're not very good at managing the tough stuff."

"Can we go home, Josh?" Jessie, her cheeks streaked with mascara, leaned back and rifled her fingers through his hair. "You're right. Some of the love stuff we are not very good at. But some of it we are very good at. And given that everybody around us seems to still be imploding, I'd kind of like to send you off to Alberta with a bang."

In an instant, it seemed the old Josh was back. The happy, light-in-his-eyes, playful Josh Jessie desperately loved, made an appearance.

"A bang, huh?" he laughed. "How about two, six, seven or nine bangs?"

"I can go all night," Jessie purred, a wide smile creasing her face. "You're the one who has to drive most of the day tomorrow."

"Charlie's tailing me. I'll be fine."

"Thank God for Charlie," Jessie breathed into her husband's neck as the song came to an end. "And thank God for Matt."

Josh didn't hear that part, but he felt his wife's body sigh into his as her words got lost in vibrations on his neck. He pulled her close, and hung on for dear life.

They made love in the pale moonlight, urging each other into sweet ecstasy with the ease and simple comfort of longtime couples.

～⁓ ⌣⁓

Kayla sank into some dark part of her soul and went to bed with Benjie and the twins. Sprawled across the bed when the fun was done, she crawled on all fours to the bathroom and puked until she was dry, then cried herself to sleep on the floor. When she awoke at four a.m., her good friend Benjie was spooning her from behind, trying as best as he could to hold her broken pieces together.

～⁓ ⌣⁓

Matt sat alone in his modern new condo; all night he smoked Jessie's brand of woodsy cigarettes and topped them off with brandy. Sleep was evasive until the pink rays of dawn appeared on the distant horizon. He flicked off his alarm as he sank into the soft duvet on his big King-sized bed. Later, he would have to meet Jessie and Josh at the tour bus. The older Sawyer children would be in school with Sam tailing them today, but Josh and Jessie would have Dylan with them as they said goodbye to Kayla. If Jacob showed up? Well, he likely wouldn't, unless he had a death wish. But he might. Matt wanted to provide all the protection to Josh and Jessie that he had available to offer.

As he drifted off to sleep he wondered whether they had made up. Were they in bed now, making love? Would they survive all the craziness life seemed to always be throwing at them?

Matt wrapped his arms around his pillow, and let himself dream that some day, even for one night, Jessie would be his. Josh wouldn't have to know...the images came fast and quick—Jessie in that dress tonight, Matt's breath on her neck as he stood behind her and slowly unzipped her...reaching his hands around her body as he urged the dress down, down down... cupping her breasts, whispering to her that he loved her...Jessie widening her stance for him as he pressed a palm against her abdomen and moved it down between her legs, her melting into him as he rubbed and teased her, until he could lie her on his bed—this very bed—and take her as his own. He could picture her beneath him, gripping the sheets, crying out, begging him to make her come, to end all those painful looks between them, to finish, as she said, "What we started in Belgium."

225

It was physically painful not to have her here with him now.

But, the thing is, it was even more painful to think of her alone tonight, at war with Josh—again.

Matt turned his face into the pillow and groaned. There was no winning in this situation. When all was said and done, Jessie needed Josh.

But one night, Matt begged the universe. *One night for a lifetime of loving this woman.*

He closed his eyes and slept.

Jacob was astounded when he got Casey on her back in her bed, which was a ground floor futon in a small messy room that served as her entire accommodations. He was going at her the way he usually went at anonymous, random sex partners—roughly and desperately. While he was clawing at the elegant gown she wore, though, trying to locate a zipper, buttons, anything, she grabbed his hands and stopped him.

"What?" he asked, looking up from his desperate movements to find himself locked in gorgeous dark eyes.

"I'm just...it's just...I'm new at this, that's all," she admitted ruefully, shyly pulling at her dress to make sure it was covering her body.

"What? What the hell?" Jacob sat back. Awareness careened over his face. "Okay. I see. You're actually a...a virgin? You've never had sex?"

"No," she whispered, eyes wide. "Never."

"You live on the Downtown Eastside."

"That don't automatically qualify me as a whore." The eyes narrowed in anger.

"I know, I know, uh, I'm...I'm sorry, Casey." The room was spinning. Jacob got up to go. "This is not happening," he said as he stood by the door.

Casey sat up on the small bed. "I didn't say I didn't want it, Jacob."

She looked so young and vulnerable sitting there. Sighing, Jacob moved back to her and sat beside her. He took her hand and kissed the backs of her fingers. "Casey," he started, "your first time should be special. It shouldn't be with someone who, let's face it, I'm sorry, but someone who you are not likely to see again. A loser like me."

"Jacob," she said, softening, "what part of 'little old me having sex for the very first time with adorable, famous Jacob Ryan'—on a night that, according to Charles Keating, will likely change my life—could possibly not be special?"

"Ah," he smiled. "I see your point."

"Good. Just slow down a little," she grinned. Lying back down on the bed, Casey reached to her side and unzipped the dress from its unusual location.

"I will," Jacob agreed, lying down beside her and reaching for the shoulders of the dress, "but if I'm going to be your first then you have to let me teach you a few things."

"Oh God, this is a dream. I'm gonna be tutored on sex by Jacob Ryan."

"Nope," he replied. "Not on sex. On men. And how to be sure they treat you right. Casey," he said, "I've made some mistakes in my life. A lot of mistakes. And there was a time that I hurt a woman. I went too far when she asked me not to. I don't ever want that to happen to you. You're too sweet," he smiled.

"You might fall in love with me yet." Casey reached up and helped Jacob ease off her dress. Nervous, she let him gaze at her and touch her, gently and with care. She was vulnerable, open.

It could have been a scary feeling, but Jacob had some wrongs to make right. The thought of Kayla and what she must be thinking gutted him. But he pushed her aside and bent over Casey, who trusted him to love her right. Pressing his lips to hers, he kissed her gently, then stayed on his own side of the bed and laid a hand on her belly. Watching her to be sure she was okay with his movements, he brought his hand up to her breast and smiled when she laid her hand over his and closed her eyes.

Soon, Jacob ripped open a condom and carefully eased into her, and Casey held him close while he taught her about physical love between a man and a woman, and the respect that very special, sacred act deserved.

Chapter Twenty-four

*I*n his fancy clothes from the night before, Jacob stood outside Casey's crumbling Victorian rooming house and listened to a seaplane buzz to a landing on Burrard Inlet far below. From where he waited for Casey to pack her bag for the tour, he couldn't see the seaplane, but its contented humming was a comfort to him. He'd missed this about Vancouver—the seaplanes landing. Not that he'd ever been on one. It was just the sound that calmed him. Like music. Closing his eyes, Jacob pictured the plane taxiing on the water and drawing to a halt by a homey floating dock. Immediately a tune took root in his head. He smiled.

Music. A universal language. A universal healer. Jacob would have a new song to piece together tonight.

He was taking Casey to a cafe in Gastown for pastries and coffee before walking her to meet the tour bus. Jacob's preference would have been a full breakfast at the Alibi Room—largest craft beer selection in the city, the old 'hair of the dog,' you know—plus they served good Elysian roasted coffee. But the Alibi only did the brunch thing on the weekends so it was not an option. In the end they chose Timbertrane, where Jacob slid into a booth and ordered a nitro cold brew.

"Best thing for a hangover," he grinned as Casey stuck to hot brew. Their conversation was easy. Music was the common denominator. "You're going places, Casey," he told her with an air of authority. "If nothing else, I can guarantee you'll be playing on some of my stuff."

"Charles Keating said last night that maybe I should do college. Get a music degree."

"You could. You could totally do that. And maybe work some on the side." His eyes narrowed. "You finish high school?"

"Yeah. I got grade twelve." Her eyes lit up. "The other students will lose their shit if my summer job is playing for Jacob Ryan." She smiled, a rarity in Casey's world until the workshops started to unravel her pain.

"Hey, Case?" Jacob started tentatively. "What's your story, anyway?"

"My story?" She frowned.

"Hey come on, we all have one. I have about ten now." Kayla's pretty face flitted back into his mind and his eyes darkened. Casey noticed.

"Jessie?" she asked.

"What? Uh, no. Actually…no. For once."

"Talia," she said carefully. "I liked her, Jacob. She was real sweet."

"I liked her too," Jacob mumbled, twisting his cool glass around and around in his fingers. "She was the real deal." He decided to take advantage of their easy rapport. "Why do you hate Jessie so much? What'd she do to you?"

"Duh! She broke your heart."

"And that's enough to hate someone you don't even know? It's totally flattering that you care that much, but hey! The Casey I am getting to know is better than that."

"I'm not the only one, Jacob. Jessie's music is amazing but she ain't the smartest cookie in the box."

He had to grin at that. But Jacob had more to say. "There's a lot of behind the scenes stuff about Jessie and me that people don't know about. They shouldn't judge. You'll learn this soon enough, kid."

Casey stared somberly at him. "What about Josh Sawyer, though? You saw that video of him at the Grammys. He scared the shit out of me."

"Hmmm," Jacob exhaled slowly. "Josh. Well, sometimes he scares the shit out of me too but he loves Jessie to pieces, and she loves him, so that's that."

"You shouldn't give up on her. It's obvious you still love her."

"It's obvious, is it?"

"Um humn." Casey was spooning yogurt and granola into her mouth. Jacob smiled and reached out a finger to wipe a misguided bit off the corner of her lip.

"You still drunk?" he asked and stuck his finger in his mouth to suck off the yogurt.

Chuckling, she said, "I was never drunk. You were. You probably still are. And yeah, why give up on Jessie?"

"This conversation is sobering me up real quick," Jacob sighed. "You know, Casey, sometimes the things we want are just not meant for us."

"Well, that just sucks."

"Please tell me you're not going to stalk me."

Tossing back her long black hair, Casey laughed. So rare it was to hear her laugh, that Jacob cocked his head to listen. *Bells.* Her laughter sounded like bells. Bells would have to be part of the new song he would write later today.

"I ain't gonna stalk you," she grinned widely. "There gotta be other rad guys out there who can teach me more than you did. About sex, I mean. I'm gonna learn what I can."

"I'm offended. That sounds remarkably like an insult."

"Call it whatever the hell ya want," she teased, flicking her yogurt-covered spoon at him. "You were sweet though, Jacob. You rocked. Is that what your ego needs to hear?"

"Did you like the, uh...you know..." He ducked his head and cracked a small diabolical grin as a pink flush lit up the tops of his breakfast date's cheeks.

"What did you think?" she asked with a wink.

"I'd say I will end this weird chat with this—enjoy your body, Casey. Respect it, be smart, try not to break too many hearts, but don't be afraid of sex. It's liberating and incredible, and with the right person it's the most amazing thing you will ever experience."

Surprising him, Casey bent over the table between them and kissed the center of Jacob's forehead. "Thanks," she said simply. "You're really somethin,' Jacob. After I play the field a bit I just might stalk you."

"You realize I'm almost twice your age."

"Don't matter to me. Finish your coffee. I need a smoke."

As he walked her to the bus after, Jacob's pulse quickened. From a distance he could see Kayla's usual ponytail bouncing as she helped sort baggage. He swallowed. This—him showing up with Casey—was bound not to go over well. But Jacob was powerless to turn back. He didn't need to be at the bus this morning but...

I just need to see her one more time, he told himself.

Jessie was there too, already, and Lordy. Josh must've gotten a good lay last night, Jacob figured, because Dylan was there too, in his mother's arms, although shortly he was handed around from dancer to dancer.

They stopped beyond the bus, before anyone spotted them.

"We good?" Jacob asked Casey.

"We are *so* good," she grinned happily. "I hope to see you again one day, Jacob Ryan. You really are somethin.'"

Bending close to her ear, Jacob whispered, "So are you, Casey 'I-have-no-story' drummer girl. You did more for my fragile ego than I did for you, by the way."

"You're too hard on yourself," Casey replied matter-of-factly, inhaling on her final cigarette before the long bus ride. "You just need to relax and let love come back to you. It will one day."

"Sounds like a song."

"It should be. Although, come to think of it, it's probably many. Nothin's original anymore."

"Go," he laughed. "Blow them away out there, girl."

A final hug between friends, and Casey walked away, her heart light and her spirit soaring.

Jacob was slower to wander into the throng of excited dancers. His appearance struck up a new energy, though, and Kayla turned to see where it was coming from.

Jacob.

Benjie was at her left side. "Let him go, Kayla. He's not worth it."

"I beg to differ," came a voice from Kayla's right. She looked over. Jessie.

"With or without Josh's influence last night, Jacob screwed me over, Jessie. I can see now why you chose Josh over him."

"Honey," Jessie tried, "Jacob needs a little time. Talia—"

"Talia, Talia, Talia. I'm so fucking sick of Talia, and I'm sick of you. Now pardon me, I need to organize our shit. Out of my way please, Jessie."

231

There was a large wheeled garment bag on the ground. Grabbing its tag, Kayla glanced at it and shoved it towards their tour manager. The dark-haired woman in turn gave it to the bus driver, who shoved it into the baggage compartment beneath the seating area of the bus.

Unsure, Jessie moved to go, but Kayla stood and faced her. "Look at Casey, Jessie. She's glowing. And Jacob's in the same damn clothes he wore to the show. I'm done. I wish me and him would have stayed in the Caribbean. The real world sucks."

Near them, two dancers had cornered Casey. They wanted the scoop, and they got it. A scream rose up from beneath the hands covering their mouths. Casey was boasting a smile so wide it reached her petite ears.

"Oh, for Heaven's sake," Kayla muttered. "Would you like to switch places with me, Jessie? I'd gladly switch with you again."

"You kicked me out. You had your chance." There was a twinkle in Jessie's eye.

Kayla groaned.

"Look, Kayla…last night at the show, I watched Jacob watch you. Your solo to his song, I mean, you dancing it. He was so lost in you. That man loves you. Your stupid brother and him got into it, that's all. Josh said some things that pissed Jacob off and he wanted to hurt Josh by hurting you. He was stupid. Look at him now. He keeps looking over here."

True, Jacob was glancing in their direction, but he averted his eyes when Kayla caught him. Shirttails hanging out and hair mussed up, he was as adorable as ever, but Kayla, at the moment, pretty much couldn't stand the sight of him. Nor was she talking to Josh, who was standing back with Matt keeping an eye on Dylan who, in typical Ryan / Sawyer male fashion, was enjoying far too much the attention of the women in the vicinity.

Jessie was silent as she watched Jacob approach Dylan. Part of her wanted to run to him and grab the child, throw him into his biological father's arms and back off so she could watch, and study the way their hair curled in the same way, and the way their small smiles curved up the same way. But Josh was nearby, and he begged watching too, so she flipped around and gave him a careful look. Before they left home, he had grudgingly agreed not to freak out if Jacob was at the bus this morning. Now, he seemed to be rather calmly keeping his word; silent, unspeaking, he was standing next to Matt just watching Jacob with Dylan, but at least he wasn't losing it.

Kayla was watching Jacob too, but her blood pressure was rising because the crowd around Casey had grown and the previous night's hurts were too big to extinguish by virtue of Jacob holding a cute two year old in his arms. His presence there, when she was trying to gather the troupe and organize everything, annoyed the hell out of her.

She did okay until one of the dancers said, a little too loudly, "You lost your virginity to Jacob Ryan. For real? Get a pic, we need to Instagram the shit out of that!"

Jacob heard too, and he saw the furor rise on Kayla's face. A quick flush and she was immediately an interesting shade of red; her lips were pressed into a tight line and her eyes were pinpricks of disaster.

"Here," Jacob said, quickly handing Dylan to Sharlyne, "take him, I'm suddenly on crisis management." Striding over to Kayla, he threw his hands up in a truce and said, "Easy, Kayla, let's go somewhere and talk about this."

Jessie was still standing next to her. Instantly her guard came up, and she glanced over at Josh for help, but he was taking it all in stride, apparently, despite the fact that when all was said and done, it was him who set the match to the firecracker last night. It was also readily apparent that Kayla had no interest in speaking with her brother over his part in this latest hurt.

It took Kayla all of two seconds to rage at Jacob and shove him back against the bus. The entire group of assembled dancers and musicians, as well as family who'd gathered to wish them well, went quiet when Kayla started to scream.

"You man-whore, was I just a stand-in for Jessie all along? Is that it? Or was I a substitute for Talia? Tell me! I need to know!"

Jacob had a new peace about him today. Being with Casey helped him realize a few things. One, love was worth fighting for. And two, the person he loved was this fiery cranberry-blonde dynamo who was currently hollering at him. Thinking she was cute when she was angry, he started to laugh at her fury until she started throwing more powerful accusations in his direction.

The first shocked him into numbness.

233

"You will apparently have sex anywhere and anytime it suits you. Including a few days after your fiancée died after she called off your wedding! With your ex, who is married to my brother!"

"Kayla, don't—" *Oh, Jesus. Tell me she won't go there.*

But she did. "And she said no. Jessie—said—no! You went for her anyway, even going so far as to hit her to subdue her so she would stop fighting you! You raped her! You fucking raped her, Jacob!"

Standing back, Kayla became aware that her white-hot rage had gotten the best of her. It hit her how bad her disclosure was when she heard Jessie gasp behind her.

Jacob was white. Eyes locked on Kayla, he stood poised like a cat at the bus, ready to fight anyone who dared fire another deadly blow.

Where was Josh? Kayla spun around and captured him solidly in her sight. He, too, was suddenly a bitter shade of pale. Matt had a grip on Josh's arm and, after last night's tension, Dan was along that morning as well to keep an eye on things, and he flanked Josh on his other side, ready to grab him if necessary.

Kayla was crying now but she pointed a finger at Josh and spoke to him through her tears. "You are my brother and I love you, but a gerbil has more sense and self-respect than you do. Don't you see what Jessie has done here? Jacob—raped—her. And instead of admitting this to you, that she tried to stop him before they had sex, she protected him. She protected Jacob from you, from the press, from his fans, from the police even, all at the risk of her marriage to you. Don't you get it, Josh? She chose Jacob—over *you*."

Nearby, Casey's eyes darted back and forth, to Jessie, to Kayla, to Jacob, to Josh. In the end they landed on Jacob. When he chanced a quick peek at her, he was sorry to see disappointment in the way she was standing, with her hands in her oversized jacket pockets and a surprised sorrow surrounding her dark eyes.

"Oh, Jesus," he thought and forced himself to look at Jessie. Jacob could see the terror playing out over her features. He knew exactly what she was thinking—*why did you tell Kayla in the first place?* There was fear in her beautiful, sad eyes. She seemed afraid to turn around, to face Josh, to see how he was reacting to this new bit of information.

Jacob scrunched up his pride, swallowed, blinked rapidly a few times, and raised up his shoulders. Fists clenching and unclenching at his sides, he faced Josh square on and waited for his adversary's temper to ignite.

The nerve on Josh's cheek was in overdrive. An unblinking, cold-hearted stare was focused on Jacob, but Josh's feet were planted. He wasn't moving. In a gruff voice, he said loudly to whoever would listen, "Somebody get Dylan out of here. Now."

A flurry of movement to his left, and two dancers moved past Josh with Dylan in the arms of one. They stopped at Josh's packed truck on the perimeter, far enough away that the child wouldn't panic over his father's potential words or actions.

Closing her eyes, trembling with the fear of the unknown, Jessie sent Jacob a frightened stare across some invisible wire before she forced her feet to turn in a slow circle. Once there, she gazed at the ground before letting her sight travel up Josh's body to land on his face.

His eyes flickered over from Jacob and captured her. What Jessie saw in Josh was not the anger she expected to see—no, it was there, all right, evident in the way his jaw was set and in the twitching nerve on his cheek, but it was completely eclipsed by unrelenting, sheer, earth shattering disappointment.

Josh was six feet away from Jessie. As she quaked before him, afraid to speak, he said, "Did you lie about Matt too?"

"No," she whispered. "No."

Shaking off Matt's arm, Josh gave him a hard shove. To him, he said, "Did you know about this? Did you know what Jacob did to my wife?"

Hopelessness crushed Matt's shoulders. "Yes," he said. "I did."

Josh was reeling. "You're family, Matt. Family doesn't keep these kinds of secrets from each other. What the hell were you thinking?"

He turned back to Jessie.

"The ranch?" He followed the dangling question with a shake of his head. His next words came from some numb place deep inside. "Don't bother coming out. I don't want to see you."

"No," she stubbornly told him. "Just—no."

Aware that others were watching and that there might be a few cell phones recording them, Josh stepped closer to Jessie. Matt, who was within earshot, crumbled at his first sentence. "Masturbating to Jacob's song is one thing. Protecting him after he—raped—you, when you and I are trying so damn desperately to hang on is a whole other shit storm." He paused. "I have to stop at home to grab a few things. Get Matt to drive you and Dylan. Take your time."

He had one final parting shot, and it was aimed at Jacob. "You've just sunk to an all time low. All that stuff you said last night about what I have that you don't? D'you ever think maybe there's a reason for that?"

With that, he pivoted around on the toe of one boot and left without a backwards glance.

Jessie watched until he was at the fence, and had picked up and cuddled his son before handing him back to the dancer, before she slowly turned back around to Kayla.

"Why would you do this to me?" she asked her in a monotone voice. "Why, Kayla? What did I ever do to you?"

Kayla had both hands pressed to her mouth. Her entire body was shaking. Helpless to explain her actions, she just shook her head.

Jessie looked back at Josh in time to catch him spinning out of the parking lot in the big King Ranch. Moving towards Matt, she stopped in front of him.

"Take me home? Please?" she pleaded.

"I don't have a car seat for Dylan," he said, his voice low and gruff. He couldn't meet her eye. The masturbation comment…

"Then fucking borrow one," she bit off, and brushed by him. "Someone here's got to have one." A step past him, she stopped and said over her shoulder, "I guess you'll have to rejig your security plans, Matt. It looks like the majority of the Sawyer family will be staying in Vancouver."

With a final confused and sorry look at Jacob, who stood by the bus, big-eyed and scared, and Kayla, who Benjie now had in his arms, Matt gathered his wits and followed Jessie.

Dan put out a call to the assembled crowd for a car seat.

While Matt collected Dylan, Jessie collapsed into the relative safety of his Audi and hung her head in shame.

Soon Dan was there with a borrowed car seat, and Matt was close behind. The car was already outfitted with a secure tether for the days Dylan rode with Matt, so between the men it only took a few minutes to get the seat and its passenger safely situated.

Matt waved Dan off and, with a heavy sigh, slid in behind the wheel.

Just as he was about to turn the key in the ignition, a small voice filled the silence.

"It wasn't Jacob I was thinking about when…when Josh caught me. With Jacob's music. It was you."

Sweet Jesus. Matt sucked in a breath and hung his head.

"I'm sorry you have to know all these bad things about me, Matt," Jessie said quietly, leaning back and looking at him from a sideways perspective. "I'm sorry to mess things up again."

"Jessie," he answered in a somber tone, "life wouldn't be normal if you didn't."

One corner of his lip turned up just slightly as he, too, leaned back and looked at her. She was so small there in the big leather seat, all sad and lost. Matt's heart melted.

Reaching out to touch her, he moved a big loose curl behind her ear.

"Don't worry, Jessie," he said softly. "He just needs some time to process this. Josh is not going to let you go again."

A last stray tear leaked from Jessie's left eye. With one quick swipe, she fisted it away. "I'm sick of this, Matt," she told him. "I'm sick of feeling this way all the time. This scared. Of losing him."

"You won't lose him," Matt smiled tenderly.

"How do you know? Can you promise me?"

"How do I know? Because, Jessie, any man who would intentionally let *you* go would have to be insane."

Jessie waited a moment before responding. She chose her words carefully. "Did you mean what you said before, Matt? In Brussels?"

"Yes. I did."

"You really love me, don't you?"

He paused. "Yes."

"I love Josh, Matt."

"I know."

"But I kinda love you too."

"Yes. I know." A sad half-smile met her eyes. Affectionately, Matt tousled Jessie's hair. "Not tonight," he said, answering the unspoken question in her sorrowful eyes. "Not tonight, Jessie. You get it mixed up. The sex thing, I mean. I want it when your heart wants it, not when you need to be held because you and Josh had a big fight."

"My heart does want it."

"I've long since learned," Matt said as he started the car, "that you have a very big heart. In fact, your heart is so big you would let any man who loves you inside."

"Having a big heart is not a bad thing, Matt."

He pointed the car out of the parking lot and turned right. "It is," he said, "when you leave a trail of broken hearts behind you. Because the thing about your big heart, Jessie, despite all the room you have in it, is that I've also long discovered that it's only happy when one man is in it. And that man is not Jacob, and he is not me."

"Josh." The tragic tears started anew as, behind them, Dylan picked up with, "Daddy."

Jessie and Matt smiled.

Matt had one last thing to whisper. "I'm not saying that if the time is right some day, I won't say yes to you, though." Taking Jessie's hand in his, he rubbed his thumb over her fingers. Even that touch was electric, for both of them. Jessie closed her eyes and held her breath. "But in my heart I hope that day never comes. Because I don't want to hurt your husband any more than he's already been hurt."

"You are a good man, Matt."

Raising Jessie's fingers to his lips, Matt kissed them. "And that, Jessie Wheeler-*Sawyer*," he emphasized the Sawyer, "is why you love me."

"Ha. Yes. You bet."

Matt signaled left, and turned north on Burrard Street. Twenty minutes later, when he nosed the Audi into the UBC house's driveway, the King Ranch had already been and gone.

Josh was leaving for Alberta, and Jessie, once again, was alone.

Chapter Twenty-five

$\mathcal{M}$att left Jessie and Dylan with a kiss on the cheek for both. From inside her UBC home, with Dylan at her hip, Jessie watched him back out of the driveway.

"Too many leavings," she said sadly to her son.

"Hungy," Dylan told her, his eyes wide as he pointed to the refrigerator.

"Men and their stomachs." Moving over to the fridge, Jessie opened the door and considered what to give Dylan. He chose an apple, and she set him down with some toys so she could slice it for him. "Men and their hearts," she grumbled, with one eye on her phone in case Josh decided to text or call.

Once Dylan was happily snacking, Jessie dropped down onto the big couch in the front room and stared at her phone. Finally, she picked it up and put in a call to Charlie.

Charlie, on his way to the barn, answered her on the second ring. "Stop worrying, I'm gonna be tailing Josh all the way to the ranch. He'll be fine."

"It's not that, Charlie. He there yet?"

"No. He's late. The two of you sneak back in bed for one last funky monkey?"

"I wish, Charlie."

Something in her voice stopped him cold. "Jessie? What is it?"

"Oh, you know us. We can't do anything the easy way. Everything's gotta hurt."

"What the hell'd you do this time? I know last night had its moments but you made friends at the end, right?"

"Put it this way. This morning at the tour bus, Kayla sought revenge for Jacob's treachery last night, which really just happened in the first place because Josh and Jacob can't seem to get past old shit, ever, and Josh tore out of the parking lot not in his happy place."

Charlie softened. "Kid, Josh hasn't been in his happy place since Christmas. And not likely since the day you and the kids got taken, if you want the truth."

"I know," she sighed. "He's so great with the kids and with that horse but it's like he's living behind a wall. He only feels safe when he disappears inside himself."

"I know someone who's like that with music." Charlie had reached the barn now. Leaning against Blue's stall, he touched the horse's nose and smiled at its big wet eyes and how they blinked sadly at him. No wonder Josh loved this horse. She was a substitute for the woman who, because of his great love for her, terrified him.

"Ha. Yeah. Thank God for music."

"So what was Kayla's revenge? What did she do?"

"Ahhhh," Jessie moaned, remembering. "My adorable sister-in-law let loose a truth that I intended to keep secret."

Charlie's groan told her what he thought of that idea. "Jessie, have you not learned by now that secrets usually find their way to the light?"

"I know, Charlie, but this one…look, Josh didn't need to know this."

Silence greeted her.

Jessie cocked her head. "Charlie? Are you still there?"

"I'm waiting. You're going to have to tell me at some point."

"Oh, for frig's sake. Ahhhh! Okay." With one eye on Dylan, Jessie watched her son talk to himself as he piled blocks up and knocked them down.

On the other end, if not for a growing fear in his belly, Charlie would have grinned at the sound of the child's happy laughter.

Jessie dove in. "Suffice it to say the sex I had with Jacob in Florida was, um, non-consensual. Well, it was at first, or I should say the whole foreplay thing was, but then…" Her voice got soft as Charlie's groan accented the already sick feeling that had her clutching her belly. "Well, I said no to him, Charlie. To Jacob. But he wouldn't take no for an answer."

Leaning heavily on Blue's stall, Charlie emitted a low *ppfffttt*. He fixed his sight on a barn kitten playing happily in a bit of straw at his feet. "The mark on your face…"

"Well, you know me, I can get pretty riled up…"

"He hit you to settle you down."

She paused. Then, "It worked," she sighed mournfully. "But it wasn't about sex, Charlie. Or love, or what we had, or any of that good stuff. What Jacob did was about anger. He blames me for the fight he and Talia were having when she pulled her car over the day they got hit."

Tenderly, Charlie said, "What I'm stuck on, Jessie, is why you wouldn't tell Josh this."

A long, slow exhale preceded her answer. Nestled deeply into the soft couch, Jessie was staring hopelessly at the ceiling when she spoke. "You know why. He already has a hate-on for Jacob. He was already mad at me for going to see him in the first place."

"So you didn't want him to say 'I told you so?' That's petty, isn't it?" Annoyed and incredulous, Charlie lightly kicked the horse's stall. Blue jumped and Charlie mouthed her an apology.

"Jesus, Charlie, no! I didn't want him to fucking kill Jacob! Josh would have gone after him with fists flying, or a shotgun in his hands, I don't know! I was scared of what he might do."

"So by avoiding the real issue, you let Josh believe you chose to have sex with Jacob which, in essence, set off a time bomb that blew up at the Grammys anyway."

"I guess." Her voice was tiny.

"What did Josh do to Jacob this morning, Jessie? At the bus."

"Ahhhh…" Jessie had to think about it. The morning's diabolical events were a hazy, painful blur. "Umm…nothing," she whispered. "He didn't touch him. I guess he learned his lesson about public brawling. But that doesn't mean this is over, Charlie."

"I find it hard to believe you can be in the same space with Jacob and not want to kill him."

"No, I mean why…" Jessie was pinching the sides of her eyes now as she relived the messed up last few months with a friend she likely should have confided in ages ago. "Charlie, we have a son together. All three of us, technically. We need to forgive and forget. Well, maybe not forget…" Her voice drifted off.

Charlie's next words were edged with caution. "And you accept Jacob's claim that the fight he had with Talia the day she was killed was your fault. You being you and all. So you took his punishment and let it go."

"Y-yeah. I guess."

"Are you okay?"

"You know, it's just been a messed up last few months. The Brussels film was so damn personal, the music we recorded for it hurt like hell to sing, and Josh has been a stranger since Christmas. If it weren't for Matt—"

"I heard about Matt." Charlie tried to keep the judgment out of his voice but Jessie caught undertones of it anyway.

"Jesus, Charlie, you sound jealous."

An exasperated sigh landed in Jessie's ear. "Get over yourself. I suppose in some ways I'm glad you've had Matt on your side, although I'm guessing you missed his company when he got banished."

"He didn't *get* banished, I fired him. Temporarily." She sighed. "It didn't last."

"By 'it didn't last' I assume you mean the affair with him." Rather pissed at what he considered Jessie's stupidity, Charlie was testing her. He waited.

"There was no affair. I've never slept with Matt. I was referring to him being banished. We needed him."

"I see."

"Look, Charlie, there's no point in hashing the Sawyer family soap opera out with you any longer. I just wanted to know if Josh got there okay. And I guess I figured I should warn you that he's not likely going to be in the best of moods when he does arrive."

"Why would he be? You constantly shove your feelings for Jacob in his face."

"Fuck off, would you?" The tears were becoming angry tears. "I didn't call you so you could side with Josh and shit all over me!"

"Jessie, listen to yourself! This isn't about taking sides! You went to Florida and made out with Jacob, which turned bad, I get that, and it scared Josh to the point of protecting himself by retreating, but then you let yourself take refuge in the arms of the man hired to keep an eye out for your safety. A little cliché, isn't it? It's like you built a huge fire, tossed kerosene and firecrackers on it, and are wondering why it exploded!"

She was quiet.

Charlie relaxed a little and spoke in a less judgmental tone. "Jess, I know you love your husband. I know the two of you have been through hell and it's taking time to put the pieces back together. You're both suffering from the hangover of your abduction, you and the kids, so there's always going to be an underlying current of fear and sorrow in your relationship. But you have to show this man of yours, who loves you unconditionally, that he comes first! There's no cause anymore to protect Jacob or go running to Matt when you need someone to hold you."

"So what am I supposed to do, Charlie? Josh is riding off into the sunset today and, by the way, he made it pretty damn clear that I am not to join him in a few weeks."

"Now you'll be on Jane's shit list too, Jessie, which means I'll be on her shit list. Thanks for that."

"A little sympathy, please?!"

"I've got news for you, Jess. Not everything is always about your spoiled superstar ass. And you know what you have to do."

She was quiet as she considered the options. "You think I should press charges against Jacob."

"And what about Matt? Is that dangerous?"

"Truth?"

"Hell, yeah."

"Very."

"Then let him go, once and for all."

"Can't do that."

"Jesus, Jessie, what is he, a backup in case Josh never wants to see you again?"

"He's my friend. He's my best friend, and right now I feel like he's all I have!" She was sobbing openly now.

"You're killing me. You are making your own bed here, Jessie. You're going to have to lie in it."

"Oh, this from the man who screwed around almost the entire eight years of our relationship!"

"Yes, I did. And look what I lost."

"Oh, Charlie. Don't go there. Please."

"I'm just saying, kid, that as a wise old man who screwed up and lost a woman I loved—love—like crazy, you'd be nuts to go down the same path. Don't go there with Matt, ever. Cut him loose and find another friend, preferably someone unattractive and safe."

"I'm getting low on those! You and Jane, may I remind you, are also going to Alberta, and Steve and Sophie are going back to God-knows-where for the duration. Jacob is off the books, Kayla hates my guts and is going on tour anyway, and you're asking me to be alone."

"Josh will change his mind. I'll work on him. You'll be here in a few weeks. In the meantime—"

Jessie answered for him. "In the meantime I'll have music."

"I'll expect some pretty soulful tunes for our new series."

"You suck."

"Look, I hear a truck. Josh is here. He's backing up to the trailer. The drive will do him good, and he'll have me and Blue. He'll be fine."

"All right. Thank you, Charlie. As always."

"Yep. You got it. As always." He smiled as Blue raised her head and let him run his fingers through her forelock. "You gonna be okay?"

"I have three kids. I have to be okay."

"Gotta go help your hubby load this crazy horse. Wish us luck."

"Be careful, Charlie."

"We will. See you in a few weeks, Jessie. Love you."

"Love you too, Charlie. Bye."

Jessie sat quietly and pondered Charlie's advice before she left the couch and sat cross-legged on the floor beside her son.

Dylan handed her a block. "Momma start building," he ordered.

"Ha. Yeah. I guess I'm back at the bottom again, aren't I, Dylan?" The way he was looking at her now, with his puppy dog eyes and droopy black curls, immediately brought Jacob to mind. Jessie reached out a hand and touched him, then she leaned in and planted a generous kiss on the top of his head. "You, my sweet, sweet boy, are going to break an awful lot of hearts in your lifetime." Lifting the block, Jessie inhaled deeply and asked, "Where should I start?"

At Jack and Lydia's Southlands ranch, Josh was just striding into the barn as Charlie was shoving his phone back in the pocket of his Columbia jacket. Slowing as he neared Charlie, Josh, who was carrying a pair of black gloves to wear while he worked with the horse, slapped them against his thigh and swallowed.

"Jessie?" he asked. Charlie always looked a little sad after a heart to heart with her. It seemed obvious she would have called her old buddy.

"What was your first clue?" Charlie asked, turning square on to the stall and leaning against it on both extended arms.

Josh took up position next to him and studied the troubled horse, who eyed him with undisguised, uninhibited love.

"The sheer joy on your face. I see that a lot on Jessie's men."

"What she said about Kayla's public announcement. Did you have any idea?"

"Nope."

"Do you get why Jessie kept it from you?"

Josh pondered that. "I think she knew I might take it public. There'd be a public outcry from Jacob's corner. It could destroy him, his career." Josh paused. "Kayla's right. Jessie was protecting him. But it's out now. This isn't the end of this, it's just the beginning."

"And you?"

"Hey," Josh chuckled darkly, slapping Charlie on the shoulder. "I always thought when she and I split up for good, she'd go running back to Jacob. But all of a sudden I am thinking otherwise. Now's your chance, buddy. Go get her back."

Charlie tossed off Josh's arm. "Some of us are happily married," he grumbled. "Don't joke about that shit."

Glancing sideways at him, a knife sliced Josh's gut. Sometimes he forgot about the old days, when Jessie was engaged to Charlie. He knew it hurt to lose her. "Sorry," he mumbled, and leaned more firmly into the stall, lifting his booted foot to rest on an overturned bucket.

"S'okay," Charlie said, a little glum at the hard memories. "She says she was worried about you, what you would do to Jacob…physically, you know. I think she was surprised you didn't go at him this morning. To be honest… I think I would have. No, I know I would have."

Staring at the horse, who was watching him almost tenderly, as if she knew he was struggling, Josh said quietly, "Charlie…I would have killed Jacob if I went after him this morning. I wouldn't have been able to stop myself. I feel a little bit the same about my wife right now. I don't want to see either one of them."

"You wouldn't hurt Jessie, Josh. I know you wouldn't."

"I wanted to this morning. I wanted to wring her stupid, stubborn neck."

"You drove away. You did the right thing."

"Alberta's not going to be far enough for how much driving away from Jessie I need to do right now. Charlie…Jessie's like this horse. She keeps you at a distance and only lets you in when she's feeling strong enough. I guess I'm a bit the same. I think that's why it's been so hard for both of us these last few months, and now I think I get why she leaned on Matt that night. I think… I think the…" He swallowed, and tried again, "I think the 'rape'…Jesus, I can't even say the word…but that's what it was, wasn't it?"

Blinking, he pondered that while Charlie remained quiet to let him process his thoughts. "I think it put her over some edge and that's why she was so quiet when she came back from Florida. I got quieter, thinking she was missing Jacob, you know? The Brussels film didn't help. But now, Charlie… my wife feels like a stranger."

Lightly, Charlie touched his arm. "Don't do anything stupid. Take whatever time you need, and make friends again. In the meantime, we have a long drive ahead of us when you consider we'll have to be stopping to give this crazy horse of yours a few breaks from that trailer. You better hope to hell she's an easy loader."

Josh stepped back from the stall and gazed sadly at Blue. "She'll be fine," he said quietly, losing himself in the tragic, loving eyes.

"I know she will," Charlie said, slapping him on the shoulder as he headed outdoors to help Josh get the truck backed up the last bit to hook onto the horse trailer.

Josh started to follow him but paused. "I was talking about the horse," he said, eyes trained on the floor of the barn.

Charlie didn't miss a beat. "I know you weren't," he said, and looked back over his shoulder to grin at his good buddy. He gestured towards the horse.

"You tell me all the time it's the troubled ones that need us the most. I'll kick your ass from here to Colorado if you even consider letting Jessie go, and I'll kick hers from here to Nebraska if she tries to run away from the two of you again. The two of you have had enough sadness and now you've got three beautiful children to consider as well. Now come on, day's not getting any younger." He softened. "Get your sorry, selfish 'poor me' butt out here. We've got a crazy horse to load."

Despite himself, Josh found a small smile lighting his face. "Charlie," he said, "you'd better stop calling my horse crazy. She'll be kicking *you* from here to Nebraska."

"I wasn't talking about your wife."

"I know you were."

Hearty laughter followed the guys out to the truck and trailer, which surprised both of them. Later, when Josh wasn't looking, Charlie snapped an iPhone pic to send to Jessie at some point.

She got it in mid-afternoon while rocking Dylan to settle him for a nap. In the picture, Josh was nose to nose with the horse, eyes closed, smiling happily, one hand on Blue's halter and one at the side of her face, just before he was about to release her from the stall and lead her outside to the trailer.

Your cowboy awaits. See you in Alberta in a few weeks, read Charlie's accompanying text.

"Ohhh!" Jessie breathed as she used her thumb and forefinger to zoom in on it. Sheer bliss was on her husband's peaceful face. "Look, Dylan. Look who it is."

Gently moving the phone in front of her child so Dylan could see, Jessie shoved away the tears pricking at her eyes.

"Daddy," said the sleepy little boy, pointing at the photo. "Daddy."

"You bet," Jessie agreed. "Your daddy." Cuddling the child closer, she bent her face to his Jacob hair and rocked him to sleep.

Chapter Twenty-six

At La Casa, Charles and Dee were having words. Behind them, Carlotta, who was digging through the cupboards and fridge assembling ingredients for a chickpea salad, was smiling widely and shaking her head at their easy argument, which boasted no traits of anything sinister. Instead, a wife's worry was sneaking through the edgy words emerging from Dee's lips.

"I talked to Jonathon. He's got someone lined up to feed you. Don't you go running off to one of those Calgary steak houses and eating red meat to your heart's content—"

"Deirdre," Charles cut her off, "I am a grown man. I am not prone to ignoring my physician's advice after almost dying. I will obey." Joking, he bowed to her.

She frowned. "I would rather you don't make fun of me. And none of that salty deep fried pepperoni they serve at those country music bars."

"All right. I'll only pick at the bowls of salty nuts." He winked.

"Charles, you—" Deirdre put one hand on her hip and scowled at her husband of many years. "You're fooling with me. You'd think I would know that by now."

Sidling around the kitchen island, Charles took his wife by the waist and smiled at her. Nearby, Carlotta snuck a peek at the power couple she pretty much worshipped. The light in Charles' eyes was bright and happy. Deirdre, too, was aglow.

Charles tapped his wife's nose and said, "Look. I am feeling well these days. I am planning to enjoy my time in the studio with Jessie before I head out to Calgary in a few weeks."

"No late nights," she admonished. "And Matt drives you everywhere. No stress."

"Fine. As long as Ulysses watches out for you, my dear, while you are in L.A."

"I'll be fine." She looked up at him with a mixture of relief and worry. "We've had a good run, Charles. I can't believe life has passed by so quickly."

"It's not over yet, Deirdre." He answered with the respect the comment deserved. "We have to be around to see our grandchildren grow up. All those school concerts…"

"And ballet recitals," she added, laughing as the front door opened and closed. Two sets of footsteps made their way down the hall and into the kitchen.

"What's this about ballet recitals?" Matt asked as he wandered in with one hand on the back of a very somber Jacob's neck. Charles wrinkled his brow. Jacob was wearing his clothes from the night before, and he looked like he'd just been run over by a truck.

"Emily-Grace has a spring recital just before Jessie leaves for Alberta," Dee said to him, her words slowing down towards the end of the sentence as she took in Jacob's sorry state and the serious lilt to Matt's stance.

Matt's lips were thin, pressed tightly together. He looked at Charles. "We need to talk."

"No stress," Deirdre said, dismayed. "What's going on?"

"Jacob has something he needs to say to you." Matt gave Jacob a little push, and the singer fell into the nearest Italian leather stool with a low grunt and a heavy heart.

Charles leaned on the kitchen island opposite him, while Deirdre took a step back and settled against the stove with Carlotta, pushing the lunch ingredients away for the time being.

Jacob started with a miserable preamble. "You're not going to be happy with me, Charles."

Hesitating, shooting a look to Matt to try to get a reading on what he was about to hear, Charles tried to relax. He took a long Yoga breath inhale. "Tell me," he demanded, no longer the happy-go-lucky husband, and now the esteemed and successful producer.

"I just…I did something a while ago that is hitting the news…today."

"And?"

Matt watched Charles for signs of strain, but the older man was holding up just fine. Deirdre remained quiet.

"Well," Jacob sighed. "It involves Jessie. And it sucks."

Charles lowered his voice and gripped the edge of the kitchen island. "Go on, son."

Jacob waited. He had to. Glancing sideways at Matt, he swallowed before Matt's gentle encouragement gave him the strength to go on.

"In Florida…the sex I had with Jessie was not consensual. She didn't want it."

Carlotta gripped Deirdre's hand as the older woman went white.

Jacob continued, a rather grey-green shade himself. "You know I hit her. I did it to get her to stop fighting me." His shoulders started to shake. "I'm sorry. I was so mad at her…Talia…" Sobbing now, he held Charles' gaze as the man he respected above all others remained quiet. "Talia wasn't gonna marry me. Jessie…" Waving an arm aimlessly in the still air, he did not need to finish his thought. They were all well aware of Jessie's meaning in Jacob's life.

Crumbling, the peace Jacob had tried to find down south disappeared, streaming onto the floor with the angst of a broken soul. It was replaced with enough strength here to be able to say those nasty words, to admit his violent wrongdoing, even though Jacob was really only coming clean because Kayla's public fury had pushed him into telling Charles before the producer heard it from the media.

Matt broke in. "Kayla announced it to the world this morning, Charles." He looked at Dee. "I would expect some damage control will need to be initiated."

Charles wasn't moving. Like Josh earlier, he was astounded and shocked. "This is why you asked me to release Jacob, Matt," he said.

"Yes," Matt said. "This is why."

"So you knew about this."

Matt paused. "I was with Jessie in Florida, Charles. She came home bleeding and angry. Yes, I knew. She told me the truth that night."

"Bleeding and angry." Charles' gaze had not left Jacob's cobalt eyes. "One of my artists rapes the other and I'm supposed to pat you on the back and, what, send you back down south so you can hide?"

"No," Jacob straightened. "No more hiding. You do what you need to do, Charles." He looked around the beautiful home. "You don't need the money. I just need to make this right. I don't know how, but I know I do."

"You will stay in the city until I tell you to go, Jacob," Charles decreed with authority. "You will stay away from Jessie and away from your son. I would suggest you also stay away from Josh's sister." He blinked and set his angry, disappointed sight on Matt. "Today? Kayla said this today? Where, at the bus?"

"Josh was there, Charles. He heard." Jacob was crushed.

Matt remained silent.

"And you're still standing? Why aren't you bruised and beaten?"

A frightened, hopeless shrug formed part of Jacob's answer. His words were dusky. "I don't know. He walked away."

"And Jessie?"

Matt spoke quietly. "Josh walked away from her too."

Deirdre closed her eyes and said a silent prayer as Carlotta hugged her.

Charles nodded and fixed flashing eyes and a set jaw back on Jacob. "Go home, son. Don't come around here until we call for you. Deirdre will be in touch."

Jacob stayed in the stool. "Charles," he said, "I don't...I don't really have anybody...right now..."

"Perhaps you can hang out with Matt."

A gasp from Dee had Charles turn around and give his wife a hard stare. "This is not the kind of covert behavior we need from our security, Dee." Back to Matt he said, "Although I expect Jessie pretty much ordered you to keep this under wraps."

"She didn't want Jacob charged. She knew what the bad press would do for his image as well as her own. Going down to see him in the first place."

"Her image or her marriage?" That came from Dee, who was trembling now as she listened to the discord as her world slipped a little off its foundation yet again.

"Her marriage," Matt sighed. "Although in my opinion I think if Josh hadn't gone off the rails at the Grammys he might have had a chance at gaining back some of the fans who wrote he and Jessie off after she went back to him a few years ago."

"Regardless," Charles said, "I don't want to see you right now, Jacob. And in case you're wondering, Jessie is not in my good books right now either. She should have come clean." To Matt, he said, "Take a few days off, then. You can thank my wife for that. We'll talk next week. Sam and Dan can handle watching our grandkids and Jessie until this new fiasco settles."

Jacob sat without moving until Matt grabbed a handful of last night's suit jacket and physically lifted him out of the chair. As he moved him towards the home's front entrance, Charles' voice floated behind them.

"By the way, Jacob. Your new song was released this morning. It's already trending. Thought you'd want to know."

Pausing, Jacob closed his eyes. "Okay," Matt heard him say. "Okay."

Together, he and Matt passed through La Casa's bright entrance, leaving a trail of new hurt behind them. Matt drove Jacob to his dingy apartment on Southwest Marine Drive, and stopped at the liquor store on his way back to his downtown condo.

Today was a day for insulation. He sat alone in front of a continuous succession of music videos, and got roaring drunk.

Chapter Twenty-seven

At home, Jacob gazed around at his messy digs. He had two choices—go to the couch, pull an old quilt up over his head, sleep for days, or...

He took number two. Retrieving his iPhone from his designer jacket's pocket, he did a quick Internet search for a local realtor.

"Hello?" he asked when a perky female voice answered. "I'm looking to buy a place in Vancouver. A condo, maybe. I'm not sure. Just a place to call home."

Kayla flitted through his mind. There would be a lot of work to do there if he had any hope of earning her trust again, but...Jacob was tired. He was tired of always pining after a woman he could never have, and he was letting guilt eat himself alive over the notion that he and Talia would never have made it anyway. Kayla was sweet, funny, bright, talented...and she could disappear inside music the way Jacob did. Yeah, she was angry right now, but Jacob would work on that. He would try to win her back.

He would just have to do it behind Josh's back, perhaps...perhaps the same way he would try to gain access to his son.

Sauntering towards the shower, he told himself that however this thing with Jessie came out in the end, it wouldn't matter. Jacob already had enough money to last him ten thousand lifetimes. If his career did a nosedive? So what. What he did to her was wrong. He needed to fix that, and his conscience and soul along with it, if he hoped to eradicate or at least soothe a troubled past that was destroying any chance at a decent future.

Stepping into the bathroom, he stripped off last night's clothes, remembering the beautiful Casey as he did so, and a tiny thrill crept up his body. Her first sexual experience...it didn't change what Jacob did to Jessie. But it was a sweet, sweet memory, for Casey as well as for him, and somehow it helped ease the pain.

The water was refreshing, hot and soothing, and as it fell over Jacob, he let it cleanse his body, and somehow, it also lifted his soul.

～～～

"So," came a gossipy female announcer's voice over the radio, "I find it interesting that Jacob Ryan's new song was released today."

"Why?" asked her male counterpart, who relished the juicy celebrity fishbowl part of their afternoon show.

"Because it's being billed as his response to the ballad Jessie Wheeler sang at the Grammy's which, as you recall, and which we all know because we all adore her and it, was an 'I'm sorry' song."

"It's about being sorry for breaking some guy's heart."

"Jacob Ryan's heart, apparently."

"Truth?"

"I expect so, yeah. Because his song is clearly a 'back at ya.'"

"So is his an 'I'm sorry' song too?"

"Yeah, but it's also about maybe only ever getting the chance to have one great love in your lifetime, although after having listened to it I would say he leaves the door open for another."

"So what's the deal about the song being released today? What's interesting about today compared to any other day?"

"What's interesting is that it also came out today that Jacob Ryan allegedly raped Jessie Wheeler around New Year's when she went to see him in Florida after his country star fiancée was killed in a car accident."

"Wait. What?"

"So his tune is truly an 'I'm sorry' song."

"He did that? They're…not a couple anymore."

"Right-o. That's the thing."

"She left him for Josh Sawyer, that hothead actor she was married to when she and their children were kidnapped. This is not likely to go down well with him."

"Not likely. It's going to be interesting to see where this lands. We'll keep you posted, listeners!"

On her tour bus, snuggled into Benjie's side, Kayla listened to the radio over the bus speaker as the opening strains of Jacob's song for Jessie filled the air around her. She put her hands over her face and cried until the bus' forward motion lulled her to sleep.

Kitty corner across the aisle in a row behind her, Casey watched her cry, turned her face towards the window, tuned her ears to Jacob's new tune, and let the glow of the sun warm her face.

She smiled.

As Jacob's song started to fill the cab of his truck, Josh turned the radio up. Clearly this was a tune meant as an apology, but it wasn't that part of the song that got to him the most. It was the chilling and angsty refrain that hurt his heart.

Jacob was posing a question. *What if we only get one true love? What if life goes by in the blink of an eye and we only get one chance at true love? What if... that love has come and gone?*

Miles of highway stretched out before Josh, Blue was behind him in the trailer, and Charlie was cruising along behind them.

A new place, a new series, a new start.

A new hope.

With Jessie? Or without?

With. No question.

Because...what if you only get one true love?

Josh didn't have to answer that question. For him there always was, and always would be, only one true love.

Jessie. His broken, troubled, lonely girl.

Like a luminescent, dying log in a fire pit fanned to flame by a warm breeze, Josh's heart revived itself, just a little.

"Thanks Jacob, ole boy," he muttered as he glanced in the rearview mirror to ensure the trailer was coming along just fine behind him. "Thanks for clearing that up for me."

The sun was just starting to lower on the horizon. Its glowing pink-orange hues bled into the earth, giving the world a solitary, otherworldly radiance that marked the landscape with a sense that something big out there in the universe was at play.

Josh was astute enough to pay attention. He slowed the truck just a little, lowered his window and waved to Charlie behind him (Charlie waved back), and he grinned. Ahead was a small motel he and Charlie had mapped out long before their Vancouver departure date. Flicking on his signal light, Josh turned right just before the natural light turned a dusky bluish-purple, and he eased into a large parking spot at the side of the graveled lot.

The radio went dead when he turned off the ignition.

Josh sat back and pulled out his iPhone. There were four messages from Jessie. She'd sent him two pictures of the kids, and two short clips of the children playing around Emily-Grace's miniature dollhouse. Josh played the videos four times each before a hard rap startled him.

Charlie.

They had a horse to feed and put to bed. They had a new TV series to look forward to, and Josh would also live like a dream on his and Jessie's ranch for six months.

With a little hope and forgiveness, surely all would be well.

Surely.

Dropping the phone into his jacket pocket, he leveraged open his door, and followed Charlie to the back of the trailer.

⌒﹏⌒

Josh didn't respond to Jessie's texts, but Jacob did. The second he got out of the shower, he sent her the link to his song. To her credit, she waited until all three children were sound asleep—all on her bed—before she slipped out of the bedroom and sat on the stairs to play it on her iPhone.

She hit 'play' a dozen times.

Then she called him.

"Hey," he answered. "What'd ya think?"

Slowly, Jessie's eyes started to dance. Maneuvering her body around, she leaned against the wall. "I think you could've done a better job on that bridge. I'm surprised Charles agreed to it."

On Southwest Marine Drive, Jacob laughed. "I came up with that when he went for coffee."

"Where'd he go for coffee, to ROAM Whistler?"

"Ha ha, Jessie made a funny." Jacob was still chuckling. "Uh, I may not have to worry about his opinion again. Matt took me by the ear to La Casa today."

"I heard. Ouch."

"You were talking to Charles?"

"Nope. Dee. Charles always needs a day or two to come down. I got Matt's take on the day as well, though. He was drunk. It was hilarious."

"And…?" Jacob didn't need to say it.

"Josh?"

"Yeah. How's he doing?"

"He left the city, Jacob. Your precious body is safe. For now."

"How mad is he?"

"I wouldn't know."

"Aww. Geez, Jess, I'm sorry."

"That's what I get for flying down to Florida to help a friend."

"It was appreciated. I just…I just…"

"Oh babe, I know. Don't you think I know? I heard your song."

"I heard yours too, Jessie. Thank you."

"You are quite welcome. It seemed to be a good idea at the time."

"Music, huh?"

"Yep. Thank God for music. Thank God to have something to disappear inside when we need it, huh?"

"You can say that again." Jacob paused. "Jessie, the world is exploding again. 'Bout you and me and this…the bad thing I did. In Florida."

"There are worse problems in the world, my darling Jacob," Jessie whispered, sniffling. "Not that I in any way condone what you did, babe, but I do understand where it came from and I take responsibility for my part in it."

"No excuse for what I did."

"Nope. And I won't let you live it down. At the very least, you will go out into the big bad world and educate others about how not to let this happen to any other women. And that it's never okay to hit a woman—or partner—and cross that line when someone says no."

"I will, Jess. I promise. I'll make this right."

"What about Kayla?" Her voice softened. "I saw you watching her. You're crazy in love with her."

"Jealous?"

"Damn straight," Jessie laughed. "Of course I am. But very happy for the two of you. I think you'd be great together if you can handle the Sawyer curse, that's all."

"And the Sawyer curse is?"

"What planet are you on? Do I really need to tell you?"

"Something to do with public displays of temper, maybe?"

"You really got to stay on the good side of a Sawyer, Jacob."

"I'm starting to get that."

Jessie's voice quieted. "But Jacob?"

"Yeah?" He lay down on his couch and crossed his ankles up over the arm. "I'm listening."

"Babe…they're really worth loving. Sawyers."

"Ah ha." He chuckled lightly. "Too bad they come with so much hurt."

"You just gotta love it outta them. That's all, babe. Just love them."

"You are one special woman, Jessie. You know that? I mean it."

"Too bad the rest of the world can't hear us now, huh? They think we despise each other."

"Not the smart, intuitive ones. Not the ones who *get* the music. They don't think that."

"No, I suppose they don't."

"Now, about that song of yours…"

It was so great to talk music with Jacob again that their conversation went on until Jessie couldn't stay awake. "I'm gonna have little kids at my feet at 5," she moaned. "I need my beauty sleep."

"Okay. Good night, sweet girl. I'd say I'll drop by the studio but Charles will have my balls."

"Call me when you need to talk."

"I will."

"I'll play you my songs and you can help sort out the bridges."

He laughed. "You got it, Jess. Luv you. 'Nite."

"Luv you too, Jacob. Sleep well."

After a bit, Jessie rose and stood by the door of the bedroom where she and Josh first made love years ago. The bed was all mixed-up arms and legs of three beautiful, slumbering children. One by one Jessie carried them back to their beds with hugs and kisses and lots of murmured love.

She fell into her own bed and hugged her pillow with a smile on her face. Josh was surely feeling lonely but he was safe—Charlie had finally texted to say they were settled in a small motel and that Blue had weathered the trip just fine so far. Jacob was now on the world's shit list, but he sounded okay. He was doing all right, lonely for sure, but okay, and so was she.

Rolling over onto her belly, she thought about Matt, and worried a little about his obvious loneliness and the fact that he was drinking when he called her. She pushed him aside and pondered her angry husband. Would they get past this latest crap?

Yes, she answered herself wholeheartedly.

Heck, yes.

As the moon rose to its full height and the sky was peppered with pinpoints of light, Jessie drifted off to sleep, and dreamt of majestic galloping horses, happy well-loved children and, above all, music.

It was good to have a place to disappear into, when life was feeling too big. When there was just so much darn *lonely*.

The End.

Thank you!

Please remember to rate and review *Into the Blue*—self-published authors rely on our readers to help spread the love!

P.S. You've made it this far…so you're officially a 'Drifterite!' Term coined by reader Amanda Grady of Ontario, Canada.

CLAIM your free excerpt from *A Song For Josh* by joining the Drifters readers' group at **www.susanrodgersauthor.com**

Happy reading!

Susan

www.susanrodgersauthor.com

Facebook: search **Susan Rodgers, Writer**

Twitter: **@srbluemountain**

www.bublish.com

email: **fatcat@pei.sympatico.ca**

About the Author

Susan Rodgers' first novel *A Certain Kind of Freedom* was a Finalist in the Writers' Federation of Nova Scotia Atlantic Writing Awards for unpublished manuscripts. Her short story from the novel of the same name, published in two anthologies, has received rave reviews, as have the Drifters novels, Susan's all-time favourite books to write.

Owner/Operator of Bluemountain Entertainment, Susan is a 'Diploma With Honours' graduate of Vancouver Film School. She produces mostly documentary style client films and short dramas with plans to one day shoot a Feature Drama based on the novel Atlantic Blue.

Formerly a Museum Curator, in winter Susan lives with her partner Steve and her striped cat Oliver (Lucy Maud Montgomery once said the only good cat is a striped cat) in Summerside, Prince Edward Island, Canada. In summer, she hides in a small trailer in Darnley, P.E.I., where she writes novels, paddles kayaks, and crafts sandcastles on the beach. She makes frequent trips to Vancouver to visit her son Christopher, where she enjoys life in the hippie city while listening to great music and sipping on good espresso.

Books by Susan Rodgers

Drifters series:
A Song For Josh
Promises
No Greater Love
Riptide
Whispers of Home
And Then There Was Silence
Let the Music Cry
If I Could Sing You Home
After the Rain
Into the Blue
A Sacred Peace
Watch Over Me

Coming Soon:
A Certain Kind of Freedom
Seasmoke
Atlantic Blue

Feature Screenplays:
The Story of Jack & Emma
Atlantic Blue
Beautiful Jane
They Were Dreamers (adapted)

Short Stories:
S12
A Certain Kind of Freedom
A Gentle Peace